ISBN 10: 1-59632-388-4
ISBN 13: 978-1-59632-388-9
DANGEROUS CRAVINGS
Copyright © 2007 by Evangeline Anderson
Originally released in e-book format in March 2006

Cover Art by April Martinez

DISCLAIMER: Many of the acts described in our BDSM/fetish titles can be dangerous. Please do not try any new sexual practice, whether it be fire, rope, or whip play, without the guidance of an experienced practitioner. Neither Loose Id® nor its authors will be responsible for any loss, harm, injury or death resulting from use of the information contained in any of its titles.

This book is an original publication of Loose Id®. The story herein was previously published in e-book format in March 2006 by Loose Id®, and is a work of fiction. Any similarity to actual persons, events or existing locations is entirely coincidental.

Printed in the U.S.A. by
Lightning Source, Inc.
1246 Heil Quaker Blvd
La Vergne TN 37086
www.lightningsource.com

DANGEROUS CRAVINGS

Evangeline Anderson

Prologue

November 22nd

"Is this what you wanted? Is it? *Is it?*"

She shakes her head frantically, *No—no!* Her eyes must be bulging with fear but he cannot see them—they are hidden behind the mask—red with black lace. Her mouth, her beautiful mouth, is sealed with duct tape. Dull silver in place of those full red lips.

"Just for you," he croons. Fingers clad in black leather caress her slender throat. Black leather—just the way she wants it. Just the way she *needs* it. That was exactly what she'd written—*It's not something I want—not just a desire or another kinky fantasy. This is something I need for me, to be who I am. To finally become the person I most want to be.*

He just hopes she appreciates the way he is helping her along. Helping her to *become* that person. He tightens his grip on her neck, feeling the frantic pulse thrumming under his fingers like a tiny, trapped animal. Something small enough to crush in his fist.

"Just the way you want it, sweetheart," he says again. "Just the way you *need* it."

She is kicking now, but not strongly enough to dislodge him. Her hands yank uselessly at the ties that bind her to the bedposts. Black satin, just the way she wrote. Attention to detail is important. He wouldn't want anyone to accuse him of not being attentive to her needs. *All* her needs.

She fishtails under him desperately as he presses deeper, squeezes harder. Black leather against pale, perfect white skin. She feels so good under him, around him. He can't imagine why he didn't do this earlier. Just because it is filthy and wrong is no reason to deny her what she needs, after all.

Her head whips from side to side in a final negation. Her neck feels like a flower stem between his hands. So beautiful. So fragile. He is waiting for the final moment, waiting to feel her push him over the edge. That edge she wrote about so often—that edge she longs for. Needs.

Then it arrives—the final moment of perfection. Her body arcs in a matchless crescendo, and her feet beat a useless tattoo on the sheets. As his thumbs press deep, deeper, deepest, she flies over the edge and takes him with her. Ah, bliss…

But the moment is too swift. Too fleeting. All too quickly over and done with. He lets her go, noticing with some concern the way he marked her. Surely those purple bruises didn't come from his hands, so cleverly encased in black leather?

He shakes her, but she is limp in his arms. Her head wobbles lifelessly, a flower with a broken stem. She is dead weight, and he pulls suddenly away from her, out of her, repulsed.

"It's not my fault." He bites his lips when he hears himself talking out loud like that. Not good to start talking to yourself. Only crazy people do that, and he is very definitely sane. He didn't mean for things to go so far—he just wanted to prove to her that it was wrong, that it wasn't something she really wanted, really needed. Now she'll never need anything again.

"Not my fault," he whispers again. But whose then? Whose?

He glances around, his eyes lighting on her computer, the slim, sexy laptop she took with her everywhere. It hums quietly to itself, open just as she left it when she came to answer the door and let him in. To let her death in.

He slips off the bed and goes to it. The screensaver, a cute one that simulates a fish tank where the fish keep changing colors, is up. He thumbs a button and the screen flares to life. He looks at her latest reading list. At the top is *Velvet Agony*. That one was hers, her first foray into depravity and also her last. Morganna Bloom, she had called herself, hiding her true identity behind the ridiculous *nom de plume* when she wrote her filth. But the others, the ones she hadn't written... *Sweet Submission, Painful Pleasures, Whispers in the Dark...* This is the kind of crap that gave her the idea to begin with, he'd bet his life on it—he has already bet hers. This is what brought him to her tonight in the first place.

He scans the list of authors, obviously pen names. Sylvestra Eden, Carolyn Sinders, Victoria Tarlatan. Three women trying to hide behind the shadow of a false name while they peddle their filth to an unsuspecting world. But those names cannot shelter them any longer, and he knows. Knows how to find the women behind those names—the women who are really to blame for her death.

And when he finds them, they will pay...and pay...and pay...

He highlights the name Morganna Bloom and hits delete. Three names remain blinking on the pitiless black screen. Just three, soon to be two.

Chapter One

Monday, December 13
Detective Cole Berkley

"Got a hot one for you." Captain Davis dropped a thin manila folder on my desk, and my partner, Alex, scooted around to look over my shoulder. The downtown Tampa PD is in a renovated bank building that was built back in the Sixties. Space is at a premium, so she didn't have to scoot far.

"What's it about?" She glanced up at Davis, who already looked pissed and tired even though it was only Monday.

The captain ran a hand through her curly, graying hair. "Remember the rape/murder Kendricks and Ramirez were working last month? The one where..."

"The victim was found tied to the bed with the mask on," I finished for her. "How could we forget? More of the same?"

"More of the same," she confirmed. "But this time the vic's still alive, or she was when her roommate called it in. The Carlton Arms down by USF, and I need you there quick. Ambulance is on the way, too, but I'd like you to get there before they disturb the scene, if you could."

"The CA," I muttered. "Where else?"

"You don't want much, do you, Captain?" Alex stood, grabbing her jacket from the back of her chair. "They're going to be sending the ambulance from University Community. We'd have to fly to get there first."

"I have faith in you, Reed," the captain said dryly. "And this case is going to belong to you and Berkley—" She nodded at me. "—from now on, since Kendricks is off until he gets out of the hospital and Ramirez moved."

"Thanks. Merry Christmas to you, too," I muttered, grabbing my own jacket and the folder off the blotter. Alex tossed me the keys, but I tossed them right back again.

"We have to go fast. You drive. I'll read."

"Hey, won't the other guys razz you if they find out you're letting a girl drive?" She grinned at me, an expression I hadn't seen in way too long.

"I'm only letting you drive because you get car sick reading in traffic," I said, grinning back at her. To be honest, she's the better driver, and I'd like to think I'm not too much of a macho jerk to admit it. Of course, I'd never say it out loud.

"I'll drive, but we're taking my car—no whining," she said, obviously seeing the look on my face.

"Fine...fine." We ran out to the parking lot behind the Tampa PD and found her bright yellow VW Bug. Not exactly inconspicuous, although that wasn't why I had a problem with it. It's a great little car, and Alex can really make it sing when she wants to—she whips around bigger vehicles like they're standing still. But "little" is the operative word. It's not easy to fit somebody my size into a car like that.

"No whining," Alex said again as I folded all six-foot-five of myself into the yellow Bug.

"I feel like I'm in a damn clown car at the circus," I grumbled, ignoring her. I closed the door, my right shoulder jammed against the glass. It's a good thing I'm not claustrophobic.

She revved the engine and peeled rubber out of the lot. "Not surprised about that, Cole—big clown like you."

"Hey," I protested mildly. "I thought I was a lug. Or maybe a lummox."

She raised her perfectly pointed eyebrows at me. "Since when are you a 'lummox?'"

I shrugged. "Don't ask me. I can't keep track of all your little pet names for me."

She punched me lightly on the shoulder and whipped around a city bus, cutting off a white Hummer that was idling along in the fast lane. The driver blew his horn and Alex muttered, "Blow your nose, asshole. You'll get more out of it."

"Alexandra!" I did my best impression of her mother. "Language, young lady."

She smirked at me, giving me a look from those big brown eyes of hers. My partner, I swear, has eyes just like Bambi—in fact, sometimes I call her that just to tease her. She hates it. But those eyes—they're soft, brown, and big enough to drown in, with a thick fringe of black lashes all the way around. To look at her you'd think she wouldn't hurt a fly.

She's short, too—well, not really, I guess. Five-seven isn't really all that short for a woman; it's just that everybody seems short to me. But she's curvy, which makes her look shorter than if she were all skin and bones like some women are. And she has those eyes, like I mentioned, and this thick, wavy brownish-blondish hair she used to wear really short. She's been growing it out lately, and it's almost down past her shoulders. I like to watch it brush over the collar of her shirt, but I'd never tell her so.

Anyway, she looks more like a kindergarten teacher than a detective first class, which is what we both are. But her looks don't fool me—I've seen those baby deer eyes narrow down over the barrel of her Browning, and I've seen her squeeze the trigger cold as ice. If the driver of the Hummer that honked at us knew Alex half as well as I did, he'd be keeping his hand off the horn and covering his nuts with it instead.

"So," I said, when she'd left the Hummer in the dust and settled in for the ride. "Got your Christmas shopping done yet?"

She glanced at me again and then back at the road. "Not really but I'm not worried. Not…" She cleared her throat, eyes locked determinedly on the road. "Not as many people to buy for this year."

I could have kicked myself. "Sorry, Alex." I put a hand on her shoulder and felt the tension running through her, just under the skin. I squeezed lightly and let go. "I didn't mean to…I have some extra Bucs tickets and I was thinking, if you didn't have anything for Jeff yet…"

"Jeff's been out of the picture for the past three months; don't tell me you don't know that." She looked at me, and I shrugged uneasily. "Come on, Cole, I *know* you know that. He wasn't even at the funeral."

"Well...yeah, I guess." Actually, I'd just been fishing for information. Alex can be really close-mouthed when she wants to be, and what with all the mess her family had been through lately, I'd never found out why her latest flame had gone south in such a hurry.

"You want to know what happened, right?" She tightened her grip on the wheel, staring straight ahead.

"Did I scare him off?" I asked, trying not to make eye contact. "I swear I didn't mean to. Didn't even give him the standard speech."

"You mean the one that goes, 'Hey, punk, if you hurt my partner, I'll rip you limb from limb, and you'll be eating through a straw for the rest of your short, miserable life'?" She was joking about it, which was good. I hadn't seen her joke much in the past several months.

"Yeah, that one." I looked down at the folder in my hands and decided to press my luck. "So if I didn't scare him off, what did?"

She sighed. "Me—*I* did, Cole. You're a nosy bastard sometimes, you know that? Just because you're five years older and a foot taller than me doesn't mean you always have to play the protective big brother."

Uh-oh, I had gone too far. I sighed. "You know I don't mean to. And give me some credit—I don't act like a macho asshole at the station at least." It had taken a while for Alex to convince me she could take care of herself. A shootout during the first year of our partnership, where she saved my ass, finally made a believer out of me. I've never treated her as less than one of the guys since, which is how she likes it.

She nodded, I thought reluctantly. "Okay, credit where it's due—you don't act like that at work. But you don't have to come gunning for every guy that breaks my heart outside of work either, you know."

I held up my hands in a "don't shoot" gesture. "Hey, I didn't, okay? I left ole Jeff strictly alone. I didn't even know what happened to him. Matter of fact, I still don't."

"Cole," she warned.

"All right, already. Sorry, I just—"

"Don't worry about it," she cut me off. "Just read. What does the case file say?"

I flipped open the manila folder and read it off. "Okay, looks like rape and strangulation. Initially it just looked like a kinky sex scene gone wrong."

"How so?" Alex glanced at me and zoomed around a truck full of laborers, probably illegal, heading for the on-ramp to 275. "Sorry," she said apologetically. "I know I should remember. I just wasn't too…with it when this case first broke."

"Understandable," I told her. I wanted to squeeze her shoulder again but restrained myself—Alex isn't as touchy-feely as I am. I went back to the folder. "Vic was a white female, Cynthia Harner, thirty-seven, upper middle class. She was found dead by the cleaning service in her new apartment. Apparently she'd just split with her husband a few weeks before."

"Okay, so what was Dear Hubby's alibi?" When a wife gets killed, you always look at the husband first.

"Air tight," I said, scanning down the page as she crossed three lanes of traffic. "He was at a conference in Denver at the time, had ticket stubs to prove it."

"And the sex?" she asked, whipping through traffic for the exit lane.

"Well, she was found tied to her bed with black satin restraints and wearing a blindfold—a sleeping mask, actually. A red one with black lace. Also had on a black silk teddy. Ramirez has notes here. Says, no forced entry and no sign of a struggle. He and Kendricks thought it looked like something consensual that went wrong at the last minute."

"So maybe she has a new boyfriend, invites him over to play…" Alex swung wide, taking us off the ramp and into Fletcher Avenue traffic, which was considerable this time of day.

"He asks if he can tie her up…" I said.

"Maybe she *asks* him to tie her up," Alex interjected.

"You think?" I glanced over at her and saw that her cheeks had gotten just a little bit rosy. Hmm, something to file away for later.

"Could be." She shrugged. "Anyway, he ties her up, they start to go for it…"

"He gets carried away. Starts to choke her."

She opened her mouth to say something and snapped it shut again.

"What?" I looked at her.

"Just that...she could have asked for that, too. Erotic asphyxiation, you know?"

Hmm, her cheeks were very pink now.

"You saying she asked for this?" I asked, directly.

Alex shrugged. "To be raped and strangled? No, of course not. I'm not saying it's her fault no matter how it went down. No means no, right?"

I sighed. "Except when it means yes, apparently."

She glanced at me. "What the hell is *that* supposed to mean?"

"I'm just saying, if you put your little theory before a jury it would sound...well, it wouldn't sound too good. For the vic, anyway."

She swerved around another car and threw me a dirty look. "Wanting to have a little rough sex does *not* mean she wanted to be killed. And it doesn't excuse the sick son of a bitch we're looking for either."

"Okay, so she likes to play rough," I said, bypassing what could have been a very interesting topic of conversation in favor of doing the job. "But not *this* rough. He gets too excited and kills her. When he sees what he's done, he gets scared and runs for it. Only now that won't fly because it looks like he's done another one."

"We'll see when we get there." Alex has always been a skeptic. "But didn't anybody hear anything at all?"

I looked at the file. "Zip, zilch, nada—but then she did have duct tape on her mouth. Looks like Ramirez and Kendricks canvassed everybody in the complex. And it's a ritzy one, too. Up in South Tampa, not too far off Bayshore."

Alex raised her eyes and made an illegal turn to get around another truck. "Dear Hubby's money?"

I looked again, ignoring the horn blaring at us from the angry truck driver. "Nope—vic could afford a nice place of her own. She was a physician's assistant to one Dr. Love, prominent plastic surgeon."

Alex raised her eyebrows again. "Seriously, that's the guy's name?"

I nodded. "Yup, paging Dr. Love, paging Dr. Strangelove."

She punched me in the arm. "Cut it out. So, no leads. The trail is cold, and Davis drops it in our lap."

"Like I said, Merry Christmas." I nodded at the apartment building that was whizzing by my window in a tan blur at the speed of light. "Hey, Dale Junior, you might want to go back, you just missed it."

Chapter Two

Detective Alex Reed

The ambulance was already there by the time I turned around and got into the complex, but it didn't matter because the girl was dead. I looked at her, hanging limply from the black satin restraints, just like the first vic had been, and wearing the same kind of sleeping mask—red with black lace around the edges. She was nude, no black nightie like the first vic, but the similarities were definitely there. Our only piece of luck was that the press hadn't picked up on them yet.

Two women viciously murdered within a month of each other is tragic but not terribly unusual in a town the size of Tampa. Last year our crime rate equaled New York City's. But if it got out that they had been murdered by the same man and the nightly news started screaming "serial killer"... I shook my head. It was better not to think about it. Better to catch this guy as quickly as possible before he got the urge again—probably in a month from now if he kept to his pattern.

I looked at Sarah Michaels closely. Her head was down, and her long brown hair hung in her face. I bent and looked under her chin; bruises ringed her slender throat. Rose petals lay scattered in a haphazard fashion all over the bedspread, and there were long, thin, bloody marks on her thighs, as though someone had whipped her with something. Our perp had stepped it up a notch.

My stomach turned over as I motioned for the crime scene tech to start taking pictures. I had a bad feeling about this one— very bad.

The apartment was a tiny two bedroom, small even by Carlton Arms standards, which is just one step up from the projects. A lot of USF students who can't afford to live on campus call it home. Unfortunately, a lot of strippers, prostitutes, and pimps also like the low rent of the sprawling, overcrowded complex. The two elements do not mix well. If I had a nickel for every car jacking, mugging, rape, and assault reported at the Carlton Arms, I wouldn't need to win the Lotto.

Cole stood in the doorway with a long-suffering look on his face as he comforted the roommate. I was betting she was all of nineteen, tall, blonde, and wearing a short cotton T-shirt that said *Hottie* in purple letters across the front, with purple panties to match, and not much else. Even accounting for the thick make-up smeared across her face, she was already looking a little ragged around the edges.

She was one of those girls who look thirty when they're thirteen and fifty when they're twenty-five. Or maybe I was just being catty because she was rubbing her obviously fake boobs all over my partner's broad chest. Myself, I've always had big ones, from sixth grade on, so I've never understood why you would voluntarily go under the knife to give yourself an extra three pounds to carry around on each side. No man is worth that.

"I just...just came home and found her like this, ya know?" The girl was sobbing like her heart would break, and I berated myself for being so cynical about her, even if she *was* coming on to Cole. After all, I really couldn't blame her for it.

Cole looks like the kind of guy he is: ex-linebacker, ex-Marine, and a damn fine detective. He still keeps his black hair military short, and he has tattoos on both biceps—Semper Fi on the right and a wicked-looking green and blue dragon with a red forked tongue curled around the left. (He admitted to me that he'd gotten that one while stinking drunk on leave one night in the Army.) He has piercing blue eyes, and his face looks like it's carved out of granite—not handsome but very solid. He's a good guy to have at your back, and I should know—he's saved my ass plenty of times in our five-year partnership. Not that I haven't saved his a time or two.

"What time did you come home?" Cole asked patiently, trying to keep an arm around the girl and keep her breasts from making too much contact with his chest at the same time. I tried to hide a smirk—he's a red-blooded guy, after all, but he does *try* to do the right thing.

"Around..." She paused for a moment to think. "Just around six a.m., I guess. I was working an all-nighter at the Mons Venus, ya know?"

Cole nodded and gave me a sidelong look. Stripper—no surprise there. Tampa's got more than its share of seedy strip clubs, peep shows, and adult novelty stores, mostly on South Dale Mabry, and the Mons was one of the more famous—or infamous, depending on how you looked at it.

I felt I'd gotten what I needed from the scene so I walked over to help with the questioning. "You came in at six but didn't notice anything was wrong until thirty minutes ago?" I raised an eyebrow at her, stylus poised to take notes on my PDA.

"Well, I was *tired,* all right?" The girl turned on me with surprising hostility. "I worked my *ass* off last night, ya know? Anyway," she turned back to Cole, meltingly sorrowful again. "The front door was locked, same as always. I didn't think anything of it—I thought maybe Sarah had been pulling an all-nighter, too—working on her thesis—and she was catching up on some sleep. Then, when I came to ask her if she wanted to order a pizza..." She gestured at the bed, with a crumpled pizza-coupon she still held in one hand, and broke into a fresh spate of tears. Cole patted her shoulders awkwardly, and she buried her face in his shirt, which was already smeared with an abundance of electric blue mascara and hot pink lipstick.

"Are you in school, too?" I asked, trying not to laugh at the look on Cole's face. It seemed an odd combination for roommates—a graduate student and a stripper.

"N-no," she sobbed, pressing harder against Cole. "But Sarah had just about talked me into taking classes next semester. She was gonna help me and everything, ya know?"

"That's too bad," I murmured, trying to sound sympathetic. "Do you know how we can contact Sarah's parents about this?"

She sniffled. "You can't—they died in some kinda accident when she was seventeen, along with her brother and sister. Sarah has been on her own ever since."

"Did Sarah have a boyfriend? Anybody who could have done this?" Cole asked her. "Somebody she would have let in with no problem if he knocked on the door?"

She shrugged and pressed a little closer to him. "I don't know—she dated some I guess."

"Could you maybe be a little more specific?" I asked, feeling irritated. She was practically humping Cole's leg.

"There might have been somebody in one of her classes, Jeremy Somebody, I think. But she hadn't been out with him in like, *weeks*, okay?"

"Fine, Jeremy Somebody. Thanks for being so helpful." Taking pity on Cole, I said, "Do you think you could look around a little and see what you think?"

"Sure." He disentangled himself from the clinging stripper with some difficulty and came forward, brushing at the wet smears on the front of his shirt.

"Don't," I said in a low voice. "You'll only make it worse. I'll tell you how to get it out later."

"Okay, thanks." He smiled at me gratefully. He's not one of those guys who's totally helpless around the house, but ever since his ex-wife, Amanda, left him, he's been learning to fend for himself all over again. He doesn't say much about it, but I can tell it's not easy for him to be suddenly single again after ten years of marriage.

I walked back to Miss Tall Blonde and Fake and kept her out of the room, so she didn't contaminate the crime scene any more than she already had. "Did Sarah say anything when you found her?" I asked, as gently as I could.

"N-n...no," she sobbed, casting a hopeful eye at Cole. My partner resolutely kept his back turned, however. "She was unconscious, but I could tell she was breathing—just barely, ya know? At least, I *thought* she was—I didn't dare touch her." Great, with roommates like this, who needed enemies? God forbid she should try any kind of first aid or CPR on her friend.

"She's cold," Cole called, placing one large, latex-clad hand on the vic's shoulder. So Miss Stripper was probably mistaken about her brainy roommate still being alive when she called it in to 911. I was betting the perp had come and gone, locking the door behind him on the way out, while she was still riding the greased pole at the Mons.

"How did you two meet?" I asked, still curious about the arrangement.

She looked at me, a dull kind of hostility in her pale green eyes. "She came to the club about six months ago—but not for the usual reasons, ya know? She was doin' research; she wanted to be some kind of sex psycho-something."

"A psychologist? Maybe a sex therapist?" I asked.

She nodded, "Yeah, that. Anyway, she was writing a paper about why people go into stripping, and she was real nice, ya know? Like, she didn't look down on us or nothing for doing what we do. She interviewed me, and we talked like, for *hours*—got to be real good friends. So about six months ago we moved in together. It was workin' out great...'til this." Her lower lip trembled dangerously, and I was afraid the waterworks were coming on again but Cole interrupted us.

"*The Psychosocial Ramifications of Female Sexual Submission Rooted in the Electra Complex, Myth or Reality?*" He was reading out loud from a laptop that lay open undisturbed on the tiny postage-stamp-sized desk at the far end of the room. He looked over at the roommate. "This her thesis?"

She nodded. "Yeah, she was doing lots of research at the different clubs around town—she was even taking some private lessons."

"Private lessons?" I raised an eyebrow at her. "In stripping?"

She shook her head. The hairspray still caked in her hair was beginning to flake. "No, something else. Bondage, I think."

"How Freudian of her," I commented dryly, looking away. My cheeks felt hot.

"You think?" I could feel Cole looking at me, but I busied myself with making notes in shorthand on my PDA. "What was the name of the teacher she took lessons from?" he asked the stripper roommate.

She shrugged, disinterestedly. "Dunno. Madam or Mistress something-or-other." I felt the tension that had been gathering abruptly dissipate—a woman then. It would take a rape kit to be sure, but I was betting the perp here was male and the same guy who'd done our first vic, Cynthia Harner. Still, Mistress something-or-other might be worth checking out. If Sarah had ties to the BDSM community, it was possible the perp did, too. I only knew from what I had read, but the scene seemed to be set up to look like a classic bondage scenario.

"Any idea if she kept a phone number for her teacher around?"

She shrugged again. "I don't think so, but I know she met her down at the Turk."

"Well, that narrows it down," Cole muttered. Turk Adult Video and Supercenter was the largest adult novelty store in the Tampa Bay area.

"Okay, I think we're done here. We should bag the evidence so they can take her to the ME." I turned to the roommate. "Do you have someplace you could stay? Maybe some friends you could crash with for a while?"

She sniffled and nodded. "Yeah, some of the other girls at the club—I could stay with them."

"That's probably the best idea, at least for now. You have a cell number? Some place we can reach you?" Cole asked. She brightened up immediately.

"Sure. And you can call me any time—or just come down and see my act. I'll even give you a dance for free."

Cole's face got a little red. "That's...very generous of you, but we really just need to be able to contact you in case we have any more questions."

"Yeah," I put in. "You know, about your roommate's murder?"

"Oh, yeah..." she half whispered, as though she'd forgotten. "Poor Sarah..." She gave the still figure on the bed a fleeting glance and looked away, biting her lip.

"Grab some things and go stay with friends; we'll see you out." Cole ushered her out of the room while I bagged the sleeping mask, duct tape, and satin restraints before they wheeled Sarah Michaels away. As an afterthought, I had them take the laptop as well. Most of the prints on it were bound to be Sarah's, but you never could tell.

When Cole came back, he was more than a little red in the face. "Let me guess, she offered you a dance again?" I guessed.

"Not really. She…" He cleared his throat, mumbling the last words so that I couldn't understand. Just then, the stripper came out of the adjoining room with a bag over her shoulder. She was wearing a pair of very tight jeans and adjusting a brief purple tube top that barely covered her artificially perky nipples.

"'Bye and thanks, Detective Berkley. Call me real soon." She banged out of the apartment as though it was just another ordinary day.

I finally got the picture. "You went with her to get her clothes, and she gave you a little taste of her act right there. What did she do, strip off right in front of you?"

He cleared his throat with embarrassment. "More or less."

I glanced down at the crotch of his pants and tried not to laugh. "Looks like you may have a little problem there, Cole."

"Give me a break." His ears were still very red. "It's been over a year since Amanda and I split. Besides, I turned around as soon as she started to, uh, take it off."

I shook my head with mock sympathy. "Uh-uh-uh. Looks like we're going to have to find you a little female companionship. I'd hate for my partner to get so desperate he ended up dating a skanky, jail-bait stripper."

"Thanks a lot, Alex." He moved down the short hall, away from the scene, still walking just a little funny. "You know," he called over his shoulder. "If I talked to you like that, they'd call it sexual harassment."

"Call it whatever you want, but if I decide to harass you, *Detective Berkley*, you'll know it." I swatted him on the butt, making my point.

Chapter Three

Cole

I was glad Alex was getting a good laugh out of the situation. It wasn't that I'd never had a come-on at work before (although rarely one that blatant) or even that I really found the girl all that attractive (I didn't). It was exactly what I'd told her—I hadn't been with anyone in a long time. Not since about six months before the divorce, actually, when things started heading south with Amanda and she cut me off.

Don't get me wrong, I'd thought about finding someone, especially after the divorce was complete. It wouldn't have been so hard—I'm no male model, but I'm not the worst-looking guy around, and a lot of women like the fact that I'm big and tall. So I could have found someone, just for the night, to take the edge off. But somehow it just felt...wrong. I'd been completely faithful to Amanda during the entire ten years of our marriage, and though she was already shacking up with a senior partner in her law firm, for me, fidelity was turning out to be a hard habit to break.

Outside it was still in the seventies although Christmas was only weeks away. It was even warm enough to take off my jacket, if I hadn't wanted to avoid showing my gun. In a place like the Carlton Arms, it's better to keep the element of surprise if possible.

"So what do you think—same guy, right?" Alex asked as we stepped out of the dank little apartment and into bright Tampa sunshine.

"Oh, yeah." I nodded. "Looks like he had a little more fun this time around, but I'd say definitely the same guy."

She nodded. "Mask and restraints match the first vic, and I'll bet my next paycheck forensics will be able to tell us the duct tape came from the same roll."

I examined the lock on the front door, which was the only way in or out of the tiny apartment unless you counted windows, and none of them had been tampered with that I could see.

"No forced entry, just like the first scene," I said, frowning.

"Either she knew him or had some reason to trust him enough to answer the door. What about Jeremy Somebody?" Alex examined the pristine door lock as well.

I shrugged. "Guess it's worth a try. Sounds like a long shot, but it's all we've got right now."

She nodded. "I'll call and try to get a list of her classes and the students enrolled in them faxed to the station. Shouldn't be too hard—graduate classes are usually small."

"Unless it was some kind of general ed thing," I pointed out. "Or something she was taking just for the hell of it to fill out her schedule."

"Can't help that." Alex sighed. "What about the mask?" She consulted the case file briefly, scanning the evidence photos, and then pulled the plastic baggie holding the mask found on Sarah Michaels out of her pocket. "It's definitely the same kind, and it doesn't look like something you could just pick up at Wal-Mart."

"Not any Wal-Mart I ever went to," I agreed. "Didn't Ramirez and Kendricks check that out?"

"Looks like…no. At least, I can't find anything in the file." She sighed and shook her head. "I'll get Matt to nose around the Internet some while we run down the leads. Maybe he can come up with something." Matt Sierens was our Internet specialist at the downtown PD. He was trained as a crime tech, but he was so good with the online stuff, he rarely left the station.

"What about the person she was taking lessons from…would that be a Dominatrix? What about that angle?" I said.

Alex's cheeks got suddenly pink, and she stuffed the mask back in the pocket of her jacket and shrugged. "Don't look at me; I don't know anything about that kind of thing. Look in the phone book under 'D' maybe."

I gave her a look, wondering why she was suddenly so defensive, but she was carefully looking away. "Canvass the neighbors?" she said.

I nodded. "I'll take one side, you take the other. Meet back here in a few." We split up, and I ended up taking the left side while she went right. I banged for a good two minutes at the first apartment to the left, one-twenty-eight, before a middle-aged Latino male finally cracked open the door.

He looked up at me, eyes widening as he took in my size. It was a familiar reaction. "Wha' choo want?" he slurred unsteadily. He clutched a bottle in one hand, and the television behind him gabbled rapidly in Spanish.

"Police." I showed him my badge, which magically sobered him up. The bottle did a disappearing act, too.

"Man, I ain't did nothing," he protested, pulling the ratty bathrobe he was wearing closer around his moth-eaten boxers. "Wha' choo bothering me for?"

"Just want to ask a few questions, Mr...?"

"Sanchez," he said suspiciously. "But I don't know nothing about nothing."

"Did you know your next-door neighbors..." I glanced at my notes. "Sarah Michaels and Vicky Connors?"

He squinted at me, as though trying to weigh the odds. "Sorta, I did. Nice ladies. Wha' they done?"

"It wasn't so much what they did as what was done to them," I said. "Sarah Michaels was murdered last night."

"That little *puta* with the dyed blonde hair and the big *tatas?*" A face popped up behind the man's shoulder so suddenly I nearly went for my gun. It was a little old Spanish woman, probably twice as old as Bathrobe; I guessed she was his mother. He turned to her and yelled something in Spanish, and she slapped him on the side of the head and yelled back twice as loud. In the background, the television continued to laugh to itself in bilingual snippets. *Telemundo.*

"Excuse me...excuse me!" I had to raise my voice to make myself heard, which is usually not necessary. They both stopped talking at the same time and stared up at me.

"Ma'am." I showed my badge again to the little old lady. "I'm investigating the murder of Sarah Michaels, your next-door neighbor. It might have happened anytime last night or this morning. Did you hear anything?"

"That the one with the blonde hair?" she asked, suspiciously.

I tried to suppress a sigh. "No, ma'am. Sarah Michaels had long brown hair. She was a student at UCH."

"Oh, *that* one." She appeared to think hard for a minute, her wrinkled features twisting into a monkey's fist of concentration. "No, officer. I never heard nothing—wish I did though, because she was nice—a good girl. Not like that *puta* girlfriend of hers." She made an exaggerated shrug. "But I'm sorry, we was watching TV all last night."

"Both of you?" I asked. At the volume they were playing it, I would have been surprised if they could hear a heard of elephants stampede through their apartment. Of course, Bathrobe might have turned up the TV, waited until dear sweet Mama was asleep to sneak next door... Nah. I just didn't like this short, potbellied guy, who was already drunk before noon, for Sarah Michaels's murder. Somehow he didn't seem the type to stage a scene like the one we'd found. Beer was probably more his scene than bondage.

They both nodded vigorously, and she said something to the man in rapid Spanish.

"Can we go now?" he asked. "Her show's on." He jerked his head back in the direction of the canned laughter coming out of the dank hallway, and I nodded.

"Okay, but here." I fished in a pocket and handed them my card. "If you remember anything suspicious, anything you heard or saw, anything at all, give me a call." I tapped the card. "Detective Berkley, okay?"

"Sure, sure." Bathrobe took the card, nodding vacantly, his attention already halfway down the hall. I turned to go, but a tug on my sleeve pulled me back.

"Hey, want to know who might hear something?" the little old lady whispered. "The lady in one-thirty-two, the other side of those two girls' apartment—she's always home, and she don't even own a TV." She nodded her head rapidly, as though she'd let me in on a particularly nasty secret and then slammed the door. Great.

* * *

I met up with Alex a while later, after doing all the apartments on my side.

"Well?" I asked.

She shook her head. "Nothing. Nobody around here hears or sees anything. You'd think the Carlton Arms had turned into a community for the deaf and blind overnight." She looked disgusted.

"What about one-thirty-two?" I asked, remembering the little old lady's statement. "Somebody I talked to seemed to think the occupant there is always home."

"Well, they aren't today." Alex looked disgruntled. "Come on, let's go see what the ME says about vic number two. We can come back later for one-thirty-two."

She was quiet on the drive to the medical examiner's office. Tired maybe, or maybe still grieving. I knew how she felt. Hell, I was still getting over my divorce, and nobody had died there. I thought of several different topics of conversation, but none of them seemed to work, so we drove in silence until I got a brainstorm.

"So, you still writing?" I asked as casually as I could, watching the road as she skillfully maneuvered us between a concrete mixer and a truck towing a trailer filled with horses.

She gave me a sidelong look I couldn't interpret. "Why do you ask?"

I shrugged, uncomfortable in the confines of the tiny car. Why can't Volkswagen make a decent-sized vehicle, anyway? Are all Europeans puny or something? "I don't know...it seemed to make you happy. Even though you'd never let me read any of it. I don't even know if it's poetry or drama..." I grinned at her. "Or torrid romance."

She looked straight ahead, eyes on the road. "Yes, Cole, I'm still writing, and no, you can't read any of it."

"Well excuse the hell out of me," I said, beginning to get mad. "You don't have to bite my head off, Alex. I'm just worried about you—that's all."

She sighed deeply and lurched to a stop at a red light. "Look," she said, turning to me (not easy, since I was taking up most of the available room in the little car myself). "I'm sorry if

I've been snappish and standoffish lately. I know I've been a bitch. It's just that...that..." She looked over my shoulder, not meeting my eyes, and her own eyes were suspiciously bright. "Just that I miss him so damn *much*," she finished, just as the light turned green. She faced front and gunned the gas, the stoic look falling back in place. "But I'll try not to let it affect my job performance. I've still got your back—you can count on me, Cole, you know that."

"That's not what I'm worried about," I said as gently as I could. I wanted to put my arms around her and hold her, to keep her safe from all the horrible things going on out there, and going on inside her, too. But I knew she wouldn't allow it.

Alex always has to be the strongest one—for as long as I've known her, she's had this kind of brittle shell around her, like a thin layer of ice over her heart. She lets me in more than anyone else, but lately even I was getting turned away at the door—that was what was worrying me. That we were losing touch—that I was losing her. But being a guy, I couldn't say all that without sounding like a stupid soap opera.

I didn't say anything. I touched her shoulder instead, daring to let my hand comb briefly through the silky waves of her hair. She tightened at first, a knot of tension under my hand, and then relaxed with a soft little sigh. I reached under the hair and massaged the nape of her neck, just the way I know she likes it, and the sigh turned into a little moan of pure pleasure as her muscles loosened. It did funny things to me, to hear that soft sound coming from my partner, but I put it down to being too long on my own. After all, Alex was just Alex, wasn't she?

* * *

The ME was Dr. Marilyn Warren, and she's one of the best. She's an African American lady who carries herself like a queen, and she really knows her stuff. Self confidence and intelligence in a woman are always a turn on, although she's probably a good fifteen years older than me.

"Time of death...judging from body temp, I'd say between eleven and one last night," she was saying as she pulled back the sheet. The smell of chemicals was strong in the air, which was fine with me—at least it covered the smell of death.

Sarah Michaels was laid out on the cool steel table, and her face had that pale bluish tinge they always try to fake on TV cop shows and never quite manage. I gave myself a minute to feel sorry for her. She wasn't even out of her twenties and some pervert comes along and cuts her life short. Empathy with your victims isn't an emotion you can afford to indulge in very much as a homicide detective, or you'll wash out in the first year. You have to keep a little distance between yourself and the crime—too much compassion is a real career killer. But still... I wanted to nail the bastard who had done this. Wanted it badly.

"So she was strangled, just like the first vic. You did the work up on Cynthia Harner too, right?" Alex asked.

Dr. Warren nodded and gestured at the body. "Mm-hm, and judging from the strangulation marks, I'd say it's a good bet that the guy who killed Cynthia also killed Sarah."

"Why do you say that?" I leaned forward, taking a closer look at the ring of purple bruises around the slim throat. It wasn't like we hadn't expected it, but it's always nice to have another professional confirm your guess.

"See the bruises?" Dr. Warren gestured, pointing with one short but perfectly manicured fingernail. "They're almost even all the way around the neck. Your guy has lots of staying power. He didn't just crush the trachea, he cut off the blood flow and exerted almost perfectly even pressure all the way around the neck—that's not easy to do. It's almost the same effect a noose gives when someone gets hanged."

I saw Alex wince and turn away. I knew she was thinking of her dad and reminded myself that the ME didn't know the circumstances of his death.

"So we're looking for a guy with a strong grip?" I asked, trying to push things along.

Dr. Warren nodded. "Mm-hm. And pretty big hands—this guy could span an octave on the piano easily."

"What about the bloody marks on her legs?" I asked, gesturing to the long, thin red lines that covered the vic's pale thighs.

Dr. Warren sighed. "Something long and thin—like a switch but with more rigidity to it. And he wielded it with a lot of force."

"Maybe a riding crop," Alex said thoughtfully. "Or a cane."

The ME nodded. "Could be. If you can find the weapon, I can match it to the marks."

"Sick bastard," I said, feeling the anger twist in my gut. "He tortured her. Tied her up, blindfolded her so she didn't know what was coming, and beat her before raping and strangling her." Oh, I wanted him, all right. Wanted to make him pay.

"Rape kit?" Alex asked.

"Spermicide from a really common brand of condom found, and some vaginal abrasions. No hair or blood, so no DNA, but

I'd say yes," the ME confirmed. "Other than that, I can't tell you much else."

"You've told us enough," I said, nodding at the body. "The scene was a little different, and we're still waiting for lab analysis on the duct tape, mask, and restraints, but we're pretty sure this is the same guy."

"I hope you find him soon." Dr. Warren drew the sheet back up over Sarah Michaels's lifeless face. "Before he decides he might like to do it again."

"Oh, he'll do it again." Alex's voice was flat. "He's got a taste for it now; he's not going to stop any time soon."

Chapter Four

Alex

I let myself into my little house in central Tampa with a sigh of relief. It had been a long day, and tomorrow would be even longer as we searched for more leads. I had spoken to a harried student aide at the University of South Florida's registrar's office who had promised me a list of Sarah Michaels's classes and classmates for the past semester, but she swore she couldn't get it to me until the next day. With nothing else concrete to look at, Cole and I had agreed to call it a night.

I live in a comfortably-sized block house that was built in the forties and completely renovated just the year before I bought it. My neighborhood is just around the corner from Lowry Park Zoo, a real kid magnet, although I think my mom has just about given up getting any grandchildren out of me. In her opinion, if I'm still single at the advanced age of thirty, I'll probably die a miserable spinster because I couldn't catch a man. My mom is kind of old-fashioned that way.

My problem wasn't catching a man, however, but keeping one once I'd gotten him. I've had my share of single white males, but none I cared enough to change my name for. I sighed as I nuked a Lean Cuisine, the single girl's favorite meal, and poured myself a glass of iced tea. Now that my dad was dead, the only guy I really felt comfortable around was Cole, and that was only because he didn't know my dirty little secret.

I sat at my desk and flipped on the computer, waiting impatiently to check my e-mail. With as much online stuff as I'd been doing lately, I knew it was time to move to broadband, but I just couldn't seem to get around to it.

When the e-mail came up, I was glad to see my latest e-book, *Whispers in the Dark*, was doing well, according to my editor. I was trying to break into print, although I knew I'd have to tone my material down considerably to get a regular editor to consider it. Erotica just isn't mainstream enough yet. Especially not erotica with a BDSM slant.

It might seem strange, a tough feminist homicide detective writing what I write, but I found it to be a release, a badly needed escape from the often harsh realities of my daily life. I started writing in the first place for my own gratification, to tell myself a story I wanted to hear, to put my needs on paper—and eventually on the computer screen. I'd been doing it since the age of fifteen and then burning the results, lest my uptight mother find what I'd written and give herself a heart attack. My father I didn't worry about—he was always too distant and distracted to notice much of anything I did, even when my efforts were aimed at getting his attention. Which didn't mean I didn't miss him like hell.

I swallowed the lump in my throat and went to retrieve my diet lasagna from the microwave. It had been almost three months since I'd found him hanging in the closet of the spare room in my parents' house. The image of his dead face still floated in my mind like a black balloon if I let it. I'd known he was depressed, but then, he'd been depressed for most of my life. I'd never expected him to take such extreme measures—I don't think any of us did. He was a kind but distant man. I felt his loss like a physical blow or a bullet lodged in my heart. A wound that would never fully heal.

"Miss you so damn much, Daddy," I murmured to myself, pushing back the tears. I knew if I let myself break down and cry I'd lose it completely, and I couldn't handle that. But the distance I was putting between myself and the grief was hard to maintain; it was putting a strain on my already tenuous emotional equilibrium. Lately I felt like I was moving in a trance, disconnected from my body in a way that was hard to explain. I knew I had to make more of an effort at work though—Cole deserved to have a partner who was backing him up one hundred percent every step of the way. Even when he was going through his divorce, he'd always been there for me, and I couldn't do less for him.

Cole, of course, had been great throughout the whole awful ordeal. In fact, he was the first person I called after making the horrible discovery. Even before my mom or 911. He'd been there to hug me and comfort me and act like the perfect big brother I'd never had. Sometimes he could be annoyingly nosy, though. Like today, asking about my writing and what had happened to Jeff, the latest in a long line of guys who just hadn't worked out.

What he didn't know, and what I would rather die than tell him, was that the reason Jeff had left in such a hurry and the things I wrote about were one and the same. Actually, Jeff hadn't gone because he found out what I wrote, but rather, because I wanted to do more than just write about it. I had told Cole that I'd scared him off, and I was absolutely serious. I didn't ever want to see that look in my partner's eyes—half pity, half revulsion—if he found out my secret desires. I could still hear Jeff's incredulous tone echoing in my head: "You want me to do *what* to you?"

I shook my head and, taking another sip of tea, opened my last e-mail. "Dear Victoria Tarlatan," it began and went on to welcome me into the Romance Writers of America. The letter was from Rebecca Pollock, the chapter president, and she went on to explain that I'd been added to their roster over a month ago when I applied, but she'd somehow lost my e-mail address. She apologized for the late notification and welcomed me to the group. I was pleased to see that the next meeting of the Tampa Bay chapter was in a little under a month, around the first of the year. I wanted to meet other women who were writing the same kind of thing I was, wanted to know I wasn't alone.

I felt a little silly, signing up under my pen name, but as a writer of erotica, I couldn't be too careful about how much of my personal information got on the 'Net. My real name was on the check and the registration form I'd sent in, of course, but I'd made it clear I didn't want it getting online. There are a lot of sickos out there combing the Internet for easy prey, but that wasn't my only reason for keeping my identity secret.

I was pretty sure that if anyone at work happened to find out what I wrote, I'd be finished professionally. Writing BDSM erotica is not something you add to your résumé if you want to go far in the Tampa PD. Oh, they couldn't really fire me because of it, but they sure as hell could give me a hard time. Women are in the minority in almost any police station. You have to be tough to make a name for yourself, and you have to be as good or better than the men you work with. I prided myself on being both. In the whole department, there were only four female detectives, and out of those, I was the only one in homicide.

And it wasn't like I was writing warm and fuzzy fluffy bunny romance either. I put my whole heart and every bit of my desire into my writing, which resulted in what you might term "hard core" books. Every one of my submissive fantasies found an outlet when I sat down at the computer—it was the only outlet I had. If the guys I worked with learned what I was writing, what I secretly craved with every fiber of my being... Well, let's just say I had to wade through enough bullshit as it was. Cole was the only person who I perhaps could have confided in, but that was out of the question.

I clicked the link at the bottom of the e-mail and was pleased to see that they'd added *Whispers* to their list of books by local authors. There was even a link to my publisher, Dark Angel Books, so anyone interested could buy and download the book immediately. Nice.

Putting the half-eaten lasagna in the trash, I got off line and pulled up Microsoft Word. It was time to do a little more work on the book I was currently writing, *Twisted Desire*. I closed my eyes for a moment, summoning the scene and then typed:

She was naked before him, trembling, helpless, wrists bound behind her back by cold silver. He was wearing the belt again—the thick black strap of leather hung low on his narrow hips. She couldn't keep her eyes off it.

"You need this belt?" he asked, one large hand caressing the flat silver buckle.

She nodded, wanting it so badly. "Use it...please!"

"You'll get what you need when you need it." His voice was soft, almost caressing. He slid his fingers into her thick blonde hair and yanked backward forcing her to expose the pale, vulnerable curve of her throat.

She gasped, heart racing, feeling the wet heat pool between her thighs.

"Don't ask me to take you," he whispered. "I'll take you when I want."

I stopped typing for a moment and closed my eyes to savor the scene. I could almost *feel* the lash of the belt, the cold silver restraints encircling my wrists, those strong hands caressing me...making me obey without question. To be that helpless, that vulnerable, with a man I could truly trust. To truly lose control... A long, slow sigh fell out of me at the thought, and I squeezed my thighs together tightly. God, just writing about it got me so worked up—if I ever actually did it, I'd probably go into total erotic overload.

I opened my eyes and took another sip of tea. And my partner wondered why I wouldn't let him see what I wrote. If Cole ever saw this, he would either laugh at me or pity me, and he certainly wouldn't approve of me ever acting like this with a man I was dating. Not that I needed his or any man's approval but still... The standard "don't hurt my partner or else" speech would take on a whole new dimension if he knew what I *really* wanted.

Worse yet, he might think I was some kind of a sick freak, especially in light of the case we were working on. It had bothered me greatly to see how much trouble the perp had gone to in order to set up the murder scene like a classic bondage fantasy. I longed to be restrained and taken by a firm but loving Master but never would I ask to be beaten and raped, let alone killed. But would my overprotective partner be able to understand the fundamental difference when faced with the ugly reality we'd seen today?

I frowned. Why was I worrying about what Cole would think about me if he knew my desires anyway? It wasn't like they had anything to do with him. I shook my head, clearing the ridiculous thought away, and went back to my book.

Chapter Five

He is quiet tonight, resting from his labors. The punishment of the second one was more enjoyable than he ever would have expected. The way she begged until he gagged her with the tape, the way her eyes overflowed, wetting the mask as he took her. It was fitting that she should die so. Fitting that she should share the same fate as the first.

And surely she had been grateful for all he had done. He had taken such pains to be certain her needs, *all* her needs, were met. The rose petals, the careful whipping of her thighs...he'd taken the scene directly from her own book, *Painful Pleasures*. And what more could she ask than that?

After the first he was shaken, fearful. Yes, he can admit it now. He was almost certain they would find him and punish him. They could never understand how necessary it was—how utterly right. But they couldn't touch him, and it made him realize something very important. A divine compulsion has entered him, and he must obey. He is entrusted with the punishment of these women and he cannot fail. And that is why the wandering finger passed over him and the watchful eye was blind.

He took a long time planning with this one. He had to wait until the roommate was out, had to cover his tracks carefully. But he is confident now—secure. It won't take nearly as long to get to the next one. She lives alone, after all. And he finds he is quite looking forward to it. Already he is reading her book, still on the laptop, and looking for an appropriate scene.

He looks at the screen of the laptop, at the list of names still blinking there. Sylvestra Eden, Carolyn Sinders, Victoria Tarlatan. He highlights Sylvestra Eden and then hits delete.

Two more to go.

Chapter Six

Cole

The day started out badly, with a call from my ex. "Cole," she snapped, as soon as I picked up the phone. "I need to talk to you." No hello, how are you, how are things going? Just straight to the point. That's always been Amanda's way—direct and confrontational. I'd found it to be kind of a turn-on when we were first dating. I liked the way she stood up to me and always spoke her mind. She knew what she wanted out of life and wasn't afraid to go after it.

Of course, this same single-minded determination was a real pain in the ass when applied to our separation and divorce. And it didn't help that Amanda was a junior partner at Catanya and Catanya, and she knew exactly how to manipulate the law in her own best interests. When we'd divorced, she'd gotten nearly everything.

It wasn't that I missed the house, although it had been a nice one. But it was too filled with the memories of us as a family, and if I couldn't have that anymore, then I didn't want anything to do with it. And I was fine with paying child support, although I was well aware that Amanda really didn't need it to make ends meet. She'd been out-earning me for the past several years, which she enjoyed pointing out whenever we had an argument. Of course, I'd put her through law school in the first place, a fact she conveniently seemed to forget once the battle lines were drawn.

What really bothered me about the whole sorry business was the fact that she was managing to keep me away from my daughter, Madison. (Amanda's choice of name, not mine.) Madison is eight and the light of my life. I adore my daughter, I really do. And I love being a dad. Of course, I'd enjoyed being a husband, too, for the most part, but when Amanda decided she was tired of our life together, there wasn't a damn thing I could do or say to change her mind.

"Cole," she said sharply, snapping me out of my unhappy reverie.

"What?" I barked back, then immediately regretted giving her any ammunition. Nobody can out-nasty Amanda when she's on a roll, but she loves the challenge when someone tries.

"Just waking up?" she said, in a voice that clearly stated her disapproval of my lethargic habits.

I glanced at the bedside clock and stifled a groan. Six a.m., and I'd been up past one, unable to sleep because my brain wouldn't let go of the damn case. "I'm awake now," I said, in a resigned tone. "What do you need?"

"To talk about Madison's birthday this weekend," she said. I could hear someone in the background asking if she wanted coffee and realized she must already be at the office.

"Is that your secretary?" I asked, sitting up in bed. "Who's taking Madison to school this morning if you're already at work?"

"She's already there. There's a before-school care program at her new school," Amanda said coolly. "And before you ask, yes, she gets a balanced breakfast as well."

I sighed unhappily. Mornings had always been my special time with my daughter when Amanda and I were still together. Because of the general craziness of my job, I was never certain I could make it home in time for supper, but we always got up early to spend a little time together before the day really started. I would make her breakfast (blueberry pancakes were my specialty), and we'd talk about school and sometimes I'd read to her if there was enough time before dropping her off. Now my ex-wife had her packed off to school before the crack of dawn, eating some institutional crap, just so she could get to the office and make senior partner a year earlier.

"How does Madison feel about that?" I asked, more roughly than I'd intended. "How does she like having to get to school when it's still dark instead of having breakfast at home with her family?"

"Actually she loves it." Amanda refused to rise to the bait. "Gives her more time to play with her little friends. She has a whole new social circle now, Cole. She's making friendships that will be to her benefit later on."

I rolled my eyes at the ceiling and gritted my teeth to stop myself from shouting at my stubborn ex. Here was the root of the whole problem—the reason she'd left me in the first place. She could say it was my job, the wild hours I worked, and the danger I was in on a daily basis that made her life too uncertain, but I knew the truth.

Amanda had left because of her goddamn ambition to get to the highest tax bracket and the most elite social circle Tampa had to offer, and she was determined to drag Madison along with her. Having a husband who was a homicide detective instead of a CEO or a senior partner was a major detriment to her plan, and she'd neatly solved it via divorce. Now I was out of the picture, and she wanted me to stay that way.

"I could take Madison to school in the morning," I offered, knowing already what she was going to say. "We could grab breakfast on the way, and I'd get her there on time, no problem."

"I don't think so, Cole. The Sylvia B. Otero Academy is way across town from where you're staying. It couldn't possibly work. But this isn't what I called to talk about anyway."

"Fine." I gritted my teeth some more—promising myself she hadn't heard the last on the subject. "What about Madison's birthday? You get her Saturday, and I get her Sunday, right?" Actually it was supposed to be my weekend with my daughter, but I'd sacrificed half of it so Madison could have two birthday parties instead of one. One with her mother and Amanda's new boyfriend, Bill Jenkins (a senior partner at her firm), and one with me.

"Actually that arrangement isn't convenient anymore." In the background I heard another line ringing and she said, "Take a message, I'll be done here shortly."

"Do you want to switch days?" I asked. It didn't really matter to me. Other than the case Alex and I were working, I didn't have anything else going on.

"No, not exactly." Amanda's voice got brisker, as it always did when she was about to deliver some bad news. "You see, Bill and I have decided to take Madison and five or six of her little friends to Disney World for the weekend. And what with travel time to Orlando and what have you, we decided it would just be easier to go up Friday evening and stay until Sunday night."

"How convenient, you *decided*," I growled. "But you didn't ask me, did you? You may not give a damn if our daughter gets to spend time with her real father, but I do, Amanda. I already gave up half my weekend so she could have the big birthday party you *said* you were planning, but I'm not giving up the other half, too. You can just forget it."

"Fine." Her voice had gone cool and brittle again. "Then *you* can tell Madison why she can't have the birthday trip her Uncle Bill planned for her. She'll be quite disappointed, unfortunately. All her little girlfriends have already been invited, and it's all she can talk about, but go ahead, burst her birthday bubble. Just don't come crying to me when she starts to hate you."

"You bitch," I said thickly, before I could get control of myself. "That's not playing fair, and you know it. You can't use our daughter's love like some kind of bargaining chip in your twisted game of emotional poker."

"Whatever, Cole. As exciting as this melodrama is, I have things that need to be attended to. I was only calling you as a courtesy, and I'll thank you to remember to keep a civil tongue in your head when we talk like this. I tape all these conversations, you know."

It was another veiled threat, and I knew it. Amanda was quite capable of taking me to court, painting me as a verbally and emotionally abusive monster and cutting me out of Madison's life for good. It was what she truly wanted although when and why she had started hating me so much was hard to understand.

"Why are you doing this, Amanda?" I said, feeling my fury dissolve into despair, a hard knot of ice in my chest that wouldn't melt. "I loved you for as long as you let me, and I love Madison more than my own life. What did I do to make you hate me this way?"

"If you don't know then I can't tell you." Suddenly she sounded just on the edge of tears herself. "How was I supposed to feel, Cole? With you always coming home late, always running around with your little 'partner?'"

"Come on, Amanda, you know there was never anything between Alex and me. That's a lame excuse," I said angrily. I'd always had an idea that my ex didn't like my partner, but I'd assumed it was because she saw Alex as an extension of the job that was taking me away from her and Madison. I'd never had any idea she thought I was having some kind of affair.

"I was faithful to you every minute of our marriage," I told her. "I never wanted another woman, Amanda."

"But I bet you're enjoying yourself now," she said nastily. "I know you moved in with her as soon as we split. Why did you even bother to get your own apartment?"

"I stayed with Alex because I didn't have anyplace else to go when you dropped the bomb," I said angrily. "But I spent every night in her guest room, not that it's any of your goddamn business."

"Not anymore it's not," she snapped back. "I didn't call to have this discussion with you, Cole. I don't care who you sleep with or how often or where." She took a deep breath. "The issue here is Madison. You can have her the weekend after Christmas and celebrate with her then." She sounded brisk and businesslike again, all emotion wiped completely from her voice.

"Sure, if you haven't planned a visit to Sea World or Universal that would make me the bad guy to interrupt," I said savagely.

"I really have to go, Cole," she said. There was a sharp click when she hung up. I sat on the bed, breathing hard and staring at the black plastic receiver sitting innocently in its cradle. Lately, it always seemed to bring bad news. I had a brief, violent fantasy of ripping the cord out of the wall and smashing the whole thing against the floor, but restrained myself.

As I was watching it with murderous intent, the phone rang again, and I snatched it up, thinking it was Amanda calling back for round two. "What do you want?" I growled into the receiver. There was complete silence on the phone and then Alex's voice came back at me.

"Whoa, Cole, are you all right? Did I wake you up?" she asked, sounding concerned.

I sighed and ran a hand through my hair tiredly. "No and no." I swung my legs over the side of the bed and stood with a half-hearted stretch. I might as well get up—I knew I wasn't getting back to sleep now.

"Well, listen, if it's a bad time…" Her voice trailed off into that sexy little half-note that always comes through so clear when she's on the phone. We like to tease her down at the station that she should be in vice with a voice like hers instead of homicide. Think of all the phone sex scams she could bust.

"It's not a bad time. I…just got up on the wrong side of the bed." I got up and searched for a towel, thinking maybe a hot shower would help take the edge off. "What's on your mind?"

"Well, I was actually calling to ask you a favor. I think I left the Bug's lights on overnight, and now it won't even turn over."

"You need a jump?" I shambled into the bathroom and turned on the hot tap full force, waiting for the water to heat up.

"I thought of that, but this isn't the first time I've let it go dead, and I think this particular battery's about shot."

"Well, I guess I could stop by an auto parts store and pick you up a new one," I offered, still keeping an eye on the shower. The tiny hot water tank in my apartment guaranteed there was never more than ten minutes of hot water at a time, and I didn't want to miss it.

"Thank you, Mr. Goodwrench," she said dryly. "But I was actually thinking more of a ride in today. And if you can drop me off at my mom's house on your way home, she can take me to get a new one. That way I can trade in the old one, too. Problem solved—that is, if you don't mind." There was a sound in the background like she was buttering toast.

"I don't mind," I said. Steam was beginning to billow out of the open bathroom door. "Look, Alex, I gotta get a shower while this piece of crap water heater is working."

"Uh-oh, did I catch you naked?" She laughed, obviously just making a joke, but for some reason the low, sexy little sound went straight to my groin. Alex has a laugh that ought to be outlawed. I'd always thought so, but I never let myself dwell on it too much before.

"Uh, guilty as charged," I admitted, feeling confused and a little embarrassed.

"I hear that note of guilt in your voice—thinking about the skanky little stripper we met yesterday?" she asked, still laughing at me. "Having a problem, Cole?"

For some reason her words pulled up not a picture of the second vic's roommate, but a mental image of Alex herself. Specifically, the way she looks when she just wakes up, with her hair all tousled and those big brown eyes half-lidded and sleepy. We'd been on enough stakeouts together where we traded off shifts for me to know the look well. For some reason my groin reacted again. If I kept this up, I'd need a cold shower instead of a hot one. Weird.

"Cole." Her voice broke into my confused thinking. "Did I lose you over there?"

"Uh, no, sorry," I said hastily. "I'll be there in fifteen. Make me some of that toast."

"With strawberry jam on it, just like you like it," she promised before she hung up.

I stood in the shower until the water got cold, wondering what was happening to me. Was I just noticing Alex in a whole different way because I hadn't been with anyone in so long, or was there something else going on?

Whatever the reason, I knew one thing for sure—I had to put a rein on this before it got out of control. Alex was my best friend and the best partner I could ask for. I didn't want to lose any of that. She was too important for me to screw up our relationship with sex.

Chapter Seven

Alex

"Yup, dead as a doornail."

Of course, Cole insisted on checking the Bug for himself, which I really didn't mind. He's a real man's man when it comes to automotive stuff.

"Sorry I had to ask for a lift," I said, climbing into the passenger side of his black Dodge Ram pick-up with the four slices of toast and a mug of coffee I'd made him as a thank you.

"'S okay." He climbed in the other side—well, stepped in, really. He keeps the huge truck not because of any macho bullshit, but because it's the only vehicle he's found that actually gives him enough leg room. I still tease him about installing a gun rack and naked lady mud flaps, though.

"Thought we could check in at the station and head out to the Carlton Arms and find out if one-thirty-two was in the night of the murder," he said, before taking a big bite of toast.

"You read my mind," I said, automatically reaching for the coffee mug so he could shift. "Hopefully that list of Sarah Michaels's classmates will be in by now."

"Great. If we don't get a bite at the Carlton Arms, we'll go check out Jeremy Somebody." He took another bite of toast. "This is really good—you're a great cook, Alex."

I laughed. "The domestic goddess, that's me. Toast is my specialty. So you want to tell me what was really going on this morning when I called?" I asked, keeping my eyes on the road. Cole is usually a very even tempered guy, but when he gets worked up, you'd better get out of the way. His surly tone when I'd called him had me concerned.

He sighed, took a sip of coffee, and told me briefly about his early morning conversation with Amanda.

"So what could I say? I guess I could've insisted on my visiting rights, but that makes me the bad guy. What kid wouldn't want to spend the whole weekend at Disney World instead of hanging around with her dad?" He stared straight ahead, his face like granite.

"What a bitch," I said indignantly. I had never liked Amanda much, although I'd tried hard to pretend while Cole was still married. Amanda, for her part, had pretended just as hard, but there was always this feeling when we were all together that she and I were only tolerating each other for Cole's sake. Near the end of their marriage, even that little fiction broke down, and now I really couldn't stand her.

"Yeah, well..." Cole sighed, his shoulders slumping tiredly. "I can see what she's doing—she's making sure I get less and less time with Madison until eventually she can cut me out of her life altogether."

"Don't let her get away with it," I said. I knew how much Cole's daughter meant to him—they had a closeness between them that I'd never had with my own father. My partner's a really a great dad. "Get a better lawyer—you're going to have to drag her into court to get your rights, Cole."

"It'll be uphill all the way if I go that route. C'mon, Alex. You know how juries react to me—she'll make me out to be some kind of abusive monster, and they'll eat it up."

"Hmm, well, you *are* a pretty scary-looking guy," I conceded. Cole is well-spoken and very intelligent, but his sheer size is intimidating. Whenever one of us has to be a witness in court, Captain Davis does her best to make sure it's me. Juries are just more sympathetic to a non-threatening, average-sized woman than a mountain of muscle like Cole.

"I have to do *something* though," he said, sounding almost desperate. "I can't just sit by and let her take Madison away from me completely."

"Aw, Cole..." I reached over and squeezed his thigh sympathetically. I'm not usually a touchy person, but he is, and it hurt me to see him looking so down. "I wish I could help, I really do. You know if you ever need a character witness..."

"Uh... I don't know if that would be such a good idea." He took another drink of his coffee, carefully avoiding my eyes. "Amanda said some things today that...well, I think she might have thought that you and I..."

"She thought you were cheating on her with *me?*" I asked, incredulously. "Are you serious?"

"Yeah, I don't know why she didn't come out with it before. Maybe she's just making up more excuses, but you can see how it would look to a jury, if she played it just right." He took another drink of coffee.

"I guess..." I couldn't believe Amanda's ridiculous ideas, but I could see he had a point. "I guess it *does* look pretty suspicious," I said thoughtfully, as Cole took another big bite of toast. "I mean, you're a man, I'm a woman. We have all the right parts, and we spend about seventy-five percent of our time together. They'd probably think I was jumping your bones twenty-four/seven." I squeezed his thigh again, making it a joke.

Cole choked, spraying toast crumbs all over the dash, and his thigh turned to iron under my hand as he braked too hard at a red light. If the mug I was holding hadn't been half empty, there would have been hot coffee all over the inside of his truck.

"You okay?" I handed him the coffee mug again, and he took a big slug of it before handing it back.

"Yeah...just." He shook his head, obviously uncomfortable about something although I couldn't tell what. "Look, Alex, d'you mind?" He glanced pointedly down at my hand on his thigh, and my gaze followed his own. What I saw made me pull back my hand in a hurry, and my face was suddenly awash with blushes. There was a very obvious bulge in the crotch of his pants. Had I caused that?

"Uh, sorry," I stammered, looking out the window so I wouldn't have to meet those piercing blue eyes. "I didn't mean..."

"'S okay," he said shortly. "It's just...been a while. That's all."

"Sure," I said, keeping my eyes glued to the traffic passing on my right. I'd teased him yesterday when the skanky little stripper had gotten that reaction out of him, but I'd never expected to provoke it myself. Was it just because it had been a long time since his divorce, and he wasn't seeing anyone at the moment, or was it something else? I shook my head, pushing the crazy idea out of my mind. Cole was Cole, my partner and my best friend and nothing more. Right?

By the time we checked in at the station, the nervousness between us had eased up a little. I was relieved. Cole was the only guy I felt comfortable around. If we started throwing sexual tension into the mix, it would screw up the only decent relationship I had.

My first item of business was to get the list of Sarah Michaels's classes and classmates that I had been promised. I settled across from Cole at my desk and called—it still wasn't ready. I had to get really nasty over the phone to convince the USF registrar's office to get a move on. The phrase "obstruction of justice" really comes in handy at times like this. The student aide I spoke to on the phone was nearly in tears when I hung up.

Cole glanced at me with a little grin. "Cast iron bitch, aren't you?"

I grinned back. "All in the name of justice." I was glad to be working a challenging case again. It almost took my mind off my own troubles—almost.

"Hey, Detectives." Matt Sierens, our resident computer geek slash crime lab tech, came wandering over. To look at him you'd think he was just another college kid with bed-head hair, baggy pants, and T-shirts advertising obscure rock bands. Today he was wearing a black T with the words *Genital Menace* printed in bleeding red letters across the front. But appearance notwithstanding, Matt is a real whiz with the Internet. He's helped vice catch over a dozen pedophiles who were using chat rooms as their stalking grounds. All in all, a pretty good guy.

"Crime lab confirms the second strip of duct tape comes from the same roll as the first," he said.

Cole shrugged. "No surprise there."

"Status report on those masks, Matt?" I asked, taking a sip of the foul coffee that seems to be all our department Mr. Coffee can produce.

"Not yet, sorry," he said. "Problem is, your masks are just generic enough that I'm having to troll through, like, *every* adult novelty manufacturer and sex toy site on the 'Net. You know how many of those there are?"

"Let's see…how many sex sites are on the Internet? That's a tough one." Cole tapped his chin, pretending to think. I grinned at him.

"Right, like, *bazillions.*" Matt waved his arms expressively. "You just gotta give me a little more time though, and I'll find it. Just wanted you to know I'm workin' on it."

"We appreciate it, Matt." I smiled at him and took another sip of coffee. Then I had a thought. "And while you're at it can you look and see if there's a local Dominatrix offering her services online? Maybe for private lessons, that kind of thing."

"Whoa, Detective Reed." His eyes widened. "Lookin' to hook up? Wanna learn how to crack the whip?" He cracked an invisible whip in the air and crooned, "Oh, Mistress, that *stings.*"

"That's enough, Matt," I said, feeling my face go red. "This is police business—an official investigation. I hope you realize I would never ask you to do research for any sort of private...fetish of mine. I would never—"

"Hey, hey, Alex, take it easy." Cole was suddenly behind me, hands on my shoulders, rubbing soothingly. "He's just joking around, that's all."

"Well, it's time to stop joking around and get serious." I shrugged off Cole's hands and turned around to glare at both of them. "Two women are dead and more are going to be if we don't stop this guy."

"Jeez, *sorry*," Matt muttered resentfully. Clearly he didn't understand why I had flown off the handle at his playful banter. To be honest, neither did I. After all, my secret was safe enough, my desires hidden behind a pen name. There was no need to let the details of the case get mixed up in my own life.

Over my shoulder I heard Cole murmuring something about the stress I had been under lately, which made me even more upset. I didn't need him apologizing for me. I took a deep breath. "Look, Matt, I'm sorry. I didn't mean to snap at you," I said, looking him in the eye. "I appreciate the work you're doing for us—this is just a very stressful case. But I didn't mean to take it out on you."

"Aw, Detective R, you don't gotta say all that." Matt dropped to one knee and took my hand in his to give it a sloppy, theatrical smooch. "You're still my favorite lady in homicide, ya know?"

"Clown, I'm practically the *only* lady in homicide," I muttered, feeling a little smile twitch at the corners of my mouth. "Get off the floor and get back to work—I need to know where those masks came from. And...the other thing, too."

"Your wish is my command." He made a sweeping bow, threw a little salute at Cole, and slouched off.

"Well, we'd better get a move on," I said, standing briskly and grabbing my light fleece jacket. It gets chilly in Tampa sometimes, but it's never exactly parka weather down here, even just two weeks before Christmas.

"Okay, sure." I could feel Cole's eyes on me. Could feel him wanting to ask if I was all right, but to his great credit, he didn't.

There's a lot to be said for a man that knows when to keep his questions to himself and give you space.

* * *

There was a ribbon of yellow and black police tape strung across the front door of Sarah Michaels's apartment, number one-thirty, but other than that, life at the Carlton Arms appeared to be going on as usual. Someone had even put one of those little door-knob pizza coupon tags you see in lots of college neighborhoods on the door. It occurred to me that Sarah Michaels was never going to eat another slice of pizza again, and I shivered. I was letting this case get to me too much.

It was one of those rare winter days we sometimes get in Tampa, where the temperature actually gets down in the low sixties, but the sun is shining and there's a brisk little breeze blowing. I wrapped my jacket more closely around my body as Cole and I made our way past the crime scene.

Unlike most of the rest of the apartments, one-thirty-two had a slender string of Christmas lights decorating the frame of its cheap plywood door. The door was painted the same tired tan color as the rest of the complex, and it opened at my first knock. A tiny little African American woman peered out at us. She was wearing a worn cotton house coat and she had a dried raisin of a face. We were immediately enveloped in a strong aroma of exotic spices.

"Good morning, ma'am," Cole said, taking the lead. "I'm Detective Berkley, and this is Detective Reed." We flashed our badges. "May we come in and ask you some questions?"

She grinned at us, showing huge, obviously fake white teeth, and stepped aside to usher us inside the tiny apartment. "Come on in, you."

"We actually want to ask about…" Cole started but she cut him off.

"No, no—cannot begin this way. Come sit down, you. Get comfortable, and then we tell each other our hearts."

Cole and I exchanged a look and sat gingerly side by side on the tiny flowered love seat the old lady was indicating. The entire front room was decorated with half a dozen long swaths of brightly colored cloth hung from what looked like plant hooks embedded in the ceiling. The cloth divided the small room into even smaller spaces, a colorful maze, almost, and the effect was both exotic and claustrophobic. There were several mismatched chairs scattered around the cloth maze, and the little lady dragged one across the generic dirty, light tan carpet and plunked it right in front of us.

"Now tell Tante Jinnie what she can do for you," she said eagerly, giving us another look at those huge white teeth.

"We're here investigating the death of—" was as far as Cole got before she hopped up again.

"Got to check my roti!" she exclaimed, and threaded her way through the colorful cloth maze to what I assumed must be the kitchen. There was a loud musical clatter of pots and pans and the spicy scent in the air became nearly overpowering. I could smell cloves and curry and cinnamon and something else I couldn't name. It made Cole sneeze fiercely.

"Bless you," I murmured, as the old lady came hurrying back and plopped herself in the chair again.

"Can't let my roti burn." She looked at Cole intently. "You hungry."

"No, actually. Thank you but I just had breakfast," he said politely. "Now, what we need to talk to you about—"

"No, you *hungry*, you," she insisted, leaning forward to poke him in the chest. "Tante Jinnie can always tell a hungry man, and you be near to starving!"

"No, really—" Cole began.

"You hungry but you a picky eater, you," she pronounced, nodding her head. "But what you hungry for the most, be right under your nose." She looked at me and then back to him, nodding slyly. "The sweetest meat be the closest to hand."

I wondered what in the world the old lady was babbling about. Cole turned red and began to cough. I pounded him on the back, certain his allergies were acting up from all the spices in the air.

"Are you aware your next-door neighbor, Sarah Michaels, was murdered the night before last?" I said before she could start up again.

The shiny white teeth disappeared abruptly, and the tiny raisin face shriveled into an expression of sorrow. "I tell her, me, that she best be careful. Tell her she let her death in by the front door, she don't watch out."

Cole leaned forward eagerly. "Why would you tell her that? Did you know someone who wanted to hurt her?"

The old lady shook her head in an exaggerated arc. "No, no! I know 'cause I know—'cause Tante Jinnie's got the sight. I try to tell her the debil got him a slippery shoe. Put it on, and you slip right in the grave." She shook her head, clucking her tongue sorrowfully. "Such a nice girl." She gestured at the colorful cloth hanging from the ceiling. "She help me fix this—everything just right. Tante Jinnie be so sad to see her pass."

"Yes, we're sure you are," Cole soothed, having gotten his coughing under control. "But we're wondering if you heard anything after nine o'clock on the night she died?"

She shrugged. "Maybe, maybe not. Tante Jinnie got the sight, but her hearing not what it used to be." She tapped a bulky tan hearing aid perched precariously in one of her wrinkled ears.

"Try to think—anything might help," I urged. "Knocking? Someone's voice?"

She turned to me suddenly, focusing her sharp little black eyes on my face in an unnervingly intense stare. "You got a secret, you," she said, poking me in the chest. Her hard little finger hurt, and I sat back abruptly.

"Look, Ms... Tante Jinnie, we need to know—"

"It be the same secret little Sarah had," she said, shaking her head and frowning. "This kind of secret put you in your grave, you. That debil's shoe already half-way on your foot."

I thought of the way Sarah Michaels had been found, bound to the bed, and of my own dark fantasies, which I was so careful to keep hidden behind a pseudonym. Those bright black eyes continued to bore their way into me, and for some reason I found myself blushing. I became aware that Cole was looking at me strangely, a questioning look on his face.

"Can you remember anything or not?" I demanded, abruptly losing my temper. "This is an official investigation, and we need some straight answers here."

She cackled softly, shaking her head. Her hair, which was almost as white as her teeth, looked like cotton balls sticking up in wispy puffs. "You don't scare me, you," she said at last. "But Tante Jinnie tell you what she hear just the same. You want some tea first?"

"*No*," Cole and I said together. "Just tell us," I added, stylus poised over my PDA.

"Very well." She nodded gravely. "Tante Jinnie tell you what she know. Long about ten o'clock that night I hear a knocking on her door. Then she come to open it, and I hear her voice and somebody else."

"Could you hear what they were saying?" Cole asked.

She shook her head. "No, but one voice be low, maybe a man? I think she let him in, and I hear her door close. After that, I take off my ears and go to bed." She tapped the hearing aid again.

Cole and I looked at each other. This almost as unhelpful as Sarah's stripper roommate. "Was there anything else?" I asked hopelessly. "Did you hear anyone leave?"

She shook her head emphatically. "When Tante Jinnie takes off her ears, time to say goodnight. After that you scream and shout all you want, you. Don't make no difference."

"So, did Sarah have a lot of friends coming and going? Any boyfriends you knew of?" Cole asked.

"Always lots of boys coming in and out of that place, but mostly for the other little girl. I think Sarah, she had a boy a while ago but by 'n by, he just stop coming around, he." She screwed up her face thoughtfully. "She tells me once, says, 'Tante Jinnie, just can't find the right man, me.' Her secret make her hungry." She nodded and poked at me again, but this time I managed to dodge the hard little finger. "Too many secrets, too much hungry."

"All right, I think that about wraps it up," I said, feeling a blush creep over my cheeks again. I stood and brushed at the front of my blouse, as though to get rid of invisible crumbs. "Thank you Ms... Tante Jinnie."

"Here." Cole produced a card and handed it to her. She took it and stared at it as though she'd never seen a phone number before. "If you remember anything else you can call me anytime," he said.

She cackled softly, rising and making her way with us to the front door. "Yes, you better go, you, before Tante Jinnie say any more."

Cole and I turned to her, her faded cotton housecoat and blinding teeth framed by the blinking Christmas lights around the door. "Do you have anything else to say?" Cole demanded, looking harassed.

"Tante Jinnie cannot answer questions you will not ask, you." She shook her head and then looked directly at me again.

As before those bright little eyes trained on my face gave me a hot, uncomfortable feeling, almost like I was under a spotlight.

"This be a secret you cannot keep, you," she said gravely, suddenly completely serious. "This secret be your death."

"I..." I opened my mouth to say something, to somehow refute her strange words, and found my mouth didn't want to work.

"Thank you, ma'am. We may be in touch." Cole took my arm and ushered me back to the truck, my mind still in a whirl.

Chapter Eight

Cole

"Finally." Alex grabbed the papers from the fax machine and sank into her swivel chair, putting her feet up on the desk. She was wearing a pair of low-slung black pants that hugged her hips and thighs like a second skin. I found myself staring at her legs and then realized what I was doing. I pulled my gaze away and got up for a cup of water from the cooler. What was wrong with me lately?

"Any hits?" I asked as casually as I could, taking a drink of water to cover my confusion. We had ridden in almost total silence all the way from the Carlton Arms back to the PD on Franklin, neither of us discussing the strange interview with the little old black lady. I had opened my mouth several times, and then closed it again, not certain how to begin. The thing that had really unnerved me was the way her bright little eyes had seemed to look right through me and see everything I was thinking...

"Cole? Hey, Earth to Cole." I realized Alex was snapping her fingers in front of my face. "I said, I think I may have a lead. Look." She pointed at the sheaf of papers she held in one hand.

"Hmm, Jeremy Bruce. Looks like he's in Sarah's psychosexual development class." I tapped the paper. "He the only Jeremy on the list?"

She nodded. "Uh-huh. And it looks like we're in luck—class starts at one so we can catch him there."

I looked at my watch. "That gives us plenty of time for lunch and something else."

"What did you have in mind?" Alex took the cup from my hand and sipped some water before handing it back.

I tapped the case file on my desk with one finger. There were pictures of Cynthia Harner and Sarah Michaels on top of it, both women found in the same degrading position, strangled to death for some psycho's sick sexual gratification. "I think I want to pay a visit to James Harner, the first vic's husband. Being dumped into the middle of all this, we never got to see him before his alibi cleared."

Alex shrugged. "Okay, good thought. Maybe we can find some similarities between his wife and Sarah Michaels. Other than both of them being Caucasian, we really don't have much to go on. Different ages, different social and economic backgrounds..."

"Both were well educated," I pointed out. "And both of them attracted this psycho somehow. I want to know why he's doing what he's doing. What's attracting him to them."

"Hey…" She touched my arm lightly. "You really want him, don't you?"

I looked again at the picture of Sarah Michaels hanging from the black satin restraints and the ring of dark bruises around her slim neck. "Oh yeah," I said, grabbing my jacket and the case file. "He won't stop 'till we catch him. I want him bad."

James Harner was home in the middle of the day. He opened the door of his expensive South Tampa mansion almost before I had finished pressing the doorbell.

"Yes, can I help you?" He was a slim, prissy little man wearing a plain white button-down shirt and gray dress slacks with expensive-looking Italian loafers. He wore black braces on his wrists.

"Detectives Berkley and Reed, Mr. Harner. Can we come in and talk with you?" Alex asked, taking the lead. We flashed our badges and waited.

"Of course, I…" He trailed off and then his nondescript face crumpled suddenly and he began to sob. "Is this…is this about Cynthia?" he managed to ask, between sobs. "Oh, God, I know you still have her personal effects…all the things you took for evidence, but I can't… I just can't come get them. That makes it too…too real, somehow. I just *can't.*"

"I'm sorry, Mr. Harner," Alex said gently. "But we didn't come about Cynthia's effects. We need to ask you some questions."

He shook his head, tears still dripping from his face. "No more, please. I'm just trying so hard not…not to think about it."

Alex's face got tighter. "Mr. Harner, I know how difficult it is to lose a loved one in such a sudden and tragic way, but we're hoping you can help us. You see, there was another woman killed in almost the exact same way as your wife the night before last, and we think the same man is responsible."

He looked up, his no-color eyes and narrow face red from weeping. "He did it *again?* That monster that killed my Cynthia—you mean you haven't caught him yet? He's still *out* there?"

I nodded. "I'm afraid so, Mr. Harner. We're trying to see if we can find some similarities between the latest victim and your late wife. Can we come in?"

"All right, all right." He stepped aside and ushered us into a quiet, tastefully furnished great room. We sat on a plush leather couch with a soft sigh of cushions, and Harner stood opposite us, running his hands through his hair. "I'm sorry I lost control of myself like that," he said at last. "It's just...so hard. What did you say your names were?"

"Detective Berkley and Detective Reed," I said, nodding at Alex and myself.

"Right...right," he muttered. "I'm sorry, I'd offer to shake hands but..." He gestured at the twin black braces that laced up his wrists and forearms.

"Carpal tunnel?" Alex asked, sympathetically.

He nodded. "Yes, I type a lot—reports, findings...I'm a consultant. Somebody always needs more information. Unfortunately, the repetitive motion has caused a lot of damage—my wrists, well, without the braces..." He shrugged. "Would either of you care for a drink?"

I shook my head and Alex said, "No, thank you, Mr. Harner. We understand this is hard for you. Just a few questions, and we'll be on our way."

He sighed and sank down across from us in one of those orthopedic massage chairs that cost an arm and a leg at Sharper Image or Brookstone. "How can I help you, Detectives?" he asked in a low, colorless voice.

"Well, Detective Berkley and I were just assigned to this case, so we're trying to get a good overview of it," Alex began. She glanced down at some notes on her PDA (I swear she takes that thing with her everywhere) and looked up at Harner again. "Now, as I understand it, you and your wife had split up just a month before she died."

"Yes, but it was just a trial separation—only temporary." Harner sat forward and gestured earnestly. "Cynthia had just finished school to become a physician's assistant and she felt like she wanted a little space. She was going to come back, though."

"She got her own apartment; sounds pretty permanent to me," I said, watching him. "An expensive one, too—off Bayshore, that's not a cheap neighborhood. You pay for any of that?"

"No..." He ran his hands through his hair and sighed. "She got a huge advance from her new boss, Dr. Love. She...she said she just needed a little breathing space. She had some new interests, some new hobbies. But she was coming back, I *know* she was."

"Or maybe you were going to *make* her come back?" I suggested, still watching.

"No...no! What's all this about, anyway? Do I have to prove my innocence all over again?" Harner stood and paced angrily out of the room. Alex started to go after him, but I stopped her with a hand on her knee.

He came back shortly with a legal-sized manila folder in his hands. "Here! My travel information—I keep it for tax purposes." He shoved the folder in my face, and I took it from him, keeping an eye on him as I did. Inside the folder were a number of ticket stubs and boarding passes. One for the night of November twenty-second and, coincidentally, one for the night before last as well, putting him in Denver again while the second murder was being committed. Both tickets were Delta, flying out of Tampa International.

"You get around a lot," Alex said, looking over my shoulder. She touched the latest boarding pass, the one for the night of Sarah Michaels's murder, and caught my eye. I nodded.

"Go to Denver a lot, do you?" I asked, looking up at Harner.

He shrugged and crossed his arms over his chest. "I told you—I'm a consultant. One of our biggest clients is there. It's not unusual for me to go there several times a month, sometimes several times a week. Are you happy now?"

"Mr. Harner, we didn't mean to cause you any pain," Alex said apologetically. "I know it must be awful to have lost a loved one, especially so close to the holidays."

"We...we were going to spend Christmas together. Cynthia said she just wanted to relax and have fun, just enjoy being together the way...the way we used to. Oh, God..." He buried his head in his hands, the narrow face hidden by the thick black wrist braces. "I'm sorry."

"Sir, we can see you're upset, so I'll just ask one more question before we go," Alex said. "Do you know if your wife knew or was in any way connected to a Sarah Michaels?"

He looked up. "No, who's she?"

"She *was* a graduate student at USF," I said.

"She was the second victim," Alex clarified. She showed him a picture of Sarah Michaels smiling for her yearbook, but he shook his head.

"I'm sorry, I've never seen her. If Cynthia had any contact with her she never mentioned it to me.

"All right. I think we've taken enough of your time." Alex stood and handed him back his travel folder along with one of her cards. "If you can think of anything else, please give me a call. My office and home number are both on the card."

"Thank you," Harner mumbled. He took the folder and got up himself, still looking a little shaky. "I'll show you to the door." He shuffled back the way we'd come, looking suddenly like a broken old man, and we followed him.

Alex turned to him once more before we stepped outside. "Mr. Harner, I promise you we're doing everything in our power to find this man and stop him."

He nodded listlessly. "I hope so, Detective. I hope you find him before he kills someone else—before it's too late, like it was for my Cynthia." He shut the door behind us with a hollow boom.

"Well, that was depressing," Alex said, stepping down the steps to my truck. "Hey, look." She snatched a pizza coupon flyer that someone had shoved under one of my wipers. "We're inside for ten minutes, and we get hit."

"Not safe from these things anywhere, I guess." I grunted, taking it from her and crumpling it into a ball. "C'mon, we still have Jeremy Somebody to trace."

* * *

Alex and I had both taken classes at USF at one time or another, so we went straight to the Edward P. Howell psych building with no problem.

"Mm-mm, takes me back," Alex murmured as we rode up to the fifth floor in the elevator.

"Back when you were just an ambitious, dewy-eyed student, determined to make a difference in the big bad world?" I asked, grinning down at her.

"I was thinking more like back to a time before I spent most of my time with a six-foot-five galloot, chasing down the bad guys," she said, punching me on the shoulder.

"Oh, so now I'm a galloot? You wound me, partner." But I was glad to see her joking again. She'd been so tense lately and besides, the joking between us felt...safe somehow. Like as long as I could keep treating her like my kid sister, that's the only way I would see her. I didn't like the way I'd been noticing her lately, her breasts, her hair, her thighs... It wasn't right; it could screw everything up. And I was determined not to do that.

The elevator chimed and we stepped out into an industrial olive green hallway, and, consulting the list of classes, took a left.

"Well, five-thirteen, this is the room," Alex murmured.

"Looks like class got out early," I said, peering in the narrow rectangle of glass just over the doorknob. There was only one girl in the room. She was short and had an armful of paperwork—maybe some kind of teacher's aide. When she saw me watching her she came to the door and opened it.

"Yes, can I help you?" she asked, giving us a bland stare.

"We hope so," Alex said. "We were looking for the psychosexual development class that's supposed to be in this room with professor..." She consulted the list. "Professor Baird?"

"This close to end of semester, we're all just doing reviews," the girl said. "But Professor Baird should be in her office. It's down on the second floor. Take a right as you get off the elevator."

"Well, actually, we aren't looking for the professor as much as we're looking for one of her students. Do you know a Jeremy Bruce that attends this class?" I asked.

"Sure I do, but why?" She looked at us doubtfully.

"Tampa PD, we need to speak to him," Alex said, flashing her badge. "Was he in class today?"

"Oh, my God, is Jeremy in trouble? Is this about Sarah?" Her eyes were wide and frightened. I heard a bell go off in my head.

"What do you know about Sarah Michaels?" I asked, leaning closer.

The girl backed away, obviously frightened. "N-nothing. Only that she was killed. It's such a tragedy, we all loved her..."

"Do you think Jeremy could have had anything to do with that?" I said, taking a step nearer.

"I don't... I don't think so..." The girl was nearly tripping over her feet to get away. Alex grabbed my arm.

"Ease down," she said, under her breath. "You're scaring the poor girl to death, Cole."

I backed off, feeling frustrated as Alex continued the questions. I tend to forget when I'm focused on a case that I can look, as Alex puts it, "pretty damn scary."

"Tell me what you know about Sarah Michaels and Jeremy Bruce," Alex said softly. "Were they having a relationship?"

"Up until a few weeks ago, yeah." The girl seemed calmer now, and Alex smiled at her encouragingly.

"Go on. What happened? Why did they break up?"

The girl shrugged. "I don't know, really. I took classes with both of them, we were all in the same cluster, you know? They've been together since the beginning of the semester then all of a sudden, like two weeks ago, Jeremy broke it off. Sarah told me they just liked different things. She seemed real sad about it."

"Was it a hard break-up—lots of bad feelings, maybe?" Alex asked.

"Well…" The girl frowned and shuffled the paperwork she was holding distractedly. "They didn't hate each other or anything like that, if that's what you mean. But they didn't talk to each other either. And it seemed like…" She frowned.

"Like what?" Alex encouraged.

"Almost like Jeremy was going out of his way to stay as far away from Sarah as he could. Like, he'd sit on the far side of the classroom from her, wouldn't ride the elevator with her. And he'd leave a room she was in as fast as he could. Stuff like that."

"That sounds like pretty immature behavior," Alex remarked. "How did Sarah feel about that?"

The girl shrugged. "I think it made her sad, but she didn't talk about it much. When we found out she'd been killed… One of the guys in class had a paper and he was reading it...we just found out today. Jeremy seemed as shocked as anybody." She shook her head. "It's just so sad."

"Do you know where we can find Jeremy Bruce?" I asked, making sure to keep my distance.

The girl glanced up at me and then at Alex, as if for reassurance. "Well, I could be wrong, but I think he's in a session with Professor Baird right now. She wanted to counsel him. It's a terribly traumatic thing to lose someone that way, especially this time of year."

Alex looked grim. "Tell me about it. You said on the second floor?"

"Take a right off the elevator. Her name's on a plaque outside her office."

"Thanks," I said, and gave her a card. "Our numbers if you need us. We may be in touch."

We left her standing in the hallway looking frightened and headed back for the elevator again. In short order we were standing outside Professor Baird's office. I had my hand on the knob, but Alex stopped me.

"Wait, let's have a look first."

There was another one of those glass rectangles in the door above the knob and we peered in, getting a feel for the situation. Inside, the office looked a bit cramped—there was a plain wooden desk with a chair in front of it, and stacks of books and piles of folders were everywhere—the ordered chaos of an academic, no doubt.

A woman with luxurious sable brown hair and sharp green eyes leaned against the front of the desk. She looked to be in her late forties, but she was in excellent shape. Sitting on a chair in front of her was a kid in his early to mid twenties. The woman, who had to be Professor Baird, wore a slinky silk blouse and a black skirt with a long slit up one thigh. As she spoke, she crossed her legs casually, baring even more thigh, and leaned back against the desk, thrusting out a pair of very impressive breasts.

Jeremy Bruce was a much less striking figure. Tall and gangly, he looked like a baby horse that hadn't learned how to coordinate its limbs yet. He had dark hair and a faintly pinkish, fairly new scar high on his right cheekbone. Dark eyes were glued to his professor's face and figure. As we watched, she said something else and he leaned forward eagerly, his face almost level with her crotch.

"Would you look at that body language?" Alex murmured as we watched, being careful to stay back enough that they couldn't see us through the glass.

"Hot for teacher," I whispered back. "Looks like our Jeremy Somebody might have a thing for older women. I wonder where he was on the night of November twenty-second when the first vic was killed?"

"Why don't we ask him?" Alex stepped forward and opened the door. "Jeremy Bruce?"

Both professor and student looked up at us, startled. The professor recovered her composure quickly. "I'm sorry, but I'm in a private counseling session right now. I'll have to ask you to leave." Her voice was low and husky with just a hint of menace.

"That's too bad because I'm afraid we'll have to insist on staying." I flashed my badge at her. "Tampa PD, we need to speak to Jeremy Bruce."

"I'm Jeremy Bruce," the kid said, standing up awkwardly. "What's this about?"

"Your girlfriend Sarah Michaels," Alex said.

"She's not my girlfriend." He threw a nervous glance over his shoulder at the professor.

"That's not what we heard," Alex told him. "How about if you step out in the hall with us and answer a few questions?"

"This is outrageous! Jeremy is grief-stricken about Sarah's death." Professor Baird crossed her arms over those impressive breasts and frowned at us, as though we were naughty students that needed to be disciplined.

"Don't you mean he's grief-stricken over her murder?" I asked, grabbing the kid by his arm. "C'mon, Jeremy, walk with us." I dragged him out into the olive-green hall, ignoring his protests.

"This is all a big mistake. I'm not even dating Sarah anymore. We broke up like two weeks ago!"

"Last I heard you don't have to be dating someone to kill them," Alex remarked.

"Why did you two break up, anyway? Maybe it was because you wanted to try a few kinky moves in the bedroom and Sarah wasn't into it?" I asked, as we led him down the hall. He was dragging his feet, literally, but that didn't bother me a bit. I made sure he kept up the pace, his sneakers squeaking along the tile floor all the way.

"You got it all wrong," he protested. "Sarah was the one who had weird ideas! I'm telling you—she was a freak. Look—I didn't want to be with her anymore, but I never would have hurt her. I even brought a box of her stuff to bring back to her today. Why would I do that if I already knew she was dead?"

"What kind of stuff did you bring her?" Alex wanted to know.

The kid shrugged. "I dunno, books, some clothes. Stuff she'd left over at my apartment. That's all."

"You mind if we take a look?" I tightened my grip on his arm.

"Sure…it's in my car."

We were halfway out to the parking lot by then, and we found his car, a shiny new candy-apple-red Ferrari, with no problem. It had a bumper sticker that read, *I like kids but I can't eat a whole one.* His hands were trembling so badly he couldn't unlock the back, so Alex took the keys from him and did it instead.

"Nice bumper sticker," I said, making sure to keep a grip on his arm, just in case he got any cute ideas.

"Sarah gave it to me. She had a weird sense of humor." He shook his head. "I just…can't believe she's gone."

"Why do I have a hard time believing that?" I asked. Besides a cardboard box, there was a ball cap with a Pizza Hut logo stitched onto it and one of those big red insulated bags the delivery guys use to keep pizzas warm on the drive to your house.

"That what you do?" I jerked my head at the pizza paraphernalia in the back of the car.

"Until I get my degree. It pays the rent." He shrugged uneasily, an operation that was made much more difficult by the fact that I had one of his arms in a lock. I wondered why he needed any help with the rent if he could afford a car like this. It probably cost more than I made in a year.

"Let's see what we have here," Alex muttered, opening a medium-sized cardboard liquor box with an ad for Absolut vodka on the side. "Hmm, a pink T-shirt, pair of sunglasses, and, as promised, a few books. More than a few, actually." She splayed out a half a dozen trade-sized paperback books like an oversized hand of cards.

I leaned closer, dragging the kid with me. "Wow, look at this. *SM 101: A Realistic Introduction. The Loving Dominant. Screw the Roses, Send Me the Thorns: The Romance and Sexual Sorcery of Sadomasochism.*" I shook the kid. "It's like a how-to library for sexual deviancy. Little light reading for you there, Jer?"

"I *told* you all this stuff belonged to Sarah! I was just bringing it back to her, honest!"

"Were you just bringing this back to her, too? Or was it a present for someone else?" Alex's face was very white as she withdrew a red satin sleeping mask edged in black lace.

"That's it," I said, pulling the kid's arms behind his back. "I think we'd all benefit from a little trip downtown."

Chapter Nine

Alex

"I told you, I didn't do it!" Jeremy Bruce was running both hands through his hair and practically crying as Cole interrogated him. Captain Davis and I watched through the one-way glass down at the PD. It had been going on for close to three hours, and the kid hadn't broken yet or even asked for a lawyer. He was sticking to his guns. I was impressed.

"Then why won't you tell me where you were the night before last?" Cole demanded, striding across the room. He had taken off his jacket and rolled up the sleeves of his navy-blue button-down shirt to expose impressively muscled forearms. Nobody can say my partner doesn't keep himself in shape.

"I *told* you, I was with friends!" It was nearly a scream. Jeremy Bruce was close to breaking.

"And what about the night of November twenty-second, were you with the same friends that night?" Cole asked, his face like granite. He slammed one huge fist down on the table in front of the kid, making him jump about three feet out of the plain wooden chair. The cardboard box full of incriminating evidence was sitting in front of him.

"I was at a party—I got really wasted!"

"Where, with who?" Cole yelled.

"Let me think...c'mon, I told you I was wasted!" There were actually tears leaking down his cheeks at this point.

"Tell me, Jeremy, how did you get that scar?" He pointed to the fresh scar high on our suspect's cheek. "Could it be Sarah cut you with her nails while she was trying to fight you off?" He was fishing there—no DNA had been recovered by the lab from under the nails, but a smart perp could always cut or clean under the nails when he was done.

"I had a mole removed." Jeremy Bruce buried his face in his hands. "Why won't you believe me?"

Captain Davis turned to me. "You think this is the guy?"

I shrugged. "The mask is pretty damning evidence but so far we don't have anything that actually puts him on the scene. And no priors, but a clean record doesn't always mean anything."

She shook her head, her close-cropped graying curls ruffling slightly. "I hope you're right, Reed. So far we've been lucky but if the press jumps on this..." She shook her head again. "It's our ass."

"We're working on him, as you can see. We're hoping to rattle him enough to give something up." I nodded at the interrogation room where Cole was still at it.

She looked through the one-way glass again and shook her head. "Looks to me like Berkley is just scaring the bejesus out of him right now."

"Yeah, he's good at that," I agreed, crossing my arms over my chest. Cole was pounding on the table again, and Jeremy Bruce was openly sobbing like a kid with a skinned knee.

"I think your partner's getting a little worked up," she said, nodding at the glass. "Why don't you go in and cool him out some? Play a little good cop/bad cop with our young friend."

I shrugged. "You got it, Captain."

"Good girl." She patted me on the shoulder. "Keep me updated, all right?"

"Will do." I opened the door to the room just as Cole was winding up for another verbal attack. I love my partner to death, but I swear to God, I wouldn't want to be on the other side of the table from him when he goes on the warpath. He'd never actually strike a suspect, but let's just say he can get very intense.

"Hey, Cole." I patted him on the shoulder. "Why don't you step out for a cup of coffee or something, and let me talk to Jeremy for a while?"

He blew out a breath and ran a hand through his hair. "Okay, sure. You want anything?"

I shook my head. "I'm good." I pulled up a chair opposite Jeremy Bruce and waited for a while until his sobs trailed off into soft hiccups. The interrogation room was small and dark and bleak, and he sounded like a lost child.

"You okay?" I asked gently. He looked up at me and shrugged, dark eyes still swimming in tears. The faint scar on his cheek was white against his red face. Suddenly I could see what Sarah Michaels must have seen in him. There was an uncertainty about him—a puppy-dog charm. He was the kind of guy you wanted to take home and cuddle, if you were the maternal type. Luckily for me, I'm not.

"You must have been really upset when you heard about Sarah," I said softly, reaching out to pat the back of his hand. I noticed as I did that his hands were rawboned and large. His knuckles were red from clenching his fists. The ME's words suddenly popped into my head: *could span an octave on the piano easily.* "Even though you two broke up a few weeks ago, you must have still had some feelings for her. Right?" I said.

He shrugged again. "I guess."

"Why did you break up?" I asked. "Tell me about it."

"She...she had some weird ideas. Like those books—she gave them to me because she wanted to do some of that stuff."

I felt my stomach turn over but managed to keep my face utterly straight. "What kind of things did she want to do, Jeremy?" Out of the corner of my eye, I noticed that Cole had slipped back in the room.

Jeremy Bruce shifted uneasily in his chair. "I dunno—it was embarrassing. I don't want to talk about it."

"Too embarrassing to talk about. Well, isn't that a shame." Cole stepped forward. "Or maybe you're too embarrassed to admit to killing her, could that be it?"

"Cole, give him a chance," I said, putting a hand protectively over Jeremy's.

"What? Give him a chance to tell us again how it was *Sarah* that was into the kinky stuff?" Cole grimaced. "You tell me what woman in her right mind wants to be tied up and beaten." His words made me sick. What woman in her right mind, indeed?

"Well she *was* taking lessons from a Dominatrix," I hissed at him. "Maybe she *did* have some alternate sexual needs."

"*Alternate sexual needs?*" He sneered. "Is that what they're calling it now?"

"What they're calling *what?*" I demanded. "Sexual perversion as defined by you? Who made you the authority on what's sick and what's not?"

Cole gave me a strange look, and I realized I was going a little too far with the good cop routine. Only it wasn't so much a routine—I felt genuinely defensive, like I was protecting both Sarah and myself from his censure. I shook my head and tried to get back to questioning Jeremy.

"Do you want to tell me what happened that night?" I asked, leaning closer, trying to get a look in his sad puppy-dog eyes.

He sighed. "I told you—I wasn't even there so I *don't know.*"

"Well, let's see if we can help you with that." Cole came a little closer, leaning on the edge of the table, arms crossed over his broad chest. "Maybe it went a little something like this. You go over to her apartment sometime between nine and ten and tell her you want to talk. You bring her roses, because you're such a sweet guy. She's a nice, trusting girl, so she lets you in. Maybe you talk about why you broke up—the things you wanted to do that she didn't. Maybe you even get her to let you try a few things, like tying her to the bed."

"No—God, no! I told you, I wasn't into that. That was Sarah's scene, not mine," he protested, but Cole just kept on talking.

"You tie her to the bed naked, and then you blindfold her, so she can't tell what's happening next. You put duct tape across her mouth so the neighbors can't hear her scream, and then you decide to have a little fun. What did you whip her with, Jeremy? Was it a whip or a cane? Maybe a riding crop?"

"No...no, I swear to God!"

"You tied her up and beat her!" Cole thundered, getting right down in his face, his blue eyes blazing. "You beat her and raped her while you strangled her to death. Then you sprinkled rose petals over her body and left her like a piece of meat for somebody else to find, because that's the kind of sick fuck you are and *it gets you off!*"

"No!" Jeremy screamed. He collapsed sobbing onto the table. "No...no, she wanted me to tie her up, but I wouldn't. I didn't want to pinch her or hit her or bruise her. She was the one who wanted to be hurt, but I didn't want to do it. She was sick...sick..." The last words trailed off into another round of sobbing.

"Cole, back down!" I pushed at his shoulder and gave him a warning look. We've played this game often enough to do it without any verbal signals, but now he was the one getting too intense, and it worried me. He really wanted this guy—it had almost become a personal vendetta.

He stepped away from the table again, rubbing his jaw tiredly. "Fine."

"Jeremy," I said softly, patting the boy's shaking shoulder. "Tell me what you mean about Sarah wanting to be hurt. Did she ask you to do all those things to her?"

"She...she did," he gasped at last, looking up again. "But not that night, I never saw her that night, I swear. The reason we broke up is because she started giving me those freaky books. I mean...she wants... *wanted* to be a sexual therapist; she believed that any expression of sexuality was valid."

"And you don't?" I asked.

He shrugged. "I guess...but I just wasn't into it. I tried to ignore her hints, and I never read the books, but one night a couple of weeks ago she came to my house with that mask and some other stuff. She wanted me to tie her up and...and...hurt her. But I couldn't... I just couldn't..."

Cole was glowering in the background, but I put up a hand and shook my head. "How did she want you to hurt her, Jeremy? Give me some examples." I felt my stomach turn over again as I waited for his reply.

"She...she wanted me to twist her nipples—really hard, too. Wanted me to whip her with my belt until I marked her...until she screamed...sick stuff like that." He shook his head. "I couldn't get into it. It...it grossed me out. But she told me it was the only way she could really get off—that she *needed* it. She said if I loved her, I'd hurt her." He rubbed the back of his hand convulsively across his mouth, as though trying to get rid of a terrible aftertaste.

"And what did you say?" I asked softly, feeling sick. Had Sarah Michaels died for the same needs I kept hidden inside myself as well as I could?

"I...I told her to leave. That if she needed something like that, she'd have to find it somewhere else. I mean... I could have stood the whole blindfolded thing, maybe even tied her up...but I...I didn't want to hurt her. I'm not into that."

"So this whole thing was Sarah's idea?" Cole asked, his voice dangerously low. He reached in the box and pulled out another book. "*The Master's Manual: A Handbook of Erotic Dominance,*" he read. "You expect us to believe that *Sarah* bought this book?"

"She bought it for me! She was hoping I could get into the whole thing—but I couldn't."

"I see." Cole dropped the book back in the box and dusted his hands together as though he'd touched something unspeakably filthy. "So we're supposed to believe that Sarah was the sick, twisted freak. That *she* was the sexual deviant and *you* were just an innocent bystander."

Hearing my partner talk like that made me feel nearly nauseous with tension and shame. Sick, twisted freak...sexual perversion...was this really what he thought of these kinds of sexual practices, or was he just doing his bad cop routine as usual? I was afraid to find out—just the thought made me feel naked.

"Detectives?" We both looked up at once to see Captain Davis's curly graying head poking in through the doorway. "I have somebody here you need to talk to."

"I'll go," I said, getting up from the table. I was grateful for an excuse to get away from the scene for a while. I thought I might puke, I felt so twisted up inside.

Outside the interrogation room was a very flustered Professor Baird. Her carefully styled sable brown hair was in disarray, as though she'd been running both hands through it, and her eyes were red-rimmed.

"Yes?" I raised an eyebrow at her. "You have something to say?"

"Me, he was with me!" she blurted out. "Now let him go, will you?"

I crossed my arms over my chest and gave her my best skeptical look. "If he was with you why didn't he just say so in the first place?"

"Because he's trying to protect me, all right?" she hissed. "Do you know what they call USF faculty members who sleep with their students? Unemployed! But I can't let Jeremy be charged with some horrible murder he didn't commit, just to save my career." She looked through the one-way glass again. Cole wasn't shouting anymore. He was whispering something too low for us to hear in Jeremy's Bruce's ear. Whatever it was, it was making Jeremy cry again.

"Can't you let him go?" she pleaded.

"So he was with you...even before he left Sarah?" I asked. "That doesn't seem right at all."

She sighed and sank down in a near-by chair. "That was how this whole affair started in the first place. Sarah Michaels could be very manipulative sexually. She started pressuring Jeremy to do things that made him uncomfortable. I'm his faculty advisor so he came to me, and I started counseling him. Before I knew it..." She threw up her hands. "I didn't mean for it to happen. He was just so hurt, so vulnerable. Everything in me reached out to him. I wanted to comfort him, and I wound up sleeping with him instead. Are you satisfied?"

"Not quite," I said. "So you're telling me that Jeremy was with you all night the night before last?"

She sighed again. "Yes, all night long."

"And the night of November twenty-second?"

"That…" She cleared her throat and seemed to have to force herself to continue. "That was the first time we…that I did more than counsel him. He called me around seven o'clock, and he was so upset. I suggested we meet for dinner and from there…well, we went back to my place."

"What restaurant did you go to?" I asked, making a note to go interview the wait staff and verify her story.

"The Three Palms. It's a charming little place off of Armenia Avenue. We went there both nights in question."

"I know where it is," I said, glancing back through the one-way glass where Cole was still talking in a low, intense voice. "That's not too far from my neighborhood, Professor. But it's pretty far from the university. Do you live around there?"

"No, I…" She shook her head. "I didn't want anyone to see us together like that. Didn't want them to get the wrong idea."

"Don't you mean the right idea?" But I could feel our case dropping out from under us. It sounded like the truth—Jeremy had an airtight alibi.

Professor Baird stiffened, obviously offended. "You know, in some societies, an older woman and a younger man can be seen together without making anyone look twice. In some African tribes, it's even expected—the older woman guides the young man into manhood. It's only here, in our repressive, sexist, puritanical, western society that—"

I sighed and cut her off. "Professor, your sexual ethics are your own concern. *My* concern is making sure that your little boyfriend didn't kill Sarah Michaels or Cynthia Harner."

"I have credit card receipts to back me up, you're welcome to look at them," she said bitterly. "Or just go ask the wait staff of the Three Palms. It's a small place—they'll remember us."

"Fine." I pinched the bridge of my nose between my thumb and forefinger, pressing back the tension headache that wanted to form. Between my head and my stomach, I felt like I'd been riding the Black Mamba at Bush Gardens all day long.

* * *

"Sure, I know her—Professor Baird. She comes in a lot, usually has students with her." The curly-haired waitress nodded positively. Behind her a neon green and pink palm tree blinked at intervals. The Three Palms was a nice little dive that I drove past every day to work. Looking around, I thought I might come back and have supper here sometime myself. It beat always nuking a Lean Cuisine.

"And was this the student she had with her on the night before last?" I held up a quick Polaroid we'd snapped of Jeremy Bruce.

She nodded again. "Good-looking kid. Professor Baird sure can pick 'em."

"So she's in here with a lot of young men?" Cole raised an eyebrow.

"Hey, I don't want to get her into any trouble—she's a good tipper. What's all this about, anyway?"

"Just a few questions," I reassured her. "Were you working on the night of November twenty-second?"

She shrugged, snapping her gum. "Sure—I own part interest in this place. I practically live here."

"Was she here that night with this same guy?" I tapped the Polaroid again.

"Let me think... I'm pretty sure, but I'd have to check the receipts to be positive. Like I said, she's in here a lot."

"You do that, would you?" Cole smiled politely.

The waitress wandered off, snapping her gum, to dig behind the register.

"Looks like Professor Baird really has a thing for the young stuff," he muttered, stuffing his hands in his pockets.

"Yeah, she fed me this line of bull about 'ushering them into manhood,' while you were still sweating Jeremy." I grinned at him.

He shook his head. "Oh boy, I'm not touching that one with a ten-foot pole."

I nodded. "Smart man. So where does this leave us?" But I knew where, even as the curly-haired waitress came back, waiving a receipt that matched the professor's.

Back to square one.

Chapter Ten

Cole

"Well, here we are," I said, pulling up in front of the rambling old brick bungalow where Alex's parents had lived for just about forever. The house was located in Old Seminole Heights, a neighborhood that had fallen out of fashion for a while but was currently making a big comeback, thanks mostly to Tampa's large gay community discovering it. Most of the houses had been built in the Forties and were solid enough to be worth the effort of redecorating.

The house to the left of her parents' bungalow had been snapped up by a couple of young gay professionals who had redone the whole thing inside and out. The old wooden siding had been painted a pale buttercup yellow with sunflower trim (I know this because Alex told me—it all just looked yellow to me), and yellow rosebushes marched proudly up either side of the front sidewalk. A single, tasteful strand of icicle lights framed the front of the house. Less was apparently more when it came to Christmas decorations.

I noticed that Gloria's lawn (Alex's mother insists that I call her by her first name) had also been recently manicured. The hedges in front of the house had been clipped into new and exciting shapes, and there was fresh mulch around the flowerbeds.

"Looks like Frank and Tawni have been working over your mom's front lawn again," I said, nodding out the window. Frank and Tawni were the neighbors who had painted their house buttercup yellow.

Alex sighed heavily. "Yeah, they love that kind of stuff—it makes Mom happy, too. I think she was always disappointed that I didn't grow up to be more decorative. But I swear, I can hardly hang a picture straight."

"You don't have to tell me—don't forget I'm the one who had to hang your pictures when you bought your house. Wore out two drill bits on that." Alex's house is cinderblock—great if you want to be safe during a hurricane. Not so good if you want to try and get a nail or a screw into the wall. At one point I thought it would be easier to Super Glue the damn pictures up.

"She said they're after her to do the inside, too—do a total overhaul." Alex looked out the window, and I couldn't see her eyes.

I raised an eyebrow. "Oh, yeah? You think she'll let them?"

"Don't know. She's thinking about it. After all, she's got all that money; might as well have fun with it." Alex's dad had left behind plenty in stocks and bonds and a private account she and her mom hadn't even known about. Alex had confided to me, in a moment of weakness, that she thought her dad had been saving up for years, until he had enough money to make sure his family would be comfortably well off when he died. She'd called it his "suicide fund."

"You know," she said after a moment of silence. "This is the first time I've been back since the week of the funeral. I just…couldn't face it. In a way I was glad that my battery was dead this morning because it gave me an excuse—a reason I *had* to come over. So I could see my mom and spend some time with her." She sighed.

"Are you sure you don't want me to pick up the battery and put it in for you?" I asked, already knowing what she would say.

Alex shook her head. "No, Cole. I may not be Mr. Goodwrench, like you, but I'm not so helpless I can't replace a stupid battery." Her voice sounded shaky, but I was betting it wasn't her car problems she was upset about.

"Doesn't look like your mom's home yet," I said. "You want me to come in for a while?"

She looked at me, and her mouth did that funny little grimace thing it does sometimes when she's trying hard not to cry. I had seen that expression on her face a lot in the past three months but never any actual tears. I wondered, as I had at her father's funeral, why she worked so hard to keep it all inside, to never let the slightest bit of weakness show.

"Alex? Want me to come in?" I said softly, when she didn't answer my question.

She gave a little shrug. "If you want to." For Alex, that was a lot. It would have been a desperate cry for help from anyone else.

"Great." I killed the truck's motor and got out. "I'm thirsty. Hope your mom has some of her famous iced tea in the fridge."

Inside her parents' house looked like something out of *Leave it to Beaver*—like stepping into a time warp to the late Fifties. Alex was an only child, and she had been a surprise to her parents, a late-in-life baby. I always got the feeling around Gloria that she loved Alex, but she'd already had a life when the baby came along, and she hadn't let having Alex change that life very much. Gloria was big into charities and bridge clubs, the whole social butterfly thing. Alex once told me she'd thought their live-in maid was her mother when she was very young. When she realized the truth, she'd cried.

Her father had been a nice guy, but very distant and to himself. He'd usually had his nose buried in a book any time I stopped by. It had been a shock to me when Alex called me and said, in a strange, flat voice, that her father was dead and could I please come be with her. But Alex and her mother hadn't seemed too terribly surprised at all. According to Alex he had been clinically depressed for years. He'd tried all of the new medications, Prozac, Welbutrin, you name it, but none of them had done him any good. His death seemed to be a lot harder on Alex than on her mom.

"Hey, here's some tea. I told Mom you'd be dropping me off—bet she made it just for you." Alex appeared, a tall, cool glass in one hand dripping with condensation.

"Thanks." I took the glass from her and took a long swallow. One thing I will give Alex's mom—she brews a mean pot of iced tea. I think maybe she spikes it with rum but she won't admit it. Anyway, it goes down smooth, especially after the kind of day we'd just had. "Mmm," I said, finishing the tea. "Perfect as always."

"Glad you like it." Her voice was listless, blank. I lowered the glass and watched her anxiously as she wandered out of the living room and down the long narrow hall that bisected the house. I put my glass on the coffee table, mindful to use a coaster lest Gloria have a fit, and followed.

I was afraid she was heading for the spare room where she'd found him hanging in the closet but Alex was standing just inside the doorway of her father's den. It was a dark little room—decorated in shabby bookcases and cracked leather chairs—the only room in the house Gloria wasn't allowed to touch. The shelves were filled with Civil War history books and some of the tiny pewter figurines her father had painted for a hobby. On the far wall was possibly the ugliest velvet painting ever made, showing a mountainside and a waterfall. Alex called it the "Mexican peeing in a waterfall" painting because according to her, if you looked at it just right, you could see a man with a sombrero standing inside the waterfall taking a leak.

"Oh." I realized Alex had made the small, hurt sound, and I looked at her, concerned. "She hasn't changed a thing," she murmured, stepping into the room as though she was entering a shrine. "I thought for sure by now she'd have cleaned this up and turned it into a sewing room—that was what she always wanted. But everything's just the same."

"Just the way your dad left it, huh?" I said, stepping in behind her. It was a small room, but still filled with his presence. The ghost of the pipe tobacco he'd used to smoke and the scent of his aftershave (Old Spice, just like my own dad) was still in the air.

Alex walked across to the cracked leather armchair that stood in one corner. "This was his chair, the one he always used." She caressed the back of the chair as though touching a lover's arm, a distant look in her eyes. "I remember coming into this room and wanting so badly to get his attention—to bring him out of himself somehow and to make him notice me."

I opened my mouth to say something, and realized I really didn't have anything to say. Alex had told me a lot about her mom, the way they disagreed, the way Gloria was always busy when she was a kid. But she'd never said much about her dad, not even after his funeral. I closed my mouth and let her talk.

"Mom was always busy, always out of the house. There was no way to get much of her time. But my dad—I could usually find him here when I came home from school. He was always here, but he was never really *here*, you know?" She looked at me and I nodded, hoping she'd go on. I got a feeling this was something she needed to tell, something that had been festering inside for a long time.

She sighed. "I wanted his approval so badly, but I practically had to bleed to get him to notice me." She looked down at her hand on the back of the chair and stroked it some more. "No, not practically—*really*, I had to bleed. I remember when I finally figured out what worked. I was six, just learning to ride a bike. Mom was gone and when I fell off and skinned my knee I came screaming into the house, you know how kids do?"

I nodded. "So what happened?"

She ran her short, shapely nails over the cracked brown leather, making a little whispering sound. "My dad was sitting here, reading like always. I think he read so much for escape, from his life, from his growing depression... Anyway, he was right here, and I came barreling down the hall, screaming like a banshee. When he saw me, saw the blood on my knee, it was like it got through to him like nothing else could. He bandaged the cut and pulled me into his lap and held me, right here in this chair." She looked up at me.

"Then I knew what worked—knew how to make him notice me. I made an art form of falling off my bike. You should hear my mom talk about the horrible 'clumsy phase' I went through, but that was it. I still have scars on my knees from that."

"Alex…" I took a step toward her, but she shook her head.

"I can still feel it—the sting of the pavement erasing the skin from my knees and elbows." She cupped her elbows in her palms, arms crossed protectively over her chest. "But I knew—I *knew* that the pain would be worth it. Because every ounce of agony, every drop of blood, would buy me his undivided attention. At least for a little while." She took a deep, shuttering breath. "A six-year-old masochist. How sick is that?"

"You're not sick," I protested, but she went on as though she hadn't heard me.

"It worked until I was about thirteen and started getting really developed. I think… I think he thought it wouldn't be proper to hold me after that. To have too much physical contact. He liked it when I made good grades, though. Sometimes he hugged me when I brought home a really good report card."

"So you started making straight A's," I guessed.

She nodded, stroking the leather. "Yeah. I was determined to be the best of the best. I wanted to be so tough—to prove I could do anything, to make him proud of me."

"That's why police work?" I asked softly.

She nodded. "Uh-huh. Becoming a cop had the double benefit of getting my dad's attention and giving my mom fits. She wanted me to go into something else—*anything* else that was just a little more feminine, I think. I never was a girly girl."

"Just as well," I said. "I don't want a girly girl getting my back when a bust goes down."

She gave me a small, wan smile. "Yeah, there is that. My dad was so proud when I made detective. It was great."

"Did you ever try to talk to him? Tell him how you felt?" I stepped a little closer, wanting to put my arm around her but not quite daring.

Alex shook her head. There was a small table-side lamp beside the cracked leather chair and she turned it on. In the soft light her face was open, vulnerable in a way I'd never seen before.

"You know in a college psych class I took, developmental psych, I think, I remember the professor saying that the father-daughter relationship is more important than most people think. Your father is the first man in your life, your model for how you're going to act with every other man you ever meet. That's why so many girls that come out of abusive homes go on to marry abusive men. They think they deserve it—that it's the way things are supposed to be."

"I guess," I said, thinking that it explained a lot. The way Alex was tougher than any of the guys I worked with. I'd rather have her getting my back than any two men from our department. No wonder she was so driven to succeed, to attain perfection and excellence.

Alex sighed and flipped off the light again, plunging us into gloom. "I don't know why I told you all that. Except..."

"Yeah?" I said, stepping toward her. God, I wished I could give her a hug, but she was so tight. Even after the funeral she hadn't let me hold her very much or very long. I think she was afraid she'd lose control if I did.

"You hug Madison a lot, don't you? You hold her?" she asked. Her face was a pale, unreadable oval in the shadows.

"Yeah, sure. As much as I can," I said, thinking of my daughter. "Not as much as I want to now, of course." I sighed.

"Well just...don't ever stop." Alex moved past me to the doorway. "Girls need that if they're not going to grow up to be some kind of stone cold bitch like me."

"Alex," I grabbed her by the arm and turned her around, trying to read her. But the pale light from the hallway was behind her, casting her face into shadows. "You're not a stone cold bitch," I told her. "That's not you, not the way I see you at all."

"Doesn't matter how you see me, Cole. It's how I see myself." Her voice had that flat, dead quality to it again that I didn't like at all. "I'm sorry." She shook her head. "It wasn't fair for me to dump on you like that."

"What are friends for if not to dump on?" Acting on impulse, I dropped her arm and went over to sit in the chair. His chair. "C'mere," I said, patting my thighs.

"Cole..."

I wished I could see the play of emotions over her face, to know if I'd pushed her too far. But this felt right to me, somehow. Like it was something she needed, although she'd never be able to ask for it.

"Come here," I said again, more sternly this time.

"I don't want..." Her voice trembled uncertainly.

"I don't care what you want. Come here, Alex, right *now*." I made it an order—a command. It worked—it was almost like something in my tone had broken some barrier inside her.

With a low, breathless moan, she stumbled across the floor to me and threw herself in my lap. I wrapped my arms around her, pulling her close, and tucked her head under my chin. She was shivering, like a puppy that's been kicked, like a wounded child. I stoked along her trembling shoulders and ran my hands though her silky hair, holding her and whispering soothing nonsense. Comforting her the same way I would have comforted my daughter if she'd hurt herself and come to me, needing me to make it all better.

"It's all right, little girl," I heard myself say, soothingly. "It's all right, Alex."

"No...no it's not all right. He's dead...he's *dead*," she whispered against my neck. And then I felt her shoulders shake as she finally began to cry. The tears, when they came, were hot against the side of my neck. Hot and desperate, like she was tearing herself up inside to let them out. She went rigid against me, with the sheer force of them, crying so hard she couldn't catch her breath, the way kids do, before finally relaxing into more steady sobs.

"Alex... Alex," I murmured, stroking her back. "It's all right, everything's gonna be all right."

I don't know how long she cried. It seemed like an eternity in that dark room, the breathless sound of her sobs, the creak of old leather, the feel of her pressed soft and helpless against my chest. I only know I wanted to comfort her, to hold her forever if only she'd let me. Alex had never let herself be so vulnerable with me before. It felt like a gift somehow, like she was trusting me with not just her life, as we did daily on the job, but with her soul as well.

At last the sobs tapered off to sniffles and little moans of pure unhappiness. And yet, I had a feeling it was just what she'd needed. I wondered if it was the first time she'd cried since her dad's death and bet myself it was.

"Cole..." She looked up at me at last. I could just barely make out her face, pale and young, her cheeks still glistening with tears. The thick fringe of black lashes around her big brown eyes was matted and wet, and the eyes themselves were like two huge pools of pain.

It hurt me, physically hurt me, to see that look in her eyes. I felt it like a knife in my gut, twisting, as she looked up me. At that moment I would have done anything for her...anything at all to wipe that look of desperation off her face. I leaned down and kissed her gently, her eyes first. Kissing away the tears, the same way I did with Madison. Making it all better.

She gave a soft little sigh and shifted in my arms. I became suddenly aware of the soft crush of her breasts against my chest, of the warm, feminine scent of her. When I bent to kiss her again, my lips found her mouth instead of her cheeks or eyes. Her lips were soft, hesitant, they trembled under mine, and I didn't know how to stop myself.

She gave another little moan, a soft animal sound of pure need. I buried one hand in her hair and held her head in place, wanting to own her suddenly, to make her entirely mine. With the other hand I stroked up her belly to the soft underside of her breasts. Some part of me still knew it was wrong, and I didn't touch them. I tried, honestly tried, not to violate this new trust she'd shown in me. But I was close. My hand hovered over her in the dark. I could feel the heat of her flesh radiating against my cupped palm. Almost but not quite touching—it was driving me insane.

But then Alex thrust up under my hands, surprising me by pressing the full curve of her right breast into my hand. Her nipple felt like a little pebble under my seeking fingertips. I brushed it lightly, then pinched very gently, provoking an intense reaction. She pulled away for a moment, breaking the kiss to gasp, "Harder!" and pressed more fully into my hands. I did what she wanted me to, twisting her nipple, probably more forcefully than I meant to, but I was rapidly losing control. Drowning in my need for her.

Alex gasped and shuddered against me, writhing in my lap like an animal. I gripped her hair tighter with my other hand, forcing her to be still, and she moaned into my mouth, a sound that sent a bolt of pure desire to my already aching shaft. She tasted like tears and pain and need. She tasted delicious.

I had a sudden blinding urge to take her right here and now. Images filled my head, thoughts of ripping down those low-slung black pants that had been driving me crazy all day, whether I admitted it to myself or not. Ripping them down and impaling her on me—forcing her to ride my cock while I took her long and slow and hard and deep. Above all, deep—I wanted to ram myself so far inside her she'd feel me for a month. Wanted to own her—to possess her completely...

"Alexandra, darling? Are you home?" Her mother's low, cultured voice shattered the intense mood for both of us. I felt Alex stiffen against me again, and then she was shoving hard at my chest, scrambling out of my lap.

"Alex, I—"

She didn't stay to hear anything else, as though anything I could say would excuse my actions. I heard a door bang open and closed and then the sound of water running as she locked herself in the bathroom.

Chapter Eleven

Alex

"Alex?"

I looked up to see Cole, standing there uncertainly in front of my desk. Today he was wearing a navy blue blazer with a pale blue shirt. A tie that had every color of blue imaginable in it brought the blazer and shirt together. It was an outfit I had helped him pick out before his last court date with Amanda. I wondered if his wearing it had any significance. Divorce, loss of innocence, screwing everything up by doing the wrong thing... He had kissed me first, but there was no doubt I had kissed back.

"Alex?" he said again, and I realized I had been just sitting there, staring at him without answering. The blue in his shirt made his eyes more penetrating than ever.

"Morning, partner," I said tightly, grabbing a file from my desk to use as a shield. I had already decided that the best thing to do was just ignore what had happened between us the night before. After all, it had been an emotional moment... I cringed in shame when I remembered just *how* emotional I'd allowed myself to get. Talk about losing control...

Cole got a determined, stubborn look on his face. "Alex, we have to talk," he said, leaning down to look in my eyes, despite my attempt to put the open file between us.

"No," I said clearly. "We don't."

"Alex, I want to apologize. And we can't just ignore—"

I grabbed the blue-striped tie and hauled the big idiot down until we were eye to eye. "Listen to me," I said fiercely. "*It never happened.* Got it?"

He looked pissed, really enraged for a moment, and then his face went granite hard again—blank. "That's the way you want it," he said stiffly, making it a statement, not a question.

"That's the way it has to be," I corrected more gently. "We're partners, Cole. That's all."

"Whoa, detectives, am I like, interrupting something here?" Both of our heads snapped to the side to see Matt watching us with great interest. He held the red satin mask, still in its plastic baggie, in one hand, and a thick sheaf of papers in the other.

"Just making sure this big lug looks presentable," I said, as calmly as I could. I made a show of straightening Cole's tie, which was rather crooked from me yanking on it. When I finished, he rose without comment and went to lean against the side of his desk.

"What you got, Matt?" he asked, as cool as I had been. As though none of it had ever happened.

Matt looked uncertainly between the two of us and then apparently decided it was safe to go on. "Uh, okay, got some good news and some bad news for you two. Number one—I found out where the masks are coming from. There's a kit manufactured by a company out of New Jersey—The Kinky Boy Scout. The kit's called—get this—Bondage for Beginners." He laughed but when we didn't join in, he sobered abruptly and went on. "Okay, so it's got the mask, the black satin ties, a pair of fuzzy handcuffs, some body oil, a feather, and an instruction booklet. Pretty kinky, huh?"

"Where can you buy this kit?" Cole asked, ignoring the last comment.

"Oh, well that's kinda the bad news." Matt shrugged. "You can get it damn near everywhere. I mean, not Wal-Mart or anything, but anywhere they sell sex toys. I even called a couple places to ask, and they've all got some in stock right now. So tracking your perp by the mask is going to be hard. Sorry, guys."

"Shit," I mumbled furiously. Damn it, this perp had all the bases covered.

"And if our little friend Jeremy was telling us the truth, Sarah might have bought that kit herself. Could be that the perp actually used her own stuff to tie her up." Cole looked as frustrated as I felt.

"But there's no whip or riding crop included in it, right?" I looked at Matt, and he shook his head. "So it might just be a coincidence, him buying the same kit she had and getting the extras—the roses, the crop or whip or whatever. But where are the fuzzy handcuffs and body oil? Or the feather?"

"None found in Sarah's apartment, but that doesn't mean anything. Her roommate could've taken them for her 'act.'" Cole frowned. "Or if the perp *did* bring his own kit, there's no reason he'd bring all of it. You know those novelty cuffs usually just have a release on them—they won't really restrain anybody who wants to get away."

I looked up at Matt. "What about the other thing I asked you to check on?"

"A Dominatrix offering lessons?" The look in my eyes must have warned him I was in no mood for joking because he said it with a straight face.

I nodded. "Any bites?"

"Well, yeah, a few. Some of 'em, I don't know if they're legit or not. It's kinda hard to separate out the ones that are for real from the ones who're just high dollar hookers offering kinky sex. I, uh, made a list for you."

Cole took the top sheet of paper from the pile he was holding. "Mistress Fantasia," he read. "Making all your darkest erotic fantasies come true. Mistress Tasty, will whip you until you beg for more...?" He looked up at Matt. "What *is* this stuff?"

Matt shrugged. "Hey, Detective B, just doin' what you told me to. Look at the fifth one down."

"Mistress Bathsheba," Cole read, looking back at the paper. "Learn the truth about S/M and the beauty of SexMagic. Release your inner Dom or sub. Hmm...sounds like she *could* be offering lessons..."

"Sarah's roommate said she met Sarah down at the Turk." I sat up straighter in my chair. "And I bet they stock a lot of those bondage kits."

He shrugged. "Worth a try. If she was giving Sarah lessons in this stuff, she might even have introduced her to her murderer."

"Hey, wait a minute, guys, I'm not done yet," Matt protested. "I was checking out the laptop they brought in, lookin' to see if there was any suspicious Internet access or e-mails, you know?"

"Sarah's laptop?" I asked. "What did you find?"

"Well, not too much with the e-mails, unfortunately, but I did find something interesting. This Sarah chick was writing a lot more than her thesis on this thing. I printed some of it for you—check it out." He passed the sheaf of papers he'd been holding to Cole who flipped through it briefly and began to read.

"I kneel before him, helpless, arms bound behind my back. I am naked, my hair hanging around my face like a velvet curtain, screening my hot cheeks.

"'Look at me.' He lifts my chin to look in my eyes, his gaze consuming me.

"'Please,' I whisper, uncertain of what I'm begging for. He begins to stroke my body, to explore me everywhere. His hands on my skin are hard as steel, as soft as silk, as knowing as sin.

"'You've been bad today,' he murmurs, still caressing me. 'I can see it in your eyes. Maybe it's time to get the crop.'

"I whimper, low in my throat, both longing for and dreading the delicious sting of leather against my bare flesh. First he will whip me and then he will take me, hard and long and utterly without mercy—"

"That's enough, Cole," I interrupted him, feeling the heat climbing my cheeks. God, it sounded like something *I* would write.

My partner looked up at me, one eyebrow raised, his blue eyes penetrating my soul.

"We...we get the picture," I managed, trying to keep a straight face. "Sarah Michaels wrote erotica."

"Well, this might have some relevance to the case," Cole argued. "We already know she was heavily into kink. Those books she was reading and this stuff she was writing..."

"Lots of women write erotica, Cole. Haven't you ever kept a diary of your secret fantasies?" I asked.

"Well, most of *my* fantasies don't involve being beaten," he objected.

"Sarah Michaels's did," I said quietly. "Are you saying that made her less of a good person? That she deserved what happened to her?"

"Hell, no, Alex! Stop putting words in my mouth. I'd never say—"

"I think we should get down to the Turk and ask a few questions," I snapped, standing and grabbing my jacket. "You coming or not?"

"Oh, I'm coming. Wouldn't miss it." Cole's face had gone granite hard again.

"Matt," I said to the computer tech, who was staring back and forth between Cole and me with eyes as big as soft balls. "Keep working the computer angle. We'll be back later."

"Uh, sure, Detective R," he muttered.

I headed for my car, not waiting to see if Cole would follow.

Chapter Twelve

Cole

I couldn't figure my partner out lately. Not that women aren't always a mystery—if they weren't, why would we bother? But Alex had always been as close to one of the guys as any woman I knew. She was tough, resourceful, and straightforward—all qualities I valued highly. Now she was changing, and I wasn't sure I liked it.

For one thing she had finally shown me a vulnerable side I had always suspected but never dared to ask about. If I closed my eyes, I could still feel the warm press of her body cradled in my arms and taste her lips, trembling and uncertain under mine.

That helplessness, that uncertainty, had awakened a part of me I didn't know I had. A primitive, possessive caveman that must have been living in the back of my skull all along, had come forward and growled, *Mine.* But a sidelong glace at her stiff features was enough to remind me that it would take more than one frantic moment of kissing and groping in the dark for me to be able to lay claim to my partner as anything more than a friend. Hell, I wasn't even certain we were friends anymore, and that was the scariest thing of all.

"Alex," I said softly. She was concentrating on the road, taking the turns way too fast, but driving with the amazing agility that had earned my respect early in our partnership. I didn't know any men who could drive like her, myself included.

"You want to talk about the case?" Her voice was flat.

"You know damn well that isn't what I want to talk about," I said.

"Then you can keep it to yourself," she said tightly. "Last night is *not* up for discussion."

"Won't you at least let me apologize?" I asked, feeling completely exasperated. "You were hurting last night, Alex— vulnerable. I feel like…like I took advantage of that, and I didn't mean to. I swear to God, I don't know what came over me…"

She swerved to the right, cutting off a semi, not smart in her tiny little Bug. We got a blast from its horn but she didn't pay any attention.

"Alex!" I protested—there's a fine line between dangerous driving and driving dangerously.

"Okay, if it'll make you feel better, I forgive you, all right? And for the record, I didn't feel taken advantage of. I'm not nearly as mad at you as I am at myself for letting it happen."

For letting yourself be weak around me, I thought but didn't say. As my dad used to say, I may be dumb, but I'm not stupid. Alex would talk about that when she was good and ready. Which might be never. So instead I reached over and patted her knee. I meant for it to be a friendly gesture but I couldn't help noticing how silky her skin was under the pantyhose she was wearing. Why did she have to wear a skirt on today of all days?

"Still friends?" I asked.

She stiffened under my touch and kept her eyes straight ahead. "Still partners, Cole, which is a hell of a lot more important."

"Oh?" I said, withdrawing my hand. "I never thought so."

We rode the rest of the way to The Turk in silence.

The Turk Adult Video and Supercenter is located on the corner of north Dale Mabry and Fletcher, not the best part of town. Still, in the time since I've joined the PD, it's grown from a tiny, seedy little shop that specialized in peep shows and dirty magazines for lonely businessmen, to a huge, "couples friendly" megamart of obscure, obscene, and blatantly sexual paraphernalia.

We stepped in the door which had a "no admittance under the age of eighteen" sign, into the well-lit interior and the scent of latex and leather invaded my nose. No more dim lighting, or hiding the really "dirty" merchandise behind a beaded curtain in the back room. Everything at the Turk is right out in the open, and there are even little hand baskets to carry your purchases in. I noticed a wall of realistic rubber vaginas to our right and dildos in every color of the rainbow to our left. It's like Wal-Mart for the sexually curious (or the sexually depraved, depending on how you look at it).

This time of the day there weren't many customers, and Alex and I didn't even raise any eyebrows, coming in together. We probably just looked like an upper middle-class couple grabbing some sex toys on an early lunch break. Even the greasy-looking counter man barely looked up from his copy of *Backdoor Lovin'*. He was reading with an avid interest that suggested there might be a test later.

"Look at this," I said, threading my way through several rows of massage oil and racks of hard-core DVDs and videos. Hanging against the far wall was a large selection of whips, floggers, canes, and crops, most of them in red or black leather.

"Doesn't look like our guy would have had to look too hard to find what he wanted," Alex remarked neutrally.

I grabbed a black leather riding crop from its peg on the wall. It had a flat, roughly rectangular leather surface perhaps two inches wide, attached to a long flexible stem that ended in a contoured handle. I slapped it experimentally into the palm of my hand. "Stings," I remarked, thoughtfully. I looked up to see Alex watching me with wide eyes. "Here," I said, "Hold out your hand—see for yourself."

Her eyes got even wider, but she did as I said. I slapped the riding crop down with medium force. She flinched but took the blow stoically enough. There was a very faint red mark when I withdrew the crop, running along the inside of her palm.

"Yeah," she licked her lips nervously. "Yeah, it...it stings."

"I think it's supposed to," I said, examining the long rod with its ominous-looking rectangle of black leather at the end. "But the question is, could it make marks like the ones on Sarah Michaels's thighs? You'd have to hit someone a hell of a lot harder than I just hit you to draw blood—and with the stem, not with the end."

"I...I don't know. I guess." She was staring at the long black leather crop in my hands as though I was holding a poisonous snake instead of a sex toy. It reminded me of a movie I'd seen with Amanda when we first got together, *9½ Weeks*. There's this scene in the movie, where the couple is trying out beds in the furniture store. The guy (played by Mickey Rourke before he turned into such a sleaze ball) makes the girl (Kim Basinger) lie down on the bed, and then he slaps the riding crop he's holding against her leg and says... *Spread your legs for Daddy*.

"What?" Alex's eyes were so wide I thought they might pop out of her head and her breathing had quickened just a little bit. I realized I'd just said the words out loud.

"A movie I saw," I explained, wondering why she was freaking out. "*9½ Weeks*." I slapped the crop against my thigh and used my lowest, most commanding tone. "Spread your legs for Daddy, little girl."

I was just joking around, of course, but Alex actually jumped and put a hand between her breasts. Her breathing was definitely more rapid—in fact, she was almost panting. A faint blush rose on her neck and cheeks. What the hell? I wondered uneasily what was wrong with her.

"Alex?" I asked. "You all right?"

"Fine, just..." She turned her back on me abruptly, obviously fighting for some kind of control. "Let's try to stick to the case here, all right, Cole?"

"Fine," I said, bewildered. "I was just wondering if a crop like this could have made the marks on our vic's thighs. Actually, I bet it was more something like this." I reached up and replaced the crop, taking down a stiff bamboo cane instead. It was long and smooth, tapered to a wicked-looking point, and it had a lot less give than the crop. It looked like a more likely weapon to me.

"At any rate, we know he wouldn't have had a hard time finding his other gear." Alex grabbed a large red cardboard box with the words *Bondage for Beginners* printed in bold black script across the front. "Look at this—just like Matt said."

I looked through the clear plastic window in the box to see a pair of fuzzy purple 'luv cuffs, some black satin restraints, a long black feather, massage oil, a how-to booklet, and, most significant of all, a red satin mask with black lace trim.

"This is it, all right," I murmured. "These are a few of our perp's favorite things."

"Help you?" The bored voice behind us turned out to belong to the greasy-looking clerk. Apparently he had lost interest in his magazine and decided to give doing his job a try for a while.

"You sell many of these?" Alex asked, thrusting the box at him.

"You kidding?" The clerk barely glanced at the contents. He gestured dismissively. "Sell so many we can't hardly keep 'em in stock. Everybody's gettin' kinky these days. You interested?" He leered openly at Alex. I couldn't resist the impulse to put myself between my partner and the creep, although I knew perfectly well she was able to take care of herself.

Having a sudden brainstorm, I said, "My...uh, fiancée and I are interested in this kind of thing, yes. But we don't know quite where to start. I heard from a friend of a friend that I might be able to contact someone here who could help us."

The clerk's eyes went flat. "Don't know nothin' about that," he said and started to move off. I made a twenty appear in my palm, and the flat eyes regained a little life.

"You sure about that?" I coaxed. "We're really interested—we understand she's the best."

I don't know if it was the money or the knowing grin I gave him, but the clerk seemed to relax. "Okay," he said, taking the bill and stuffing it into the pocket of his grimy gray pants. "Could be I remember somebody who might be willin' to help ya. For a price."

"Money's not a problem," Alex said, stepping forward and looking around my arm, obviously wanting to be included in the conversation.

"It ain't always money she's worried about," he said darkly. "You got to keep things quiet, ya know? Some people don't understand and if word gets around..." He made a graphic gesture.

"We understand," I said quickly. "Just give us her number, and we'll get out of your hair.

"Fine, buy a hundred bucks worth of merchandise—minimum—and I'll put the number in the bag with your purchases."

"A hundred bucks?" Alex protested. "But he just gave you—"

"You want the number or not? Thought you said money wasn't no problem?" The flat eyes narrowed suspiciously.

"No—no, that's okay," I said hastily. Turning to Alex I took her by the shoulders and said, "Just go pick out anything you want, sweetheart, and don't worry about the cost. My treat."

"Yeah, but who's going to treat you?" Alex muttered under her breath. I knew she meant we'd have a hell of a time adding these types of purchases to the expense report. Captain Davis might be willing to pay out money for information, but not necessarily for sex toys. But I didn't see any other way to get the number of the Dominatrix who had been training Sarah Michaels. If I was a hundred bucks out of pocket, it would just be too bad—it was worth a lot more than that to me to get this guy off the street.

We got to the register in record time with one of the bondage kits, the cane I had been examining, a black leather bra-looking thing that looked to be Alex's size, and a slender leather collar studded with small silver hearts. The total came to over two hundred and fifty dollars.

I gave Alex the eye as I handed over the money, muttering something about women and shopping, which made the clerk cackle. "Yeah, the ladies spend more in here than the guys do," he assured me, wrapping the leather bra and collar in tissue carefully before placing them in the bag. "They get in here, and they just can't help theirselfs."

"Right," I said shortly. "The number...?"

"In the bag," he assured me. "Be sure to tell her Ted sent you—she don't take clients without referrals."

"Will do." I took the surprisingly heavy bag from him, and we got out of the store.

"What now?" Alex wanted to know when we were crammed into her tiny Bug again. I was beginning to wish something harder to fix than a dead battery had been wrong with it—at least we'd have had room to breathe if we were in my truck.

"Now I'm going to call and make an appointment with our Dominatrix friend. Which, by the way, *you* can pay for since I just bought you a complete set of leather underwear."

She smirked. "You did say to get anything I wanted, *sweetheart*," she reminded me. "And besides, if we're making an appointment with the Dominatrix, we might have to look the part. I was just planning ahead."

"You mean I actually get to see you in that leather bra thing?" I asked, beginning to enjoy the teasing. Were we beginning to get back to normal?

Alex paled a little. "For your information, it's called a bustier. And if I end up having to wear it anywhere in your presence, I expect you to act appropriately."

"Jeez. Yes, ma'am," I said sarcastically. Message received, we were definitely *not* getting back to normal. Not yet and maybe not ever. For the umpteenth time since it had happened I kicked myself for giving in to my impulses and treating my partner like a woman instead of just a pal and co-worker the night before. And yet, now that I had seen her softer side, I couldn't un-see it. Just the thought of her in all that black leather had me hard as a rock.

Trying to push those thoughts to the back of my brain, I found the crumpled slip of paper "Ted" had slipped into the plastic bag, and flipped open my cell phone. It was a local number; that much, at least, was good.

I dialed and a voice as smooth as sex on a stick dipped in dark chocolate answered on the second ring.

"You've reached Mistress Samantha, how may I help you?"

"I...uh, my fiancée and I were given this number by a friend who said you could help us," I said, pretending to be nervous. Because Ted had been so reluctant to give us the number, I thought it was advisable to go on playing the sexually curious couple for a while longer. We might get more information out of the Dominatrix going in that way, than flashing our badges and waving our guns.

"And who exactly referred you to me?" she asked, the smooth, dark chocolate voice sharpening just a little.

Taking a chance I said, "Sarah. Sarah Michaels. I'm taking a class with her at UCH." I was hoping she hadn't read the paper or watched the news in the last couple of days.

There was a long pause before she finally spoke again. "Very well. If Sarah referred you I'm willing to give you a consultation at least. When would you like to come in?"

"What's your next available appointment?" I asked, trying not to sound too eager.

"Actually, I have a cancellation at seven tonight. Would that be convenient?" she asked.

"Perfect," I assured her. "Thank you for getting us in so quickly. We're very eager to begin."

"I'll just bet you are," she purred. Then her voice changed abruptly, becoming all business. "Be at the address I give you at six-thirty sharp to fill out paperwork. And I want it understood that I don't engage in any actual sex play with my clients. I am not some kind of a prostitute—I'm a licensed sexual and mental health counselor and as such I am prepared to instruct you, not to fuck you. Understood?"

"Uh, yes, ma'am," I said shortly. Her tone took me all the way back to boot camp and for a moment I had a strong urge to drop and give her fifty. "Is...should we bring anything?" I asked hesitantly.

She sounded amused. "Besides your checkbook, I only require that you bring yourselves and any toys you may have already acquired that you wish to learn the proper use of." She gave me the address.

"Thank you, um...?" I fumbled, genuinely not knowing how to address her.

"You may call me Mistress," she said coolly. "I'll see you at six-thirty sharp—mind you're not late. Oh, and do dress appropriately, you and your fiancée both." Then she hung up.

"Well, what's the story?"

I turned to Alex who was staring at me expectantly. "We got an appointment for seven tonight, but we have to be there at six-thirty to fill out paperwork. Oh, and it looks like you get to play dress-up after all."

Chapter Thirteen

Alex

"Okay," I said, taking as deep a breath as the black leather bustier would allow. I had on a jacket to keep me warm, but it was still chilly in the brief leather top. "We're going in there as a couple, but let's not get carried away." We were sitting outside the upscale Hyde Park home that was the address the Dominatrix had given us, and I was feeling more nervous by the second.

Cole gave me a withering look, and I almost felt ashamed. "Give me *some* credit, Alex. One little mistake, and you're treating me like the Boston Strangler. I can control myself."

"Okay, all right, I'm sorry," I said, struggling to keep my voice level and firm. "It's just that…this makes me a little nervous, all right?" That, for the record, was the understatement of the year, maybe of my entire life. The ironic thing was that going to an actual Dominatrix for instruction was something I would never have done on my own, despite my natural inclinations. It was too real, too scary. It was one thing to write about bondage and discipline but something else entirely to go to a professional and take a class in it. I would no sooner sign myself up for a class like this on my own than I would sign up for a class on masturbation—it was that private.

"What do you think we should expect?" Cole looked at me, one eyebrow raised, and I felt myself flush.

"How should I know? I'm not into this kind of stuff." A blatant lie, but I felt compelled to keep hiding behind my tough girl persona. My partner had already seen more than enough of my soft side, and where had it gotten us? In a tangled-up mess, that's where, I told myself sternly, when my body wanted to remember how small and deliciously vulnerable I'd felt in his arms.

I became aware that Cole was looking at me strangely. "I didn't say you were into it—I just thought you might have more information since you spent some time in vice, and I haven't," he explained shortly.

"Oh, sorry." I felt stupid. If I wasn't careful my defensiveness was going to blow my cover. "Uh, mostly what I remember was from the gay leather scene at the Castle." The Castle is a gay bar in Ybor City, Tampa's party district. We had busted it occasionally in the year I worked in vice, mostly in a joint deal with narcotics, looking for illegal drugs. I told Cole as much.

"Yeah, I've heard a river of X and coke runs through that place," he said.

"Pretty much." I fiddled with the leather collar, which was just on this side of too tight. Why had I really bought it? I had told Cole I wanted to dress the part if we had to, but that wasn't the whole truth by a long shot. How long had I fantasized about wearing something like this? But in all my fantasies it was placed around my neck by my Master, a man whom I could give complete control of my body, my pain, my pleasure— everything that was in me—to do with as he saw fit.

Fantasies and foolishness, I knew I would never find such a man—adding the collar to the shopping basket had been stupid and unrealistic. And yet, a girl can dream, can't she? Well, not in this situation, not if I didn't want my most private and shameful desires exposed to the one person who meant more to me than anyone else in the world. I was desperate to keep my sexual appetites hidden from Cole, which was probably what motivated my next statement.

"I *do* know," I said, looking down at the black leather skirt I was wearing, "that one of us has to play the top and one gets to be the bottom." I looked up at him. "We go in there as a couple, then I'm the top."

He gave me an unreadable look. "Don't you think that's kind of unrealistic?"

"Why?" I asked. "Because you're a big bad man, and I'm a helpless little girl? That's pretty sexist, Cole."

He held up his hand in a "don't shoot" gesture. "Okay, fine, that's the way you want it."

"It is."

"Just try not to spank me too hard." He grinned.

"Ha-ha," I said dryly. That's Cole, always good for a laugh, but my sense of humor seemed to have taken a permanent vacation.

I looked at the unassuming Tudor-style house at the address the Dominatrix had given us. She was living in Hyde Park, one of Tampa's more exclusive neighborhoods, so she must not be doing too badly. How much were people willing to pay for this kind of thing? It made me think of that credit card commercial—*Leather bustier—one hundred dollars, whipping cane—fifty dollars, bondage and domination lessons from a real Dominatrix—two hundred dollars. Acting out all your most secret and perverted fantasies—priceless.* It almost made me smile.

Cole looked at his watch. "You ready to do this?"

I nodded in what I hoped was a confident way. "No problem." It was dark in the interior of his truck (he had insisted on driving this time—unusual for him), but I could make out his serious blue eyes by the light of the dash.

"We'll play the curious couple as long as it's getting us somewhere. We won't pull our badges unless we have to—right?"

"Right," I agreed, taking a deep breath. We'd done this kind of thing before—gone undercover, even played a couple. It was no big deal, honestly. So why was I nearly trembling? I clenched my hand tightly—the one he had smacked with the riding crop. I could still feel the slight burn where Cole had hit me and the sound of his voice, deep and commanding, when he'd quoted that line from the movie. I knew he was just joking and yet... No, I told myself firmly, this was definitely *not* the time to be having erotic flashbacks, especially about my partner. We were on a case—I had to get hold of myself.

"Let's go," I said, shedding the jacket and sliding out the passenger side door in the same move. It was almost cold enough to see my breath, and my skin pebbled into gooseflesh immediately. The sidewalk grated under the stiletto heels of my black leather boots. I had worn them hoping they would make me look tougher and more sexually dominant. But they were so high I actually stumbled and Cole had to catch my arm to keep me from falling.

"Whoa, you really look the part," he murmured admiringly, his eyes raking up and down my body with appreciation. "Where'd you get the other stuff?" He nodded at the boots and short leather skirt. I was beginning to regret wearing both.

"Um... I got them for a Halloween party one year," I improvised rapidly.

"Why wasn't I invited?" His eyes were still glued to me, and I realized how very exposed I felt without my jacket on. The black leather bustier pushed my breasts up and out. They wobbled with every step I took, like some exotic fruit on a tray. The real reason I'd bought the boots and skirt was the same reason I'd bought the collar—dreams and fantasies. I'd never actually expected to wear them out anywhere.

Cole was wearing a much more prosaic outfit than mine. His clothing consisted of a pair of simple black dress slacks, a wine-red shirt, and a black leather vest. The red shirt brought out his dark coloring, and made his eyes even more piercing. He looked tall, menacing, dangerous...dominant. No! I couldn't let myself think like that.

"You have the things?" I asked, meaning the bondage kit and the cane he'd picked out.

"Got 'em right here." He showed me the heavy plastic bag, and I nodded.

"Good, let's go. We don't want to keep Mistress Samantha waiting."

A young woman in a demure knee-length skirt and white silk blouse greeted us when we rang the doorbell, and I abruptly felt ridiculous. She looked like she could have been a hostess at any nice restaurant in town, and here I was dressed up like some kind of leather slut.

"Oh..." I hung back for a moment. "Mistress Samantha?" I asked, uncertainly. "I guess I'm not really dressed correctly."

She laughed good-naturedly. "Oh, no. I'm just her assistant, Melissa. And don't worry about the way you're dressed—it's quite appropriate."

"Thanks," I said, feeling relieved.

She beckoned us both inside, and we entered a large rectangular foyer that had been decorated as a reception area. Against the walls were plush leather benches, similar to but nicer than the kind you'd find in any doctor's waiting room. There was an intricate oriental rug on the marble-tile floor, and the walls were painted a soft beige with burgundy accents.

"Not exactly what I expected," Cole remarked, looking around.

The girl laughed again. "Oh, everybody says that on their first visit. Don't worry, the dungeon will more than meet your expectations. Please, have a seat, while I get your paperwork."

"The *dungeon?*" Cole muttered as we settled on one of the leather benches.

I elbowed him. "Keep it down—she's coming back."

"Please be sure you fill out front and back and sign the bottom." The smiling girl handed us each a legal-sized clipboard with a pen attached, before disappearing into another room.

I looked at the clipboard. There was a questionnaire attached with a list of questions as long as my arm. At first glance they all seemed to be medical in nature. At least until I looked on the back.

"Do you have a history of heart disease?" Cole read in a low voice. "Have you ever been diagnosed with any form of breathing disorder such as asthma?" He looked up at me. "It's like the doctor's office."

"Look on the back," I said, scanning a second list of questions. "I guarantee you never went to any doctor that asked you this kind of stuff."

He flipped his form over and frowned. "Dom/sub/switch?" He looked at me, raising an eyebrow.

"Just mark sub," I said, putting a bold black X in the box marked Dom. Sighing, he did so.

After a moment he complained, "I don't understand half of what they're asking here. What the hell is 'age play?' And when they're asking about 'cock worship,' I hope to hell they're asking if I want someone worshiping mine. I'm damn sure not prepared to go the other way, even to solve this case."

"Just do your best," I said tightly, still marking boxes. "We'll tell her we're new to the scene and she can explain. Remember we're only having a consultation tonight."

"Right, a consultation," he grumbled, and went back to his own questionnaire.

To tell the truth, some of the questions were confusing to me as well, but I wasn't about to admit it. I kept my head down and continued reading. Breast whipping, nipple clamps, spanking, paddling, restrictions on speech and behavior... Everything from various forms of bondage to various forms of servitude was covered. Some of the prospects gave me a dangerous little thrill. Others just left me cold. Infantilism, legal/permanent name change, plastic surgery, sleep deprivation, body modification through corseting or scarification...none of that did anything for me.

The long list of sexual preferences and predilections did make several things clear to me, however. One, I wasn't nearly as kinky as some people out there. And two, writing about bondage and discipline and actually living the lifestyle were obviously two different things.

I didn't even have any tattoos or piercing, let alone own any fetish equipment aside from my current outfit. I had toyed with the idea of having my nipples pierced for a while. But in my line of work, going through metal detectors is not uncommon. What would I say when I'd taken off my gun and turned out my pockets and the detector kept going off? Nope, it was a naughty pleasure I would have to deny myself.

"Mistress Samantha is ready for you now." The smiling receptionist came back in and led us up a long flight of stairs to the top portion of the two-story house. I had never heard of having a dungeon on the second floor but I assumed it was for practical reasons. There was no way to have a basement in South Tampa—not so close to the bay.

There was a tall plain wooden door at the end of the stairs and the receptionist opened it and ushered us inside. "Mistress

Samantha will be with you shortly. Please have a seat," she chirped, and closed the door behind us.

"Wow." Cole's eyes were wide and when I turned from the door to examine the room, I could see why. The "dungeon" looked to take up the entire top half of the house. Someone had knocked down the walls and created a huge, customized space and every available corner of it was filled with sexual devices.

"What *is* this?" Cole wondered aloud, walking slowly around the perimeter of the room. "I mean some of it's obvious." He pointed at a hefty black leather paddle that was riddled with holes like a wiffle ball. "But some of this…" He stood before a large wooden frame, which was about seven feet tall, and had restraints at both ends. It was shaped like a capital X and was highly burnished, as though someone had taken great care to keep it in good condition. As I watched, Cole reached up to stroke the glossy wood.

"I see you're admiring my Saint Andrew's cross." The low voice startled us both and we turned to see a woman who could have been anywhere between thirty-five and fifty walking toward us. She was dressed in a conservative suede skirt that fell to mid-calf, dark brown boots, and a white silk shirt, much like the receptionist's. Her dark auburn hair was pinned into an elegant French twist, and her pale green eyes snapped at us. This must be Mistress Samantha.

"It's…something all right," Cole said dryly, looking from the Dominatrix to the cross and back again.

"It's so useful, particularly if you're playing with more than one person." Her voice was casual. "Just string one submissive to the cross and he or she is more or less out of the way while you torment another. Why, they can even watch each other." She laughed, a rich throaty sound that sent chills skittering down my spine.

"I see." Cole jerked his hand away from the cross as though he'd been burned. I sympathized with him.

"Come with me." She gestured to the far end of the dungeon and I saw that one small corner held a table and several chairs. We walked over, with the Dominatrix at our backs, trailing us like a cloud full of lightening, ready to strike. I felt tense, and not just because of my own hidden sexual proclivities.

This was an unknown situation, and I was unarmed. Between the leather bustier and the tiny black leather mini-skirt, there was nowhere to hide my gun. Cole was still wearing his Glock, his shoulder holster concealed beneath the black leather vest. But I felt naked in more ways than one, without the solid weight of my Browning under my arm. Not that we expected to run into any trouble but still…

I took some comfort from the feel of Cole's large hand at the small of my back as he guided me toward the table and chairs. It was a friendly gesture, and a protective one. He always tends to touch me more when he senses I'm upset. Despite the weirdness between us in the past twenty-four hours, I found myself soothed by that warm touch. *We're together*, it said. *And as long as we're together, everything is going to shake down okay.* He'd touched me like that before more than one big bust, and it always calmed me down like nothing else could.

"Sit down." We had come to the card-sized table. Two large, comfortable-looking wingback chairs upholstered in oxblood leather faced each other across from it. The Dominatrix settled herself in one and gestured at us. We walked awkwardly around the table, and I saw a low wooden stool beside the other chair. Cole is a big guy, so I sat on the stool myself and gave him the other chair.

When we were settled, apparently to her satisfaction, Mistress Samantha produced our paperwork and a tiny pair of wire-rim glasses and began to read. I thought she looked more like a strict schoolteacher than any kind of exotic sex devotee but I kept it to myself. The wooden stool was uncomfortable and I shifted uneasily, wondering what she would say.

"We're here because—" Cole began, obviously more impatient than I was.

She held up a hand. "I know perfectly well why you're here, Mr. Berkley. Be still a moment while I finish looking over this." Her low voice held a note of command that indicated she was used to being obeyed. It was the exact same way I talked to a suspect when I was making an arrest. Interesting. From the slightly sour look on Cole's face, he didn't find the situation quite so fascinating.

At last she finished looking through our questionnaires and glanced up. "All right," she said briskly, addressing Cole. "Can you tell me please, in your own words, Mr. Berkley, when you first became interested in sexual submission?"

"I...uh, I guess I've just—" he began haltingly.

"You can't, can you?" she snapped, cutting him off. "Because you're *not.*" She laid the paperwork on the small table in front of her and frowned at us both. "Mr. Berkley, Miss Reed, we are going to get nowhere fast if you begin by lying to me about who you are and what you want."

Cole and I exchanged uneasy glances. What the hell? We'd been in her presence less than ten minutes and our cover was already blown.

"I…uh, I'm afraid I don't understand," Cole said carefully. I shrugged, to indicate my own confusion as well.

"Really? Well, what *I* fail to understand," Mistress Samantha said, green eyes flashing over the wire rimmed spectacles, "is why you would waste your time and mine as well as a considerable sum of money pretending to be something you're not, the both of you. You—" She pointed at Cole. "—are clearly a dominant—a top, in layman's terms. And you—" She pointed at me. "—you wear your submissive tendencies like a thorny crown, my dear. They make you terribly uncomfortable, but you can't get rid of them."

"I…but…" I couldn't seem make my mouth say anything coherent.

"What makes you think you know so much about us just from a few simple questions?" Cole demanded, black eyebrows drawing down dangerously low as he glared at the Dominatrix.

"First of all, my questionnaire is anything but 'simple.' When used correctly it can be a powerful tool for delving into your psyche. Secondly, I used only your own body language and non-verbal clues in making my deductions." She stared at us coolly. Great, we were in the presence of a sexual Sherlock Holmes.

"Would you care to explain exactly how you drew your conclusions?" Cole challenged her, still looking decidedly red in the face. I personally wasn't saying anything because I was horrified. Were my secret sexual tendencies really that transparent? Could anybody look at me and see what I wanted? What I needed?

"I'll be happy to tell you." She settled back with a little smile. "It started on the telephone." She looked at Cole. "*You* called and made the appointment, Mr. Berkley, not Miss Reed. You took the initiative. Were she really dominant to you, it would have been the other way around. Second—" She looked at me. "—I told you to dress appropriately, and *look* at you." I felt myself blushing as her eyes raked me, taking in the whole outfit. "You're wearing fetish gear, openly displaying your needs while Mr. Berkley feels comfortable in more standard clothing. He is dominant to you, therefore, he has no need to display his body for you as you clearly need to display yours for him."

"That's...that's ridiculous. I feel no need to..." I began but she cut me off.

"Then when you walked across the room, I saw the way he guided you. He touched you the way any good Dom with a nervous sub would—calmed you down, let you know he would take care of you if things got frightening."

I blushed harder, remembering my almost subconscious pleasure in Cole's warm hand on the small of my back. It did comfort me, although not for precisely the reasons she was citing.

"What else?" I asked, fascinated. I couldn't help myself— this woman seemed to know me better than I knew myself and in only ten minutes time.

She smiled, her full red lips curling almost contemptuously. "Look at where you're sitting, my dear." She gestured between us. "No self-respecting dominant would take the hard wooden stool and give her sub the comfortable chair."

"So what does all this prove?" Cole asked, his face still as dark as a thundercloud.

"It proves that I've passed your little test, such as it was. Now, we can proceed with this consultation only after you assume your proper places." She steepled slender, elegant fingers tipped in crimson and stared at us.

"I don't understand what you want us to do," I said, hesitantly.

"Take your place by your Master's side, my dear," she said. Her voice was still commanding, but almost warm. "Don't fear or be ashamed of your needs. They're a part of you as much as your fingerprints or the color of your eyes and hair."

I looked at Cole who shrugged and beckoned to me. The gesture said, "humor her." It was obvious he had no idea how accurately she'd seen into me, which calmed me somewhat. Still, my heart drummed rapidly in my chest as I rose from the uncomfortable wooden stool and went to him. Was I supposed to sit on the floor at his feet or what?

My question was answered when Cole pulled me onto his lap. I stiffened for an instant, then allowed myself to melt against him. I made sure I was leaning on his right side though, so I wouldn't get in his way if he needed to go for his Glock. See? Still thinking like a cop, despite the burning fire raging through my nerves. Still on the job, I reminded myself desperately.

"Now." Mistress Samantha smiled brightly at us. "Isn't that better?"

Cole shrugged and stroked my arm, the way you might absently stroke a cat that had jumped in your lap. "I guess."

She frowned sternly. "You may answer me, 'Yes, Mistress,' or 'No, Mistress.' Respect is essential in the type of relationship we are considering."

"Only considering...*Mistress?*" Cole asked, his fingers tightening around my arm.

"Indeed." She smiled at us coolly. "I haven't said if I'm willing to take you as clients or not, and I reserve the right to be particular in my selection."

"Maybe this was a mistake." Cole frowned, and I felt his fingers reaching for his badge, his movements hidden by my torso.

"No...no, let's give it a chance, please..." I hesitated, uncertain what to call him in front of her.

Again, the Dominatrix seemed to read my mind. "Call him what he is, my dear. Your Master," she urged, almost gently.

I closed my eyes and swallowed hard. Inside I was on fire. That I should have to call Cole, of all people, by that title that I most feared and longed for. He was my partner, damn it! If I started letting myself have feelings for him outside of work everything would be ruined. And yet, in order to do my job, I was going to have to put my personal feelings on the line. Irony, anyone?

"Say it. You know you want to," Mistress Samantha urged, obviously sensing my reluctance. I could feel Cole's eyes on me too, boring into my soul. He was probably wondering why I wasn't playing along.

I could say it, I told myself. I could do this. But not if I had to look at him. I buried my face in his neck, hiding from his piercing blue eyes and breathing in his warm, masculine scent.

It reminded me entirely too much of the night before when he had held me close while I cried, and then kissed me like he would die if he didn't, but I couldn't help that.

"Please, Master," I breathed. "Please, I want to stay. I think...I think Mistress Samantha can help us."

"All right, Alex. We'll stay if you want to...because you asked so nicely." Cole stroked my back, getting into the part.

"Thank you, Master." I pulled my face away from his neck, my cheeks burning.

"Excellent, now we're getting somewhere." Mistress Samantha looked pleased with both of us. "Now that we all know what to call each other, let's begin at the beginning." She looked at Cole sharply. "How much do you know about the lifestyle?"

"Uh, the lifestyle?" He looked at her blankly.

"The community? The scene?" When he still looked blank, she gave a long-suffering sigh. "I can see I'm going to have to start at the beginning. Well, that's all right. We all have to start somewhere. "Why don't you begin by telling me exactly what you and your fiancée have tried so far?"

"Um...sexually?" I could feel the muscles in Cole's chest and thighs tensing.

"That is generally the basis of BDSM play," she said dryly. "Although if you're doing something that involves bondage and control issues in a non-sexual manner, I'm willing to listen to that as well."

I gave Cole a look from the corner of my eye. He's usually as cool as a cucumber whenever we go undercover, but I noticed that his face was decidedly red. The Dominatrix had really put him on the spot. I hoped he could come up with realistic enough scenarios to satisfy her. Personally, I could think of dozens but she hadn't asked me, and it was fairly obvious that in the "dungeon," a submissive only spoke when spoken to.

"Well? Must I remind you again that I can't help you if you won't let me?" She raised one perfectly sculpted auburn brow at him, and I felt Cole shift restlessly under me. I knew if he didn't feel we could gather some valuable information this way, he would have pulled out his badge right then and there. But I had as much as begged him not to—he was forced to play along no matter how uncomfortable it might be for either one of us.

"When we make love…" He cleared his throat. "When I take Alex, sexually," he amended, his voice becoming deeper and more confident. "When I take her, I sometimes like to tie her up so she can't escape. I tie her hands to the headboard with black satin ties. That way she can't get away from me, and I can do whatever I want to her. Sometimes I make her wear a mask so she can't see what I'm going to do next."

I realized that in a round about way he was describing our crime scenes but just the thought of him doing that—of tying me down and doing unspeakable things to me, made my body flush all over.

Mistress Samantha made some notes on his questionnaire. "Go on," she murmured, nodding for him to continue. "Why would she want to get away from you?"

"Well…" Cole seemed to be thinking hard. "Alex has…issues about oral sex. She wants it, but she's afraid to admit she wants it. I enjoy cuffing her hands behind her back or above her head while I taste her."

Oh, my God—I couldn't believe he was saying this. I wriggled in his arms, wishing I could get away somehow. Maybe I could have listened to him talk this way if I was sitting across the room from him, but I was too close—literally in his lap. This was too damn much to bear!

"Alex, be still," he commanded, and I went rigid in his arms before forcing myself to relax. Something hard and hot poked me in the thigh, and I became abruptly aware that talking like this was turning him on, too. I moaned inwardly...there would be absolutely no getting over this or living it down. It would haunt our partnership like an unquiet ghost forever.

Apparently undaunted by the specter I saw looming large in our future, Cole put a proprietary arm around my waist and continued. I could see him out of the corner of my eye; he was looking at me as he talked. But no matter how hard I tried, I couldn't make myself meet those steady blue eyes.

"I love the way she feels under my mouth and hands when I take her like that...the way she squirms and begs to be free when we both know she just needs to submit to me, so I can give her what she needs." He shifted, and I could feel his shaft throbbing beneath my ass. "She tastes so sweet, and she comes so hard. I like to wait until she's coming, until I can taste her heat on my tongue, before I spread her legs and ram inside her. Before I fuck her."

His eyes bored into me, and he was breathing harder; I could feel the rapid rise and fall of his chest against my back. God, he was turned on by the thought of this...maybe almost as turned on as I was! My body felt like it had turned to molten lava from my nipples down, and I couldn't help squirming again. This time he said nothing, only took a firm grip on one of my thighs and squeezed warningly. With a small, frustrated moan, I subsided in his arms again. God, he was killing me!

"Hmm... Most interesting." Mistress Samantha didn't look surprised or offended in the least at my partner's frank statements. She made a few more notes in what I was beginning to think of as "Cole's file" and turned to me. "And how do you feel about this, Alex. Do you enjoy what your Master does to you?"

"I..." My throat felt like sandpaper, but I knew that somehow I had to answer. If Cole could rise to the occasion (in more ways than one), then I could certainly do no less.

"Go on, you're allowed to speak," Mistress Samantha encouraged. "Do you feel that you're getting a lot out of these games you two are playing?"

"I...yes," I answered at last. "At first I was frightened of...of what my Master wanted to do to me. But he...I know he'd never hurt me. At least, not more than I need to be hurt." Then I bit my tongue savagely. Why had I added that last?

Mistress Samantha nodded, unfazed by my statement. "I see. It sounds like you two are already having a very satisfying relationship. So why come to me?" She was looking at Cole again.

"Because," he answered, much more readily than before. "Sometimes Alex is disobedient, and she needs to be punished. But she's so soft...so vulnerable." His large, warm hand stroked over my inner thigh, making me moan again despite myself. "I don't want to hurt her," he said, more softly. "At least...at least not any more than she needs to be hurt."

Hearing my own words in his mouth was almost too much. I bit my lip against the little cry that wanted to come out and willed myself to stay relaxed against him, despite the way he was caressing my thigh.

"Mmm-hmm." The Dominatrix made another note. "So you're interested in sensation play—perhaps a little erotic pain."

"Perhaps," Cole said cautiously.

"And what about you, Alex? Does this interest you as well?" She looked at me intently.

I bit my lip, wishing I could hide my face in Cole's neck again. It seemed cruelly ironic that I should have to admit to my most secret and shameful fantasies in front of the one man I never wanted to know about them.

"Answer me when I ask you a question." Mistress Samantha's voice was sharp, commanding. I found myself responding to her tone, spilling my secrets into her lap uncontrollably.

"I... I need to be disciplined, Mistress," I said softly, keeping my eyes on my hands, now twisting in my lap. "Not just when I'm disobedient, but because...because..." I felt my face burning but forced myself to go on. "When my Master disciplines me, when he whips me, I feel all his attention centered on me—all his love, all his hate, every emotion—all for me. And when he ties...ties me down and uses me, then the pleasure I feel...it isn't my fault. He's in complete control of me and...well, he makes me feel things I can't let myself feel any other way."

Then I buried my face in Cole's neck again, miserable and throbbing with shame and need. I didn't dare look at his face to see what he thought of my statements, but he ran his fingers through my hair and stroked my back gently, soothing me.

"Very good, Alex. You've been a very good girl." She sounded pleased, and the praise in her voice made my body react helplessly. Not for the first time I wondered what was wrong with me. Why was I hardwired to need such extreme treatment?

"Can you teach me to discipline her effectively, Mistress?" Cole asked, his hands still running gently over my back. "I think you can see how much…how much she needs it." The words seemed to stick in his throat, and I felt him tense beneath me. God—if he had any idea that what I was doing and saying tonight wasn't an act he would think I was sick.

"I can." Her voice hardened. "The question is, will I?" I looked up to see her pale green eyes dissecting us slowly. "Before I answer that question, Mr. Berkley, Miss Reed, I want you to answer a few questions I have for you."

"Well?" Cole asked and I could feel the tension thrumming through his muscles increase a notch. I realized I couldn't see the Dominatrix's hands anymore. They were under the small table. It made me nervous—put my already tightly strung senses on red alert.

"What do you know about Sarah Michaels's murder?" Mistress Samantha said, slowly and distinctly. "And before you go for the gun I know you have beneath that vest, Mr. Berkley, let me tell you I have a gun of my own pointed directly at you under the table. A Lady Smith and Wesson to be exact. Not as big as that cannon you're trying to hide, but I assure you it will do the job quite effectively."

I had been getting ready to move fast if I had to but now I froze in place. Looking under the table I could just see the cold glint of steel in its concealing shadows. She wasn't bluffing.

"Answer the question," she barked. "Did you kill her?"

"Actually, *Mistress*, we came here to ask you the same question." Cole's voice was deceptively mild but his next words weren't. "You see, we're homicide detectives from the Tampa police department and if you don't put that gun on the table in about five seconds flat you're going to be under arrest for assaulting an officer."

"Why should I believe you?" The green eyes never wavered and the gun stayed in position. The lady had guts, I had to give her that. Cole would have said she was "ballsy."

"If you'll allow my partner here to go for her badge, we can prove it." Cole jerked his chin at me and I raised my eyebrows in silent question.

She considered for a minute and then nodded. "All right, but no funny business."

"Wouldn't dream of it," Cole said dryly. "Alex?"

"Got it right here." I dug the gold detective's badge out from where it had been pressing uncomfortably between my breasts and showed it to her. She studied it for a moment and then relaxed.

"All right. I believe you."

"The gun?" Cole reminded her, still tense. "And you damn well better have a permit to carry."

"I have a permit," she said coolly, placing the Lady Smith and Wesson, which looked as well cared for as all the other equipment in the room, on the small table top. "It's for self protection. I can't be too careful in my profession."

"I just bet," I said, leaning over and grabbing the gun. I felt better the minute I had it in my hand. "Now tell us what you know about Sarah Michaels. We know she was taking lessons from you."

Mistress Samantha's eyes flashed. "Any information I have would be covered under patient confidentiality. I *am* a licensed therapist, as I believe I told you on the phone."

"We can always get a court order to help you loosen up a little." The menace in Cole's tone was unmistakable, his breathing rapid again. Abruptly, I realized I was still sitting in his lap. With a mixture of relief and regret, I moved back to the stool, still clutching the gun.

"That won't be necessary." Mistress Samantha folded her arms across her chest and sighed. "I want whoever did it caught as badly as you do—probably more. I'll tell you everything I know, but I'm afraid it won't be much."

"We're glad you're willing to cooperate," I said, nodding at her. I was feeling more in control of my emotions and the whole situation by the moment. It's amazing what a shot in the arm holding a badge and a gun can be. "When she came to see you, was she bringing anyone with her?" I asked.

"Once." She reached up and smoothed her hair. "A young man from her class—which is why I was so suspicious when you called and made the appointment."

"His name?" Cole asked, eagerly.

"Jeremy...something."

"Bruce," I supplied, feeling my hopes drop flat on the floor. "We already checked him out."

"Oh, I don't think he could have done it or I would have made an anonymous call myself." She sat up straighter. "But he was...very reluctant to have anything to do with all this." She made a sweeping gesture that took in the whole of the "dungeon."

"Big surprise," Cole said sarcastically.

"And *that*, Detective, is why my call would have been anonymous. That's the kind of blind prejudice I encounter on a daily basis." She leaned forward, her green eyes snapping. "Did you know that in recent studies it was revealed that forty-four percent of men have had fantasies of dominating a partner? Other studies found that fifty-one percent of women fantasized about being forced to have sex. What I do here is simply to act on those fantasies in a healthy and productive way. This isn't about rape—it's about sexual control. We're not exactly the lunatic fringe you'd like to make us out to be." She slapped the table for emphasis, a red spot of color glowing high on each cheekbone.

"Your statistics are fascinating but they aren't helping our case." Cole frowned. I said nothing, being too busy trying to digest what she'd said. Were there really that many other women who wanted what I wanted? No *wonder* my e-books were selling so well.

"Since we've ruled Jeremy Bruce out, is there anyone else you can think of that might have had some reason to do this? Maybe someone she met in the, uh, the scene?" Cole asked.

The Dominatrix shook her head positively. "No, Sarah wasn't all the way out in the scene yet. She came to me with her needs and desires still vague and undeveloped." She sighed. "She was like a beautiful butterfly, trapped in a cocoon. I was helping her break out."

"Out into this." The contempt in his tone was unmistakable. Inwardly, I cringed.

"Yes, into this," she replied with dignity. "There were things she needed that "normal" sex couldn't give her. The tragic death of her parents and siblings had scarred her. She'd buried the anguish she felt and tried to move on—but she couldn't. She needed physical pain to reconnect with the emotional pain she'd been repressing for so many years. Only then was she able to work through it."

"I guess that sounds reasonable in a twisted kind of way," Cole said grudgingly. "But what makes you so sure that someone involved in all this...in the lifestyle, didn't kill her?"

"Because we're not monsters!" Her words were a whisper but her voice had the intensity of a shout. For a moment I thought she was going to get up and make some dramatic gesture, try to slap him or stomp out, but she didn't. "Look." She ran a hand over the elegant French twist and massaged the back of her neck wearily. "There's a principle in BDSM—a rule we all live by. *Safe, sane, consensual.* All right?"

"And what does that mean to us?" I asked pointedly.

"It means that whoever did this to Sarah might have *wanted* to be in the scene, but he wasn't—not really. Nobody who knows how to play properly would ever go so far, and I don't believe that Sarah would have gone with anyone who didn't know what he or she was doing. She'd taken several lessons with me; I'd taught her all about safe words..."

"Wait a minute, explain that please," Cole said, shifting in his seat. For my part, the wooden stool was getting uncomfortable again, but I wasn't about to go back to his lap.

"A safe word is a predetermined verbal signal agreed upon between the top and the bottom before a scene ever begins and that means 'stop, this is too much for me.'"

Cole shrugged. "Why not just say stop then?"

She sighed again. "During this kind of sexual play, the sensations and emotions you experience can be very extreme. A submissive, or bottom, needs the freedom to beg and plead—to say 'stop, don't, I'm afraid,' without actually stopping the action. It allows the dominant to push the envelope, to take the submissive to the limits of their endurance and sometimes beyond."

"Whoever did this to Sarah Michaels put duct tape on her mouth. Hard to say your safe word when your lips are literally sealed," Cole remarked.

"Precisely my point." She nodded. "They might have had an agreed upon hand signal but if she made it, he clearly ignored her. No responsible and experienced dominant would do such a thing. If they had anything to do with the BDSM community at all, they would have been on the fringes, a hanger-on, what we call CHuDWas."

Cole raised an eyebrow. "Going to have to ask you to explain that too."

"CHuDWas," Mistress Samantha said derisively, "are Clueless Het Dom Wannabes—usually heterosexual men who think all they need to be a top is an extra helping of testosterone. There's considerably more to being a good dominant than cracking a whip and barking, 'On your knees, bitch!'"

"You don't say," Cole said dryly. "And you're sure Sarah couldn't have been involved with one of these...uh, these CHuDWas?"

She frowned. "Not that I knew of. The only person besides me that she revealed her desires to was the boy from her class.

But as I said, he really wasn't interested. It made her sad—and reluctant to look for anyone else who was."

From my own experiences with my ex-boyfriend, Jeff, I knew exactly how Sarah Michaels had felt. Nothing turns you off and douses your self-confidence quite like being told what you want is sick and disgusting. I looked up at the Dominatrix, wishing I could get up the nerve to ask some private questions of my own. But there was no way I was risking anything with Cole in the room and besides, we weren't here for me. We were here for Sarah Michaels and Cynthia Harner.

"Sarah had some marks on her thighs—as though someone had been beating her," I said. "Since you're the expert on…ah, erotic pain, do you think you could have a look at the autopsy pictures and tell us what you think?"

Mistress Samantha shrugged. "I suppose I could try."

"Good thought, Alex." Cole got up. "I'll go get the file out of my truck."

"Take your time, Detective." The Dominatrix gave me a penetrating look. "I'll be happy to talk to Alex…ah, Detective Reed, while you're gone."

He gave us a strange look but then shrugged, and left the dungeon by the single door in the far wall. We sat quietly for a moment, and I was intensely aware of her eyes on me. Normally I would have stared back but somehow, I just couldn't. She had forced me to say things out loud I never would have dared to admit to anyone, and I felt in some strange way that she knew me. It was a scary, vulnerable feeling I wasn't sure I liked.

At last she shifted in her chair, making the oxblood leather creak. "How long, Alex?" she asked softly, her eyes still trained on me. I could feel the weight of her gaze.

"I don't know what you mean," I said, keeping my own eyes on the comforting cool metal gun in my hands. A symbol of authority, of power. All the things I had. All the things I wanted to give to someone else, at least for a little while.

"Come, my dear, no one could fake your extreme reaction to my questions earlier. Admitting your needs, especially in front of your handsome partner, must have been devastatingly difficult, and yet you did. You couldn't hold them inside."

"I was playing a part," I said uneasily. "We thought we could get more information from you if you didn't know we were the police."

"Why, because of the business I'm in?" She looked offended.

"No, because the man that gave us your number indicated as much." I sat up straighter in the stool and met her eyes, relived to be off the subject of myself. "He seemed to think that you were a very secretive person and that you resented authority."

She laughed that rich, throaty laugh again. "My dear, I *am* authority—to most of my clients, at least. But I'm assuming the man you talked to was Ted? An older gentleman who works at the Turk Theater?"

I nodded. "He made us buy over a hundred dollars worth of merchandise before he'd give us your number."

She frowned. "Now *that* is uncalled for. I'll have to talk to him." She sighed. "Ted is harmless, really—just a busybody who thinks he can curry favor by handing out my name. Anytime he sees someone shopping in the bondage section of the Turk, he sends them to me, hoping I'll see him."

"But you won't?" I asked.

She shook her head. "No, I told you I'm very selective in my choice of clients. There has to be a spark—an interest. I'm afraid Ted holds neither for me, although I seem to hold considerable fascination for him." She sighed.

"Was he the one who referred Sarah to you?" I asked, eagerly.

"Come to think of it, yes." She tapped the tabletop with one long red nail, obviously following my train of thought. "But I wouldn't get your hopes up too much, Detective. I believe on the night that Sarah was killed he was working. He called me quite late, around midnight in fact, to say he was sending me another client and to beg for an appointment." She pursed her lips. "I turned him down, but he keeps trying, of course."

"We never told you that she was killed at night," I said blandly.

She shrugged. "I assumed it was done after dark sometime. Otherwise Sarah's roommate would have been in the apartment with her, probably sleeping. Indolent creature." She made a face, and I almost smiled. Apparently she had formed the same opinion of Sarah Michaels's stripper roommate that I had myself.

"Well, are you sure it was midnight and that he was calling from The Turk?" I asked.

She nodded. "He woke me up, and I remember looking at the clock. I almost didn't answer because I know that when I see The Turk's number on my caller ID, it's always Ted." She grimaced. "And usually, he's drunk."

"All right, here we go." We both turned to see Cole coming through the plain wooden door with the manila file folder in his hand. He sat back at the table and opened it, carefully arranging the photos of Sarah both before and after she'd been cut down from the restraints in her bedroom.

"What you're about to see is confidential," he warned, pushing the stack of glossy eight by tens across the table to her. "And much of it hasn't been released to the press. We have an on-going investigation and—"

"Detective," she interrupted him, her eyebrows arched haughtily. "Do you really think I could succeed in my chosen profession if I didn't know the value of a confidence? Don't worry—your secrets are safe with me."

Cole frowned. "Fine. This first set was taken at the crime scene—in Sarah's bedroom. The second was taken in the medical examiner's office, detailing her injuries."

She sifted through the photos, stacks of violence lovingly depicted in vivid color, an expression of detached horror on her face. By unspoken consent, we gave her a while. You see this kind of photograph all the time in the movies and in TV crime dramas, but it's different when the picture you're looking at is of someone you once knew and cared for.

When she looked up at last, her eyes were suspiciously bright but her voice remained steady. "It's as I thought—no one in the scene had anything to do with this. No one who had any idea what they were doing, at least."

Cole and I leaned across the table eagerly. "Explain," he said.

"Well, look at this." She tapped a picture that was a close-up of the black satin restraints tied around Sarah's wrists, binding her to the headboard.

"What about it?" I asked.

"The knots—they're all wrong. Anyone who's into any kind of restraint play can tell you that there's an art to bondage. A safe way and an unsafe way to restrain your submissive. Look." She got up and went to a small bookshelf at the back of the room and brought back a trade-sized paperback book. On the cover was a woman's bare torso covered in white rope, tied into intricate knots.

Cole took it from her. "*The Seductive Art of Japanese Rope Bondage*," he read and looked up. "People actually study this kind of thing?"

She nodded. "Any good dominant does his or her homework, Detective. Parachute cord is the safest and most maneuverable rope to use, not the cheap crap this person used on Sarah." She gestured derisively at the photographs.

"Those are satin," I objected and reached for the bag at Cole's feet. "Look, they came out of a kit like this." I showed her the large cardboard box containing the Bondage for Beginners kit.

"As I said, cheap crap—garbage. This is the kind of thing that leads to injury and death. People playing with things they don't understand." She frowned and shook her head, green eyes glinting angrily. "Low grade satin like this is too slippery to use effectively. Look at how tightly he had to tie her to keep her from escaping." She pointed at the picture of Sarah's bound wrists. "He cut off her circulation—her poor little hands are blue! No good, knowledgeable dominant would ever do such a thing."

"What about the marks on her thighs?" Cole asked, looking through the pile of pictures and picking out the one he wanted. "Our medical examiner thought they might have been made using a whip or a cane of some kind." He pulled the cane we'd bought at the Turk out of the bag and showed her. "Something like this, maybe?"

"More cheap crap," she said, dismissively, but bent her head studiously over the picture he was indicating. "Well," she said after a moment of intense concentration. "It's certainly possible, I guess. Although whoever did it must have been a barbarian. At any rate, he certainly didn't know what he was doing."

Cole rolled his eyes. "Let me guess—there's an art to caning too."

She sniffed. "Of course there is. And there are different styles as well. There's American caning, English caning, power caning…"

"We get the picture," I said, holding up a hand to stop her.

She frowned. "No, I don't think you do. There's a proper, civilized way—a *controlled* way to cane someone you are punishing. When I'm working over a submissive, I generally have a very specific pattern in mind. Here." She took the cane from Cole and beckoned to me. "Stand up, and I'll show you."

"I'd rather not," I said, feeling my mouth go dry. Suddenly the investigation was the last thing on my mind.

"Come, I won't hurt you if you don't want me to, Alex." She smiled at me, a small, knowing smile, and I felt the world go dim and far away. *I know you*, that smile said. *I know what you want, and I'm more than willing to give it to you.*

I found myself standing suddenly, on unsteady legs. Mistress Samantha stood as well and took my feverish hand in her cool, smooth one. "Over here," she said, leading me to the large polished wooden X, the Saint Andrew's cross that Cole had been looking at when we first stepped into the dungeon.

"Alex…" Cole's voice was low and uncertain.

"You come, too, Detective Berkley," she called over her shoulder. "What I'm about to show you may be valuable to your investigation."

I didn't really believe her, and I don't know if Cole did either. But I was caught in the spell of her voice, in the pain and pleasure she was offering me. The loss of control. I went with her willingly and stood quietly while she buckled my wrists and ankles to the wooden cross. With my arms raised over my head and my legs wide apart, I felt utterly helpless, utterly submissive. I leaned forward, resting my forehead against the cool polished wood, trying to drive back the throbbing ache of need that threatened to consume me.

"Look," I heard her say to Cole. "The action is all in the wrist. You want to work your submissive starting at the buttocks, the most padded area, and move gradually down to the tender backs of the thighs. When you do it properly…" There was a whistling sound and a sharp *crack*. I felt a stinging blow to my backside as the cane connected with the leather skirt stretched tightly across my ass. I let out a soft cry but didn't move. I felt my body clench inside like a fist.

"Hey—you'll hurt her!" Cole's voice was angry. "Alex, are you all right?" he demanded, putting a hand on my shoulder and peering anxiously into my face.

I wished he wouldn't make me talk. I was afraid that if I opened my mouth all that would come out was a plea for more, and then my whole shameful secret would be out in the open.

"I...I'm fine," I managed to say, nodding at him. "Let...let her go on. We might learn something important."

"If you're sure..." He withdrew with a last, uneasy look at my eyes, still half closed, as I savored the sting left by the cane.

"As I was saying," Mistress Samantha continued, as though she'd never been interrupted. "When properly wielded, a cane makes a very distinctive mark." I heard the high whistling again and barely had time to tense my body before the blow fell, a little higher than the first. "Perhaps you would care to see? You could compare the marks on your partner with the ones in your pictures."

"Well..." I could hear the hesitation in Cole's voice as he realized that looking at the marks she'd made on my skin would mean taking off my skirt. Her hands were at my waist, the long fingers cool against my heated abdomen as she waited for his decision.

"Go...go ahead," I said, feeling like my tongue was too thick and clumsy for my mouth. "It's all right." She didn't wait for Cole's consent as well, but deftly unzipped the leather. It was the kind with a zipper running the entire length of the skirt, and she was able to take it off without unbuckling my ankles from the cross's restraints. I felt a cool breeze across my bottom and upper thighs and was dimly aware of being glad that I had worn my best black silk panties under the skirt.

"Look," I head her say to Cole, and then those cool fingers were tugging down the wisp of black silk to expose the tops of my buttocks. I felt her trace the heated lines left by the cane, and I knew they were completely straight and perfectly parallel to each other. She would be a perfectionist in this as, I was certain, she was in all things.

"That's...those...the marks are perfectly even in diameter. The ones in the picture are more tapered." I thought Cole's voice sounded rather strangled. I wondered what he must be thinking, seeing me, his tough feminist partner, spread out like this, half naked with red welts showing plainly on my vulnerable ass. I hung my head and closed my eyes against the delicious humiliation of it. God, to see the look on his face... But I couldn't bring myself to turn my head. What if I saw pity or revulsion on those strong features? What if I saw disgust in his bottomless blue eyes?

"The marks might have been made with something more like this." Out of the corner of my eye, I saw her put down the cane and reach for another implement, a long, tapered, expertly woven leather baton. She handled the tool with reverence, as though it deserved respect.

"What's...?" Cole's voice died away behind me.

"There's a flexible metal rod at the center that adds several degrees of ferocity to this particular tool." Her voice was dry, almost lecturing, but my body was already tensing for what was to come. "It's a very intense piece of punishment equipment. Shall I?"

"I don't—" Cole started to protest, but I cut him off with a whispered,

"Yes."

"Very well." I heard a low whooshing sound behind me and a flat crack as the leather collided with my flesh, just at the tender junction where my buttocks met my thighs. I had to bite my lip to keep from screaming—the sensation was that intense. And yet, even as the pain burned and raged along my nerves, I could feel myself getting wet. Moisture gathered in the shallow well between my thighs as the throbbing, aching need grew inside me.

"Hey!" Cole's voice was an angry roar. I felt him step between me and the perceived threat, his body heat like a line of fire along my back. "Damn it—that thing could really hurt her." I felt his hand, rougher and warmer than hers, reach out to caress the new welt forming on my skin, still covered by the lower border of the black silk panties. I jerked and stifled a moan as his callused fingertips explored my pain. Agony followed by ecstasy—it was like coming home. I felt another flood of moisture to my sex and groaned softly, my hips working against the smooth, unforgiving wood in front and his warm palm behind. My hands clenched into useless fists, fixed high above my head.

"I assure you, Detective Berkley, that Alex is quite all right. Do you see what I mean by the different marking?" Mistress Samantha's voice was still cool and detached but my partner's breathing behind me was ragged. He was still standing between me and the Dominatrix but now I felt a cool rush of air as he stepped back a little and bent to see what she meant.

"Here," she said and those long, chilly fingers tangled in the fragile wisp of silk between my legs. With a decisive motion and a low ripping sound, she tore the panties completely away.

I gasped out loud, feeling the sudden coolness of air against my unprotected sex. The shame was almost too much to bear. The knowledge that Cole was looking at me, that he could see me as he never had before, so bare, so helpless…

"Goddammit!" he growled. "Don't—"

"Look." Her voice was dry and implacable. "Lean forward, Alex," she commanded. "Let us examine the mark." Mutely, I did as she demanded, leaning my upper body forward and pressing my ass outward, spreading my legs wider for their inspection. I teetered on the black boots, at the very edge of my balance in more than one way. I felt the edge of her nail trace a line of fire over the red ridge I could feel growing at the tender backs of my thighs. "Look," she said again, and this time, I knew he was.

"Jesus…" Cole's voice was hoarse and strained. I felt his breath, warm against the backs of my thighs and cool against my heated sex as he leaned forward to examine me. Slowly, hesitantly, one callused fingertip traced the same line Mistress Samantha's red fingernail had, as he explored the welt the wicked black baton had raised on my flesh. I bit my lip against the pleasure/pain/humiliation/desire that flowed through me like a river of molten lava. I knew he could see how wet I was, that he could see how I was so swollen with need that my flesh was opening of its own volition, as though begging for some rough entry.

I moaned low in my throat when his fingers caressed my inner thighs, drawing a tentative pattern in the moisture collected there. He jerked back at the sound, as though I had burned him.

"Doesn't… Damn it, Alex! Doesn't that hurt?" he demanded. His voice sounded angry and uncertain and hot enough to melt steel all at the same time. I knew it was melting me.

"Yes," I whispered, keeping my eyes tightly closed. God, how I wanted him!

"It's supposed to hurt. Pain is the point of everything you see here. Pain and pleasure." The Mistress's voice was still dry and lecturing, but I thought I heard a laugh somewhere far back in her tone. I understood suddenly that she enjoyed this. Enjoyed revealing my secrets—pouring my private treasures in a gaudy, glittering handful into Cole's lap, like so much cheap, tawdry jewelry. Her voice lowered, becoming seductive once more. "Here—would you like to try?"

By the clattering sound of the baton hitting the polished hard wood floor I knew what Cole was going to say, and he didn't disappoint me.

"Hell, no! Get her down from there—*now.*" Strong hands yanked at the wrist restraints as he spoke, and I felt more competent hands releasing my ankles. I could have cried. I didn't want to go. I wanted to stay, wanted to feel that sting across my flesh again and know that it was *his* hand holding the cane or baton or whip. Wanted to give up control to my partner, my lover, my Master…

"Here—Alex, a little help here. What's wrong with you?" Cole's hands fumbled to get the leather skirt rezipped and onto me, and his last question brought me back to myself. He was only my partner and friend, nothing else, and I was acting like a fool if I thought otherwise.

"Not feeling so well," I mumbled, making an effort to come out of the bizarre lust trance I'd somehow fallen into. I'd read somewhere that it was called "headspace." As in, I had somehow gotten into a submissive headspace and now I couldn't get out of it. "Sorry…" I murmured.

Somehow he gathered the folder, the bag of sex toys, and me, and made his way down the narrow stairs leading from the dungeon to the first floor. My last sight was of Mistress

Samantha waving at us, still holding the braided leather baton on one elegantly manicured hand.

"Goodbye, Alex," she called softly. "Call me again when you're ready to admit what you need. I'll be more than happy to work with you again, anytime."

Chapter Fourteen

Cole

I couldn't understand it. It was like the weird red-haired Dominatrix bitch had cast some kind of spell over Alex. She was so far away from me I could barely bring her back—she was acting like she'd taken three hard blows to the head instead of to her ass. Oh, God, her ass... I closed my mind to the picture that kept wanting to pop up behind my eyes.

Her softly curving naked ass, marked by those three perfectly parallel lines... The way she'd spread her legs and thrust backwards, showing me what I never dreamed I'd ever see. What I never even allowed myself to think of while I was married to Amanda, and even afterwards, when my divorce was final, for fear of ruining our friendship. Hot, pink, wet... She was so fucking *wet.*

Why or how the caning had made her that way I didn't want to know. But I *am* a man, damn it—there's only so much I can take. I wanted her in a way I'd never wanted anyone before, but I pushed the wanting away savagely. She was my partner, my best friend. I didn't want to ruin that.

She was silent on the way back to her house, except for a few little gasps and moans when the truck hit a pothole and bounced. I knew the welts on her ass were stinging as they rubbed against the leather of her skirt, causing her pain. But the soft, animal sounds coming out of her only made me that much harder. By the time we got to her place, I felt like I had a telephone pole shoved down the front of my pants.

I pulled into the gravel driveway in front of her house and parked, gripping the wheel so tightly my knuckles were white. It had long since gone dark but I could see her face, naked and needful, by the light of the single street lamp.

"What the hell," I said, slowly and distinctly, "was that about?"

She turned to me and there was so much need, so much pain and confusion and shame in her eyes, that I felt my insides clench. God, she'd never even hinted at anything like this. Or maybe she had, and I just wasn't paying attention... Maybe I was ignoring her because I didn't want to know.

"Cole..." Her voice was soft and tentative. The look on her face said she expected me to hit her at any time. I wanted to shake her, this vulnerable stranger. Shake her and demand what she had done with my tough, no-nonsense, takes-no-crap-off-anyone, one-of-the-guys partner.

"Never mind," I said, feeling the muscles in the side of my jaw bunch and tense. "Just get out."

"No." Her eyes cleared a little, my rough words seeming to bringing her back to her senses. "No, I'm not leaving like this. I need…I need…" Her mouth worked uncertainly.

"What?" I asked, my voice dangerously soft. "What do you think you need, Alex?"

"I need you to understand," she burst out, desperately. "I need you to know that I'm not…that I don't…"

"Don't what? Don't get off on—"

"Don't say it." She slid across the seat and pressed her small hand over my lips. In the dim glow of the lamp her eyes were wide and drowning deep. I felt in danger of falling in and never getting out again. I wanted her so badly I ached. But I didn't want to lay her down and take my time—didn't want to bring her gently or take her softly. I wanted what she wanted. I wanted to be rough with her. I couldn't let myself want that.

I pulled back from her, afraid that her touch, the press of her small, warm fingers against my lips, would set me off. "Get out," I said again. I felt like a loaded gun with three pounds of pressure already on the trigger. "Get out, Alex."

"No." She was trembling but determined. "No, come in with me."

"I can't." I heard a low grating sound and realized it was me, grinding my teeth. "I can't—I'll hurt you."

She looked up at me, eyes wide and serious. "I know."

I could hear the steering wheel creak beneath my palms as I gripped it. I was holding it like a life preserver, knowing that if it left my hands, and my feet took me into her small dark house, I was lost. *I can't let that happen.* I said it to myself over and over.

"Cole," she said, stroking the side of my face. "Cole, please..."

My control snapped and somehow my traitorous hands left the steering wheel and buried themselves in her silky hair, the same way they had the night before. I was again conscious of wanting to own her—of wanting to possess her totally. Her mouth was as sweet as a bruised berry. I crushed her to me, wanting to own and if I couldn't own, wanting to mark. To leave a sign on her skin that would let the world know I had been there.

She melted under me, all the rigid, prickly, feminist exterior gone. It was like peeling a cactus and finding the soft sweet heart under its hardened, thorny hide. I pushed my tongue in her mouth, demanding entrance, tasting her like I owned her already. Like she would never belong to anyone else. Her breasts were crushed against me, pressed up and out by the ridiculous leather bra, and I cupped them roughly, rolling the nipples between my fingers. I made her moan and swallowed the small sound eagerly, greedy for more.

I pulled away at last, panting to see that she was in a similar state—flushed and out of breath. "Please," she whispered. "I want...I need...please..."

"We can't," I said, feeling suddenly desperate. "If we do this we'll regret it forever. You'll hate me tomorrow. I don't want that."

"Let tomorrow take care of itself." Her small shapely hands were all over me, stroking my chest through the shirt and vest, running down my thighs to cup the aching heat between them, stroking the throbbing in my groin.

"Stop!" I grabbed her wrist, squeezing hard until I felt the small bones grind together. She made a tiny sound of protest and I eased up but didn't completely let go. I looked at her, at the look on her face. I'd seen the same look on the faces of junkies and prostitutes I'd arrested. It was a hungry, needy, desperate look, and seeing it on her face only made me hotter and more enraged.

I saw she was willing to throw it all away—our partnership, our friendship, any love that might ever have existed between us. She was willing to burn it all to ashes for one night of fucking. It made me furious with her—it made me want her even more.

"Please," she whispered again, her small hand still caught in my grip. "Please, Cole."

"Fine." I released her abruptly, and she shrank back over to her side of the truck, rubbing her wrist and staring at me. She looked like some wild, hurt creature, staring at a predator and wondering when the final blow would come.

The few times I'd ever allowed myself to imagine what sex with her would be like, it had never been anything like this. I had thought it would be slow and gentle—Alex is a control freak and I was more than willing to let her be on top. I had imagined her rising over me, her breasts swaying softly to our mutual rhythm as I stroked inside her. Never had I thought to see that hunted, hungry look in her eyes—the look of a junkie desperate for a fix. I was the hunter. I was the drug. I was on fire, as sick as she was. Sick with wanting her.

"You want it, fine," I said, hearing the words come out of my mouth but not registering them as my own. "We'll do this, but on my terms. Understood?"

She nodded, eyes wide, willing to comply with anything I asked. What the hell was wrong with her? What the hell was wrong with *me?*

"You'll go in the house and strip—take everything off. I want you completely bare-assed naked," I told her, my voice dropping into a predatory growl. "Go to your bedroom. Get on the bed on your hands and knees and spread your legs for me. Don't look around. When I come in, you better be ready to take me. *Do you understand?*"

She nodded again, wordlessly, and slipped out of the truck. Her eyes never left my face as she stumbled blindly to the front door, hobbling in the ridiculous stiletto-heeled boots. I saw her fumbling with the key and then she was inside, leaving the door cracked, an open invitation.

I closed my eyes and gripped the steering wheel, still tasting her bruised berry mouth. It was a cold night but I was sweating. The big muscles of my arms and thighs jumped with tension. I squeezed the wheel until it groaned beneath my fists. "I can't," I said. "I can't. I *can't.*"

I could see it all in my mind. I was going to turn the key and shift into reverse. I was going to back out of her driveway and get the hell away. I would drive home and beat off. The next day we wouldn't mention it. We would never mention it again.

I raised my hand, the hand I'd touched her with at the house of that damn Dominatrix, to rub my jaw, to massage the tension out of my aching face. But then I caught it—the slight, feminine musk. Her scent, still on my fingertips. My hand was trembling. I inhaled deeply, knowing I was lost.

Hopelessly, helplessly lost.

Chapter Fifteen

Alex

I knew Cole was mad at me—enraged was more the word. My partner is generally a sweet-tempered guy. I tease him about being a big teddy bear. But get him worked up, and all you can really do is stand back and hope the train doesn't hit you. This time the train was coming down the track at full speed, and I had jumped directly into its path.

I must be insane—I have to be crazy, I told myself as I stumbled in my front door, drunk with need and danger. What was wrong with me, provoking him like that? It was obvious— more than obvious what he thought about what I was, what I needed. Sick, desperate, twisted, demented...how many ways can you say it? His disapproval was a heavy weight, a stone around my neck, dragging me down.

And yet...and yet, I needed so *much*. Needed *him*. I staggered to the bedroom, shedding clothes along the way.

Ripping off the skirt, yanking at the elaborate laces of the bustier, awkwardly toeing off the boots. The panties, of course, had already been taken care of. The collar I left on.

Tonight I didn't want to worry about how he would look at me in the morning. I didn't want to worry about the loss of respect and friendship and yes, love, if there was that between us. I didn't want to think about how we'd both probably have to ask for transfers, for new partners who didn't know us quite so well, at least in the Biblical sense.

Tonight I only knew what I wanted, what I *needed*, was finally within reach. After years together I could admit to myself that I wanted Cole, not as a partner or as a friend, but as a lover. As a man. The things that had happened to me tonight had made me admit it to myself. Admit that I wanted him just as my own dirty, shameful secret was being revealed, smashing any hope I could ever have of having him—at least on any kind of a permanent basis.

But *this* I could have—one night of passion. One night of his body sheathed within mine. One night of pleasure and pain to remember forever. I felt drunk and high and desperate. I opened the door of my bedroom and doused the lights with a careless flick of my hand. Then I crawled onto the bed naked and waited, shivering. The bedspread felt cold and rough against my palms and knees and my skin crept into gooseflesh at every little sound.

I had almost decided he wasn't coming when I finally heard a fumbling at the front door and then it slammed, and I knew he was in the house. Heavy footsteps crossed the threshold, creaking on the old floorboards. It was the thunderous sounds of a monster making its way to the prey. I started to turn my head, to try and catch a glimpse of his face.

"Turn around and stay on your hands and knees." There was a controlled fury in his voice that made me shiver. I huddled on the bed, legs spread and nipples hard with fright in the chilly air. I hadn't turned the heater on before I left that morning and the house was cold—freezing. I felt like a little girl in a fairy tale, about to be eaten by the big, bad wolf. And yet the need still throbbed between my legs, and I had never been so wet or so ready.

"Alex..." He was behind me suddenly, large hot hands caressing my shivering skin. He stroked me like a cat and my back arched upwards in mute supplication. His fingers traveled over the throbbing welts on my ass and I hissed in pain, writhing without pulling away. The word, "Master" rose to my lips but I bit it back, swallowed it. My need was huge—it consumed me.

His hands on me turned forceful, grabbing me and pulling me into position. "Your hands," he said roughly. "Put them behind your back—now." I did it, although it pressed my shoulders and face into the mattress. I thought he might cuff them behind my back but instead of cold metal, hot flesh encircled my wrists. His fingers dug into my arms as he held me easily with one hand. I heard the low, menacing purr of his zipper sliding down.

I wanted to ask about a condom. I was on the pill and I pretty much knew Cole hadn't been with anyone since Amanda and no one but her the entire ten years of their marriage but still...you're supposed to ask. You're supposed to do a lot of things and none of them involve kneeling naked on the bed with your legs spread wide, vulnerable and terrified and needful, as the man who's been your best friend and partner for five years prepares to do unspeakable things to your helpless body. But God, how I needed him!

I felt him nudging between my thighs, huge and hot and naked. His sheer heat threatened to consume me as he swiped the broad head of his shaft against my wet folds, making me jump and gasp. The tender bundle of nerves at my center throbbed as he rubbed over it again and again, deliberately making me crazy. Then he stopped and I felt him settle into position.

He began to breach my entrance, pressing upwards and inwards, thrusting into me, filling me with himself. I could feel the heavy weight of his thick shaft forcing me to stretch to accommodate him already, and he wasn't even halfway inside me. The pain and pleasure mixed and became a new, confusing emotion my brain couldn't process. I wriggled under him, trying to be open enough to endure it. He pressed harder, deeper, his grip on my wrists tightening. The side of my face was pressed hard against the cool bedspread.

A small cry broke from me then. A tiny, helpless sound that got past my lips before I could call it back. Behind me, Cole froze in position, still only partially inside me. I felt him trembling with urgency, but somehow he held back.

"Alex?" His voice was deep and uncertain. "Am I...am I hurting you?" he asked.

I turned my head, unable to see him in the darkness. My whole world was pleasure and pain—the pleasure of finally being pinned beneath him, spread and filled and fucked by my Master. And the pain of receiving his brutal shaft into my body.

"Yes," I whispered, unable to hold back the truth, unable to hold back anything from the man who was mastering my body so sweetly and completely. "Yes, but don't stop. I want it. I *need* it," I told him, baring the most secret part of my soul, letting him know that I wanted not just the pleasure he was giving me, but also the pain. That I needed to be forced—made to submit.

"No." His voice was a growl—more a vibration along my spine than a sound in my ears. "No—not like this." He pulled back from me, out of me, and I cried again. A sound of disappointment and loss.

"No," he said again. "No, I can't." He turned and left, slamming the door behind him.

Left me filled with need, aching for him. Unfulfilled, unwanted, unloved.

The ringing of the phone woke me up at six o'clock in the morning. Looking blurrily at the clock, I realized I'd barely managed three hours sleep. I fumbled the braying receiver to my ear, mainly to shut the damn thing up. I felt miserable and then I remembered why—the scene last night. God, what a mess. What a horrible, horrible mess.

"Hello," I said, or rather, croaked. My throat was hoarse from crying half the night.

"Alex." Cole's voice was rough and scratchy too, but I doubted it was from crying.

"What do you want?" I asked and before he could answer I added, "I don't want to talk about it."

"Alex," he said, his voice almost breaking. "I'm sorry—God knows I'm so sorry about last night but this isn't about that."

"What's it about?" I snapped. "Wanted to get an early start on finding a new partner? I guess this is a courtesy call, or did you already wake Captain Davis up and let her know while she was still in her PJs?"

There was a long pause in which all I could hear was deep, ragged breathing. I was about to hang up when he spoke again. "I don't want a new partner but I'll understand if you do. What I did, the way I acted—Hell, there's no excuse I can give you." He paused and took a deep breath, I could hear it over the phone. "But that conversation is going to have to wait. Alex—he did another one. We have another dead body on our hands."

Chapter Sixteen

Cole

Someone had tipped off the press and they had finally managed to play connect the dots. I could hear them baying for blood like a pack of wolves as Alex crossed the police line and entered the Bayshore Avenue residence that was our latest crime scene. Captain Davis would not be pleased.

I was standing in the bedroom with my hands encased in latex when she came in. Her silky hair was tousled by the breeze whipping off the bay and the big brown Bambi eyes were red-rimmed, as though she'd been crying all night. She looked like she felt like shit. She looked beautiful.

"Alex," I said uncertainly but she cut me off, all business.

"What've we got?" she asked, whipping out her PDA and preparing to take notes.

I sighed. "Take a look for yourself. Same pattern, same MO—but he's stepped it up again." I walked to the nude body of

Lauren Schafer, attorney at law, and pointed. She had been a beautiful woman in her mid to late thirties with deep auburn hair cut just above her shoulders. Now she was stiff against the headboard, her hands tied with black satin and the signature red mask with black lace edging covering her eyes. There were no whip marks this time. But all along her inner thighs and the mounds of her breasts were reddish, hardened blobs of dried wax.

"This is...bizarre." Alex came closer, her eyes narrowing as she took it in. The perp had concentrated on Lauren Schaefer's nipples, turning them into cherry capped peaks, and there was also a mound of wax between her thighs, obscuring her vagina.

"No marks on the thighs this time," I said, struggling to keep my voice level. "But why the wax?"

"Sensation play." Alex's voice was flat and her eyes were hard when she looked at me. "Hot wax stings when you drip it on your skin but it's a pleasurable kind of pain. At least some people think so. But I guess you wouldn't know anything about that. You're not perverted enough, are you?"

"Alex, give me a break," I said, feeling helpless and angry and hurt all at once. "Damn it, how was I supposed to know?"

"You weren't," she almost shouted. "No one was. But it was your damn idea to go in like a couple last night. And after all the things you said..."

"I was playing a part," I protested. "I thought you were, too, until..."

"Yeah." She turned away again to stare at the body. "Until." She took a deep breath and blew it out. "We don't have time for this right now. We have a case to work and a sick bastard to catch. After we catch him, then we can reevaluate our working relationship. Until then, let's just try to be civil."

I wanted to grab her and shake her. Wanted to tell her I wanted to be a whole lot more or a whole lot less than civil. I wanted to push her up against the wall and have her right then and there and I hated myself for it. What was wrong with me? Alex had been my best friend and partner for five years. In all that time, I'd managed to work with her on a daily basis and ignore any sexual thoughts or urges by treating her like one of the guys. Now just looking at her made me crazy.

I took a deep breath and put some distance between us by walking around to the other side of the bed. I tried to think about the facts but my feelings kept intruding. I wasn't sure if Alex was angrier with me for what I had done to her the night before or what I hadn't done. I hated myself for almost raping her—hell, I'd been halfway inside her—penetration equals rape. She hadn't been exactly unwilling, but she hadn't been in a very sane state of mind either—neither one of us had. She hadn't borne any resemblance to the woman I had grown to know and love over the past five years. And I had been holding her down, no doubt hurting her. But she acted like she *wanted* to be hurt...

I closed my eyes briefly. I don't have time for this, I told myself. I don't have time for pain and self-loathing. I don't have time to analyze this relationship, if there even is a relationship left to analyze. I have work to do.

"Something else new over here." Alex's voice brought me back to myself, and I looked up to see that she had donned a pair of latex gloves herself and was peering under the mask.

"What is it?" I edged closer, looking at what she was pointing to.

"Some bruising around the eyes and the bridge of her nose—looks like it's been broken," Alex said. She dropped the mask and made a note in her PDA. "Well, we already knew our perp had a mean streak."

"Looks like it could be old, though," I said, lifting the mask myself to have a look. Sightless blue eyes stared back at me. The bruises had that faded look—they were a greenish color that contrasted with the dark necklace of fresh reddish-purple marks she wore.

"So somebody worked her over before last night? But she was a lawyer—what the hell was she doing?" Alex frowned.

"She was a personal defense attorney. Maybe she defended the wrong person. Some bottom-feeder that fixated on her. Think it could be a copy-cat?" But even as I said it, I knew it couldn't be.

Alex shook her head. "No, the black satin restraints, the positioning of the body. And the mask." The mask we were holding back, hoping to weed out the sickos who just wanted attention from any real tips that might come our way. No one but the actual perp would know about the mask.

"I don't see any signs of a husband." Alex was looking around the room. "Did she live alone in this big old house?" It was a valid question. Bayshore Avenue, which runs right along the curve of the bay, is hands down the most expensive neighborhood in Tampa and most of its residents count their fortunes in the millions. On a Monopoly board, it would be Boardwalk.

"Husband's dead, at least according to the maid that found her. Heart attack two years ago, but he left her well off and apparently she still practices law. Check out the paintings on the wall."

Alex whistled. "Looks like…wow, is that an original?"

"If it's not, it's a pretty damn good fake," I said, stuffing my gloves in my pocket. "No forced entry, and it looks like nothing's been taken."

She shrugged. "Well, we already know our guy isn't into this for financial gain. Hello—what's this?" She was speaking mostly to herself but I came over anyway, drawn by her tone. Alex bent and pulled something out from under the bed— something that looked like one of the implements we'd seen hanging on the walls of Mistress Samantha's dungeon the night before. It had a thick handle made of leather, dyed red and black, with many long, buttery-soft leather laces hanging from the end.

"Hmm," I said, noncommittally. Just looking at the whip, weapon, whatever the hell it was, made me feel hot and cold all over. I looked at Alex and saw that her face was very pale and she wouldn't meet my eyes.

"Better bag it," I said at last. "No way to know if he used it on her or not—not with all the damn wax in the way."

"Yeah." She bagged the instrument carefully, still avoiding my eyes, and then wandered over to the other side of the room. We worked in silence for a good twenty minutes before she spoke again. "Hey, Cole." I turned to see that she had found a day planner lying just inside a small roll top desk in one corner of the large master bedroom. "Look at this—somebody who actually keeps their plans on paper instead of in a computer for a change."

"We can't all be as high tech as you, Bambi," I said, giving her a smile.

She almost smiled back before she caught herself and then it was suddenly awkward again. But I felt a small stirring of hope. We still worked well together—still played off each other's ideas. If we could just stay in the groove on this case, maybe everything would blow over, and we could go back to normal by the time it ended.

"Looks like...she had plans last night." Alex was looking at the planner, carefully not meeting my eyes. She read aloud. "'Scribblers Ink meeting, B&N, 7:30.'"

I raised an eyebrow. "Scribblers Ink? What the hell is that?"

"Sounds like a writers' group to me. And look at this—a list of their numbers. Nice that she was so organized."

I came around and looked over her shoulder, careful to keep some space between us. "In alphabetical order, yet. She was meticulous. Well," I looked at her. "Let's finish the scene and start at the top of the list, what do you say?"

She nodded shortly. "I say, let's do it."

* * *

We worked the scene the way we've done a hundred others, by the book and right down the line. At times I got so caught up in the minutiae of the evidence that I could almost forget about the unresolved tension between us. Almost.

Alex was quiet but there didn't seem to be any rage simmering under her silence. Rather, it was a resigned kind of quiet, a pensiveness that I found got on my nerves even more. I would always rather have her blow up at me and get it out of her system than let it fester like that. But this time I didn't know if anything less than a nuclear meltdown could clear the air between us so I let it rest. There would be time to discuss everything later—I hoped.

We decided to case as many of the names on the list as we could before going on to the ME's office. The first person listed was Jessica Broward, a CPA who we visited at her office. When we told her the news about Lauren Schafer, she nearly fainted.

"Oh, my God, oh, my God," she kept saying over and over. "I just saw her last night—she was so happy, so upbeat. Oh, my God, are you sure? Are you really sure it's her?"

"I'm afraid so, Ms. Broward." Alex stepped forward and put a steadying hand on her arm. "We saw in her day planner that she had a meeting with you and the rest of your group, Scribblers Ink, last night. Can you tell us what time the meeting broke up?"

"Oh, God, let me think…" She ran a hand through her medium length blond hair distractedly. "We always stay late—reviewing each other's material, you know? Barnes and Noble was closing as we left, so say, around eleven, I guess."

"And did she have any plans, anywhere she was going afterward that you know of?"

"Well, no, I don't think so." She put a hand to her chest. "As far as I know she was just going to give Tate a ride home and then go home herself. She had an early court date today, she said." She pressed her palm to her forehead. "Oh, God, I can't believe it."

I looked down at the list of Scribblers Ink members. "Tate Zimmerman—that was the girl she gave a ride home to?"

Jessica Broward looked up, troubled. "Oh, no. Tate's a guy—the only one in our group."

Alex and I looked at each other. Bingo. Despite a last name of Zimmerman, Tate instantly moved to the top of our list.

* * *

"Yes, can I help you?" A pleasant-faced young man somewhere in his mid-twenties opened the door when I rang the bell. He was tall and lanky with short, curly blond hair and big blue eyes. At first glance I thought he was much younger, maybe even somewhere in his mid-teens—he had that kind of young, innocent face most women would kill for.

"Tate Zimmerman?" Alex and I flashed our badges and he nodded, the blue eyes filling with concern.

"Can I help you?" he asked, stepping aside to usher us into the spacious loft apartment. A German shepherd rushed up as we entered and began barking its head off. The echoes inside the large space were murder on my head.

"You mind?" I asked as the dog jumped excitedly. I put myself between it and Alex instinctively even though I knew it would piss her off. She doesn't like big dogs.

"Cybil, bad dog! Down!" Tate Zimmerman said sharply and the dog subsided to a low whining growl and slunk into a far corner, never taking its eyes off of us.

"Cybil Shepard—that's cute," Alex said, stepping pointedly out from behind me and giving me a dirty look for protecting her.

"You'll have to excuse her—she's still just a big puppy. Now, how can I help you? This...this isn't about one of my parents, is it? Are you here to tell me something's wrong?" One pale, slender hand fluttered to his chest and the big eyes got even bigger.

"Your parents are fine as far as we know," I said. "We're here about your friend, Lauren Schaefer. We understand she gave you a ride home last night after the meeting. Is that right?"

"Well, yes. But she almost always does. It's our writers' night routine. I work in Orlando, so I commute with a friend who drops me off at the bookstore where we meet, and then Lauren takes me home." He made a flowing gesture that took in the whole of the sparsely but expensively decorated loft. "It's on her way."

"So what time did she drop you off last night?" Alex asked, rapidly taking notes.

"Well around eleven fifteen, eleven thirty, I guess. It doesn't take that long—we meet over at the South Dale Mabry Barnes and Noble. It's just a hop skip and a jump, really. But please..." The hand went to his throat again. "Has something happened to Lauren? Is she all right?"

"We'll talk about it in a minute," I said. "Did you go anywhere else after you got home?"

"Well, no—I just had a glass of wine, read a book for a while and went to bed."

"Is there anyone who can verify that you came home when you said you did last night and that you didn't go out again?" Alex asked, still scrawling on her PDA. "Roommate, wife, friend?"

He shrugged. "Well, yes there is but can you *please* tell me what's going on with Lauren? She was perfectly fine when she dropped me off last night—she was even hungry. Said she was going to order some Thai food."

I frowned. "There's a place that delivers Thai food at eleven o'clock at night?"

He nodded. "Sure there is—a little place called Ruby Thai on Gandy. They stay open until three every night. *But what about Lauren?*"

If he was acting, he was doing a pretty good job of it. I thought we'd better break it to him gently—he seemed like the excitable type.

"Mr. Zimmerman, is there somewhere we can all sit down?" I asked. He nodded stiffly and led us to an eclectic collection of white leather furniture. There was a chair, a love seat, and something that looked like a couch with all but one arm cut off. Alex and I settled on either end of the love seat, presenting a united front but careful not to touch. (It was a small piece of furniture so this involved some scrunching on my part.) Tate Zimmerman settled onto the weird one-armed couch across from us.

"Mr. Zimmerman, I'm sorry to have to tell you this but Lauren Schaefer was murdered last night," Alex said. I watched carefully for his reaction to her words.

"I'm…I'm sorry, what did you say? I know you didn't say that, did you?" Both hands fluttered up to his throat this time and the blue eyes abruptly filled with tears, looking almost crystalline in their clarity. The dog came to him, whining, and laid a head on his blue-jeaned knee. "Did you say she was dead?

Did you?" he demanded, and abruptly began to sob noisily. "Oh, my God…"

"Hey, what's going on in here? Who…" A taller man, probably about the same age as Tate or maybe a year or two older hurried into the room and stopped short at seeing us sitting on the couch. He had a lot of thick dark brown hair that flopped over a high forehead and suspicious hazel eyes. I thought he looked a lot like that actor that had played Wolverine in the X-Men movies.

He moved quickly to Tate and put a comforting arm around him. "What's wrong, Tator-tot?" I heard him murmur gently into the other man's short blond curls.

Tate looked up abruptly, his pale complexion blotchy and red with tears. "I'm…they're…" He gestured at us helplessly, trying to go on while the dog whined uneasily at their feet. "They're saying Lauren is dead, Patrick. They're saying someone murdered her."

The second man, Patrick, looked up angrily, keeping a protective arm around Tate's shoulders. "Who are you people, anyway? You've got a lot of nerve coming in here, telling such awful lies."

We flashed our badges again. "I'm afraid it's no lie, Mr…"

"Brighton," he supplied shortly. "Patrick Brighton."

"Well, Mr. Brighton, unfortunately it's true that your…" I gestured uncertainly. "That Tate's friend, Lauren Schafer, was murdered last night in her home. Apparently Tate here was the last person to see her alive, so we're trying to verify his whereabouts last night."

Tate looked up, blue eyes still swimming in tears. "Surely you don't think that I..." He shook his head violently. "I couldn't do that to anyone, let alone someone I knew. Lauren was a *friend*."

"We understand your feelings, Mr. Zimmerman, we're just doing our job."

"Is it your job to come around harassing innocent people?" Patrick's hazel eyes flashed.

"It's called establishing an alibi, Mr. Brighton, and if your friend here doesn't have one he'll have to come with us," I said, getting fed up with the protective boyfriend routine. Personally, I didn't like Tate Zimmerman for the murder—he didn't seem the type at all. But at this point with the press on top of us and Captain Davis breathing down our necks, I wasn't willing to take any chances.

"Lauren dropped Tate off around eleven-thirty last night—I know because I was here. We drank a glass of wine, made love, and went to bed. He slept in my arms all night last night and didn't leave the house once. Now, are you satisfied?" Patrick raised a well-molded chin and glared down his nose at us.

"Patrick!" Tate's fair skin turned red again, this time, I was sure, out of embarrassment.

"Well, they wanted the truth—this is it. I'm not ashamed to admit it, and you shouldn't be either." This sounded like an old argument, and I raised my hand to stop it.

"All right, we get the point. You couldn't have been assaulting and murdering Lauren Schaefer if you were at home all night doing...whatever." I could feel my own face getting a little red at this point. I'm a progressive kind of guy, and the large gay element in Tampa doesn't really bother me. For the most part they're pretty peaceful except when they get a skinful at their pride parade. But being progressive doesn't mean I want to know all the nitty-gritty details of what goes on behind their closed doors at night. If I were interested in that kind of thing, I would've asked for a transfer to vice.

Tate's full lower lip trembled—he had a mouth like a girl's. "A...assaulted? Do you mean someone raped her? Oh, God..."

"That hasn't been determined yet, Mr. Zimmerman. We're so sorry to have to give you this news, especially at this time of the year," Alex said softly. She reached out to pat him on the hand. The dog, who had been sitting quietly at their feet, growled loudly and snapped at her. She drew back hurriedly.

"Bad dog!" both men shouted in unison and the shepherd subsided, whining miserably.

"I'm sorry," Tate said. "I think she thought you were hurting me. She didn't get you, did she?"

Alex shook her head. "No—no, I'm fine."

My partner might have been fine, but I wasn't. She was wearing a long-sleeved sweater, a deep brown one that brought out her eyes and hugged her curves nicely (I didn't seem to be able to stop noticing details like this lately). But when she'd reached out to pat our suspect's hand, the long sleeve had drawn back from her arm and I saw something that made my stomach churn. A bracelet of dark, finger-shaped bruises encircled her slender wrist. And I knew damn well who had put them there. Me.

"Mr. Zimmerman, we'll be in touch." Alex produced a card but it was the boyfriend that took it, handling the small piece of cardstock as though she'd given him a dead rat.

"Thank you, if there's nothing else we'd like you to leave now," he said stiffly, rising from the couch where Tate still crouched, the very picture of abject misery.

I nodded, wanting to get out of there almost as much as they wanted us gone. I needed to talk to my partner.

"Wait," Alex stood too, still looking at Tate Zimmerman. "We noticed that there was some facial bruising around Lauren's eyes and the bridge of her nose. Do you know anything about that?"

"Oh, so now he beat her up before he killed her? You people are too much." Patrick Brighton gave us a thoroughly disgusted look.

"No, it's all right." Tate looked up at us and took a deep breath. "She'd...she just had her nose done. She said that it was something she'd wanted to do all of her life, and she was going to finally do it. It...it was supposed to be her Christmas present to herself..." He broke down sobbing again, and buried his face in his hands, hunched shoulders shaking with the force of emotion.

"Could you *please* leave now?" Patrick Brighton said. He stood protectively in front of Tate, arms crossed and eyebrows raised.

"We're going," I said, heading for the door. "But don't be surprised if you hear from us again."

"Whatever, just go. You know where the door is." He turned back to his sobbing boyfriend and I heard the soft sounds of comfort being given as we shut the door behind us.

Chapter Seventeen

Alex

The minute we got back out to his truck, Cole turned to me. "Push up your sleeves." There was a steely quality in his voice that I usually only heard when he was interrogating a suspect.

I lifted my chin. "Why?"

"Because I said so," he growled.

I laughed, but it wasn't a happy sound. "You've known me long enough to know that isn't a good enough answer for me, Cole."

"Damn it, Alex! Just push up your goddamn sleeves. I want..." His voice got suddenly lower. "I need to see how badly I hurt you."

"You want to see? Fine." With swift, jerky motions, I pushed up the long sleeves of my favorite brown sweater and held out my arms for inspection. "There, are you happy now?" I demanded.

For a moment, he didn't answer. To be honest, it looked a lot worse than it felt. I have fair skin so I've always bruised easily, and the rings of dark marks around my wrists where he'd held me down the night before were more tender than actually painful. The fading welts that still striped my buttocks actually hurt more, but I wasn't about to broach that subject with him.

"Oh, God, Alex…I never meant to…" The anguish in his eyes was like a thorn in my heart. I had spent all morning alternately hating him, wanting him, and trying to forget what had happened between us so I could do my job effectively. But no matter what he thought of me now, he was still Cole. Still my best friend and partner—the man who's seen me through the death of my father, the man who'd gotten my back and saved my ass on the streets a hundred times over. The man who'd held me in his arms and stroked my back while I cried. I had always prided myself on being strong—emotionally invulnerable—but if I couldn't show my weakness around Cole, then who could I show it to? I just wished he didn't see it as a perversion. Even more, I wished *I* didn't see it like that.

"Cole, it's all right," I said awkwardly. I wanted to pat his arm but I couldn't quite make myself touch him. There was too much desire and fear in me still for that.

"No," he said, his face going hard. "It's *not* all right. Look what I did to you." He lifted my hands gently in his, and a warm fire ran up my arms at the feel of his skin against mine. God, his touch never affected me this way before…before last night, that was.

"I bruise easily," I protested. "And besides, it really doesn't hurt at all."

"Bullshit," he said, his blue eyes growing dark with anger and self-loathing. "I ought to go turn myself in right now for what I did to you. Hell, you ought to report me, I don't know why you didn't. I just..." He shook his head remorsefully. "I just got so crazy. I didn't know I had it in me to do anything like what I did last night—especially not to you."

"I think we both did things we didn't know we were capable of last night," I said quietly. Wanting to make him understand somehow, I cupped his cheek, turning his face toward mine. "Cole, you didn't do anything to me last night that I didn't want you to do." In fact he had done considerably less, but I wasn't about to go into that right now. "Everything..." I cleared my throat, self-consciously. "Everything that happened between us last night was consensual. Rough, but consensual."

He cupped his hand over mine and frowned at me, puzzled. "See, that's what I don't understand. I *hurt* you, Alex. And that woman, the Dominatrix...the marks she made on you..." He shook his head. "I don't...I can't accept that anyone would want that."

"Would *need* that," I corrected him softly. I sighed. This wasn't going to go away—we had to talk about it. But it would have been easier to go through a root canal with no Novocain. "I don't know why I need what I need," I said dully, feeling the burning ache of shame in my heart. "I only know that I need it."

"It was that Dominatrix—she cast some kind of weird spell on you. You weren't like this before." His eyes hardened. "You weren't..." He shook his head, obviously unable or unwilling to go on.

"I wasn't what, Cole? Twisted? Perverted? Sick?" I pulled my hand away from his cheek, feeling the sandpaper of his whiskers against my palm as I did. "I have news for you—I've been this way for as long as I can remember." I crossed my arms defensively, looking down at the floorboard of his truck where a couple of burger wrappers were crumpled into tiny balls. "I've just never...acted on it before."

"What about the way you kept saying you didn't know anything about this...scene? You got so rattled last night when I just asked..." He trailed off. "It was a front, wasn't it?"

"Great detective work there, partner," I said angrily. "I didn't want you to know. I didn't want *anyone* to know. It's been my own dirty little secret for years. I only ever tried to share it with one other person."

"Who?" He looked at me, blue eyes blazing. If I didn't know better, I'd think it was jealousy I saw in their depths. But that couldn't be.

"Jeff," I said shortly. "Remember you asked if you scared him away, and I told you no, that I did?"

"Sure, but..." His eyes widened. "Oh, you asked him to..."

"Yeah." I looked away. "He thought I was sick—a freak. He didn't want anything to do with it—or with me after I asked him...what I asked him to do."

"But...but why? Why do you want...?" His voice sounded helpless, lost. Like a kid asking why there isn't any Santa. I realized that I must have shattered some ideal of his. He probably couldn't have been more shocked if he'd suddenly found out that I was gay or some kind of a transsexual.

I sighed deeply. "I told you, Cole, I don't know *why*. Oh, I've taken plenty of psych classes to try and figure myself out. I can give you all the standard answers—I had a distant father and a domineering mother who was absent a lot during my formative years," I recited rapidly. "I probably have an unresolved Electra complex, and I grew up associating pain with rewards and pleasure—I told you the way I used to get my father's attention when I was a kid. Do I really have to go on?"

"No," He shook his head and ran a hand over his jaw. "No, I don't mean why are you like...like the way you are." He looked at me earnestly. "I mean, why *pain?* Why do you...how could you *want* someone to hurt you? The way you got last night. I wouldn't have believed it if I hadn't seen it myself. You were so..." His voice grew low and embarrassed. "I think that's part of what made me lose it. I'd never seen you so... Hell, I don't know."

"Aroused?" I felt the dull red blush creeping into my cheeks but there was no other way to say it.

He took my right hand and gently traced the circlet of bruises he'd put there the night before with one warm finger. "Yeah. I just don't understand how pain, how having someone hurt you, could get you that way. Could make you so hot."

I looked up at him again, forcing myself to meet his eyes, which were full of concern for me. "It isn't about the pain, Cole. Well, I mean, that is a big part of it but..." I took a deep breath. "Mainly it's about control."

"But you *are* in control," he protested. "Alex, you're more in control of yourself than anyone I've ever met."

"That's the *point*," I told him, earnestly. "It's not about *getting* more control over myself or my life. It's about *giving up* some of that control—giving it to someone else for a while." I put a hand to my throat, imagining I could still feel the faint loving squeeze of the leather collar I had been wearing the night before. "If I..." I looked away from him and out the window, ashamed to meet his eyes as I spoke. "If I could give control of myself, mind and body and spirit, even just for a little while—if I could give it to someone else. Someone I trusted..." I shook my head.

Just the thought of giving up my control to someone—to *him*—while he traced the marks he'd made on my skin was overwhelming. Marks of passion, marks of ownership. But how can a die-hard feminist, a tough, street-wise cop, admit she wants to be owned, even for a little while? I couldn't. Just the thought of it shamed me, and made me unspeakably hot. I shifted in the seat uncomfortably, feeling the ache and wetness growing between my legs.

Cole let out a breath. "I thought it was about wanting to be..." He shook his head frowning.

"You thought I wanted to be tied up and raped and strangled, like these poor women we're investigating, is that it?" I asked, my voice growing hard.

"No, I never thought—"

"Listen," I cut him off. "There's a big difference between wanting to give control of your pleasure and pain to another person for a little while and having a death wish. I don't want to be raped, and I certainly don't want to be killed. I may be twisted and sick and perverted, at least in your eyes, but I'm not stupid!"

"No, Alex—I don't see you that way," he protested, but I thought his voice sounded weak and indecisive.

"Can we just go?" I said, staring out the window at the mostly deserted street. The lampposts in this part of town had been fitted with those giant tinsel stars and candy-canes that seem to be the city's idea of festive holiday decorations. "We have a murder investigation to conduct and a killer on the loose," I reminded him. "This is hardly the time to be arguing over petty personal problems."

"Fine," he said, twisting the key in the ignition. The large truck roared to life around us, and he pulled out into the non-existent traffic. "We'll leave it alone—for now."

I knew that was as good as I was going to get so I kept my mouth shut and let him drive.

Chapter Eighteen

Cole

At the medical examiner's office, Dr. Warren had already finished the autopsy.

"I got a call from your captain, asking me to make it a priority," she said dryly, nodding at the recently de-waxed body of Lauren Schaefer, lying cold and still on the stainless steel table. The Y incision looked fresh and raw in her pale, pale skin and without the mask and duct tape, her face looked naked. The familiar smell of chemicals stung my nose.

"We appreciate it," I told her. "This guy's an animal and he's not even holding to any set pattern. It was a month between vic one and vic two. Now he's done another in less than a week."

"He's on a roll, all right." Alex looked grim. "Anything you can tell us would help. Did the marks on her neck match both Cynthia Harner's and Sarah Michaels's?"

Dr. Warren nodded. "Exactly. And she was raped as well, although I couldn't be sure at first."

"Why?" I asked and then the penny dropped. "Oh—the wax."

She nodded grimly. "He must have spent some time with her after…afterward. He filled her full of it—it was hell getting it out."

"But why?" Alex said. "Obscuring evidence?"

"Making a point." I looked at the reddish blotches on the breasts and torso of the body—the places our vic had dripped hot wax over Lauren Schaefer, no doubt while she writhed in agony. What Alex had said about "sensation play" was one thing but I was fairly certain even the kinkiest player wouldn't want to be filled full of the stuff.

"He hates these women for some reason—this has to be personal," I said. "The way he stages them…the rose petals, the whip marks, the wax…it's all a message to us somehow." I turned to Dr. Warren. "Speaking of that, we found some kind of a…a whip like thing at the scene, but we couldn't tell if he'd used it on her. Wax was in the way. Did you find any evidence of a recent whipping? Maybe on her back, shoulders, buttocks?"

The ME shook her head. "If there was, I didn't see it. You can test what you found but my guess is nothing but the candle wax was used on her."

I shook my head again. "Maybe it belonged to her then. I can't imagine our perp would bring it and not use it. And he takes what he uses with him when he goes. We didn't find any evidence of the candles he used to drip wax on her or whatever he used to whip Sarah Michaels's thighs. He's clean—wears gloves, doesn't leave any DNA. No hair, no fluid."

"But there was none of that, no wax, no whip marks, on the first vic, on Cynthia Harner," Alex protested.

"Because he was just getting started." I stared at Lauren Schaefer's face, cool and dead. "Just feeling his way through the first one. Now he knows what he likes, and he likes it a lot. We have to get inside his head. We have to find out why he's picking them—there must be a pattern, some reason... And why are they opening the door to him? No forced entry on any of these cases even though all three women were alone."

"Maybe they all knew him somehow," Dr. Warren offered. She had been standing quietly by, watching with interest while Alex and I lobbed ideas at each other.

I shook my head. "They were from all over the place. I could see Cynthia Harner and Lauren Schaefer running in the same circles—they were both upper middle class, white, rich professionals who lived in or around South Tampa. But Sarah Michaels, the second vic, was poor, a student. She lived clear across town in the Carlton Arms."

"What about..." Alex walked over to the body and looked hard at faint bruises still visible around the eyes and nose. "One of the vic's friends told us she'd just had plastic surgery." She looked at Dr. Warren. "Can you confirm that?"

The ME nodded, and crossed her arms, the white lab coat she wore wrinkling as she did. "Yes, I looked up her medical records when I saw the bruises. Recent rhinoplasty performed by one Dr. David Love."

I looked at Alex. "I know that name."

She snapped her fingers. "Sure—it was the name of the plastic surgeon Cynthia Harner had just taken a job with before she died."

I shook my head. "But what about Sarah Michaels?"

"I'm on it." She was already on the cell phone and I heard her say, "Matt, Detective Reed here. You still have Sarah Michaels's laptop? Good—I want you to comb through it and see you find any references to a Dr. David Love. Uh-huh. All right, thanks." She got off the phone and looked up at me. "He's checking."

I nodded and looked at my watch. "Okay, in the meantime, we'd better get our asses back to the PD. Captain Davis wanted to talk to us both as soon as we left the ME's." I turned to Dr. Warren. "Thanks again, Doc. You find anything else, call us."

"Absolutely." Her face was drawn as she pulled the sheet over Lauren Michael's still face. "I want you to catch this guy."

"You and me both," Alex said. "Come on, Cole."

"Oh, there's one other thing." We both turned back to see Dr. Warren smoothing the sheet thoughtfully. "Stomach contents were partially digested noodles of some kind—possibly Pad Thai. Time of death was between one and three a.m., and she ate barely an hour before she was killed. I don't know if that helps any but…" She trailed off with a shrug.

Alex and I exchanged a glance. "Thanks, doc," I said. "It might help—we'll see."

Chapter Nineteen

Alex

"I don't have to tell you the press is breathing down our necks on this one." Captain Davis looked grim, and I could swear her curls were considerably grayer this afternoon. "But that's not even the bad news," she continued, getting up from behind her desk and coming around to lean on the front of it. Cole and I and several other detectives she'd had to pull off other cases were crammed into her office, a small, glass-walled space, where every available spare surface was covered in paperwork. Captain Davis has her own filing system, which pretty much amounts to organized chaos. If she ever dies or retires, we'll never find anything again.

"What's the bad news?" Cole growled. He looked surly and rough—probably because we'd had to fight the press, who were camped outside looking for a statement, on the way into the station.

We'd barely had time to cram down some burgers (not my lunch of choice), on the way from the ME's office to the downtown PD. The tension between us was still running high although we were concentrating on the case. He'd brushed my hand when reaching for a napkin while we ate and then pulled back as though he'd been burned. It was just a little thing but it made me feel like shit. I had to remind myself that I couldn't afford to concentrate on my own feelings just then.

We'd spent the rest of our abbreviated lunch time talking about the case like our lives depended on it which was just as well—we'd actually come up with some pretty solid ideas. It continued to amaze me that Cole and I could keep functioning as a team when I couldn't decide if I wanted to strangle him or tie him to the bed and never let him go. Of course given the details of our case, either option sounded equally sick. Captain Davis's brisk alto voice pulled me back to the present.

"The bad news is I got a personal call from Mayor Serrano. Seems she went to law school with the last vic, and she wants results yesterday." She clapped her hands together briskly. "So— tell me something good. I've got a press conference in half an hour and we need some progress. Where are we, people?"

This was our cue. "We've got a few leads we're pursuing," I said, counting them off on my fingers. "First, we know Lauren Schaefer had plastic surgery not long before she was killed—a nose job. The surgeon who did it is apparently the same doctor that our first vic, Cynthia Harner, had just taken employment with before she was killed."

Captain Davis nodded. "Excellent. Any connection to vic number two?"

"Matt's working on that," Cole answered. "He's combing her laptop for any mention of him and we're checking the phone records, too, to see if there were any calls between them."

She nodded and tapped her sensibly short nails on the wooden desk. "Good, what else?"

"Lauren's friend told us she was talking about ordering Thai food last night, and the ME confirms that she ate barely an hour before she was done. She might have ordered out from a place called Ruby Thai on Gandy," I said.

Captain Davis raised an eyebrow. "Are we thinking delivery boy?"

"Could be," I said. "Probably not but it's worth checking."

She nodded. "Anything else?"

I shook my head. "We're still trying to draw parallels between the vics. We want to keep interviewing friends and family, find out how he's picking them. But first we'd like to see if Dr. Love pans out—he's the best lead we've got going so far. Looks like he had an alibi for the first vic but it's pretty weak— he was up at the office late with his receptionist working, and nobody else saw them. We'd like to lean on her and see what gives."

Captain Davis nodded. "All right, let's see if Matt—" Just then, as if on cue, her office door opened and Matt's shaggy head popped into view.

"Hey, I know you're in a meeting, Captain, but I found something I think you're gonna like." His voice was tense with excitement, and he was practically bouncing on the balls of his feet.

"Okay, come on in." She gestured impatiently. "What've you got?"

"This." He waved a sheaf of papers he was holding in one hand and then read from it. "Body Beautiful—Self-Mutilation in America Today. In Pursuit of Perfection Through Plastic Surgery." He looked up at us excitedly. "It's a paper she wrote, and guess who's cited as her main source?"

"Dr. David Love." Cole and I exchanged a look.

"You got it." Matt bounced like a rubber ball in the small room. "That means he knew all three of the vics, huh?"

"That's exactly what it means, but we're going to be keeping a lid on it for now." Captain Davis gave Matt a warning glare that effectively took the bounce out of him and then addressed all of us. "Listen up, people. We can't afford to drop the ball on this one. I'm going to go out and stall the press as much as possible and we're going to keep Dr. Love to ourselves until we're sure one way or another. Anybody who leaks anything and I find out—your balls are mine. Got it?"

We all nodded, and there were murmurs of assent from everyone assembled. Captain Davis didn't get where she was by playing Ms. Nice Guy. If she makes a threat, you can be sure she'll live up to it.

"Jeffries, Barkett," she said, nodding at the two detectives sitting to Cole's left. "I want you to go check out the Thai restaurant and find out who delivered the food and what time they left. Reed and Berkley, go make nice with Dr. Love and shake down that receptionist. The rest of you, run the LUDs and check background." There was some general grumbling, and she raised her hand for silence.

"I know I've pulled some of you from other cases but it can't be helped. We've got a serial killer on our hands, and I've got the press and the mayor up my ass—everything else is on the back burner until we get him. I've also called for federal help. No—wait a minute," she said, as the groans became louder. "I just asked for a profile of our perp, that's all. Other than that, it's all ours so let's work it, people. Dismissed." She clapped her hands loudly once, and her office began to clear. Cole and I were in the lead.

* * *

"I'm sorry, but Dr. Love is in a consultation with a patient." The waiting room was decorated in minimalist chic with nothing but *GQ* and *Men's Health* in the magazine rack and the receptionist was pretty in a blond fake-Amazon kind of way. It was obvious she'd had just about everything that was humanly possible done to her in the way of elective surgery. From her pert button nose to her super flat tummy-tucked stomach and the D cups in between, she was more plastic than person, and the smile she flashed us was just as fake as her chest. But from a man's point of view I knew it would be pure eye candy.

I saw Cole give her the once over and a sharp little knife stabbed me somewhere in the region of my heart. It was funny, I'd never been jealous before when I saw him sizing another woman up. I wished for the hundredth time that I would have been more in control of myself the night before. If only I hadn't invited him in, if only the weird, almost-sex hadn't happened between us. Our partnership was on the rocks because of me—because of my sick needs and desires—and it made me feel guilty as hell.

"Well, we want to talk to you, too, Ms..." Cole raised an eyebrow at her.

"Ms. Honey. Lola Honey." She leaned forward across the expensive mahogany desk and simpered at him, flashing teeth that were perfectly straight and blindingly white.

"Well, isn't this the office for cutesie names?" I said, showing her my badge. "We'd like to talk to you about your whereabouts on the night of November twenty-second."

She paled suddenly, and the bright red lipstick that ringed her mouth stood out like a circle of blood in her paper-white face. "I...I already talked to the police about that. Two very nice officers that..."

"That aren't on the case anymore," I said, frowning. No wonder Kendricks and Ramirez were so willing to swallow Love's alibi if it came from this blond bombshell. What man wouldn't want to work late with Naughty Nurse Honey, they must have reasoned.

"My partner, Detective Reed, and I just got assigned the case. We'd just like to get your statement for the record. I'm Detective Berkley, by the way." Cole smiled at her charmingly and she calmed down and smiled back, batting her lashes for all she was worth.

"Oh, well, if that's all." She looked around the empty waiting room, and nodded as though satisfied. "I guess it's all right," she said. "I already told the other officers that I was here with Dr. Love going over some billing information until late."

"Very late," I said dryly. "Conveniently late, as a matter of fact. Let me ask you something else. Can you check the good doctor's schedule and tell us where he was the night of December thirteenth and last night, too?"

She shook her head. "He doesn't have appointments during the night. I don't know—"

"But a good receptionist always knows how to get in touch with her boss. What if there was an emergency at the hospital with a patient he'd worked on? Wouldn't you know where to reach him?" I pushed. "Or were you with him on the other nights, too?"

She looked at us uncertainly, the confidence she'd gained when Cole smiled at her was visibly leaking away. "Well, I don't exactly...I mean, I'd have to check. If you'll just give me a minute..." She started to rise.

"You mean give you a minute to ask your boss what you're supposed to say?" I asked, grabbing her wrist to stop her. "No, I think you'd better answer the question now. Were you with him on all the nights in question? And what does his wife think of that?"

"He's not married," she said sullenly, yanking her wrist away from me and sinking back into the chair. "I...I'm the only one he sees. I'm with him most of the time."

"So then you shouldn't have a problem telling us if you were with him last night and the other nights we asked about," Cole said reasonably. "Do you two have a relationship outside your professional one, is that what you're saying? If you do then you should certainly know where he was on the nights in question."

"I...I..." She shook her head, looking confused.

"This isn't rocket science, Barbie," I said. "Are you seeing him or not? Is it sexual favors in exchange for the perfect body? Or is it true love?"

"It's not...he doesn't..." She shook her head.

"Were you *really* working on billing until two o'clock in the morning on the night that Cynthia Harner was murdered?" Cole asked softly. "Do you know how they did it, Ms. Honey? Someone tied her to her bed, blindfolded her, and raped her while he strangled her to death. Did you know her very well?" His voice was still soft but his eyes were hard. I was glad to see that her sex-kitten act wasn't pulling the wool over his eyes as it obviously had with Kendricks and Ramirez.

"I didn't... She only worked here for a month or two before... Oh, God..." She covered her mouth with one perfectly manicured hand and shook her head violently, which almost made her helmet of perfect blond hair move. Almost.

"Did you know that providing a false alibi is a felony, Lola?" I stared hard at her, using my blankest, most frightening face. I can never look as scary as Cole, but I do my damndest. From the look on her surgically perfect features, I wasn't doing too badly—something was about to give.

"We could get you on accessory to murder," Cole said softly. "I bet you wouldn't like the nose job you'd get in prison nearly as well as the one Dr. Love gave you."

"All right, all right!" She held up a hand to stop us, her bee-stung lower lip trembling. I was betting two to one on collagen injections against Mother Nature on those lips. "He...wasn't with me. We weren't together at all, any of those nights. We're not together—not like that."

"Okay, tell us where he was." Cole leaned forward on her desk, and I pulled out my PDA, ready to make notes.

She shrugged helplessly, her wide eyes beginning to leak crocodile tears. "I don't know where he goes. I just know if anyone asks, I'm supposed to say he's with me. He...he *wants* people to think we're sleeping together but we're not. We're *not...*" She shook her head. "It was part of the deal when I took this job. He gives me as many free procedures as I want, and I pretend to be his girlfriend at banquets and award ceremonies and Christmas parties..." She gestured. "Stuff like that. I've had my nose and lips and breasts done so far, plus he pays me really well."

"I bet he does," I said grimly. "So you're saying you have no idea where he was?"

She shook her head earnestly, and this time the blond helmet did move, just a little. "Honestly, no. I really don't. But I don't think he did any of that...that horrible stuff to Cynthia. She was a good physician's assistant, and they seemed to have a lot in common. He *liked* her."

"Uh-huh. I think we'll ask the good doctor exactly what he thought of her and where he was." Cole started around the desk.

"Wait, you can't go back there! He really is in with a patient!" she protested, half rising from her cushy chair.

"That's too bad, isn't it?" I grabbed her shoulder and pushed her back down, firmly. "We're going back, and you'd better not warn him or we'll charge you with obstruction of justice. Is that clear?"

She nodded and sighed. "I really liked this job, you know? Next month I was going to get my butt done."

I shook my head. "What a shame."

"Hey, back here." Cole jerked his head at a closed door near the back of the office. We pressed our ears to it, and I could hear a man's voice right behind it, talking in a high, soft tenor.

"What I'm going to do is just lift them a little—right here, so the nipples are more evenly aligned…"

I nodded and whispered, "Now."

"*Police.*" Cole shoved open the door, and we saw a fit, youngish-looking man with sandy hair who was probably in his late thirties, sitting on a little rolling stool in front of an oldish-looking woman, who was probably the same age, sitting on an exam table. He was holding her sagging breasts in both hands like he was weighing fruit at a supermarket. The woman squealed and raised her arms to cover herself with the blue paper drape in her lap. The man, who had to be Dr. Love, withdrew his hands and crossed his arms over his chest, staring at us.

"What is the meaning of this? I am in the middle of a consultation." His voice was severe, but I thought I saw a flash of fear far back in his gray eyes.

"The meaning is we'd like to ask you a few questions about your whereabouts last night." I showed him my badge. "Start talking."

"I was out with my receptionist, Lola. She's the girl sitting just outside who should have stopped you from coming back here." He was still perfectly cool but there were small white dents on either side of his nose and his lips were a thin and trembling line.

"Wrong answer, buddy," Cole snarled. He reached down and dragged the doctor up by the collar of his expensive Egyptian cotton shirt.

I jerked my head back in the direction of the waiting area. "Your receptionist decided the nose job and the free boobs weren't worth time in prison, so if you've got another alibi you'd better come up with it fast."

Dr. Love turned to his patient, not an easy maneuver when Cole was holding him like a dirty little boy who's been caught stealing. "Mrs. Farnsworth, I'm going to have to ask you to excuse us while I talk to these *people*."

"Oh...oh, certainly." Nodding wildly, she gathered the paper drape more closely around herself and edged out of the room, her wide frightened eyes never leaving our faces. I was betting that was one patient who wasn't going to reschedule.

"Now." Dr. Love gave Cole a withering look, which had no effect at all. "If you'd let me go, I'd be more than happy to talk to you."

"Fine." Cole pushed him back down onto the rolling stool he'd been sitting on and stepped back, effectively blocking the doorway. "You can start by telling us where you were between twelve o'clock and two a.m. last night and ten o'clock and midnight on December thirteenth."

"I was...I was home alone. I have to go to bed early when I have to perform surgery the next day." The gray eyes were beginning to look hunted.

"And *did* you have a surgery the next day?" I asked, stylus poised to make notes.

"Well, I...I...Just let me check with my receptionist."

"You mean the one you were supposed to be with when you were supposedly home in bed?" Cole asked. "I gotta tell you, doc, so far your alibi sucks."

"But...but I don't even know what this is all about. Why should you care where I was last night, or...or..."

"The night of December thirteenth," I supplied for him. "Maybe this will ring a bell." I reached in the manila file I'd been carrying and pulled out the smiling yearbook picture of Sarah Michaels. I slapped it down on the exam table in front of him, where his patient had been sitting. "Or this." I put a picture of Lauren Schaefer that we'd gotten from the Law Review.

He stared at them blankly for a moment before nodding his head. "Yes, I know them. This one," he pointed to Lauren's picture, "is a patient of mine. I did a routine rhinoplasty on her several weeks ago. It came out just fine—not a single hitch. And this one," he tapped Sarah's smiling face, "was a young lady who wanted some information on elective surgery. I had done a breast augmentation on her friend and she contacted me, asking if she could get a brief interview. I contributed to a paper she was writing for some sort of class. I, uh, really can't recall their names right now. If you'd just let me check my records—"

"Their names were Sarah Michaels and Lauren Schaefer and this is what they look like now." I pulled out two autopsy photos and slapped them down in front of him. "Does that jog your memory?"

"Oh, my God." Love's face got very pale. "I didn't...I don't...surely you don't think that I..."

"That's exactly what we think unless you start giving us a good reason not to." Cole's voice was a growl. He was really taking these murders personally.

"The first victim, Cynthia Harner, worked for you," I said, ticking them off on my fingers. "The second came to you for information and cited you as a main source for her research paper. The third was a patient of yours. So far you're the only person we've been able to tie to all three women."

"But...but..." He looked from Cole to me and back again a little wildly. "But what about... Don't you people always look for a reason? What possible reason would I have to...to kill any one of these women, let alone all three? For example, Cynthia— I was very pleased with her work performance. I had absolutely no complaints."

"You mean *motive*, Doctor?" Cole gave him a shark-like grin. "In cases like these the motive generally speaks for itself. You don't go to the trouble of tying someone to the bed, blindfolding her, beating her, covering her in hot wax, and raping her if you're dissatisfied with her work performance."

"Tying...? Raping...? Hot...hot wax...?" His face was so pale now, I was almost afraid he was going to pass out. "Oh, my...oh, my," he half whispered. "Oh, no, but I didn't...I couldn't..."

"Tell us why you couldn't," I said softly. "Give us a reason, give us somebody who knows where you were on the nights in question."

"Somebody other than your receptionist," Cole added.

Love looked up at us, his pale face naked with fear. "I'll...if it gets out I'll never practice medicine again."

"Look," I said reasonably. "We're not interested in your under the table dealings whatever they may be. That would be for the IRS or maybe narcotics, depending on what you're doing. But all we want right now is to catch the man who's doing this." I tapped the autopsy pictures with my nail.

"All right. I...I'll tell you. But you have to swear to keep it out of the papers and off the news."

"We'll do what we can," Cole said neutrally. "But you better start talking."

He looked at us uncertainly. "Maybe...should I have my lawyer?"

"I don't know—do you need one?" I asked. "Feel free to call him and have him meet us at the downtown police station."

Cole shrugged. "Of course, if we have to take you down to the station..."

"There were seven news crews down there last time I counted," I finished for him, looking at Love meaningfully. "So if you don't want to end up with your face plastered across every TV set in town, you'd better talk, *now.*"

"Fine. I...I was with..." He covered his face with both hands so that his words came out muffled. "I was with my lover, all right? I'm *gay.*"

I frowned and saw Cole doing likewise. "All three nights?" I asked skeptically.

"*Every* night." He took his hands away from his face, and his eyes were suspiciously red. "I hired Lola to be my beard, to go with me to public functions and that kind of thing. She was just a more convenient alibi when all the...when those horrible things happened to Cynthia."

"Those horrible things were rape and murder," Cole grated. "And I'm still not convinced you didn't have anything to do with them."

"I don't understand," I said, tapping my fingernails on the exam table. "A lot of professionals are out and proud these days.

Hell, my gynecologist is a lesbian, and she doesn't care who knows. Her partner works right in the office with her."

Cole shot me a look. "That doesn't bother you?"

I shook my head. "Why would it?"

He shrugged. "No reason, I guess. But if I found out that my proctologist or somebody like that was…well…" He see-sawed a hand in the air.

Dr. Love looked up at us. "See? That's what I mean. I can't have my patients finding out, especially since…" He shook his head, biting his lip.

"Go on, Doctor," I prodded gently. "Especially since what?"

"Especially since even by the standards of the gay community, the relationship I'm in would be considered extreme," he finished in a rush.

"I don't understand," I said blankly.

Cole frowned. "I don't either. And you better start explaining quick. We were just telling your lovely receptionist how providing a false alibi is a felony, so I hope your boyfriend can stand up to close examination."

"He's not my boyfriend." David Love looked at us with a strange mixture of pride and misery on his face. "He's my Master."

Chapter Twenty

Cole

"David comes home every night between six and seven. If he's going to be later than seven he has to call me. If he doesn't call, he knows he's going to get a punishment."

I stared in disbelief at the thin Latino man who sat on the couch opposite us, in the plush Bayshore apartment complex that catered to rich singles. The walls were painted a pale mint that contrasted with the rich forest green Berber carpet and expensive-looking modern art hung on the walls. Here was yet another reason that Love would have made the perfect perp—he wasn't even a mile down the road from Lauren Schaefer's house—the latest crime scene. But I was beginning to believe we had hit another brick wall and every word the weird "Master" guy said was another nail in the coffin of our perfect perp theory.

"Could you please explain that?" I asked, preparing to take notes. "How exactly do you, ah, *punish* him?" From the corner of my eye I could see Alex's expressive face going from red to pale and back to red again.

"Cole, do you really think that's relevant to the case?" she said in a low, choked voice.

"I think we have to know why he wouldn't sneak out to do whatever he wanted after his uh…" I coughed into my hand. "After his Master was asleep for the night."

"I am a very light sleeper." The Master, whose name was Carlos Montero, twined an arm around David Love's shoulders and raised a sharply pointed eyebrow at us. He had black eyes and most of his long hair was pulled back in a thick ponytail at the nape of his neck. "And besides, David would never dare to go out without permission. The consequences would be most severe." He grinned, showing sharp white teeth that looked almost vulpine. He couldn't have been more different than the clean-cut Dr. Love, and I wondered how the hell they had gotten together in the first place. Opposites attract, maybe?

"Consequences?" I raised an eyebrow at them but Alex hastily interrupted me.

"Did anyone else see you together the nights in question? Particularly the first night, the night of November twenty-second?"

"November twenty-second…that would be a Monday, correct?" He smiled at us again. "Why yes, over a hundred people saw us together. That was the night of our Thanksgiving get-together down at the club. We were there until nearly two, and then we came straight home."

"You got together with over a hundred other people at what club?" Alex asked, making notes on her ever-present PDA. She had laid out the pre-autopsy photos of all three victims in front of them on the highly-polished teak-wood coffee table.

"The Liar's club in Ybor City," David Love volunteered. It was the first time he'd spoken since we walked in the door and from the stern look on Montero's face, I thought it might be the last.

"Did someone ask you to speak, David?" he asked. His tone was soft but there was menace in his voice.

"No, sir," Love almost whispered. "I'm sorry, sir."

"We'll see about that later," Montero said. He ruffled the sandy hair and gave Love an affectionate kiss on the cheek.

"Okay, can we please get back to the questions?" I said blandly. It wasn't just the fact that they were gay that was weirding me out. Hell, Tate Zimmerman and his lover hadn't bothered me at all. The whole dynamic between these two was getting to me.

I looked at Alex out of the corner of my eye. Was this what she wanted? To have a "Master" controlling her every move, telling her when she could come and go, what she could and couldn't do and say? I couldn't imagine my independent, ballsy partner wanting anything like what Dr. Love and his "Master" seemed to share but then, I never would have guessed that being caned would turn her on, either.

She caught me looking at her and went red again, but when she spoke, her voice was icy-calm. "This party you were at, what kind was it? Who was in attendance?"

"It was our annual Saint Jude's Thanksgiving mixer. We have several, ah, get-togethers every year and just about everyone in the Tampa Bay area who's into the lifestyle attends."

"In other words, the BDSM community," I said, making a note. "And I guess you go as the Dom and Dr. Love here is the sub."

"Oh, Detective, I'm impressed." Montero smiled at me coolly. "You're even getting the terminology correct. Now why haven't I seen you around the scene before?"

I grinned at him nastily. "Oh, I'd hurt you. I play too rough."

Montero stared at me with frankly appraising eyes. "I just bet you do," he murmured. It was a little unnerving—I'm not used to being sized up sexually by other guys.

"I think we're getting a little off subject here. Can you give us the names of some other people at this, uh, party who can back up your story? " I said.

Montero frowned. "Well, generally, people in the community don't like to be outed, but I think in this case we'll have to make an exception. I can give you the names of two or three people who live the lifestyle twenty-four/seven. They won't mind."

"One of them wouldn't happen to be Mistress Samantha, would it?" I asked, hazarding a guess.

"Why, yes." Montero looked pleased. "Everybody in the community knows her. We've even taught a few classes together."

"Classes?" Alex asked, her lips tight.

He nodded. "Oh yes, let's see... There was a class in erotic biting that we taught together, and then we also did some workshops on resistance play, rope bondage, and spirituality and S/M. Oh, and I was teaching a class on flogging two years ago while she did a workshop on the sensuous art of caning. She's the *best* at that."

"Um..." I cleared my throat, not looking at Alex. "So we've heard." God, just the memory of those red stripes on her ass and the way she had gotten so hot and wet... I shifted uncomfortably in my seat. This was definitely not the time—we were in the middle of an investigation.

"Okay, so she was there that night," I said.

"With this one." He pointed at the picture of Sarah Michaels and nodded decisively. "We went over to say hello because David had helped her with some kind of a school paper or something. Anyway, she was sticking close to her Mistress, didn't leave her side all night that I saw."

"Uh-huh." As much as I hated to do it, I made a note to get back in touch with the elusive Mistress Samantha. I could see from the look on my partner's face that she wasn't looking forward to a second meeting with the Dominatrix either.

"Let's talk about something else." Cheeks burning red, Alex pointed at the pre-autopsy pictures of Cynthia Harner and Lauren Schaefer. "Have you seen either of them before?" she asked Montero.

He leaned forward, pushing thick blue-black bangs out of his eyes, and studied the pictures carefully. "Well, this one looks a little familiar—I may have seen her hanging around the fringes, so to speak, from time to time." He nodded at the picture of Lauren Schaefer. "And this one worked for David until a month ago," he said, pointing at the picture of Cynthia Harner.

"Until she was killed, you mean," I said, feeling my voice go low in frustration.

He raised a perfectly pointed eyebrow. "There's no need to get belligerent, Detective. I think we've established that neither David nor myself had anything to do with her rather unfortunate end."

"She was raped and strangled." Alex said quietly. "That's a little more than unfortunate, don't you think, Mr. Montero?"

"Yes, well…" He waved a hand airily. "All I know is that the poor woman was still alive and kicking last time I saw her."

"And when was that?" I asked, leaning forward.

"The same night you're asking about. She was at the mixer. David here was actually mentoring her—showing her how to be a proper submissive. Oh, I was so proud." He gave Love another affectionate kiss on the cheek, and the doctor actually blushed. I shook my head. God, the dynamics of this relationship got stranger and stranger.

"Our notes don't indicate that she was anywhere but at work and home that day." Alex frowned earnestly at the manila envelope in her hand.

"I'm not surprised." Montero shrugged. "As I said, many of the people in our community don't want to be outed."

"But David knew," I said flatly. I turned to the doctor, sitting submissively curled in the crook of his "Master's" arm. "How did you find out about Cynthia Harner's, ah, sexual proclivities in the first place?"

Before answering my question, Love looked at Montero, who nodded gravely, obviously giving permission. "Well." He cleared his throat. "She actually came in for an interview, and I liked her list of credentials. She'd gone back to school a little late in life, but I think life experience is valuable, and she said she was looking to make big changes in her life. 'Sweeping' changes was how she put it, I think. She told me frankly that she had just separated from her husband and that she had some new interests she wanted to pursue. I thought she was interesting and well qualified."

"Okay, fine, but how did you find out that her new interests included kink—" I looked at Alex who was staring at her hands, her cheeks still flaming a dull red. "Ah, that her new interests included alternate sexual practices," I amended, feeling stupid.

"Why, Detective, how very PC of you." Montero smiled at me again, that predatory smile I wasn't used to being on the receiving end of.

"I'm speaking to Dr. Love right now," I said, giving him a look of my own. "You'd do well to remember that your boyfriend—excuse me, *submissive*—is still under suspicion of triple homicide until we can find someone to verify your stories, Mr. Montero."

He nodded gravely. "Very well. David, answer the man."

Love shifted in his seat. "We—actually, I—had a feeling about her, but we didn't say anything. I might never have known if we hadn't literally run into each other outside the elevator right after the interview when I was going for lunch. She, ah, dropped a book she'd been carrying, and I caught a look at the title before she could pick it up."

"And that book would be?" Alex raised an eyebrow, stylus poised over her PDA.

"A true classic—*The Complete Slave: Creating and Living an Erotic Dominant/submissive Lifestyle*, by Jack Rinella." Love got a dreamy smile on his face. "It was one of the first books I read when I became interested in the lifestyle, so I knew right away what her 'interests' were. She was mortified, of course, until I let her know it was all right. After I hired her, we spoke more on the subject, and she revealed that she had gotten interested when she was doing research for some kind of article or short story she was writing. She had done a lot of reading but hadn't actually experienced the scene yet. I ended up inviting her to the Thanksgiving mixer. It was supposed to be her first real event." He sighed. "Unfortunately, it was also her last."

"How late was she there?" Alex asked, checking the file again. According to our notes, Cynthia's time of death had been somewhere between midnight and two a.m.

Love frowned. "Let's see... I'd say she left around eleven because the party was just getting started."

I frowned. "Wasn't she enjoying herself? Why did she leave?"

He sighed. "Well, now that's the strange thing about it. She was doing fine and having a great time—I thought she might even, uh, hook up with one of the men there—a Dom, by the looks of him. But then she got a phone call and said she had to go."

Montero nodded. "I remember, she went tearing out of there like her hair was on fire and her ass was catching. The Dom she was about to hook up with was *very* disappointed."

"Disappointed enough to go after her?" Alex asked sharply.

Montero shrugged. "I really couldn't say, Detective. At that point we got involved in some other, rather engrossing activities. As I recall, it was our turn at the whipping post." He grinned lazily at us, and I stared back stonily while Alex dropped her eyes, blushing again.

"LUDs show a call from the Tampa airport," she said, sitting up straighter with a rustle of papers, and scanning the file. "Must have been the DH leaving for Denver. A sudden attack of remorse, maybe."

Love looked at Montero briefly and said, "If you mean was she running back to her husband, well, I doubt it. She'd confided to me that he wasn't at all interested in the scene. It was one reason they separated."

I raised my eyebrows at Alex, and she nodded back. That wasn't exactly the story we'd gotten from the grieving widower. Yet another witness to re-visit. I was beginning to feel like we were chasing our tails all over town.

"Can you describe the Dom, uh, man that Cynthia almost left with?" Alex asked, moving on.

Montero thought for a moment. "Big, beefy guy, maybe a little shorter than you, Detective," he smiled at me in what I guessed was supposed to be an enticing way. "Heavy black beard, several piercings I could see, and I'd bet there were several I couldn't. A real 'leather daddy' type, if you know what I mean."

Love looked up eagerly. "Don't forget the tattoo."

Montero frowned. "I was just getting to that, David. Yes." He nodded. "There was a tattoo on his upper arm—his right I think. There was a ring of barbed wired around his bicep and under it was something about fresh meat or something."

"It said, 'I like it raw,'" Love offered, and then cringed at the look on his Master's face.

"David, I think we're going to have to have a serious discussion about speaking out of turn," Montero said, the soft menace back in his voice.

"That's going to have to wait until we go." I frowned at them both, not anxious to witness any "punishment" that Montero might dish out to his sub. "Now, Cynthia Harner was an upper-class, well educated woman. Do you really think this is the kind of guy she would've chosen to go with?"

Montero grinned at me, that irritating, sultry baring of teeth that had me itching to knock them all down his throat. "Didn't you hear David say she wanted to make 'sweeping changes,' Detective? Sometimes we all long for a little crude discipline to take our minds off our hum-drum lives. Those of us who are living hum-drum lives, that is." He sniffed expressively and turned to give Love another lingering kiss, this time on the mouth. Love melted against him, visibly surrendering completely to his Master's oral assault.

"Okay, that's enough." I stood, feeling violent enough to pound both of them. "That *crude discipline*, as you put it, might have cost a good woman her life, but I'm glad you find it so goddamn amusing. I also want to point out that if the Dom who may or may not have followed Cynthia out of the party is responsible for her death, you could have stopped two other brutal murders by making a phone call."

"Wait a minute, don't try to put this on us." Montero rose but Love stayed seated, eyes down on the forest green Berber rug. "I *told* you, people in our scene don't like to be outed."

"Well nobody in any scene likes to be murdered," Alex said, rising as well.

"There's such a thing as an anonymous tip," I said. I pointed at both of them. "We're going to be checking your story front, back, and sideways so don't even think about leaving town."

"We wouldn't dream of it, Detective." Montero made a little half bow, and I shut the door in his leering face on the way out.

Chapter Twenty-One

Alex

There was dead silence when we got out to the truck and then Cole turned to me and exploded.

"Is that what you want—what those two have? Some kind of sick fantasy about control and domination? Somebody to tell you what to do and where to go and if you can speak or not?" His blue eyes blazed at me angrily, accusingly.

"Cole," I said, holding on to my temper with both hands. "Do I need to ask you what to do and where to go? And when have you ever known me not to say exactly what was on my mind? I don't need anybody's permission for anything I do and say and for you to imply otherwise is goddamn insulting."

For a minute our eyes locked and we just glared at each other. Then, he took a deep breath and pinched the bridge of his nose, as though trying to push back a tension headache.

"You're right, I'm sorry," he said at last. "It's just that...this whole thing has me rattled. The way they were acting up there, it was so fucking *weird*."

I knew he was upset when I heard the F-bomb. Unless he's really worked up, Cole usually lays off that particular four-letter word. He told me once that he was afraid if he got in the habit at work, he'd forget and talk that way around Madison. So for an ex-Marine, he's got a pretty clean mouth.

"That kind of twenty-four/seven relationship isn't for everyone," I said, keeping my voice low and steady. I knew for sure it wasn't for me. I had fantasies of being mastered, of giving up control. But they were *sexual* fantasies—I wanted to lose control in the *bedroom*. If some man actually tried to tell me where I could go and when I could talk, I'd cut off his nuts with a dull butter knife. I thought about telling Cole that, but I just didn't know where to begin.

"I just don't understand how anyone could want that," he said at last, in a low voice.

"Sorry about that," I said neutrally. I'd tried to explain to him earlier when he noticed the bruises he'd made on my wrists earlier, and he still didn't get it. I wasn't baring any more of my soul—not to him or anyone.

"Alex." He looked at me, blue eyes burning. "I don't understand but I *want* to. I want to at least try."

"Try on your own time," I said, keeping my voice cool and impassive. "We have a case to solve. I think we ought to make another visit to Mistress Samantha, don't you?"

"Why, so she can show you more about the 'Sensual Art of Caning'?" he snarled.

I gave him a level look. "That was uncalled for and you damn well know it."

"I don't know anything anymore," he said, the anger leaving his voice suddenly. "About you or our partnership or even myself."

"That's because you're getting your personal life all mixed up in this case," I said tightly. "You need to remember that I'm not one of the victims, Cole. Stop trying to protect me and just do your job and I'll do mine. All right?"

He sighed deeply, pinched the bridge of his nose again, and finally started the truck. "Fine." He looked for a moment as though he was going to say something else but then he just shook his head and drove.

After a while the heater kicked in, which was good—it was getting late, and with the sun almost down, it was chilly. But even with the warm air blowing on my face and hands, I still felt cold.

* * *

Our second meeting with Mistress Samantha was considerably less eventful than the first. She met us in the waiting area of her Hyde Park home, almost as though she'd been expecting us.

"Detective Berkley, Alex," she greeted us, a small smile playing around her full red lips. "I'm surprised to see you back again so soon. Have you finally come to terms with your needs?" She stepped forward and lifted a hand, I thought to caress my hair.

"Hardly." Cole frowned and put himself between me and the Dominatrix protectively. "And have the courtesy to call my partner by her title, please, *Mistress*."

I sighed and stepped out from behind him. "Why didn't you tell us you'd taken Sarah Michaels out with you to the clubs?" I asked, meeting her level green gaze with a look of my own. "You said she wasn't out into the scene yet."

"Well she wasn't, not solo anyway." She shrugged. "I took her out on a few fieldtrips, yes, but she never left my side. I didn't feel she was ready yet and frankly, neither did Sarah."

"While you were out on these 'fieldtrips,' did you ever notice anyone noticing Sarah? Did anyone try to get close to her, make contact with her in any way?"

She stiffened. "Only once, now that you mention it, and it was very insulting as she was obviously with me."

I flipped open my PDA. "Was it the night of November twenty-second, at a party at the Liar's Club, in Ybor?"

"Yes it was, why?" She frowned, her perfect auburn eyebrows lifting.

"Just answer the questions," Cole said shortly. Obviously he still hadn't forgiven her for the scene in her dungeon the night before. "While you were at the party, did you happen to see a Carlos Montero and his, uh, submissive, Dr. David Love?"

"Absolutely." She settled herself on one of the plush benches and looked up at us. "Master Montero is a well-respected Dom in the community and his little sub is rather adorable, don't you find?"

I sighed. "Actually no, we didn't. And we're looking for a man that Montero and Love described to us. He would be a little shorter than my partner, here, with a black bushy beard, several piercings and a tattoo that says, uh…" I consulted my notes, "'I Like It Raw.' Was he the man that came up to you and Sarah and tried to, ah, cut in?"

Mistress Samantha nodded. "That was him, but I sent him away immediately."

"All right, and when he left you, did you happen to notice him bothering this woman?" I dug in the file and held out a picture of Lauren Schaefer.

She took the picture from me and studied it closely. "Not that night but I have seen her around the clubs once or twice. I remember she had that tentative quality—she was obviously new and inexperienced."

"Well, did you ever see her talking to the man we're looking for?" I looked at her hopefully.

"It's entirely possible." She sighed. "As I said, she looked new and a little uncertain—that probably would have attracted him."

"Any idea who he might be?" Cole asked, obviously frustrated.

She sniffed disdainfully. "He was an overbearing asshole—I never got his name. I don't know everyone in the scene, you know, although most of them know me. I *can* tell you where you might find him, though."

"Where?" Cole leaned forward eagerly, and I reflected that almost anyone else would have been intimidated by having my huge partner hulking over them like that. But the Dominatrix simply looked up at him coolly, completely unruffled.

"You won't find him tonight, Detective, if that's what you're thinking. But tomorrow's Friday and there's going to be a Christmas get-together at the Liar's Club. Everyone who's anyone and everyone who *wants* to be someone in the community will be there." She looked him up and down. "Of course, if you go in dressed as vanilla as you are right now, anyone with a guilty conscience is going to go straight out the back door as you come in the front."

"What does that mean to us?" I asked, feeling my heart sink and my gut twist. I already knew what she was going to say.

She smiled at me slowly. "It means, Alex, excuse me—*Detective Reed*, that you'll have to let your inner submissive out to play again, at least for a little while. If the man you want is preying on pretty little subs, he'll be after you in a heartbeat, especially if you appear to present a challenge."

"If you think I'm letting her go alone into some perverted club—" Cole began, and I elbowed him angrily.

"Since when do you say what I do and where I go?"

"It's not safe," he objected, his eyes narrowing. "I'm not letting you go in there alone, especially dressed like you were last night."

"I'll do whatever I have to do to catch this guy, and if that means going in alone then—"

"Detectives, *please*." Mistress Samantha rose and put out a hand to each of us, as though stopping an argument between two quarreling children. "It will do no good for Alex to go in alone—you'll need to go in together."

"I don't understand," I said. "Won't Cole scare him off?"

"Not if he's the kind of man I think he is. He'll be interested in the conquest of taking a woman away from another Dom—a power play." She nodded thoughtfully. "Be here around eight tomorrow night dressed as you were when you first came to see me, and we'll see what we can do."

"I don't like it," Cole growled. "I think we should go down to Ybor tonight and turn the place upside down. This guy is bound to be around somewhere."

"He might be," the Dominatrix said coolly. "But people in the community tend to stick together. So in all probability if you go around asking for him, all you'd be doing is giving him a heads up. Then you'll never find him."

Cole looked at her for a moment, his eyes blazing and finally said, "Fine." He stomped out of the house and I followed him, hearing the small, satisfied *snick* as Mistress Samantha's front door closed after us.

"She's right, Cole," I said, sighing. I dared to lay a hand on his broad back and felt him thrumming with tension. "I'm sorry but it's this or nothing, I'm afraid."

"Damn it." He kept his back to me so I couldn't see his face. "You're not half as afraid as I am, Alex."

* * *

We went by James Harner's South Tampa home, but he wasn't in and he didn't respond to any of the numbers we had for him.

"Probably back in Denver at another conference." Cole sighed heavily as we headed back to the station. "What now?"

"Back to the station, and then if we're lucky, we go home. I only got three hours of sleep last night, and I'm beat." I sighed. "We can try Harner again tomorrow. Before, uh, before we go to Ybor."

"Yeah. Well, at least we have our link—all three vics had ties to the, uh, the community. This son of a bitch was staking them out in the local BDSM bars. Bet you my next paycheck we find Mr. 'I Like It Raw' and we've found our perp."

"Yeah." I sighed. "Just wish we could get him tonight."

"You and me both." He was quiet for a minute and then he gave me a little half-glance out of the corner of his eye, a gesture I knew was a prelude to an uncomfortable question.

I sighed. "Go on, Cole, spit it out."

"I just…" He shook his head. "I just wondered if you know more about this than you're telling me—the lifestyle, or scene, or whatever the hell you want to call it. I mean, since you're into this kind of thing…"

I stared at him. "I don't believe this. You think I'm holding out on you? You think I know something I'm not sharing?"

"No, I just…" He shrugged uncomfortably.

I didn't know whether to laugh or cry. This was exactly what I had been afraid of—the exact reason I didn't want Cole to know about my secret desires. He didn't trust me anymore, and now I was certain I'd lost his respect as well. What did he think I was doing? Going out to bars every night looking for somebody to spank me?

"Have the common courtesy not to question my professional integrity," I said tightly. "Did I or did I not tell you that I'd never acted on my impulses before the other night when I was forced to by our little role playing scenario? Do you really think I'd keep anything about this case from you if I thought it would help to solve these crimes? Have I fallen that low in your opinion?"

"No, Alex. Dammit, you're twisting everything I say. I never thought—"

"I guess you didn't," I cut him off. "But just in case you're wondering, Cole, I've never been part of the 'scene' in any way. I've only ever…fantasized, and I've never acted on my fantasies. All right? Does that answer any questions you may have?"

"Yes," he said, and after a moment he added in a low voice, "I'm sorry." He fell silent then, which was a relief because the last thing I wanted to do was talk. I had too much on my mind, none of it pleasant.

It occurred to me that writing and publishing books on the subject, even if they were only e-books, was considerably more than fantasizing, but at that point I would rather have died than told Cole about my writing. It was just one more link in my own personal chain of perversion, a link I would just as soon keep to myself. Our professional relationship was already screwed up enough—maybe even unsalvageable. But we had to keep going until we caught whoever was killing these women. We owed the victims and their families that much at least.

Back at the station we reported to Captain Davis who was looking more harried by the hour. She wasn't happy that our best lead had turned out to be a dead end and was only marginally mollified when we outlined the sting for Friday night. After all, the man we were looking for could be the perp, or it could be someone else entirely—anyone, really, who'd had the opportunity to look over all three vics at the local BDSM bars.

The delivery angle had also turned out to be a bust. Lauren Schaefer had indeed had Thai food delivered to her house about an hour before she was killed, but the delivery boy turned out to be a girl who had then delivered to two other houses on Bayshore before going back to the Ruby Thai.

Every lead looked like a dead end, and with nothing left to chase, the captain sent us home, exhausted. Cole and I exchanged no words as we headed for our separate vehicles— there was a wall between us that hadn't been there before this whole mess started. I wanted to make things right with him, but I was so damn tired and my emotions were in such a tangled snarl, I just couldn't face it.

I felt beat as I unlocked my front door and my mind was in a fog. Someone had put one of those doorknob pizza coupon things on my front door and for a moment I actually considered ordering something. Then I realized I was way too tired to sit and wait for a pizza to come, let alone eat it. I drank a glass of milk, brushed my teeth, and went to bed, hoping tomorrow would be a better day.

Chapter Twenty-Two

Cole

Driving home I couldn't stop thinking about the sting for Friday night. More specifically, I couldn't get the image of Alex in that skimpy leather outfit out of my mind. Damn it, we'd been best friends for years; I respected her as a person and as a detective. And yet now, whenever I thought of her, my mind kept wanting to show me slow motion pictures of her sliding out of that tight leather bra, of me cupping her tits in my hands and sucking those ripe pink nipples. I thought of her tight wet heat, her soft, yielding body, the way she'd gasped like a hurt, wounded animal under me as I pressed inside her...

Ultimately, it had been that small gasp of fear and pain that stopped me, that kept me from pushing all the way in and fucking the living hell out of her. I've known guys that got off on hurting women—actually, I've arrested a lot of them. But I've never been wired that way myself, thank God. When I realized I was hurting her—actually causing her pain—I just couldn't go on.

And that was what was bothering me, of all things. My inability to hurt Alex, the woman I...what, loved? She was my partner; was I going crazy here? I shook my head, but the thought persisted. What if she wanted me to hurt her, *needed* me to, and I couldn't do it?

"Get a grip," I told myself out loud as the truck's big engine purred around me, and the silent streets, colorfully decorated for Christmas, flashed past my windows. I'd be lucky if Alex ever wanted to speak to me again after we wrapped this case, let alone have any kind of a permanent or lasting romantic relationship.

The sight of a familiar silver Lexus parked in one of the two allotted parking spots in front of my apartment ended my train of thought abruptly. *Oh, no.* I nearly groaned. Not tonight. I just couldn't deal with my ex tonight.

But when I let myself in, there she was, sitting rigidly on the very edge of the couch arm, as though to actually sit on the cushion itself would contaminate her. She had a romance novel in one hand—her one escape, as she had called it when we were married. Escape from what? I had never asked. Apparently she had been reading to pass the time while she waited for me.

"Amanda," I said tiredly, running a hand over my stubbly jaw and wishing I could just kick her the hell out. "What do you want?"

"That's a nice greeting. I've been waiting for hours." She tapped the face of her expensive Lady Rolex, no doubt a gift from senior partner Bill, and frowned accusingly.

"What are you even doing here?" I snapped irritably, taking off my jacket and slinging it over the back of a chair. "I guess you let yourself in with the key I gave Madison."

"It was better than waiting out in the cold." She sniffed. "Marginally. I have to say, Cole, this place is a dump. You're even more of a slob now that you don't have anyone to pick up after you."

"Great," I growled. "I'm a slob, my place is a dump. Did you just stop by to pick a fight for old times' sake, or is this a new form of entertainment? I don't come into your house unannounced and uninvited."

"I should hope not." She stood up and brushed imaginary lint from the back of her black business skirt. She was wearing one of those severely tailored executive women's suits, and the platinum blond hair that our daughter had inherited was up in a tight bun at the back of her neck. When she turned I could see by her profile and the gaunt lines and angles beneath the expensively tailored fabric that she had lost more weight.

Amanda's always been on the thin side, but when she started gunning for partner, she began working to exclusion of everything else, even sleeping and eating. I had been worried about her in the six months before she left me. I opened my mouth to say something then closed it again. She had made it clear that she wasn't my worry anymore. Still, the sight of her stick-thin body moved something in me. Not love, exactly, but the ghost of love.

I sighed, suddenly too tired to fight. "Whatever you want, can't it wait? We've got a really nasty case going right now, and I'm all in." I sank onto the couch she had just vacated, pushing a T-shirt and the towel I had used to dry off that morning aside to do so. She was right—I was a slob. The thought made me feel even more tired—weary almost to the point of not caring.

"Well, isn't that the story of your life? Work always comes first." Her mouth pursed in a thin line, and she crossed her arms over her chest, her elegant French manicured nails tapping an impatient rhythm.

"Amanda," I growled, losing my patience. "Just tell me what the hell you want and get out."

"*I* don't want anything from you but your daughter does." Raising her voice she called, "Madison? Your father is finally home."

"Daddy, 'zat you?" My little girl came wandering out from the direction of the bedroom, rubbing her eyes sleepily.

"She fell asleep on your bed waiting for you. I told you we've been here for hours." But at the sight of those sleepy blue eyes and that tousled blond hair, Amanda's thin, strident voice and my own weariness lost all importance.

"Hey little girl, it's me all right." I grinned at her and stood, holding out my arms.

"Daddy!" She ran at me like a miniature freight train, and I pretended to be knocked backward as I caught her in a bear hug and swung her around the room. She giggled and screamed excitedly. I caught a glance of my ex-wife's face, frozen in a frown of disapproval, but I didn't care. She had always complained that I worked Madison up into a lather right before bed time on the nights I did get home in time to see her.

"Hey, Sugar Bear," I said at last, holding her tight and relishing the feel of those small arms wrapped around my neck. She seemed bigger than she had just two weeks ago, her legs wrapped around my waist like a little monkey. I buried my face in her pale blond hair, like the finest silk, and breathed her in. God, I loved her so much!

"Hey, Daddy," she murmured and gave me a smacking kiss on the cheek, then made a face. "Oh, you're rough!"

"Sorry, baby, I didn't get a chance to shave today." I grinned at her and tweaked her nose. "It's good to see you, I didn't think I'd get to see the eight-year-old Madison ever again. I thought next time I saw you the nine-year-old Madison would've taken over."

She giggled. "I'm still eight. At least 'til Saturday."

"I know," I said, hugging her tighter. "But you're getting old so fast your old man can't keep up with you. You looking forward to your trip to Disney World?" I kept an eye on Amanda as I said this, and she had the good grace to blush and look away.

"That's what we came about tonight, Daddy." Madison looked at me earnestly, her big blue eyes so much like her mother's, but so full of the love that was lacking now in Amanda's. "I won't go if you don't want me to," she said simply, and hugged me tighter.

"You won't? Who told you I didn't want you to go?" Over the top of her head, I glared at my ex-wife.

She shrugged her thin shoulders and glared back at me. "Don't look at me—this was her own idea. She insisted on coming over here tonight to tell you."

"Sugar Bear, what makes you think I don't want you to go have fun at Disney World for your birthday?" I asked her, looking into those big blue eyes earnestly.

"Nobody, Daddy, and I was real excited to go but then I 'membered I was s'posed to spend some time with you, and it made me sad." She buried her face in my neck and squeezed tightly. "I miss you, Daddy," she said in a husky little whisper that was just short of a sob.

"Ah, Madison." I hugged her back helplessly, feeling torn. "I miss you too, baby, more than I can say," I said, feeling a lump in my throat. "But I don't mind you going to have fun on your birthday. I'll see you the week after Christmas, and we'll celebrate then."

"Don't want to wait." She nuzzled closer, and her breath was warm and peppermint-scented against my neck. She must have been eating candy canes. "I want to see you on Christmas. Why can't you come be with us, Daddy?"

"Madison, we've discussed this over and over." My ex-wife tapped her fingernails impatiently. "Mommy and Daddy aren't together anymore, so we have to do things separately."

"But why? Why can't we be together anymore?" She looked at me, blue eyes filling with tears. "A girl in my class, Rachel McManus, her mom and dad split up but then they got back together. Why can't you and Mom get back together, Daddy?"

"Because we just can't, baby." I tweaked her nose softly. "I'm sorry, but sometimes it happens. How about if instead of waiting for the weekend after Christmas you spend Christmas Eve with me and Christmas with your mom?"

Her eyes lit up but my ex was already shaking her head. "That's going to be impossible; we have plans with Bill's family." Her voice changed, becoming softer and slightly sing-song. "Don't you want to see Grandma and Grandpa Carrington? They already told me they bought you lots of presents, Madison."

"Don't want presents, I want Daddy," my daughter said stubbornly. She wiggled to get down then leaned against my legs. She was getting so tall her head just about reached my hip. "I wanna spend Christmas Eve with him, like he said."

"See what you started?" Amanda glared at me and reached over to grab Madison's hand. "Come on now, you have school tomorrow, and it's getting late."

"I don't wanna go!" Madison's voice was low and tense. "Don't wanna go back there. It's never any fun with you and Bill."

"Come on right now, young lady." Amanda pulled her toward the door.

Madison dug in her heels and got a sly look on her face. "Say I can stay with Daddy on Christmas Eve, and I'll go."

I had to suppress a grin; when Madison went head to head with her mother, the sparks always flew. The thing that amused me was that Amanda never seemed to recognize that her own bargaining skills were being used against her. In so many ways Madison was a miniature of Amanda, complete with a stubborn personality and a will to win. I usually just stepped back and let them fight it out.

"We'll talk about it," Amanda ground out, tugging on Madison's arm. "Now come on, *we have to go.*"

"When you say that, it always means no!" Madison yanked her hand out of her mother's and ran back to me, catapulting herself into my arms for one last hug and kiss. "I love you, Daddy," she said breathlessly.

"Love you too, Sugar Bear." I kissed her back, feeling the childish smoothness of her cheek against my own rough one. I squeezed her until she squeaked in protest. "Now run out to the car. I'll see you later."

"'Kay!" She jumped down and ran out to the waiting Lexus, scrambling into the front seat and buckling herself in. Amanda followed her with poor grace, still frowning.

"Amanda," I caught her arm as she was reaching for the car door.

"What?" She turned to face me, and I wondered for the hundredth time what had happened to the woman I used to love. The facial features were there, thinner and a little more lined but still beautiful. But all the emotion we'd had between us had soured somehow. Had gone as rancid as old milk.

"Let her come," I said quietly, knowing it was no use demanding. One of the things that irked me about the divorce was that my ex had the final say over visiting rights. I couldn't demand anything, only appeal to her heart, and lately I was wondering if she even had one.

"We have plans already," she said tightly, her eyes on the hopeful face of our daughter in the front seat.

"Let her come," I said again. "Don't punish her because of your feelings." I thought of what Alex had said to me the other night, of the way she had cried in my arms. "I may not have been the best husband, but I'm a damn good father," I told my ex. "And it's important that a girl has a good relationship with her father. It's going to affect her relationship with every other man in her entire life. Come on, Amanda, you know it's true. You were close to your dad."

She sighed and for a moment her thin shoulders sagged and she looked tired and haggard instead of just bitchy. "We'll talk about it," she repeated again, hooking her fingers into the door handle and giving it a tug. I knew what that meant.

"I'm not going to let you cut me out of her life, Amanda," I said, dropping the charm and letting my eyes grow cold. "We may not love each other anymore, but I love Madison too much to let you separate us completely. If I have to, I'll drag you back to court."

"You do that and you risk losing her altogether. Who do you think a judge is going to award sole custody to, Cole?" Her gaze, so much like Madison's, but cold as ice, flashed into mine. "A hardworking mother who keeps regular hours, or a man who spends all his free time running down murderers and rapists?"

"It's my *job*, Amanda. It's what I do." I held on to the car door, keeping it shut, not wanting our daughter to hear the harsh words between us although she would certainly be able to tell by our tense facial expressions what was going on.

"It's *always* your job," she hissed, yanking ineffectually at the door. "Always your job and your partner and your life that comes first."

"That's not true." I tried to keep my voice steady. "I know I couldn't always make it to dinner on time or make all of Madison's school functions, but I made damn sure I saw her every morning. I always made time for her."

"For her, Cole, but not for me." She yanked on the door again, and this time I let it go so she could get it. "Think about that," she said, sliding into the plush leather interior of the Lexus. "And maybe you'll understand how you lost us in the first place." She slammed the door in my face and gunned the engine, backing out of the small space so fast she scraped the back wheels over the curb.

The last thing I saw was my daughter's small face pressed longingly against the passenger side window, staring out at me.

Chapter Twenty-Three

He has been out scouting, time well spent, especially when those in authority are so eager to find him. He has spent time outside of the house of his one remaining name. Carolyn Sinders, also known as Lauren Schaefer, was ridiculously easy, almost a joke, and he found the punishment most enjoyable. In fact, he uneasily admits to himself, he may have gone a little overboard with the wax. But it had been *her* fantasy he was acting out, after all. *Her* becoming that he facilitated. Now she is an altogether different creature, she has become what she longed to be, and he is the cause of that.

He still feels the divine compulsion within him, the need to scour the earth of these women, and with it, the certainty that he cannot be stopped. But still, there's no harm in planning ahead. He sat for a long time outside the last one's house the night before. Sat and watched her walk up to her front door and unlock it, examining the little present he left for her on the knob. For a moment he thought she might actually order something, and wouldn't that be a fine joke? But after a while the lights went out and he knew she was in bed. The same bed he will bind her to when he visits her, to punish her, to help her become.

After she was tucked in, snug as a bug in a rug, he left her alone. Alone in the house dreaming her wicked dreams and writing them down to corrupt others. Soon, very soon, he will stop all of that. But he must have a day of rest—the work of punishment and becoming, while exhilarating, is very tiring. So he will give himself a day or two to get ready, so that he can be in top form. So that he can enjoy himself completely.

He has been scanning the story of his final project—she has more prosaic tastes than the last two, but that is all right. He doesn't mind. As he read her work the night before, a scene had jumped out at him, the perfect one to help her become what she needs to be. The perfect scene to punish her for her words of corruption. When he is finished with her, she will be pure at last, pure and perfect and altogether different from the vile creature who wrote the trash that started all this in the first place.

Two names are blinking on the laptop in his bedroom. Carolyn Sinders, and Victoria Tarlatan. He highlights Carolyn Sinders and hits delete.

Only one more to go.

Chapter Twenty-Four

Alex

"I don't know what you're talking about. That's *disgusting*." James Harner looked beyond offended, as though we'd suggested that his dead wife had been into Satanism and child sacrifice instead of just kinky sex.

"That's not what we heard, Mr. Harner," I said, a little surprised at his violent reaction. "Our understanding was that one reason you two separated in the first place was her interest in...ah..."

"Alternative sexual practices," Cole finished for me, not meeting my eyes.

"Right. So?" I looked at James Harner, who was throwing clothing into a small suitcase, obviously getting ready for another business trip. We had followed him into his bedroom to talk to him as he showed no inclination to sit down with us this time. He still wore the black carpal tunnel braces on both wrists. They made his arms look alien, almost insectile, I thought, as they flashed back and forth, between the dresser and the suitcase.

"I don't know who you've been talking to but my Cynthia wasn't into anything like that. She was a saint—she never would have...have..." His mouth was a thin, tight line, but when he looked up, the pale, no-color eyes were brimming. "Please," he said appealingly. "Isn't it bad enough that I lost her? Do you have to go dragging her memory through the mud too? It's...it's all I have left."

"I'm sorry, Mr. Harner," I said as gently as I could. "But we're trying to establish some link between your wife and the other victims."

"Victims? Plural?" He stopped his frenzied movements and looked up at me and then at Cole, as though to confirm the terrible news. "You mean he's killed another one?"

"You must not watch the evening news," Cole said dryly. He was leaning against the doorframe, nearly filling the entire space with his broad shoulders. "It's all channel eight's been talking about. And channel nine, and channel five, and *Good Day, Tampa Bay...*"

"I've been busy. I've been keeping my mind occupied with work because it's the only thing that blocks out what happened to Cynthia. When I try to watch TV or read a book..." He shook his head. "I just can't let myself think about it too much. It's too painful."

"We're sorry, Mr. Harner, but another woman was killed the same way your wife and Sarah Michaels were killed the night before last. As you can see, our perpetrator is escalating his behavior. Now, we have a theory that he may be involved in the BDSM scene here in town," I said.

"I'm sorry, the *what?*" he glanced at me sharply.

I cleared my throat uneasily. "BDSM is sort of a catch-all that stands for bondage, discipline, domination, submission, sadism, and masochism. It's a term used to cover any sexual activity that involves one partner being in control and one partner being controlled." I could feel my cheeks flaming, but I resolutely continued, keeping my eyes on Harner, not on Cole, though I could feel his blue eyes piercing straight through me. "Did your wife ever express any interest in being tied up or held down while you made love? Maybe in being blindfolded or gagged during sex?"

Cole spoke up from his post by the door. "Did she ever ask you to hurt her in any way? Spanking, whipping, maybe with a belt or riding crop...was she into erotic pain?"

Harner looked back and forth between us, horror growing on his narrow, mild face. "Certainly not!" he exploded. "My Cynthia would never be interested in anything like that, and even if she was, I wouldn't..." He broke off, shaking his head in disgust. "We were a normal couple. We loved each other, took care of each other. Expressed our affection and our...our sexuality in *normal* ways."

"Until she finished school and took a job with Dr. Love?" I asked softly. "He took her under his wing, and suddenly she felt free enough to explore a side of herself she'd never been able to release before, isn't that right, Mr. Harner?"

He threw a half-folded shirt in the open suitcase. "No! No, it's not."

"It must have been rough," Cole took up the narrative. "I mean, you're faithful to her all those years, you even put her through school, and then she repays you by demanding you do things that disgust you. Perverted sexual scenarios that make you sick…"

"No…*no!*" Harner insisted. He looked wildly between us.

I almost couldn't continue the act. I couldn't look at Cole—was he just trying to get under Harner's skin, or was he stating his own view on S/M practices? Were his words aimed indirectly at me? My stomach twisted in knots, but I forced myself to go on.

"She left you when you wouldn't, didn't she? Left as soon as she could afford to because you weren't meeting her needs?"

"That's it." Harner squeezed the pair of black dress socks he'd been about to pack so tightly that the knuckles on his right hand popped like small gunshots in the large bedroom. "If you don't stop harassing me—and that's what this is, harassment, plain and simple—I'm going to call my lawyer. How do you think *Good Day, Tampa Bay* would like to know that the detectives assigned to solve my wife's murder are spending their time bothering me instead, implying that I'm some kind of a…of a pervert?"

Cole and I shared a look. "All right, Mr. Harner, we apologize." He held up both hands in a calming gesture. "We're just looking for a lead, any lead that might help us here. So far this is what we've got."

"Well then, I suggest you go back to the drawing board and start again." Harner threw the pair of socks after the shirt, and I reflected that he was going to look like hell in his business meetings—all his clothes were crumpled into little balls.

"Mr. Harner," I began, and then broke off coughing. "Excuse me," I said at last. "Could I have a drink of water, do you think?"

"I'll get you one." He turned stiffly and strode out of the tastefully decorated bedroom, and I followed him, knowing that Cole would take the opportunity to give everything a once over while Harner and I were gone.

"We really didn't mean to upset you," I said soothingly, as Harner poured me a drink of cold water from one of those filtration pitchers he'd pulled from the stainless steel refrigerator. The kitchen was large and airy, all the appliances done in the same brushed stainless steel and the counters in black marble. It looked like whoever had designed it was a serious chef, not just a dabbler.

In the center of the large space was a four-by-four-foot butcher block table. On it was a scatter of coupons, most of them for pizza places. I walked over and picked one up idly. "You order out a lot? This kitchen looks like it was designed by a gourmet."

He shrugged stiffly and handed me the water. The glass was cool against my fingers. "That would be Cynthia. She loved to cook, before she went back to school, that is. The past several years we've ordered out a lot. She...didn't have time, you see."

"I see," I said neutrally. "Lot of coupons for a man alone—you ever have any company?" I asked.

He grimaced. "Most of those were given to me by one of Cynthia's patients—a young man. I don't know his name but he came by to offer his condolences soon after...soon after it happened."

"I see. Could you describe him?"

Harner shrugged. "I don't know—I was in a haze. Tall, maybe? White with brown hair. That's the best I can do. Sorry."

"That's all right." It was probably nothing, but the description gave me an uneasy prickle at the back of my neck. Still, he could be describing almost anyone, and the one suspect we'd had that remotely fit that description, Jeremy Bruce, had an alibi. I shrugged it off—it probably was just a concerned patient. I drank half the water and handed the glass back to him. "Thank you."

"You're welcome." He placed the glass carefully in the sink. "Now if you don't mind, I really have to pack."

"Of course." I followed him back to the large bedroom, decorated in highly polished cherry wood, clearing my throat along the way to let Cole know we were coming.

My partner was examining an airline ticket that was lying on the dresser beside a set of gold and ruby cufflinks. "You always fly Delta?" he asked, looking up as we entered the room.

"My company has an expense account with them. That way whenever the clients need me, I can go immediately without waiting for any kind of authorization."

"Going to Denver again, I see," Cole murmured.

Harner snatched the plane ticket and the cufflinks and jammed them both in the side pocket of the suitcase. "Yes, for the third time this week. I was just there the day before yesterday, and I didn't get back until this morning. Now they're calling and saying their system is crashing again." He sighed heavily.

"Wait a minute, I thought you said you were a consultant?" I raised an eyebrow at him.

"A computer consultant—more of a systems analyst, actually." There was a faint trace of pride in Harner's voice.

"So if they're having trouble, can't you just do some kind of a remote fix? Hook into their system down here, use the Internet?" Cole asked, arms crossed over his chest.

Harner sighed again. "It's not that simple, Detective. Unfortunately, our client is having trouble with the hardware, not the software. It's a hands-on kind of fix."

"Oh, mmm." Cole nodded thoughtfully. "Well, I guess we've taken enough of your time, Mr. Harner."

I nodded. "Our apologies if we offended you—we're just trying to find the guy who's doing this."

"Well I hope you do." Harner's narrow face was no longer flushed, and he appeared to be mollified by my apology. "And now if you'll excuse me, my flight leaves in half an hour."

"We may be in touch," Cole said, leaving a card on the dresser, where the ticket had been.

James Harner nodded stiffly and escorted us to the door without another word.

"I don't like it," I said, as soon as we were back in the unmarked sedan. I was driving today, but the unmarked was my silent concession that I no longer felt comfortable enough with my partner to sit in the close confines of my Bug with him. At least the sedan gave us both breathing room, and we weren't so…on top of each other. Being physically close to Cole had never bothered me before, but now I couldn't seem to stop the crazy skittering of my heart whenever we were in each other's space.

"What don't you like?" Cole raised an eyebrow at me as he buckled his seat belt.

"He's holding out." I buckled my own belt and turned to face my partner. "If what Love said is true…"

"Right, *if.*" Cole snorted.

"What's *that* supposed to mean?" I asked, feeling put on the defensive. "You think Love is lying?"

"I don't know what to think, but I'm just saying I can see Harner's side of it. He supports his wife for years, puts her through school. Then—bam—she leaves him. Decides he isn't what she wants anymore." Cole shrugged. "You want a motive for murder, there it is—you don't need to throw kinky sex into the deal. If he didn't have such an airtight alibi…"

"Cole," I said softly. "Are we talking about James Harner or about you?"

His face got red, and his lips narrowed to a thin white line. "That's a low blow, Alex."

"I'm just saying you shouldn't let your own life intrude into this case," I said, trying to keep my voice low and non-confrontational. "I think we've both been dragging too many personal issues into it, and that's bound to muddy the waters."

He snorted again. "Oh, you mean the way you get so defensive and start blushing while we're questioning witnesses? I have to tell you, partner, *you're* the one who looks guilty when you're asking those questions about their sex lives."

"Are you accusing me of being unprofessional?" I demanded. "Because maybe it would be a little easier for me to keep a straight face if you weren't talking about how perverted and sick—"

"That was part of the act—I was just trying to get him to react," he protested. "You know I didn't mean—"

"I have no idea what you meant, and I don't care." I stabbed at the ignition with the key and ground the motor to life, lurching out onto the quiet suburban street. "I'm just saying let's try to keep our personal lives out of this."

"Hey." He held up his hands. "I'm doing the best I can over here."

It didn't seem like it to me, but I just shook my head and concentrated on driving. I had already decided I was going to make some calls to the Delta counter at TIA. I didn't like Harner's attitude, and there was no harm in double checking, no matter how airtight his alibi appeared to be.

Chapter Twenty-Five

Cole

"Well, well, like lambs to the slaughter." Mistress Samantha gave us a once over coupled with a slow smile that made my gut twist. All in all, not a very promising beginning.

"We're here," I said, unnecessarily. "Now let's get down to the club and catch this bastard."

"Not so fast, Detective, there is more to playing your roles than just dressing the part." She stepped aside and motioned for us to enter her waiting room foyer. "Please come in."

I sighed and followed her in. I would have exchanged a glance with Alex, but I was trying as much as possible to keep my eyes off my partner tonight. She was wearing the same skin-tight leather skirt, black leather bra, and high-heeled boots that she'd been wearing the other night when things had gone so disastrously wrong. The black leather bra left her arms bare, and the bracelet of bruises she still wore filled me with shame. They were fading but still visible, and Alex didn't even seem to notice them. Was she really so unconcerned by the way I had marked her?

Just looking at her in that outfit made me think of everything that had happened and, worse, everything that had *almost* happened between us. To make a long story short, I was fighting a losing battle with my libido, and I didn't need to throw any more fuel on the fire.

"Now, where to begin?" The Dominatrix clasped her hands behind her back and inspected us. I almost felt like I should stand at attention, and I squashed the impulse with a surge of annoyance. I was wearing the same outfit I had been the night before, albeit with a slightly smaller gun tucked into my shoulder holster. Alex was unarmed. I didn't like that one bit, but she pointed out, as she had before, that there was literally no place in the skimpy leather outfit she wore to hide a firearm. I mentally promised myself I'd be watching her back, despite my intention not to look directly at her if I could help it.

"We're here to catch a serial killer, not take lessons from you." Alex's voice behind me was soft but firm, catching me a little off guard. I actually flinched when she took a step forward and her arm brushed mine. From the corner of my eye, I could see the subtle hurt on her face as she took a step away. When I looked forward, I could see that Mistress Samantha had noticed my reaction to my partner's proximity as well. She was studying us with a slight frown on her sculpted red lips.

"Alex," she said abruptly, taking a step closer to my partner. "I don't think the outfit you have on quite does you justice. After all, we want to really put you on display tonight. Every Dom in the club must want you, that way you'll present an even greater challenge—a more coveted prize." She turned and clapped her hands sharply twice. "Melissa?"

Immediately the foyer door opened, and the pleasant-faced girl we'd seen on our first visit stepped into the waiting area. "Yes, Mistress?" she asked without a trace of irony.

"Alex is in need of something a little more extreme for tonight's outing." She cupped her chin in one hand, one dark red eyebrow raised for a moment as she considered my partner, who was standing silently before her. "Something in red leather, I think? And some very high boots. Something eye-catching without being completely obscene."

"Of course, Mistress." The assistant nodded and held out a hand for Alex. "Come, let's get you changed."

Alex took her hand mutely, and they left the room without a backward glance. It bothered me that my forthright partner didn't even object once. It wasn't like her to do as she was told so quietly, to agree absolutely with what anyone said. But then, I reminded myself, she *wasn't* acting like herself very much lately—at least, not like the Alex I knew.

The Dominatrix waited until the door had snicked shut after Alex and her assistant and then turned to face me, hands on her hips. "It bothers you greatly, doesn't it?" She looked at me, pale green eyes piercing in their intensity.

I shifted uncomfortably. "I don't know what you're talking about."

"Your partner's need to submit, it bothers you." She sat on one of the padded benches, her own leather clothing creaking gently at the motions. She was wearing a more sedate version of Alex's outfit, a black leather skirt that came down to her knees and a black cut-away jacket that revealed a generous amount of creamy, slightly freckled cleavage.

"She doesn't need...any of that," I said stiffly, crossing my arms over my chest. "She just has these crazy ideas, which *you* probably put in her head. She'll get over it."

Mistress Samantha shook her head. "Don't fool yourself, Detective Berkley. My influence has done nothing but force her to admit her desires out loud. But the need had been there a long time before you two ever walked into my dungeon." She patted the bench beside her. "It's going to take Melissa a little while to get her looking just right. Why don't you sit down and we'll discuss it."

I felt like we ought to be discussing the case instead, mapping out a strategy, but without Alex in the room it was a moot point. Besides, she and I had handled this kind of sting before—we could do it with our eyes shut. I settled uneasily beside Mistress Samantha, not willing to admit that I desperately needed some answers for my partner's bizarre behavior lately.

"Why does it bother you so much?" she asked softly, keeping her eyes fixed on my face. "You obviously have some dominant tendencies yourself. I would think the fact that a woman you love has submissive tendencies would be intriguing to you."

"First of all, I'm not in love with Alex—she's my partner and that's it," I said flatly. "And secondly, the reason it bothers me is...is...because that's not Alex! This isn't the way she is— she's tough and in control..." I broke off and ran a hand through my hair in agitation. "You don't understand. Alex and I have been partners for five years. I trust her with my life—I'd rather have her guarding my back than any three of the male officers I work with, and now, all of a sudden..."

"It's like you don't know her anymore. As though she was suddenly a stranger," she said softly.

I nodded, feeling miserable. "I guess, in a way."

"Detective Berkley, the way you've described your partner—tough, in control, as good or better at her job than any of the men you work with—would it surprise you to know that almost every woman who comes to me matches that description?"

I looked at her in surprise. "You're kidding."

"No, nor am I exaggerating in the slightest. If you think that the only kind of woman I see on a professional basis is the stereotypical 'Bambi bottom,' you're completely misinformed." She tapped her nails on the leather bench for emphasis. "The women that come to me have high-stress jobs—lawyers, doctors, CEOs, and the like. They come to me for a relief from their daily pressure, from the never-ending grind of their chosen vocations, to escape the burden of always being in control of themselves and others."

I jumped, almost as though she had pinched me. "Alex..." I cleared my throat, looking down at my hands. "She said something about needing to lose control—I didn't really understand. I guess I still don't."

"But if you truly love her and value her friendship, you'll try." She looked at me, one perfectly pointed eyebrow raised. "*Some people need to be tied down to feel free,*" she emphasized. "Even the toughest, most competent woman needs to be able to feel vulnerable sometimes. If she trusts you enough to show you that side of herself, you should feel honored and try to be a little more accepting. You have no idea how much courage it takes to admit to such feelings. It's a hell of a lot harder to admit it than to keep everything bottled inside and just pretend you don't care…pretend you don't *need*."

"I guess…" I crossed my arms over my chest uncomfortably. "I guess I never thought of it like that. When you put it that way, I sound like a selfish jerk, not wanting to let her express her emotions."

"Is that how you see yourself?" Tap, tap, tap went her fingernails.

I thought of Alex crying and helpless in my arms, of her tears wetting my chest and her lips trembling under mine. I had wanted so badly to protect her then, to wrap her up and keep her safe forever. No, it wasn't necessarily her need to be vulnerable, as Mistress Samantha put it, that bothered me.

"It's not that," I said aloud, standing to pace the limited space of the foyer.

"Well then?"

I looked down at her, and she was staring at me, fingernails still tapping.

"Go on, Detective, this particular session is on the house." She nodded at me. "What bothers you the most about your partner's desires? About her needs, other than the fact that you never suspected them before a few days ago, that is."

"Pain," I said, hearing the work break from my lips in a short, bitter syllable. "It's the fact that…that she wants me…wants someone, I mean, to hurt her. To punish her. I just can't…that's not…it's not normal," I finished weakly, my shoulders sagging.

"Normal as defined by whom?" she asked sharply. "There are many levels of eroticism, Detective, and not all of them fit neatly into the ideas of our culture. But that doesn't make them any less valid. However…" She paused and tapped one finger thoughtfully just beneath her pursed lips. "It's my guess that it isn't so much the pain your partner is seeking, as the undivided attention that comes with it. Did you listen at all to the answers she gave to my questions the other night? You might have been making yours up but Alex's came from the heart. She said, 'When my Master disciplines me, I feel all his attention centered on me—all his love, all his hate, every emotion—all for me.' Do you remember?"

I did, vividly as a matter of fact. Of course, at the time I had thought Alex was just play-acting, as I had been myself. Although I had to admit that the idea of doing some of the things I had described to her was an amazing turn-on. But damn it, I wasn't supposed to feel that way for my partner, my best friend.

"I do remember," I said at last, when I realized Mistress Samantha was still looking at me.

"And does the idea of that—of doing what Alex described, what she *needs*, really revolt you?" she asked quietly.

I scowled, unwilling to admit the answer, even to myself. All the possessive, controlling emotions, all the sexual heat I felt for my partner that I'd been trying to suppress for the past several days, rose up like a tidal wave and threatened to drown me. I couldn't speak so I simply shook my head.

"It doesn't, does it?" she said softly. "Quite the opposite, in fact, I would think. Food for thought, Detective Berkley." She rose from the bench and went to the door just as it opened and her assistant stepped through, followed closely by Alex. "Come in, my dear—don't you look *lovely*."

Despite my reluctance to listen to anything the Dominatrix had to say, her words hit home with me. It wasn't fair for me to expect Alex never to change. And maybe it was time to start re-evaluating our relationship from a personal rather than a professional level. Was it really so bad to let myself look at her not just as my partner, but as a woman? Of course, to start with, I had to make myself look at her in the first place and try to get over the guilt I felt when my body inevitably reacted to the sight of her. I was just so used to seeing her as one of the guys, but now...

I forced myself to look up and take in the new outfit Alex had on. Nope, definitely not one of the guys anymore. A leather mini skirt, much shorter and more revealing than the one she'd been wearing, barely covered the tops of her thighs, and her top was a brief leather halter with a plunging neckline that came very close to revealing her nipples. In fact, when I looked closely, I could see a flash of the dark pink ring of areola on either side of the creamy swells of her breasts as she breathed. Thigh-high, spike-heeled, leather boots that nearly brushed the brief hem of her skirt completed the outfit.

The boots were black with thick silver buckles but the skirt and top were the color of fresh blood, vivid and unmistakable. She was no longer wearing the black silver collar, and her slender neck looked smooth and kissable.

I let my eyes travel up from the boots to the top, taking in every luscious curve in between and finally forced myself to look Alex in the eye, a thing I had been avoiding all night.

"Well?" She shrugged uneasily and made a slight gesture, indicating the outfit. "What do you think?"

I became acutely aware that three pairs of female eyes were fixed on me, waiting to hear what I had to say. "You look like Barbie does Bondage in that get-up," I said, walking over to her and letting one finger trail down the brief halter. I heard her quick little breath as my fingertip traced over the swell of her breast, catching the hard little nubbin of her nipple, barely hidden by the red leather. I leaned closer, never letting my eyes leave hers. "But it works," I said softly. "Every man at the club is going to want you tonight—I know I do."

"Cole!" She slapped at my chest lightly, obviously wanting to turn the words into a joke but I wouldn't let her.

"You look hot, Alex. So damn desirable it takes my breath away," I told her, catching her small hand in mine. I pressed a warm kiss to her soft palm, enjoying her little gasp of mingled pleasure and apprehension as I did.

"Th-thank you," she stuttered, dropping her eyes. "I think."

It wasn't like her to let me get away with making what she would normally consider sexist remarks. She'd once kneed a guy for saying a lot less at work—a real jerk named Manzetti who worked in narcotics. He'd told her a dirty joke and then asked if she wanted to act out the punch line with him. I'd been all set to deck him, but Alex had beaten me to the punch—literally. Manzetti had given her a wide berth after that, as had a lot of the guys in the department.

But now, instead of going for my balls, she was blushing and dropping her eyes, acting shy with me, of all people. I couldn't figure it out and yet, I found that it didn't bother me quite so much. I decided to just let myself go with it, at least as far as Alex was concerned. Our first priority was apprehending the suspect; allowing myself to relax with her would help me sharpen my focus on the objective. Besides, it felt good to interact with her this way—natural, although it certainly wasn't our usual MO.

"Are we ready to go?" Still blushing, Alex glanced at Mistress Samantha, who was looking at us both with an unreadable expression on her ageless face.

"Not quite." She seated herself on one of the benches again and indicated that we should do the same.

"What now? Time's wasting." I sat across from her and Alex sank down beside me, the bare skin of her side brushing briefly against my arm. This time I did not jerk away. In fact, I could barely restrain myself from putting a protective arm around her and pulling her closer.

"Patience, Detective." Mistress Samantha gave me a stern look and adjusted her skirt with a brief rustle of leather. "I just want to give you a few tips before I send you into the lion's den. If you want to blend in with others in the lifestyle, you'll have to play your parts a good deal more convincingly than you did the other night."

"Fine." I settled back on the bench, prepared to listen. "What do you suggest we do differently?"

"You need to be a little less stiff with each other, for one thing." She gestured at us, sitting close but not touching on the bench. "A dominant needs to show ownership. Touch Alex like you own her, as though she was your most cherished possession."

I almost looked at my partner for permission and then caught myself—a real Dom wouldn't ask—he would be confident enough to know his advances were welcome. I pulled Alex close to me, as I had wanted to earlier, and was gratified to feel her melt against my side. She put her arms around my waist and pressed her cheek against the side of my chest, as though listening for my heart.

The Dominatrix looked at us for a moment and then nodded critically. "Good. Remember, the more you flaunt your ownership of your beautiful sub, the greater the challenge you convey. Now, a few ground rules for being a Dom or a sub." She looked at me first, ticking the points off on her slender, scarlet-tipped fingers.

"One—be quiet and patient with your sub. You look like you spent some time in the military, am I right, Detective?"

"Marines," I said.

"Good." She nodded. "Then I'm certain you remember your time in boot camp, and the drill instructors that trained you quite well."

I grinned despite myself. "I'm not likely to forget it."

"Good, now picture the toughest drill instructor you had—have you got it?"

I nodded.

"That," she said, leaning forward. "Is exactly what you *don't* want to be like as a Dom. So many men think that shouting and posturing are what it takes to assert your dominance when in fact, it's exactly the opposite. To be really effective you need to be quiet and controlled. Lay down the ground rules with your sub ahead of time and make it clear that if she breaks one there will be consequences. If she breaks a rule anyway, don't wimp out—give her the punishment you promised. Be tough but be fair—consistency is important.

"Now you." She turned to Alex who was watching silently with wide eyes. "The proper submissive is constantly aware of her dominant at all times. Be alert to his moods and in tune with his needs. Be aware that when you give him control of yourself that includes both your pleasure *and* your pain. If you disobey his rules, he has the right to punish you in the way he sees fit. Accept the punishment gratefully and gracefully and don't try to get out of it or second guess your Dom—that kind of behavior is called topping from the bottom, and it's generally frowned on in the community.

"Now, you may be wondering why I'm telling you all this when you're just going in for one night, pretending to be in the lifestyle when you're really not." Her gaze took in both of us now. "It's because to pull this off effectively, you have to believe it yourselves. You have to get into the right mindset—we in the scene call it 'head space.' You," she pointed at me, "have to be really dominant. You have to believe in your ownership of Alex. And you," she pointed at my partner, "have to be really submissive. Give yourself totally to Detective Berkley, acknowledge him as your Master. Obey him, and submit to him completely. Have you got it?"

I nodded and Alex murmured assent but Mistress Samantha looked unsatisfied. "What did you say?" she asked, a slight hint of menace in her tone.

"Yes, Mistress," Alex said, slightly louder.

"Yes, Mistress," I echoed. I still felt slightly ridiculous using the title, but it was coming more easily to me than it had at first.

"Good." She stood and dusted her hands together, obviously ready to get started. "I think we're ready to go, but there's one more thing. Melissa?" She nodded at her assistant who had been sitting quietly by, watching the lecture, and the girl stood and came forward, holding something in her hand. When she got closer, I could see that it was a slender leather collar, about an inch wide with a delicate silver buckle in back. The collar was made of the softest suede that felt smooth and supple. I knew because the assistant handed it not to her Mistress, but to me. I examined it closely, it was dyed a rich black and from it hung a heart-shaped ruby crystal about the size of a nickel.

"What's this?" I looked at the Dominatrix questioningly and she nodded at Alex.

"Your sub's collar. Put it on her, Detective Berkley. Claim her." She smiled at me, the expression never quite warming her sharp green eyes. From the corner of my eye, I saw Alex turning red. The collar must have a special significance I didn't quite understand.

I turned to my partner, feeling the softness of the leather band in my palm—no matter its significance, it would look beautiful around her slender throat. "Turn around and raise your hair," I said in a low voice, not asking but telling. A slight tremor ran through her, but she did as I commanded. Turning, she put her back to me and raised her thick fall of golden-brown hair submissively to bare the tender nape of her neck.

Besides breasts and legs and ass, which all men look at, I've always found a woman's throat to be very erotic. It's a sensitive area, vulnerable, especially if the hair is pulled up and it's bare. I read in a book once that the geishas in Japan deliberately leave a quarter inch at the back of their necks, just below the hairline, free of the thick white make-up they use, in order to tantalize prospective patrons. That kind of thing would definitely work on me.

Now as I fastened the butter-soft strip of suede around Alex's throat, I felt a surge of ownership and possessiveness I couldn't explain. Her skin was silky and pale, and her pulse skittered rapidly under my fingertips, letting me know I wasn't the only one this little performance was affecting. I spent a moment massaging her shoulders, and then I dared to lean down and place a soft kiss on her vulnerable nape, just under where the collar buckled. She made a soft gasp and would have turned to face me, but I held her in place, my hands on her shoulders, wanting to preserve the sense of pleasurable uncertainty just a moment longer.

She stilled under my touch and then leaned back, so that her shoulders were resting against my chest—a gesture of trust. Her unspoken submission was an almost palpable thing in the air between us. It sent a chill down my spine. If we let this go on, what might happen between us?

At last I let her go and whispered, "You can let your hair down now, Alex."

She did and turned to face me, a heated blush burning high on her cheeks.

"What do you say, Alex?" Mistress Samantha murmured, still watching from the sidelines.

"Thank you…" Alex took a deep breath and looked up at me, her brown eyes deep and wide and vulnerable. "Thank you, Master," she almost whispered.

"You're welcome," I said softly. The ruby heart dangled beautifully just at the hollow of her throat, and I had to fiercely suppress the urge to pull her close and take her mouth with my own. We were still on a case, I reminded myself. Better not get too far into the "head space" Mistress Samantha had spoken about. Or at least, not so far that we couldn't see our way out again and remember our number one goal—apprehension of the man who was very possibly our killer. It wouldn't do to forget that.

"Come on," I said softly, taking Alex's hand. "Let's go—it's time." This time Mistress Samantha didn't contradict me.

"All right—so we understand the plan?" I looked at Alex, shivering in the chilly air in the tiny leather outfit and felt another surge of protectiveness. She looked so defenseless, so vulnerable. And I still didn't like the fact that she wasn't armed.

"We'll go in, make a lap with you displaying your ownership of me very clearly." Alex's cheeks were red, whether from embarrassment or the cold, I couldn't tell. "Then you'll leave me alone by the bar, and we wait for our perp to show. Then we grab him."

"I just don't like leaving you alone unarmed. Be careful." I didn't intend to let her out of my line of vision for a second, but I still didn't like the idea of using my partner for bait to lure out a possible serial killer.

Alex sighed. "I'll be fine, Cole. But look—I think we might be able to do even better than just nabbing him. Give me some time with him before you jump in. Maybe I can get him to talk a little."

"We'll see," I growled. "If he starts manhandling you, I'm coming in."

She sighed again. "In case you've forgotten, I can take care of myself."

I grinned at her. "I never said you couldn't. I just don't want anybody messing with my property." I reached out to brush a strand of hair out of her serious brown eyes, but she ducked my hand, her cheeks growing even redder.

"Don't."

"Don't what?" I asked her, mystified.

"Don't joke like that." She dropped her eyes, her hands twisting nervously in front of her.

"Hey, who says I'm joking?" I lifted her chin and brushed her lips lightly with my own. "For luck," I said.

Alex looked down, still not meeting my eyes. "I'm freezing out here—let's go do this, okay?"

"You got it." I slid my hand down to the small of her back, cupping her body heat in my palm, and guided her toward the entrance of the club. Usually this gesture seemed to calm her down but tonight I could feel her trembling under my touch, her bare skin smooth and soft against the pads of my fingers.

The Liar's Club is one of the few free-standing structures in the Ybor City strip. Most of the other buildings are connected in some way, leaning like elderly, tired drunks against each other, wall to wall, one solid line of grayish-brown grime lit from within by garish neon lights. But the Liar's Club is located in the husk of what used to be one of the largest cigar rolling factories in town, and it stands a little apart from the rest of Tampa's party district, its grayish-white walls rising like a monolith in the gloom.

I could hear the steady beat of techno music coming from inside. Outside the large double doors, a tall black bouncer/doorman wearing nothing but a brief pair of leather shorts and a red Santa hat was standing watch. Alex and I joined the line to get in, and I was glad that Mistress Samantha had taken the time to see that we were briefed. It was clear the bouncer wasn't letting anyone who didn't look and act like they belonged on the scene into the club.

A few spaces ahead of us in line were a couple of college kids wearing University of Tampa sweatshirts and jeans. They looked like typical jocks; one had sandy blond hair and the other was dark. When they got to the door, the bouncer shook his head and scowled. "Please—you expect to get in here dressed like that? I don't *think* so." He tossed his head, and the bell on the end of his Santa hat jingled brightly in the crisp air.

"What? What's wrong with how we're dressed?" the blond kid demanded angrily.

"We supposed to dress like *you?*" The dark-haired kid made the question an insult.

"If you want to get in here, honey. Club rules—nobody vanilla sets foot inside tonight." The bouncer drew himself up to full height, which was considerable, and looked down his nose at the two kids. "Now, I suggest you run along."

The dark-haired UT student spat on the sidewalk. "C'mon, Mark, let's go catch the action down at Club Joy." To the bouncer he sneered, "*Fag.*"

"And proud of it, honey. Merry Christmas to you, too. Next." The bouncer looked for the next person in line, completely unruffled. He probably had to put up with worse than a few insults on a typical Friday night in Ybor.

The next two couples in line passed inspection and then the couple right in front of us were turned away for being "too vanilla." I was beginning to get worried about my own state of dress. Alex certainly looked the part, but I was just wearing black dress slacks with my red shirt and a black leather vest. Hardly hard-core bondage material. I should have taken off my shirt and left the leather vest on to let my tattoos show, but that would have meant wearing the shoulder harness for my gun against bare skin which chafes like a son of a bitch.

When we reached the bouncer, I did my best to look cool as he gave us the once over. If we had to resort to flashing our badges to get in, our cover would be blown before we walked through the front door.

"Well, well, aren't you a lovely lady?" He was speaking to Alex, who dropped her eyes and blushed modestly.

"Thanks," I said, taking credit for her beauty as though I had every right.

The bouncer looked up at me, lip curling slightly. "And aren't you a big, strapping motherfucker," he said, giving me the eye. "Dressed kind of plain tonight, aren't you? It's a shame you don't match your pretty little lady." He turned back to Alex. "Maybe you should just go on in by yourself, sweet thing. Find yourself a man who dresses a little sharper."

"Please." Alex looked up at the bouncer, taking one of my hands in both of hers. "I don't want to find anyone else and besides, I can't go in without my Master. He'd *punish* me."

"Oh, he would, would he?" The bouncer looked at me with new eyes. "Mmm, and I just bet he can hand out some pretty stiff punishments too."

"You have no idea," I growled, looming over him. He was a big guy, but I was bigger. I usually am.

"I might like to find out, though." He smirked at me and then blew out a breath. "Oh, all right—you can come in since it's Christmas time. Don't want anybody saying I'm a Grinch."

"Thank you." Alex smiled at him and tugged me into the club before the verbally abusive bouncer could change his mind.

"Well, here we are," I said under my breath as we mingled with the leather-clad crowd filling the large open room that comprised the main dance floor. "Good thinking with the whole punishment thing," I added.

She ducked her head. "Thanks."

The club was decorated, not surprisingly, in black, and the thumping beat of the music seemed to jump in time with my heartbeat. There had been some half-hearted attempts at Christmas decorations but the few strings of silver tinsel and glowing lights couldn't detract from the charged atmosphere. Everyone seemed to have piercings and tattoos, and I wished again that I'd left off the shirt and let my own ink show. We wandered around for a moment, and I noticed that there were various rooms leading off from the main area, all of which we would have to look into, as I didn't see our suspect anywhere in the crowd.

"You're new here, aren't you?" I turned to see a tiny elf of a woman clad in black leather with a whip curled at her side. Her frosted hair was spiked into points, and her eyes were taking us in greedily.

"We just moved to the Bay area," I said, taking a firmer grip on Alex's hand. "We thought we'd check out the scene down here, but it's our first time to this club."

"I'm Clair." She held out a hand so small it felt like a doll's inside my own. I pumped firmly twice before letting go—not too friendly. She didn't offer to shake hands with Alex.

"I'm Cole, and this is my sub, Alex," I indicated my partner a bit awkwardly.

"Excellent." Her smile included both of us this time. "So, would you like to play?"

"Um…" I shook my head, not certain of what to say. I wasn't sure what this woman's definition of "playing" was, but I was pretty sure I didn't want to find out. Of course, I didn't want to blow our cover, either.

"I'm sorry, maybe that was a bit sudden. It's just that your sub is so luscious." She fingered the whip at her side and the look she gave my partner managed to reduce Alex to a sexual snack. I stepped in front of her, putting myself between them and shook my head.

"She's new—I'm still showing her the ropes so I'm afraid I can't share." I shrugged, trying to look genuinely regretful. "Sorry."

"That's all right." She nodded at me, the smile never leaving her face. "I'm a switch—think you can handle me?"

A switch? I remembered the term from Mistress Samantha's questionnaire, but I still wasn't completely positive as to its meaning. But this Clair person seemed to be asking if I thought I could dominate her—I decided to bluff. I took a step closer and looked down at her, using my height to advantage.

"Oh, I know I could handle you, little girl. The question is, do I want to?" I gave her my nastiest grin and had the satisfaction of seeing her pale, just a little. Well, not quite as self-confident as she wanted to appear, then. It was a good thing since I didn't have any idea what to do if she took me up on the veiled threat.

"Maybe you'd like a tour of the club while you decide?" She crossed her arms under tiny pointed breasts and looked up at me.

I almost turned to get Alex's reaction before I caught myself. As the "Dom" here, I would be making all the decisions, not asking my "sub" what she thought. "That would be great," I said, gesturing for her to lead the way. Maybe we would see our suspect as we looked.

"Come on, then." She turned and wove her way into the crowd, heading for one of the smaller, dark rooms to our right. I grabbed Alex's hand again and pulled her along. I didn't want to risk losing her in this freak show.

"This is the Lesbifriends room," our guide said, pulling aside a black curtain and gesturing into the small, dark space where several leather-clad bodies were writhing together. A pair of faces looked up at me from the gloom, both pretty, with cat-like eyes, dilated from the dark. Maroon lipstick smeared both their mouths, and it was impossible to say which one of them had been wearing it in the first place. Obviously our guy was not going to be in here.

"Nice, isn't it?" Clair gave my partner another longing look before she let the curtain drop back into place. Apparently she was a switch in more than one way. She led us along the wall until we came to another curtained-off room. From inside I could hear a flat smacking sound and a low, masculine groan.

"What's this?" I looked at our guide, and she smirked and drew back the curtain.

"This is the Naughty Boy room. It's where your Mistress takes you if you need a punishment or a spanking."

As my eyes adjusted to the gloom, I could see a man about my size chained naked to the wall. Luckily, his back was to us. Standing in front of him was a woman even smaller than Clair, holding a large, wicked-looking black paddle in one hand. It was padded black leather with holes drilled in it to cut the air resistance. There were red marks all over the man's back and…other areas I really didn't want to see. The main thing was that the man had no beard or the telling tattoo—not our suspect. As we watched, the petite pixy of a woman hauled back and really let him have it with the paddle. His body jerked as though he'd been given a jolt of electric current, and he groaned again, more loudly. I was relieved when Clair let the curtain fall.

The next and final room on the right side of the dance floor was the Orgy room. The reek of sweat and other bodily fluids hung heavy in the air and a tangle of half naked flesh of both sexes writhed on several futons that had been pushed together and thoughtfully covered in rubber sheets. It was hard to tell, but I was fairly certain our suspect wasn't in the room, unless, of course, he was at the very bottom of the pile.

"This doesn't look very…safe," I said, gesturing to the mingling of body parts.

Clair pointed to a small table on my left. "Condoms, lube, and dental dams right there. Everybody here plays safe," she assured me. "Interested?"

I shook my head, trying to look intrigued although I was anything but. "Uh…not right now."

She shrugged. "Okay, let's finish the tour."

The back wall of the massive open area was taken up with the DJ's equipment and the music was nearly deafening as we walked past it, through the crowd of dancers, to the other side of the room.

"Now this room I *know* you'll be interested in." Clair drew back the black curtain to reveal several benches lining the walls. Various devices hung from pegs on the back wall, including a large variety of hairbrushes, which seemed strange. I wondered if this room was for hair fetishists.

"What is this?" I asked.

Clair walked across to the back wall and took a large, silver handled brush down from its peg. She slapped the back of it hard, into the palm of her hand and grinned at me. "One guess, my friend." Suddenly the use of the brushes became clear.

"Excuse me." A short, barrel-chested man, with a handlebar mustache, wearing leather pants and not much else came past us into the room, holding a tall blond woman firmly by one arm. He grabbed a hairbrush, sat on one of the benches, in plain view of us, and pulled the woman over his lap so that her ass was facing in our direction.

I started to leave but Clair stopped me with a shake of her head. "Stay—it might do your pretty little sub some good to see what goes on in this room."

"All right." I pulled Alex around in front of me and put her back to my chest, the same way we'd been standing when I put her collar on. She'd been following me around as silent as a ghost, being the proper subservient sub, I supposed. I had been so busy scanning for our suspect I hadn't even considered how all this must be affecting her. Now as we watched the mustached man pull up the blond woman's skirt, I could feel my partner trembling against me. Was she trembling with fear or desire…or both?

"Claudette, you've been a very…very…naughty…girl." Mustache punctuated each word with a slap from the back of the hairbrush. The woman in his lap writhed and made high, sexual noises. She didn't have any panties on, and I could see that the "punishment" was turning her on. Alex flinched against me each time the hairbrush connected with the blond's ass, which was soon glowing like a sunset. I watched with a kind of horrified fascination. He wasn't hitting her lightly—this was obviously a serious punishment. But she was loving every minute of it.

The scene couldn't fail to remind me of the way Alex had submitted so readily to the caning Mistress Samantha had administered in her dungeon. I wondered if this was what she wanted, for me to drag her over my knee and punish her soundly. And if she did want it, could I do it? I imagined myself pulling up her skirt and baring her softly rounded ass, imagined the feel of her writhing in my lap, vulnerable and full of need. I could almost hear her soft moans as I punished her, could almost taste her panting lips against my own…

I became aware that the volley of blows had increased and with it, the pitch and intensity of the blond woman's cries. From the way she was moving and gasping, it was clear that she was reaching some kind of completion. Could she have an orgasm simply from being spanked? If not she was putting on a damn good show.

I couldn't help picturing Alex in that state. I realized suddenly that I was hard as a railroad spike, and I was pulling my partner back against me, pressing myself against her leather-clad ass. I had a sudden, blinding urge to reach under the brief, tight skirt and touch her, to see if this display was making her as hot as it was me. But it wasn't watching the blond woman get punished that was turning me on—it was imagining doing the same thing to Alex.

The realization was like a wake-up call. I stepped back and away from my partner, disturbed at the turn my thoughts had taken. Did I really want to do that to her? She looked back at me, her big brown eyes wide and drowning deep, and I saw a need there that matched my own. Was this turning me on because I wanted to please her, to do what she wanted? Or was a darker, more twisted part of my psyche that I had never dared to explore, perhaps never even dreamed existed, rearing its head in this strange place?

Alex turned back to the couple who had finished their performance. Mustache pulled down the blond woman's skirt and pushed her gently off his lap. He reached up to re-hang the hairbrush and then turned her to face us. Her fair skin was red and tears wetted her cheeks but her face was serene—as calm as one of those marble statues of the Virgin Mary you see in cemeteries and Catholic churches.

"Thank the nice people for witnessing your punishment, Claudette," the man instructed her.

She didn't hesitate a bit. "Thank you for watching my Master punish me," she said in a soft, low voice that belied the high-pitched cries we'd heard just moments before. I didn't answer. This, more than the whipping itself, disturbed me. That he should make her thank us for watching her humiliation and degradation… It was too much.

"You're very welcome, Claudette." Clair, who I had almost completely forgotten, patted the blond woman's cheek and smiled at her. "I wouldn't mind punishing you myself sometime."

Mustache grinned at her. "If you're serious, we're headed for the whipping post next. I always like to get her warmed up and in the mood for some real punishment first."

Real punishment? The whole thing with the hairbrush had been just a warm-up? I glanced at Alex to see what she thought of this but her face was impassive.

Clair turned to me. "You want to watch?"

I shrugged, not sure how to get out of it. "All right." We followed Mustache and Clair who were talking and Claudette who was trailing behind her Master like a faithful blond terrier. I heard Mustache talking to Clair, who was fingering her whip eagerly.

"You have to go a little easy on Claudette with the whip—she's back shy. Some asshole wannabe worked her over too hard with a crop before I met her. She's especially sensitive between the shoulder blades."

"No problem, I can concentrate on the ass," I heard Clair reply easily. Claudette, who could surely hear their plans as well as I could, kept a serene little smile on her face the whole time. It was bizarre, but then, the whole place was.

I tried to ignore the conversation ahead of us and keep an eye out for our suspect while we made our way to the far room where, apparently, the whipping post was located. On the way we passed by another curtained area where exclusively masculine groans were drifting from behind the black drape. Remembering the Lesbifriends room across the dance floor, I was pretty certain what was going on inside and breathed a sigh of relief that our guided tour didn't include this particular room.

"Well, it looks like we came at a good time—the post is free." Clair looked very pleased as we ducked into the slightly larger room at the end of the wall. There were several couples standing around, waiting, I guessed, to see someone get whipped. Clair and Mustache were already fastening Claudette face first to a cross like the one Mistress Samantha had in her dungeon.

"Cole!" Alex was standing in front of me, and I felt her sharp elbow connect with my stomach.

"What?" I leaned down, pretending to nibble on her neck, trying to speak inconspicuously. Her hair smelled like flowers and felt like silk.

"Two o'clock," she hissed, jerking her chin toward the far corner of the whipping post room.

I looked up and saw a shaggy, bearded face staring back at us from the shadows. His attention was divided between Claudette, being strapped to the cross, and my partner. But increasingly, his eyes seemed more drawn to Alex than to the blond sub in front of us. He was wearing a leather vest with nothing underneath it, and I could barely make out what looked like a tattoo on his right upper arm. There was barbed wire, all right, but we were too far away to read the words inked above it. My gut was telling me this was the guy.

"He's staring at you," I whispered. I lifted the hair from the side of her neck and began to kiss her throat, long, slow, hot kisses, tasting her salty/sweet flavor and making her squirm against me.

"What are you doing?" she gasped under her breath. Her hips twitched back and her ass pressed against my groin.

"Keeping his attention." I nipped her earlobe sharply, then sucked it to take away the sting. "Look at him, make eye contact while I touch you—while I *claim* you."

She stared into the dark corner obligingly while I ran my hands up and down her arms and thighs. I let my fingers travel over the full swells of her breasts and then cupped them from behind, pushing the creamy mounds up and out—an offering, an invitation.

It was a come-on—I was deliberately trying to draw our perp out. But it was more than that, too. Touching her, tasting the soft skin of her throat, I wanted her so badly I could hardly see straight. The roles we were playing began to mix with reality, running together like the colors in a child's finger-painting.

"Cole..." She shivered helplessly while I touched her and sucked her neck. She was so sweet, so utterly delicious that I almost forgot why we were doing this. It was easier just to let the possessive emotions take over. "*Cole*," she gasped again.

"What did you call me?" I growled in her ear, running my palms down her flat stomach to her inner thighs. I wanted to feel the heat between her legs, wanted to know that she was utterly helpless under my hands. Maybe Alex wanted the same.

"Master," she whispered, her voice breaking just a little. "Master, please..."

I withdrew from her a little, although I didn't want to. What I wanted was to push her up against the nearest wall, rip up her skirt and take her in front of everyone. I pushed the urge away, ignoring the ache in my balls. We were on a case, we had an objective to accomplish, I reminded myself. And besides, she was my partner. Not my lover—my *partner.*

"Come on." I grabbed her hand and dragged her out of the room, fairly certain that our bearded suspect would follow. Near the end of our little performance, his eyes had been glued to Alex, completely ignoring the spectacle of Claudette preparing to be whipped.

"What...?" She stumbled after me as I pushed my way to the long, sticky black marble bar in the center of the room. I ordered two whiskey sours, keeping my back to the room we had just vacated. Around us the music pulsed and throbbed and people swayed and shoved and visited the different rooms. The smell of leather and sweat and other things was strong in the air. But all I could smell or feel or taste was Alex. Again I pushed the need for her away and tried to concentrate on the case.

"Is he back there?" I spoke out of the corner of my mouth, still keeping a possessive hand on Alex's arm.

She ducked her head and looked back. "I see him against the wall, he's staring in our direction."

"Good." The drinks arrived, and I took a gulp of mine, feeling the burn all the way down, and pressed hers into her hand. "I'm going to leave now, but I'll be keeping you in sight, all right?"

"Got it," she whispered back, her lips barely moving. "Give me a little time to get him interested before you come back."

"He's already interested," I told her. I cupped her cheek and turned her face up to mine, taking her sweet red lips in a possessive kiss. She melted against me, and I almost didn't have the strength to pull away. If I didn't really watch myself, this was going to get out of hand. Our professional relationship was already shot to hell, but I didn't want to lose her friendship, too—if I still had it at all.

I made myself pull back. "I'll be watching," I said, as a parting shot. Then I left the bar and walked purposefully in the direction of the men's room. Once I got lost in the crowd, I turned, putting the wall to my back, and watched the action I had left behind.

It didn't take our suspect a full minute to take the seat I had just vacated. He moved in on Alex like a lion stalking an antelope in the Serengeti. I saw him lean in, talking to her, obviously trying to convince her of something. Alex was looking up at him from under those long lashes of hers. She was doing her "little girl lost" act which is so effective until the suspect realizes she's got him by the balls. But this time she wasn't armed, and he was easily twice her size—almost as tall as me, just like Montero told us.

The suspect said something else and reached up to touch Alex's cheek. She ducked away, still playing shy, and he grabbed her wrist instead. I felt a surge of angry possessiveness and moved closer. The bracelets of bruises that I had put on her myself were fading but still visible—now his meaty hand covered them completely. Covered my marks. His bicep flexed, and I could see the words, "I Like it Raw" in blue ink clearly above the barbed wire. This was our guy all right, and he had his hands all over *my* partner. It was going to be a pleasure to take him down.

I moved even closer, coming up from his blind side, watching the action through a red haze. His hands were still all over Alex, pawing her, and inside my head a low, snarling voice was saying, *Mine, she's mine, asshole!* I was just about to grab his shoulder and yank him away from her when Alex caught my eye and gave her head a slight shake of negation. I paused, momentarily confused. What was she up to?

"Punishment?" she asked, in that trembling, little girl voice. "I don't understand. My Master—"

"Your Master can't work you the way I can, baby." His voice was low and nasally, like Robert DeNiro with a head cold. It took every ounce of my willpower not to grab him by the back of his leather vest and yank him backward off the high bar seat.

"I don't even know you. How do I know you'd be as good as my Master?" Alex looked at him wide-eyed, not making any attempt to free her wrist from his grip. She somehow managed to convey fear and intrigue at the same time.

"You want to know if I'm experienced, baby? Let me show you a little bit about myself." He drew her closer, obviously about to make lip-lock and though Alex struggled, she didn't make any use of the hand-to-hand training I knew she had. That in itself told me she thought we might get more out of Mr. "I Like it Raw" if we worked the scene right, and I trusted her judgment. So when I broke them up before the kiss could really get started, it was her shoulder I grabbed, not our suspect's.

"Goddammit, can't I even leave you alone for five minutes before you start flirting with another man?" I yanked on Alex's shoulder, pulling her back before our suspect could get make any real contact. "Well, what do you have to say for yourself?"

She looked at me, big eyes filling with fear. "I'm sorry, Master. Please, I didn't see you…"

"Shut up," I barked, deliberately being the drill-sergeant Mistress Samantha had advised against. I had a feeling this was the kind of "Master" our suspect liked to play, and I thought it would be the best way to establish a rapport. I turned to him, still keeping a punishing grip on Alex's shoulder.

"You'll have to excuse my sub—she's always looking for attention. Or maybe…" I pulled Alex closer. "You're looking for a punishment. Is that it, Alex?"

"Master, *please*," she gasped again.

"Quiet, Alex." I turned to our suspect and held out a hand. "Name's Cole. I'm sorry this little bitch came on to you like that."

He took my hand warily. "Tony Cullen."

I threaded the fingers of my right hand through Alex's hair and yanked backward, exposing the pale length of her slender throat. "It's almost like she wants me to catch her," I told Cullen, who was looking at us from under bushy black eyebrows. "You ever have a sub like that?"

"Sure." He had been tense at first, obviously bracing for a fight. But now that I was putting all the blame on Alex, he seemed more relaxed. "Sure, I've had subs like that. The kind that can't get enough." He stroked his beard and smirked at her.

Of course I was hoping for some specific details but he didn't seem inclined to say anything else. I wondered how I could get him talking—bragging really, about his past exploits. If we worked this right, we might even get him to convict himself. It would save a hell of a lot of trouble if he handed himself over in a neat little package. Kind of an early Christmas present.

"Master, please. Please don't…"

I turned my attention to Alex, still held in the stiff, neck-stretching posture by my punishing grip on her hair. There was something in her big brown eyes—a spark, maybe a plan. Knowing she had to be thinking along the same lines I was, I decided to play along.

"What do you want, Alex? I shouldn't even allow you to speak. You're in the presence of two Doms—your only function should be to shut up and serve." I shook her once for emphasis.

"Master, I just wanted to apologize. I…I was wrong and I'm sorry. But please…please don't punish me. At least not…" She swallowed, fear filling her eyes. "At least not in front of him."

"Shut up!" I shook her again, giving myself time to think. I knew what my partner was doing—trying to get me to whip her or punish her in front of the suspect. She had a point—sharing an experience like that would form a bond and probably make him feel free to open up and brag about his past. But I wasn't sure I wanted to do it, even to catch our killer. With the lines of reality and fantasy blurring between us, I just wasn't sure if I was ready to go there with her. Frankly, I wasn't sure if I'd ever be ready. It all came back to the question I had been asking myself ever since I began to understand what she needed sexually—could I hurt her if I had to? If she needed me to?

"Master, I'm begging you." Alex let her eyes fill with tears, and I reflected that she was a damn fine actress when she wanted to be. Or were the tears real? Could she want me to do this and yet fear it at the same time? She hadn't begged for a beating when we visited Mistress Samantha the first time— she'd simply submitted to it without all the pleading and crying that was going on now.

"Ya know." Our suspect leaned closer. "It's been my experience that the more they beg you not to, the more they need a good whuppin'." One look in his blank, black eyes, and I knew I'd have to go through with this scenario, like it or not. Alex's instincts were right on the money with this guy—if I could get him interested in what we were doing, he'd talk.

"You're right." I dragged Alex off the high stool (by her arm, not her hair) and steered her toward the room with all the hairbrushes. I turned my head and nodded at Cullen. "You coming? I think she needs an audience to make this lesson stick."

"Wouldn't miss it." He slid off his stool and followed us, still grinning under those bushy brows. It occurred to me that this guy must have established a fair amount of control over the women that had been killed in order to get them to open the door to him in the middle of the night. He was definitely what Alex would have called "creepy" what with the bushy beard and eyebrows. He had the whole Manson vibe going on.

Our little parade between the bar and the punishment room didn't even raise any eyebrows. Apparently this kind of thing was accepted behavior here at the Liar's Club. Yet another reason to avoid it in the future.

I dragged Alex into the curtained room, relieved to see that it was currently unoccupied, and then stood there, gripping her arm, uncertain how to begin. Should I drag her across my knee and raise her skirt as Mustache had with his blond sub? But I didn't want to do that, didn't want to expose her that way to the sick pervert that was coming to watch the show. And besides, such an action seemed too intimate—dangerous somehow. Cullen was right behind us, and I had to make up my mind fast.

Alex seemed to understand my problem. As the curtain twitched aside and Cullen entered the room, she began twisting in my grip and begging again. "Please, Master, not the belt. Don't use your belt on me!"

I stared at her and fingered the black leather belt at my waist. Could she be serious? She wanted me to use the belt? Was this her answer to my no-paddling problem, or did she genuinely desire such a whipping? Not for the first time that night I thought that this particular undercover assignment would be a hell of a lot easier if I didn't know about my partner's hidden sexual appetites.

"Not the belt!" Alex begged again. Behind us, Cullen smirked.

"Like I said—whatever they don't want is most likely what they need."

"You really know your stuff," I said, trying to make my voice admiring. Feeling slightly sick, I pushed Alex face first against the wall. "Assume the position," I barked.

Alex spread her arms and legs like a suspect waiting to be frisked and leaned her forehead against a clear space on the wall. The red leather skirt pulled taut against her ass. She was breathing raggedly and again, I couldn't tell if she was acting or if this was really affecting her.

With fingers that felt numb and fumbling, I unbuckled my belt and slid it free of the loops with a small hiss of leather against fabric. I grabbed the buckle firmly in one hand—no way in hell was I going to hit her with that—and looped it several times around my fist.

I swung the remaining length of belt experimentally, letting it just lick against the back of her legs. There was a small strip of bare skin on her thighs where the high black boot ended and the short leather skirt began. The belt fell there, not hard, but she seemed to feel the impact all the same because she hissed and flinched.

"Tell me, Alex, why am I doing this?" I said, and swung the belt again, harder this time.

"Because...because..." She seemed unable to finish and I licked her with the belt again.

"Speak up so Master Cullen can hear as well," I commanded, playing on our suspect's ego. I let the belt fall again, right across her ass and considerably harder this time. Alex flinched and pressed her ass outwards, almost as though she was asking for more.

"Because I was bad. Because I flirted with another man, Master." She gasped as I whipped her again.

"And what happens when you're bad that way, Alex?" I demanded, swinging again, this time aiming for the tops of her thighs. As she leaned forward, the short skirt rose even higher, and I was treated to the sight of the soft under-curves of her ass. Either she wasn't wearing panties tonight or she was wearing a thong—I couldn't tell in the dim room. The sight of her bare ass sent a surge of heat to my groin I couldn't ignore. I swung the belt again, getting into the rhythm now, and aiming for those tender curves of exposed flesh.

"Answer me!" I demanded.

"When I'm bad you whip me." Alex was almost moaning now, and I thought this had to be affecting her. Even she wasn't that good an actress—was she? The problem was, it was affecting me, too. With every swing of the belt, with every soft moan and whimper I forced from between her lips, I was getting harder. I swung again, hearing the flat slap of leather against flesh, and she cried out, a soft, sexual sound that came from deep in her throat.

"And why do I whip you, Alex?" I asked, making my voice low and harsh. Her bare flesh was red now, criss-crossed with the marks of the belt. I wasn't holding back—I was really whipping her—giving her what she had asked for. Maybe what she needed.

"Oh!" she gasped as I swung the belt again. "Because I deserve it, Master. Because the only way I learn is through punishment."

"That's right." I swung the belt again, but this time I deliberately aimed for the soft, open area between her legs. The belt licked up and kissed her sex with a sharp snap. Alex cried out, her knees buckling as she collapsed against the wall.

I threw down the belt and grabbed her around the waist, feeling half-crazy with lust and anger. I forgot all about Cullen, still watching the show, and covered her smaller frame with my body, shielding and supporting her. How was it that she had gotten me to do this to her? And how was it that we had both enjoyed it? *Had* she really enjoyed it? I needed to know.

"Master, please..." Her voice was weak and faint, meant for my ears alone.

"Alex, you've been so bad. You deserve a lot more than this," I whispered, rubbing my shaft hard against her ass to let her know exactly what she deserved. I held her around the waist with one arm and reached down with my other hand to pull up her skirt. I touched the soft skin of her inner thighs, needing to know what she felt beyond the shadow of a doubt.

My seeking fingers encountered a wet warmth, and she gasped and jerked against me. I pulled back, but I knew what I needed to know—the cries and moans hadn't been all for our suspect's benefit. Alex was wet...as wet as she'd been that first night in the dungeon of the Dominatrix. I closed my eyes briefly and tried to get hold of myself. I felt like I could fuck a hole through a concrete wall.

"She's a hot one, all right." Cullen's voice pulled me out of my own private rush of thoughts and emotions and forced me into the present. His tone was definitely interested. We had him hooked—now to reel him in.

"Yeah, she's hot—hard to control." I tried to make my voice steady and even. I made certain that Alex could stand on her own and then turned to face him, keeping myself between her and our suspect, giving her time to straighten her skirt and regain her composure. "I guess you've had experience with this kind of sub. Maybe you can give me some pointers?"

"Sure." He stepped forward eagerly. "I kinda favor using a whip or a crop over the belt though."

"Oh, uh...I think she's had enough for right now—she's still pretty new to the whole scene," I said apologetically. "But why don't you let me buy you a drink, and you can tell me what you know. We can play again later." I looked over my shoulder, giving Alex a leer. "You hear that, baby? Something for you to look forward to." And then to Cullen, "I like her to anticipate the pain—keeps her in peak condition."

"Mind games, I like that." He grinned back at me, stroking the beard. "If there's one thing I've learned it's that you got to dominate the mind as well as the body."

"Come to the bar and tell me." I opened the curtain and ushered him out, trusting Alex to follow us. "I want to hear all about it."

Chapter Twenty-Six

Alex

"You're going to tell me what I want to know, you scum-sucking son of a bitch!" Cole slammed our suspect, Tony Cullen, up against the wall of the interrogation room with enough force to make the one-way glass rattle in its pane. I started to go in and try to calm him down and then decided to wait and see how the situation played out.

I hadn't seen my partner this upset since we'd apprehended the man who'd raped and murdered a twelve-year-old girl two years before. The perp had left her body in a rain-filled ditch, effectively washing away all DNA evidence. We knew it was him but we couldn't prove it—not beyond a reasonable doubt—not without a confession. Cole got one using the same methods he was using now on Tony Cullen. He worked on the guy until he gave it up. My partner can be very persuasive when he wants to so I decided to sit back and let him persuade.

"You got him?" Captain Davis was suddenly at my elbow. Although we'd called her from home, it was clear she hadn't been getting any sleep. Her graying curls were in wild disarray and there were bags Samsonite would have been proud of under her bloodshot eyes.

"We think so," I said cautiously, not wanting to get her hopes up too far. "We did the whole routine at the club, got his interest, got him talking…" I trailed off, feeling my cheeks heat when I remembered exactly how far Cole and I had gone to hook our suspect.

"And?" She looked at me impatiently.

"Sorry. And he gave us a few juicy tidbits about some of our vics. Seems he knew all of them in one way or another and he claimed to have had, uh, sexual encounters with all of them, too. Of course, now he's singing a different tune." I nodded through the one-way and pulled Cole's jacket tight around me, as much for the amount of skin it covered as for warmth.

I was glad for the jacket, which Cole had draped across my shoulders before we went into the PD. There had been no time to return the kinky red-leather bondage outfit to Mistress Samantha in the middle of the bust, and I was pretty much resigned to wearing it until I got home. But that didn't mean I wanted my superior officer to see me dressed like this. Another thump and rattle of the one-way glass focused my attention back to the situation at hand.

"Looks like your partner is in full avenging angel mode," Captain Davis commented dryly.

"Yeah—Cole wants this guy bad, and the way he was talking at the club…" I shrugged. "We like him for all three murders, Captain. Like him a lot."

"Tell me again how you knew Lauren Schaefer," Cole demanded, still pressing Cullen hard against the wall.

"I told you, man, I met her in the club, and she wanted to interview me for some kinda book she was writin'. That's *all*."

"No, that's not all." Cole slammed him into the wall again. "Back at the club you told me that she was your bitch, Cullen, your *slave*. You said she'd do anything you wanted and come begging for more. Now tell me, you sick fuck, did she beg to be murdered?"

"Whoa—hey, man, I done told you—I don't know nothin' about that! All that other stuff I told you, that was just braggin'. Just macho bullshit—everybody does it. Don't mean I killed her." Cullen's black eyes widened, and he hunched his shoulders.

"Doesn't mean you didn't, either." Cole pulled him by the lapels of his greasy black leather vest and slammed him down in a chair. "Look at these." He stabbed an accusing finger at the autopsy photos of all three victims, spread out like a macabre deck of playing cards on the rough wooden table top. "Do any of these look familiar?"

"I seen all of 'em at the club at one time or another, but that's *all*," Cullen insisted. "Swear to God, man, that's all I know."

"Your guy seems to be sticking to his guns." Captain Davis ran a hand through her bushy hair.

I nodded. "Yeah, I'm surprised he hasn't lawyered up yet."

"What about alibis?"

"Fuzzy at best," I assured her. "We know he was at a party at the Liar's Club the night Cynthia Harner was murdered because several people saw him there. But we don't know what time he left—we think he followed her home. He claims he was with friends in a pool hall on South Howard the night Sarah Michaels was killed, got uniforms checking that, and he claims to have been at the club again until four the night of Lauren Schaefer's death."

She pursed her lips. "That's awfully late for a club to be open on a week night."

"That's what we thought," I said. "Which is why we're also checking it out."

"So it looks good. I don't mind telling you, Reed, that my ass is on the line here. The mayor's been calling for hourly reports and the press…forget the press, it's a nightmare. If this is the guy it could really save our bacon."

I nodded. "Let's wait and see how the alibis check out, but so far it looks good." I ticked the points off on my fingers. "He knows or claims to have known all the vics, he's in the BDSM scene here in the Bay area, and he's got three priors for aggravated assault and battery. And, as a bonus, we happened to find a condom on him that was lubricated with the same type of lube found in all the vics. It's a common brand, but still…"

Davis nodded. "Yeah—every little bit helps." She clapped me on the shoulder. "Proud of you, Reed—and Berkley, too. You two have been working your asses off on this one."

"Yes, ma'am, just hope it pays off." Just then my cell rang. I fumbled through Cole's pockets to find it and finally yanked it out and open. "Reed here."

"Hey, Detective." The voice was familiar—Mac McMurtry, one of the uniforms I'd sent out with our suspect's picture to check alibis while Cole and I worked him. Mac was a good guy, a career cop due for retirement in a few more years and one of the most conscientious policemen I'd ever known.

"Hey, McMurtry, tell me the good news."

"Wish I could, Detective." His voice sounded regretful and my hand tightened on the phone.

"Ah, come on. Don't tell me."

"Well, seems your guy has a talent for getting himself noticed. 'Course, with the beard and the tattoo, that ain't hard. On the night of the first murder he was at the club 'til it closed. The bouncer remembers him 'cause he practically had to kick 'im out."

"So that was when...?" I asked hopefully.

"'Round about four, four-thirty a.m. I asked why the club stayed open so late but apparently they don't have a set closing time. They stay open as long as there's enough people, uh, 'playing' I think they called it, to make it worth their while."

"No chance he could have left and come back, made a scene to attract attention and establish an alibi?" I asked, still hopeful.

There was a rustling of paperwork on the other end as McMurtry checked his notes. "Uh, nope, no dice. The bartender remembers your guy, too. Said he was a fixture for most of the night, gettin' drunker and drunker and tryin' to pick up women, but none of 'em took the bait."

"All right." I sighed. "What about the other two nights?"

"Well, turns out on the thirteenth he really was at a pool hall—Johnny Be Good's on Howard that was—'til round about two a.m. Owner remembers him and his good-time buddies 'cause he finally had to kick 'em out to close the joint. He said it looked like they were gonna go hit a few more bars down the road, and he didn't think your guy, Cullen, was in any condition to kill anything but another beer, if that."

"He was pretty soused, huh?"

"Completely shit-faced according to the owner. Uh, excuse my French, Detective."

I sighed again. "That's okay, McMurtry, your language doesn't offend me. I just wish you had better news."

"Me, too," he said glumly. "We all want this guy caught. Hell, I got a daughter same age as that second vic, that Sarah Michaels, and she just moved out not a month ago. Wants to try gettin' by on her own." He sighed deeply.

"That's a rough age," I said sympathetically. "Berkley and I are doing everything we can to nab this guy." I ran a hand through my hair. "Well, just for the record, where was our guy on the night of the last murder?"

"Same as the first—at that damn freaky club all night long. Stayed 'til closing again, around four. You know what I'd do if I caught my daughter at a place like that? I'd turn her over my knee and give her a whippin' she wouldn't never forget."

I had to bite the inside of my cheek to keep from telling him that if he caught his daughter at the Liar's Club, that was probably the kind of treatment she was looking for in the first place.

"All right, well thanks, McMurtry. I appreciate your running all over town at this time of night," I said.

"No trouble at all, Detective. Just wish I had better news to give you. You let me know if there's anything else I can do."

"Thanks, Mac. Will do." I ended the call and turned to face Captain Daniels who was shaking her head.

"Gone to shit, hasn't it?" Her face looked gray and dried up, as though she'd aged ten years in the last ten minutes.

"Afraid so," I said. "Cullen's got airtight alibis for all three nights in question—just like he claimed." There was another bone-jarring thump and the one-way glass rattled again. I sighed. "Look, I better get Cole before this guy starts screaming police brutality."

"Yeah, you do that. Do we have any other leads?" She looked at me hopefully.

I shook my head. "I'm sorry—we're still interviewing family members and loved ones, trying to get a handle on why this guy is singling these women out. The BDSM angle still looks like the strongest lead we've got. We know that all three women were at that club at one time or another so it seems likely that they met the killer there."

She sighed tiredly. "Well, keep working it. I've still got the whole department on it, and the feds are supposed to be giving us that profile any year now. We'll station people inside the damn club every night if we have to."

"Sorry, Captain." I rapped sharply on the one-way glass and turned to open the door.

"Not your fault. I meant what I said, Reed, I know you and Berkley are having a rough time with this one. You're still two of my best—just keep at it." She turned away. "At least I didn't tell the mayor we had the right guy yet, although she's probably already heard it from her pet reporters." Her voice trailed off as she rounded the corner.

I opened the door and stuck my head into the interrogation room where my partner had our now-cleared suspect by the lapels again. "Cole, let him go."

"Dammit, dammit, *dammit!*" Cole slammed his fist against the wheel of his truck and then had to swerve suddenly to avoid a large SUV that was trundling along like an oversized beetle in the fast lane.

"Whoa!" I grabbed onto the dash, glad I hadn't neglected my seat belt. "Watch it, okay? You may have a death wish, but I don't."

"Sorry." He sighed deeply and ran a hand over his face, which was showing signs of a heavy five o'clock shadow. "It was just that Cullen looked so *good* for it—for all of it. And now..."

"Back to the beginning," I finished for him. "I know, I know. But at least we know that the club is probably the link. We find the guy that chatted up all three of our vics, and we probably have our killer. What we need to do is go back and interview everybody who works there from the bouncer to the bartender and everybody in between. Someone is bound to have seen something."

"And what would they do if they *did* see something?" Cole demanded, his face set in grim lines. "Nothing. He could have dragged them kicking and screaming out of the club and nobody would've thought a thing of it. You saw that place, Alex. The way they acted..."

"Yeah," I said quietly. "Yeah, I saw."

Cole seemed to realize he'd said something wrong because the look on his face abruptly became one of concern. "Look, I didn't mean... Oh, hell." He scrubbed a hand tiredly across his jaw.

I looked out at the night streaming past the truck's window and shook my head regretfully. We had spent hours with Cullen before his alibis cleared and hadn't had time to get into what had happened between us at the Liar's Club. The way Cole had mastered me, the way my body had responded to him... I thought of his seeking fingers between my thighs and a shiver ran through me. He knew exactly how much what we'd done had affected me, and I was more than a little ashamed of that. What must he think of me now? I wasn't sure I wanted to know.

Half of me had been hoping we could forget the whole thing—just leave it alone forever. When we were working a suspect, and trying to figure out the angles on a case, Cole and I fit together as neatly as ever—like two halves of the same person. It was almost as if none of the craziness in our personal life had happened at all. But the minute we started getting into each other's space or discussing emotions—watch out.

I wished for the thousandth time that none of it had ever happened, that I hadn't allowed myself to start having feelings for my partner, the one man in the world I should have avoided becoming romantic with. If you could call what happened at the club that night romantic. I closed my eyes, and I could still feel the rigid heat of his erection pressing against my ass, could still hear the low whistle and feel the snap and crack of his belt as it fell on my flesh. I could smell his scent, like animal musk and clean sweat, enveloping me as he covered me, my back to his front. I could feel his heat against my skin, his hand reaching between my thighs...

"...sorry, Alex."

I opened my eyes and looked away from the dark blur outside my window. I had allowed my fantasies to carry me away. Cole was looking at me, an uncertain expression on his face. It was the look he got when he wanted to comfort me, and I knew if things weren't so uneasy between us he would've been massaging my neck or my shoulder right now. I missed that, I realized, missed the casual, gentle touching between us that used to happen on a daily basis. Had we screwed up things so badly that we could never touch again without some kind of sexual undertone?

"Cole, it's okay." I reached for his hand, hovering uncertainly over my thigh, and squeezed it tightly once, before letting go. "You can say what you want without offending me. That place...the Liar's Club...that's not what I really want, anyway."

He looked baffled. "It's not? But I thought...and the way you acted..."

I felt my cheeks go hot with a blush. "Look, it's not that I didn't...enjoy myself, enjoy what we did there. But...I just think that it ought to be private, you know?" I was blushing so hard it was a wonder I didn't spontaneously combust, but I forced myself to finish anyway. "I don't...don't really get off on having other people watch me, is what I'm trying to say."

Cole got a look something like relief on his face. "Really? That's...that's good to know."

I didn't know why it should be, except maybe because it made him think I was a little less perverted. I still got off on the idea of being punished and mastered—did it really make that much difference if I did it in the privacy of my own bedroom or if I went to a kinky sex club and did it there? I shrugged. "Look, can we just talk about the case? We're still got this guy out on the loose somewhere, and who knows who's going to be next?"

"You're right. We really need to brainstorm this one." He pulled into my driveway and killed the engine. "What do you say we order some take-out Chinese and really hash it out? The way we did on the Jensen case."

"Sounds good to me." I opened the door and slid out of the truck. "Come on, *mi casa es su casa*, partner."

"Always showing off your superior language skills, aren't you?" He grinned at me, and I felt a surge of affection for him. This was the way it was supposed to be between us—this was the friendship I hadn't wanted to screw up. Maybe by concentrating on the case it would be possible to just go back in time, before all the sexual tension that threatened to drown us came into play. I knew I could never reverse my own feelings but maybe in time Cole could learn to treat me like one of the guys again. Maybe he could forget what he knew about me, or at least push it to the back of his mind. If only we could just go back...

Cole beat me to the door and unlocked it with the spare key I had given him when he stayed for a while after Amanda had first announced that she wanted a divorce. I had never thought to ask for it back and he never offered to give it. It just seemed like a good idea for him to have my spare key in case I got locked out or needed help. Watching him open the door and wave me inside with a flourish, I realized how much my partner and I depended on each other. Not just at work but in our day-to-day lives.

"You got anything to drink around here? I'm parched." Cole made himself at once and entirely at home, rummaging through the refrigerator before I could even answer.

"There should be some orange juice in there. Last time Mom was at Sam's Club, she picked up about fifty gallons of the stuff, and she's determined I'm going to drink at least half of it. Help yourself," I added unnecessarily as he took out the carton and began looking for a glass.

"Thanks." He was already pouring the juice, and I felt another twinge of sorrow as I thought how familiar this whole scene was. Working an all-nighter, bouncing ideas off each other, just being comfortable in each other's presence. I missed the easy camaraderie between us so damn much, I was almost willing to forget that I cared for my partner in a more than friendly way now. Almost.

"I'm going to freshen up," I said. Cole made a "go on" arm motion since his mouth was busy guzzling juice. I ducked into the bathroom, grinning despite myself. Same old Cole—it was me that had changed. Or rather, the part of me that I only let out in my books. My books!

I charged out of the bathroom to find my partner deep in the middle of my latest chapter of *Twisted Desire*. Dammit! Why the hell did I leave it up in the first place? I'd been so engrossed in the case I hadn't touched it in the last several days, but I just kept thinking I'd get back to it...

Cole looked up at me, a strange expression on his face. I couldn't tell if what he'd been reading had turned him on or repulsed him. Probably the latter. "What's...uh, what's this?" He gestured uncertainly at the screen and my pen name, which was on the header along with the novel's name on every page. "Who's Victoria Tarlatan?"

"She's a local author," I said, truthfully enough. There was no need to let him know she was me. Cole already thought I was perverted enough without knowing that I published my secret desires for anyone on the Internet to read. I thought quickly. "I, um, I'm doing some research," I said, keeping my face as straight as possible. "Remember that Sarah Michaels had some, uh, some erotica on her laptop? And Cullen said Lauren Schaefer was interviewing him for a book she was writing…"

"He just said that tonight," Cole objected.

"Oh, well…" I reached around him and got out of Word with a click of the mouse. The screen went abruptly and blessedly blank. "I just thought it might be another angle. But now that the BDSM thing looks so good…"

"Yeah, the BSDM scene is the most likely one but how is he getting them to open the door?" Cole took the bait as I'd hoped he would, striding up and down the formal dining room that I'd turned into my computer space. "I mean, they must not look like Cullen, or else these women are really desperate. Do you really think if that Charles Manson wannabe showed up at your door you'd let him in, even if you'd met him the night before or whenever at that club?"

"Absolutely not." I crossed my arms over my chest. "But then, I work with this stuff all day long. I know most rapes and homicides are committed by someone the victim knows."

"Yes, but these were intelligent, savvy women," Cole objected. "They wouldn't open the door to just anyone."

"Intelligence doesn't always equate with street smarts," I reminded him. "Somehow he got under their guard. I mean, all it takes is to open the door just one inch, just enough for him to get a gun or a knife in their face and then…" I spread my hands. "The rest is history."

"So he gets in the door, threatens them. Controls them somehow…" Cole shook his head. "I don't like it—I can't see it. I need to know the how and the why of it, need to get inside this guy's mind."

"Act it out," I said, before I thought about it.

It was something Cole and I did on a regular basis, one of us taking the role of the victim and the other taking the role of the attacker. We'd gotten to the heart of a lot of cases that way. You can talk until you're blue in the face and still not get the "how and why" of a particular scene as Cole had put it. But put the steps in motion and reenact the crime, and sometimes something will break lose from the ice-jam inside your head and the pieces with suddenly click. That was what I was suggesting now. Only…I wasn't really sure I wanted to act out this particular scenario with my partner, not with all the tension that had been between us lately. But it was too late, Cole jumped on the idea.

He looked at me, blue eyes sharp with interest. "Victim or attacker?"

I opened my mouth to say "attacker," which was my usual choice, but what came out was, "Victim." I looked down, unable to meet his eyes. "I'll be the victim this time."

He looked at me a little strangely and then nodded. "Okay. Let me go outside, and we'll take it from the top."

"Fine." We went back to the front door and he stepped outside, closed the door behind himself and then knocked.

I acted like any woman alone at night would've. "Who is it?" I called as I went to the door and looked through the peep hole. The sight of Cole, looming on the front step, still wearing the leather vest and sporting a heavy beard shadow, would not have inspired trust in anyone but me. I opened the door anyway, as all of our victims must have although why we didn't know.

"Okay, now why did you open?" Cole frowned and rubbed his jaw, producing a sandpapery noise from his whiskers.

"I know you," I said, still playing the part of the victim. "I probably met you at the club."

"What, once or twice? Are you going to open the door to me on the basis of such a casual acquaintance?"

"Maybe we had sex," I said as blandly as I could. "That's more than casual."

"Not for everyone," Cole pointed out. "Now think, Alex, *why?* Why did you open the door for me?"

"Maybe you played the Master for me—fulfilled my darkest sexual fantasies." I couldn't believe I was saying this, but the words seemed to come flying out of my mouth without checking in at my brain first.

Cole was looking at me sharply, blue eyes narrowed, but I kept on talking. "Maybe..." I licked my lips, which were suddenly dry. "Maybe you ordered me to open the door for you. You used that tone you have, the low, commanding one—your 'Master' voice, and I couldn't refuse. When...when I opened the door, you told me what a good girl I was. And you told me you had a special treat. You showed me the roses, or the candles, or the riding crop you were holding behind your back and you said..."

"Come into the bedroom," Cole finished for me. He stepped inside the doorway, looming over me as he always did, but there was something different in his demeanor now. He had assumed the role of a sexual predator, of our perp, and I felt a shiver run over my skin at the look in his eyes.

I was still wearing his jacket but Cole took it off me now, sliding it from my shoulders and letting it fall carelessly to the floor. Under it, the red leather bondage outfit seemed to cover almost nothing. My skin broke out in a rash of goose bumps at once.

"Now I'm inside." Cole's voice was soft and deep, but his eyes still blazed with intensity. "At this point if I don't have complete mental and emotional control over you, I'll use a gun or a knife." He reached for me so quickly I didn't have time to duck out of the way. Suddenly he was behind me, with one arm locked around my neck. "I've got a knife at your throat, Alex," he almost whispered, still in that low, mesmerizing voice. "You're going to do exactly what I tell you."

"Please don't hurt me." My words were little more than a gasp. I felt his large frame pressing against me, his arm around my neck, his body heat like a line of fire along my spine, and my fear was not imagined. Nor was my desire. God help me, as sick as it was, this was turning me on.

"Come into the bedroom," Cole said again and began to move me in that direction. I couldn't help remembering what had happened, or almost happened between us, the last time we had been in my bedroom together. The memory made me shiver again—*helpless on my hands and knees, waiting for him. The feel of his hand encircling my wrists, holding me down, his thick shaft parting my warm, wet folds, my body struggling to be open enough for him as he moved inside me...*

We were in the bedroom now, lit only by a single lamp on my nightstand. The room was filled with shadows, highlighting my queen-sized bed, with its solid oak frame and dark green bedspread. The headboard and frame were antiques, inherited from my grandmother on my father's side, and the dresser to one side of the room matched. Out of the corner of my eye I could see myself in the long oval mirror hanging over the dresser, looking small and fragile as a doll with Cole's massive arm around my throat.

"At this point, I make you strip." His breath on the back of my neck was hot, and I felt my heart pounding in a frantic rhythm against my ribs. The victims would have known what was in store for them when their clothes started coming off. I wondered what was in store for me.

"The first one had on a black nightie," I protested, remembering the first crime scene.

"But after that one, I decided I like it better when you're naked. Naked and completely helpless." Cole's voice slid into a lower register, deep and commanding and impossible to disobey. The Master voice. "So strip for me, Alex. Take everything off."

He released me long enough for me to obey his directions. At this point, had the attack been real, I would have tried to go for my Browning, which I kept in the drawer of my nightstand on the right side of my bed where I slept. But I was long past any such show of disobedience now. I did it.

Numbly, I began unlacing the intricate ties of the red leather outfit. It had taken Melissa, Mistress Samantha's assistant, the better part of twenty minutes to get me into it. The halter was tight enough to leave red marks on my skin, which looked pale and innocent in the dim light. Surprisingly, the top and skirt came off easily, and the boots were the hardest. At last I had to sit on the bed and fight with the buckles to get them off. I felt like a fool until Cole knelt before me and helped, his hands warm against my shivering skin. I pressed my knees tightly together, feeling more than naked with him so close to me.

"I like this look," he said softly, looking me in the eye intently. "I like you naked except for the boots."

I didn't know what to say to that so I kept quiet. Was he talking as the perp and attacker, or as Cole? We had never taken a crime scene reenactment this far before, and I wondered where it would end. I wondered where I wanted it to end. But it was out of my hands now. I felt as helpless as any of the victims must have. Were they playing a sexual game with a man they knew? Or were they being coerced at gun- or knifepoint? I tried to think, tried to get inside their heads as Cole was getting into the attacker's role. But somehow all I could feel was me—the stir of chilly air over my naked skin and my partner's blue eyes branding me with fire.

"Scoot up on the bed until your back is against the headboard," Cole commanded after looking at me a long time. I did so and then crossed my arms and legs self-consciously. We'd been naked in this room before together and in a considerably more intimate position but it had been dark. Now he could see me—all of me, and it made me feel shy and vulnerable and terribly hot.

Cole shook his head. "No, don't hide yourself from me. I want to look at you. In fact, let's get your arms out of the way entirely. Put your hands over your head."

I did as he asked, very aware of the way my nipples jutted out in front of me, hardened as much by fear as the chilly air. I only hoped he wouldn't make me uncross my legs. I didn't want him to know how this was affecting me—that I was actually getting turned on by this reenactment of the crimes we were investigating. These women had been in mortal danger, and had probably been terrified as well. Yet, as we continued, I couldn't seem to think of anything but the way *I* felt—the way being naked and helpless with the man I wanted so much was affecting me whether I wanted it to or not.

Cole had no satin ties to bind me to the headboard but he made do with his handcuffs, which worked just as well. The feel of the cool silver restraints around my wrists was almost too much to bear. It was the same way I had felt at the Liar's Club when he had wound his fingers in my hair and yanked my head back to expose my throat. The way I had felt when he positioned me up against the wall and whipped me with his belt. It was almost as though he had read my mind and knew exactly what I wanted—what I needed. God, I wanted him, but I didn't dare let him know it.

"Now we need to blindfold you. I don't want you watching me work." Cole's voice was thoughtful, but he was still in predator mode. Somewhere he found an old silk sash to tie around my eyes. I thought it might be from a robe I had discarded long ago, but I wasn't certain. Once I couldn't see anymore, all of my other senses seemed heightened. The clink of the handcuffs against my oak headboard was loud in my ears, and I could hear a slight rustling as Cole moved around the room. The cool air around my body seemed to caress my skin with ticklish fingers, and I could smell a faint hint of the lavender sachet I kept in my pillowcase to help me sleep at night.

At last there was a dip in the bed, and I knew that Cole was sitting beside me. I pressed my knees together, my head turned toward him blindly. What was he going to do next? How far was he prepared to take this? I was suddenly aware of how completely I had given him control of this situation and of myself, and the knowledge gave me a surge of fright even as I felt the wet heat between my legs growing.

"What should I do with you now, I wonder?" Cole's voice was almost in my ear and I jerked, aware that he was right over me, almost on top of me. The question was rhetorical so I didn't answer him. My heart was banging against my ribs as though it wanted to get out and make a run for the door. But I was trapped, handcuffed to my own bed by a man I trusted—didn't I?

"I don't have any roses or candles and I don't have a crop. I already used my belt on you once tonight, and you enjoyed that, didn't you, Alex? Answer me!" he demanded when I remained silent.

Hesitantly, I nodded and then, realizing he wanted verbal confirmation I said hesitantly, "Yes."

"Yes, what?" His voice was a low, silky rumble. I felt my heart rate climb another notch.

"Yes…Master," I almost whispered.

"That's better. You know, Alex," he continued. "I've never seen you naked before—not like this, all spread out so I can really look at you." He shifted closer, and I could feel his warm, cinnamon-scented breath blowing across my bare breasts.

"Please," I gasped. I struggled for a moment, making the cuffs clink dully against the oak of the headboard before I subsided, panting.

"Please what? Please don't look at you?" He laughed, a low chuckle filled with a frightening promise. "Don't you know how often I've stopped myself from doing exactly that? From looking at you the way I wanted to—as more than just a partner, more than just one of the guys? Now I can look at you as much as I want. Now that I've got you cuffed up, naked...helpless." He let the last word hiss between his teeth, and I felt the warm brush of his hand against my cheek. I jerked back, then nuzzled forward, wanting the touch more than I wanted to keep my dignity.

"Do you like it when I touch you, Alex?" There was a genuine uncertainty in his voice now, despite the low tone. I realized he was asking for permission—perhaps for absolution for what we were doing and what we were about to do. We were out of the reenactment now—the crime scene left far behind. This scenario had become nothing more than a reason for us to act on the feelings that had been growing between us for the past week. At least, it was for me. I wasn't sure what it was for Cole. But I wanted to find out.

"Yes, Master," I said softly, letting him know that I wanted this—that I *needed* it. "I...I like it when you touch me."

"That's good to hear." His hand, large and warm and slightly callused in the places where he gripped his gun, slid down my throat and cupped my left breast. I gasped, feeling the sexual tension course through my body.

"I've always thought you had beautiful breasts," he said, his voice low and almost thoughtful. He pinched the nipple gently, and then harder, sending a sharp jolt of pleasure/pain to the warmth between my thighs. "Isn't that the way you like it, a little bit rough?"

I wished that I could see his eyes, that I could tell what expression accompanied those words. Was he disgusted by my needs? I didn't know.

"Answer me, Alex," he said again, twisting both my nipples now, making me writhe on the bed helplessly.

"Yes, Master," I gasped, before I could call the words back. "Yes…please…"

"Now what are you asking please about?" His low voice was amused and, I thought, aroused. "Do you want me to stop…or not?" The fingers on my nipples pinched tighter, sending shockwaves of erotic pain through my trembling frame before abruptly releasing the tender nubbins of flesh.

I couldn't answer his question, but it didn't seem to matter. He was cupping my breasts again, gently now, as though weighing them in his hands. My head was back against the headboard, my knees still pressed together tightly as I struggled to control my emotions.

His next question startled me. "Did I hurt you, Alex?" This time I knew he would demand an answer.

"Yes, Master," I said truthfully. It had hurt, but it was a good kind of hurt, a low sexual ache I could still feel pulsing like a second heartbeat under my skin.

"And did you like it?" His stern tone demanded I tell the truth once more.

My voice breaking with shame, I repeated, "Yes, Master. Yes...I liked it." I expected him to ask me more, to ask me why, as he had after discovering the bruises he'd put on my wrists but he didn't. The silence between us stretched like a warm thread of honey, thoughtful and not entirely comfortable.

"Do you want me to do it again?" he asked at last, sounding genuinely curious. Oh, God, what would he think of me if I said yes?

"If...if you want to," I said hesitantly.

"But what if I don't? What if I'd rather do this?" The warm, cinnamon-scented breath moved down from my throat abruptly, and I felt a hot wetness enclose one of my nipples, soothing the low ache he'd caused. I moaned out loud—I couldn't help it—and arched my back, wanting to give him fuller access to me, to my breasts. I wished with all my heart that I could see him, that I could watch his dark head bending over me, sucking my ripe, red nipples into his mouth. They were so hard, so sensitive from the pain he'd inflicted earlier, that every sweep of his tongue over my flesh felt like a million prickles of light burning through my body.

"I've always wanted to do that," he said at last, after spending a long time licking and sucking each nipple. His voice was rough—almost ragged. "Always, I just couldn't admit it. Not even to myself and certainly not to you. My tough, one-of-the-guys partner. Not so tough now, are you, Alex?" The words were incendiary, but his tone was gentle, almost soothing.

"No," I said softly. I pulled on the handcuffs again, feeling the tension in my arms and shoulders and the roughness of the carved oak headboard behind my back. "No, I'm not. I...I don't always want to be. Tough, I mean." It was an admission to myself almost as much as to him. I didn't always want to be tough, to be in control. I wanted to lose it—lose it all in a rush of passionate pain. But how could I explain that to Cole?

"I know," he said simply. His hands caressed lower now, stroking my sides gently, almost teasingly. "It's hard to give up that toughness—that control though, isn't it? Even if you really want to."

"I guess," I whispered, wondering where he was going with this. His hands were moving lower, stroking my hips and thighs, which were still pressed tightly together. "But...but I'm afraid." It was the truth—my body was electrified by terror almost as much as pleasure. I didn't know what this would do to our relationship, to our partnership, but I no longer cared. I was so caught up in the sensations Cole was provoking in me, in the fantasy he was giving me, that I could barely think anymore.

"That's all right," he said softly. "It's all right to be afraid, as long as you obey. Now—I want you to spread your legs for me."

My breath caught in my throat. "What? But why?" I asked before I thought. Then I tensed, waiting for his reaction to my disobedience.

"There's something else I've always wanted to do to you." His voice didn't sound angry, only very firm. "Remember what I told Mistress Samantha when we were pretending to be a couple? When she asked what we liked to do?"

I felt my breath catch in my throat, and I pressed my legs even more tightly together. Surely he couldn't mean...

His voice continued, low and thoughtful. "You know, I couldn't believe how hot you got...how *wet*, just from her caning you. But it was more than that, wasn't it? More than just the pain. It was being tied and helpless—being forced to submit.

Just the way you're going to submit to me now." His hands on my thighs became more insistent and his voice dropped down into that lower register again—commanding, dominating. "Spread your legs for me now, Alex, I want to see how wet you are. I want to taste you."

I shook my head, feeling my hair brush in frantic wisps over my bare shoulders. This was going too far—this would change our relationship forever. And yet, I wanted it so badly, wanted to give him what he was demanding, what I knew he wouldn't take by force no matter how much he was acting like the Master of my dreams.

Cole didn't say anything, but he didn't stop touching me either. His hands, large and warm and rough, roamed over my body, over my breasts and hips and legs, caressing and patient. I realized that he was prepared to wait all night, if he needed to. Prepared to wait until I gave in.

His hand dipped low, touching the apex between my thighs where the soft patch of curly golden-brown fuzz grew. "I want to touch you here, Alex. I want to taste you." His breath was in my ear again, and then he moved to the side and I felt it puff against my lips. "I want to put my tongue inside you," he said. "I want to feel your heartbeat in your clit." His mouth covered mine suddenly and the kiss was soft and slow and gentle, his tongue pressing carefully between my lips while he cupped my cheek to hold me in place. I knew he was showing me the way he would do it—the way he would taste me when I finally gave in. It was too much.

With a low moan I relaxed the tension in my thighs, letting my knees fall apart, baring myself utterly to him. "Good," he whispered, pulling back from me, and I felt his hand cupping my mound, just resting against me at first. "You're such a *good* girl, Alex." The words of approval sent such a sexual charge through my body that I actually cried out and arched against him, pressing myself hard into his large hand.

"That's right, baby, give it up for me," he growled softly, grinding the heel of his hand into my damp heat. "Let me see how wet you are."

I gasped in the darkness created by the blindfold, arching my back even more as I felt his mouth travel down my body, taking exactly what he wanted. What I wanted so desperately to give him. I knew that I was risking it all—our relationship, our partnership, everything that had ever been between us, with this one reckless act of submission. But I couldn't help it— couldn't stop myself. I felt exactly the same way I had that first night when he had almost taken me and pulled back at the last minute. Like I would die if I didn't do this—like I couldn't live without his touch on my skin one minute more.

"So beautiful. So goddamn beautiful," I heard Cole mutter and then everything else was lost in a tide of sensation. I felt his hands on my thighs—my inner thighs now, stroking gently, kneading and caressing the tender flesh. I felt his breath, hot and eager, against my center and then he was parting my folds, spreading me, baring me completely. I writhed restlessly in need and shame. That he should look at me now, that he should see me like this, so utterly exposed, was almost unbearable. But he didn't look for long.

I felt a warm, wet sensation as his lips made contact, and then he was kissing me. Kissing me every bit as gently and carefully as he had kissed my mouth. I moaned out loud, pressing my hips up and toward him, and he seemed to understand what I needed. His mouth on me became firmer, more insistent, and I felt his tongue moving restlessly, tasting me the way he'd wanted to. Then he moved lower, slowly and deliberately. I bit my lip, holding back a shout as he pressed inside me, penetrating me, opening me, *owning* me the way I needed him to.

He pressed into me deeply, making slow, rhythmic motions with his tongue until I felt like he was reaching for my heart with every thrust. I pulled against the handcuffs, feeling the cold steel bite into my wrists as I thrashed on the bed under him. Then his hands were on me, holding me still, making me lie there and submit as he tasted me.

"Such a good girl," he whispered again, pulling back for a moment. "I want to feel you come. Can you do that for me, Alex?"

I wanted to say I could do anything for him, I could jump over the moon, as long as he didn't stop. But all that came out of my mouth was a low moan. My voice was shaking as badly as my body was. I needed him—God, so much! Needed to give in to him, to give him this final and utter surrender.

Cole seemed to take my moan as assent because I felt him bend over me once more. I could feel the silky-coarse brush of his military short hair against my inner thighs and then he was gathering me close, pulling me up to meet his mouth. He spread my thighs even wider, making me feel vulnerable and hot, before pressing his lips to my center once more.

This time I felt his tongue darting inside me for just an instant. Then he drew back a little and began drawing exquisitely slow spirals starting at my outer edges, circling closer and closer to my throbbing clit. I moaned breathlessly and arched my back, feeling like it was too much. Too much sensation, too much need, too much pleasure centered on the tiny tender bundle of nerves that was my core.

It felt so good, so right, and yet I needed something more. Just a little more to push me over the edge, to help me come. As though sensing my need, I felt Cole's fingers, long and strong and relentless, pressing inside of me. I bit my lip, and my hips bucked with pure, raw need as he thrust deeper and deeper, exploring that secret part of me as though he were drawing a map of my soul.

At the same time, his other hand slid up my body and found my right breast and the tender, vulnerable nipple. Hard, relentless fingers gripped my nipple and twisted, shooting a stinging bolt of pleasurable pain down my spine, electrifying my entire body. This was no gentle tug—Cole was actually hurting me, was using his strength rather than holding it back, to give me what I wanted, what I so desperately needed. He was recognizing my need and was acting upon it. That, more than anything else, finally pushed me over the edge.

"Cole... Oh, God!" His name burst from my lips as he pressed hard and deep, his tongue never stopping its gentle assault. The pleasure rolled through me in waves and behind the blackness of the blindfold, huge glowing stars exploded in my vision. I thrashed under him, twisting my hips uncontrollably, feeling like I was being electrocuted by pleasure. It was too much. Too, too much...

At last Cole pulled back, and I could hear him panting, could feel the hot bursts of his breath against my trembling stomach. His fingers were digging into my thighs, hard enough that I might have bruises there to match the ones on my wrists before long, but I didn't care.

"God, Alex..." I felt the movement of the bed as he sat up suddenly. Without warning, he ripped the blindfold off my eyes. I blinked, almost blinded by the dim light coming from the lamp on my night table. As my eyes adjusted, I could see him. He looked wild. He had taken off the shirt and vest and was naked from the waist up. A light sheen of sweat glimmered on his muscular torso and the tattoos on his upper arms rippled with the nervous flexing of his muscles. His mouth was wet from tasting me, and his blue eyes had turned a deep, dark cobalt, filled with savage need.

"Cole?" I asked, suddenly uncertain. He looked like a man on the edge of some steep precipice, like someone trying to make up his mind whether or not to jump.

"I need you now," he said, without preamble. "But not with the blindfold. I want to look in your eyes while I do this. While I fuck you."

His words sent a shiver through me as I realized he was through asking. He was telling me now, telling me what he was going to do to me. My eyes dropped to the bulge in his tight black pants, and I remembered how huge he was, how thick and solid.

He unzipped the pants in short, jerky motions, pulling them down, baring his engorged shaft. The angry purple head beckoned me, his thickness rising from between his muscular thighs. I bit my lip at the size of him. I had never seen him before, and had only begun to feel what that part of him could do to me. I gripped the headboard behind me, hearing the clink and rattle of the cuffs as I did. I had never felt so open, so utterly vulnerable to any man. Again my desire was tinged with fear but it heightened my need, the way pain enhances pleasure.

"Now," he growled again. He came forward on the bed, gathered my hips in his hands, and positioned himself at my entrance. The brief thought of asking for a condom zipped across my mind and was lost—a shooting star. Then he was pressing inside me, spreading me wider and wider, pushing ruthlessly into my body and forcing me to make room for him.

"Cole," I gasped. I moaned at the mingled pleasure and pain and squeezed my eyes shut, almost unable to bear the sensation.

"No," his voice was rough with passion. "No, open your eyes. I want to watch you watching me take you."

I opened my eyes, forcing myself to meet that piercing blue gaze. He held me, held all of my attention intently focused while he pressed even deeper into me, while he penetrated me to the core. At last I felt him reach the end of my channel, stretching me to the limit with his thickness, bottoming out inside me. I wrapped my legs around his hips, feeling utterly dominated, utterly owned.

"Cole," I whispered, but he shook his head.

"Call me Master when I fuck you like this. Isn't that what you want? Someone to master you? Someone to fuck you long and hard and deep and tell you what a 'good girl' you are for taking it all?" he demanded. His voice was harsh, and his gaze penetrated me completely, making my very soul feel naked.

Unable to answer, I nodded my head. But his eyes wouldn't leave mine until I murmured, "Yes, Master."

"That's right." His voice softened somewhat. "But that's all right, Alex." He pulled out of me just a little and thrust back in, hard. I gasped, feeling the ripples of pain and pleasure course through me. "That's all right," he continued. "Because you are a good girl, such a *good* girl for taking all of my cock inside you. You're *my* good girl. All mine now." He bent and took my mouth in a hot, possessive kiss that took my breath away. I could taste myself on his tongue, salty and sweet, and then he pulled back and began to move inside me, his eyes never leaving my face.

It was unnerving to be watched so intently while he thrust into me. Unnerving but unspeakably erotic. I felt all of his attention focused on me, all of his interest, his emotion, his need, everything he had or could ever be all centered on my face, through those blue eyes, as piercing as a laser beam. It was as though my pleasure were the most important thing in his life.

With other lovers, there had always been the tendency to shut my eyes and let my fantasies carry me away during the act. But here and now with Cole, I had no need to imagine, no wish to fantasize. This *was* my fantasy, to the last degree. Even the thought that we were probably doing irreparable harm to our professional relationship and our friendship couldn't stop me from reveling in it.

Cole worked me hard, his hips pumping and his shaft grinding into me, demanding I be open for him, taking me the way I needed him to. I rolled my hips, trying to press back, helping with the slow, steady, absolutely maddening rhythm he had set up. I wanted to feel him inside me forever, wanted never to forget this moment of mutual madness when we gave in to our baser instincts in the name of need.

"Oh, God... Oh, God...ohgodohgodohgod!" I couldn't stop the noises, couldn't seem to shut myself up. The sensation of his thickness buried inside me was too intense; I was too close to the edge of losing all control. I felt my orgasm fast approaching, a deeper more encompassing feeling than before, and I knew I was going to come harder than I ever had. Cole must have seen it in my eyes, or felt it in the quiver of my body under his own.

"Can you come for me again, Alex?" His voice had a low, grating quality and a light sheen of sweat covered his body, the muscles flexing rhythmically as he pumped into me. "I want to feel you come around me," he said. "Come around me while I come inside you. *Now!*"

With a final desperate thrust, I felt him pressing hard against the mouth of my womb at the same time that my own climax broke and shattered over me. I cried out—screamed, really—and lost myself in the intense sensation of his warm wet heat bathing me and my own pleasure overtaking me yet again.

The orgasm shook me as none before it ever had, maybe because I knew it might mean the end of our partnership—the end of our friendship. Because how could my partner respect me now? Now that I had allowed him to do this to me? To handcuff me to the bed, to hurt me and pleasure me and fuck me? I told myself I didn't care; I only knew what I needed and he had fulfilled that need. Cole had dominated me and mastered me, had held me down and fucked me until I couldn't see straight. No wonder I felt like I was exploding inside.

For a moment everything went gray and I felt him withdraw from my body, leaving me feeling empty and spent and full of regret.

"Alex?" His voice was distant, a soft sigh bringing me back to myself. "Alex, are you all right?" He sounded concerned. After a moment I realized why—I was crying. "Alex?" He said again. "Oh, God, did I hurt you?" He sounded almost panicked now. I made myself look up at him and saw the concern darkening his eyes.

I shook my head, unable to speak, but not wanting him to worry. I wasn't exactly sure myself why I was crying. Maybe because of the intensity of the orgasm, but I thought it was more than that. It was the fact that I had ruined our partnership, had destroyed any respect my partner and best friend had ever had for me by allowing what had just happened between us. I could lie to myself all I wanted, tell myself that it didn't matter, that I didn't care. But I did—desperately. It wasn't physical pain that was making me cry but a deep, emotional hurt that nothing would ever be able to cure. I was losing him, and it was all my fault.

I knew now for a fact that there was no going back for Cole and me. As soon as this case ended we would have no choice but to go to Captain Davis and ask to be reassigned to different partners. And then we would inevitably drift apart. Because how can you be best friends with someone you can't look in the eye?

"Dammit, Alex, are you hurt or not?" Cole put his hands on my shoulders and ducked down, trying to get a look in my eyes.

"I'm fine," I managed to say. "Just…just uncuff me."

He fumbled for the key, which he had placed on the nightstand, and knelt over me to unlock the cuffs. I had been pulling on them fairly steadily during the entire encounter and my wrists were ringed with red marks. Cole's eyes grew worried again and he took my right hand, massaging the wrist gently. I snatched it back, pulling both arms in close to my chest to cover myself. Suddenly I felt even more naked than before, and this time it wasn't a good feeling.

Cole's face hardened. "I'm sorry. I thought...I thought I was doing what you wanted. What you needed. I didn't mean to hurt you, Alex, you have to believe me."

"I believe you," I whispered. "And you didn't hurt me—not any more than I wanted to be hurt." That, of course, was part of the problem. I tugged at the bedspread he was sitting on until he got up. I covered myself with the deep green spread, trying to salvage the tattered remains of my dignity.

I cowered under the covers and Cole knelt beside the bed, still trying to get eye contact. But I was too ashamed—mortified really. It was bad enough that I had allowed him to know I had such desires, but the fact that I had practically invited him to act on them with me... I squeezed my eyes shut, refusing to look at him. What must he think of me now? I remembered his words, "Not so tough now, are you?" he'd said. How could he ever trust me to get his back again having seen me at my weakest and most vulnerable?

"I'm sorry...Alex, I'm so sorry." I felt his hand, large and hesitant, stroke over my hair. I scooted further under the covers so he couldn't reach me. I was smothered by the nearness of the fabric and my nose was stuffed up with crying. I was miserable.

"Please, just go." My voice was muffled by tears and the bedspread but he must have heard, anyway. I heard the sounds of him dressing, the slight rustling of fabric, the creak of his leather vest and the minute noises of adjustment as he returned his gun to his holster.

Then it was quiet, but I sensed he hadn't left yet. He was standing beside the bed, hovering over me, probably trying to think of a way to make things right. But there was nothing he could do or say that would undo the last half hour. Nothing that could take back the things we had said and done. I felt disgraced and dirtied, not by his actions, but by my own desires. By my own needs. Why was I like this? Why did I need to be mastered and controlled and hurt to get turned on? What was wrong with me? Why was I so weak?

"Alex..." His voice was soft and uncertain, nothing like the commanding "Master" tone he had used earlier to such effect. "Please, just tell me what's wrong."

"I shouldn't be like this. I shouldn't *need* this. We shouldn't have..." But I couldn't go on.

"It's going to be okay." His tone was placating now, soothing. The same tone he'd used when he held me and let me cry against him in my father's chair. The memory made me even more miserable—it had been the first time I let him see my weakness. The beginning of the end.

"It's never going to be okay ever again," I told him. "Go—get out. How many ways do I have to say it?" I buried my head further under the covers. I heard his short, frustrated breathing, and then heavy footsteps as he stalked to the door.

"All right," he said from somewhere near the vicinity of the bedroom door. "I'm going but this isn't over. We're going to talk about this later."

"Like hell we will!" I flung at him. My shame turned suddenly to anger. "Get the hell out of my house, Cole. *Now!*"

I heard the slam of the bedroom door and then a muffled thump as he slammed the front door as well. There was a muted roar as his truck fired to life and then he drove away, leaving me alone, just like I had wanted. I cried myself to sleep.

Chapter Twenty-Seven

Cole

All the way home I tried to figure out what the hell I had done or said to set her off. Hadn't I acted the way she wanted me to? Hadn't she enjoyed what we'd done together? If she hadn't, she certainly could've fooled me, with the moaning and writhing, the way she'd moved under me... Just the thought of it was enough to have me half hard all over again.

I wished like hell she hadn't gotten so upset. I wanted to be back in her bed with her, holding her. I wanted another chance to make love to her—softly this time. Gently, the way I'd always dreamed of doing it with her, whenever I'd let myself imagine it, which wasn't often.

I knew what we'd done wasn't exactly kosher, and I don't mean just the kinky cuffing her to the bed and twisting her nipples part either. I mean in the long run, for both our careers at the PD. Ideally, as an officer or a detective, you don't start sleeping with your partner. It almost always screws up the professional relationship. Case in point, the wary way Alex and I had been treating each other since our first semi sexual encounter, when I'd held her and kissed her at her mom's house. We'd been best friends before the fact and dancing around each other like we were waltzing in a mine field ever since. Things had only gotten worse after our second encounter, following our visit to the Dominatrix.

That time I hadn't been able to follow through because I'd been so afraid I was hurting her. This time I had hurt her on purpose—not a big pain, true, but enough, apparently, to get her engine revving. The same way whipping her with the belt at the Liar's Club had turned her on. But the pleasure she'd gotten from it, from my dominance over her, had been more than enough for me to overcome my fear of hurting her and to go on to do the deed.

Now I wondered if I should have listened harder to that little voice inside my head, the one telling me that I ought to watch out—to be careful because I might be screwing up the best relationship I had in my life.

I slammed the steering wheel with my fist—my mind was running in circles. Was Alex upset because I had really hurt her? Or was she upset because we had gone too far and probably ruined our partnership and friendship? With the way she liked to clam up whenever she had personal problems, I might never know. But I knew what would happen next.

There would be a quiet shuffling of paperwork somewhere in the background and before I knew it I would be reassigned to someone else and Alex would be, too. She'd be with another partner, someone who wouldn't appreciate her, who wouldn't protect her and watch her back, someone who didn't deserve her. I already hated whoever it was, and I didn't even know him or her yet.

I was going to lose her.

"Dammit! I can't lose her—I *love* her." The words came tumbling out of my mouth, and if I hadn't been stopped at a red light, I would have wrecked the truck. It was true—absolutely true, I realized. All this time I had been fooling myself, telling myself that I didn't care for Alex in more than a friendly way, that I didn't love her because I wasn't *allowed* to love her. First because of Amanda and then because of the job. But I couldn't lie to myself anymore. I wanted her as more than a friend and partner. More even than a lover. I wanted to set up new parameters for our whole relationship.

I nearly turned the truck around on the spot until I remembered that one, Alex might not feel the same for me. (In fact, she probably didn't.) And, two, she was still angry and upset at me for reasons I hadn't pinpointed yet.

Well, hell, was I a detective or wasn't I? Although getting inside a woman's mind is tougher than any homicide investigation you're likely to run across. I sighed tiredly and ran a hand over my face, feeling the pull of my five o'clock shadow, which was more like a five a.m. shadow now. Suddenly the adrenaline I'd been running on since the start of the long evening drained abruptly away, leaving me feeling like a limp dishrag. I sagged in my seat, my body feeling like it had been dipped in lead—I was physically and emotionally exhausted.

My partner's sudden mood swings were a mystery I wasn't likely to solve tonight. I probably had enough time to go home and catch a couple hours of sleep before we started running down fresh leads on our serial murdering perp tomorrow. Tomorrow, which was actually later on today.

"Tomorrow, I'll talk to her tomorrow," I mumbled, pulling into my parking slot at the apartment complex. I stumbled out of the truck, almost overcome by weariness.

It all seemed perfectly clear. I would tell Alex how I felt about her and find out why she was so upset. I would tell her I loved her and if she, by some miracle, returned my emotions, I would ask her to think about moving our relationship in a different direction.

I would tell her I couldn't lose her.

Chapter Twenty-Eight

He is frustrated. He waited outside her house for hours tonight, waiting for her to be alone, but the stupid man she calls her partner wouldn't leave. He has everything in readiness, and he is there until the early morning hours and yet the huge black truck stays stubbornly in her driveway, like an unwanted dog that won't go away.

At last he is forced to drive off in disgust. All his careful plans ruined. All his careful preparations for nothing. Her punishment will have to wait for another night.

For tonight, he decides suddenly, studying the last name on the list, blinking on the laptop's screen. Tonight will be her night. Tonight is the night of her punishment and redemption— of her becoming. He cannot wait any longer. The need to punish is strong in him. It surprises him how strong.

Beside him on the tabletop is another list, this one printed on paper. On it are dozens and dozens of names. Names as ridiculous as Morganna Bloom and Carolyn Sinders. And beside those false names, the real ones. He has had this list for a while but lately he has taken to studying it more and more.

The punishment and becoming of the three guilty ones is almost complete, true. But there are dozens more like them—hundreds in the Tampa Bay area alone. So many hundreds spreading corruption and filth and mental disease across the world through the Internet. It hardly seems fair that he should have been granted a divine mission to go after only three of them, four, if you count the first.

He puts the paper list away and studies the laptop, the single name blinking in its screen, Victoria Tarlatan. Tonight she will become what she has only dreamed of; tonight she will be purified through his trial of fire. When her punishment is complete, he will turn his attention to the others. But for tonight all his attention is on her. His bag is packed with all the right equipment, the kit he always buys for the mask and ties, and all the disgusting props to reenact the scene straight from her own twisted imagination as well. Yes, tonight is the night—he can feel it.

Victoria Tarlatan. The name looms larger and larger on the screen, and his finger itches to hit delete. Tonight.

Chapter Twenty-Nine

Alex

It was hard, terribly hard, to go in to work and act as
though nothing had happened between me and my partner. It
didn't help, either, that we were in the middle of one of the
most publicized murder investigations ever to hit the Bay area,
or that I had gotten barely two hours of broken sleep, either.
But as my mom always says, this is the kind of day you prove
what kind of woman you are.

Actually, that's something she used to say when I felt too
sick to go to school, and she didn't want to be stuck home with
me and miss her important club and charity meetings. But I still
carry it with me as a sort of armor against weakness. I had been
giving in to myself entirely too much lately, I lectured inwardly,
as I navigated the one-way streets of downtown to get to the
station. I had broken my own rules, had let myself be vulnerable

emotionally, physically, and worst of all, sexually. All of that had to stop.

"It stops here and now," I promised myself out loud. I was determined to toughen up and keep going. I would finish out this murder case which, please God, had to break soon, and then I would ask to be reassigned to another department and another partner. As much as it hurt me, Cole and I would have to go our separate ways, because there was no way back to a good working relationship now. Not after last night.

The minute I walked into the PD, I knew my resolve was going to be severely tested. Cole caught me before I could even get to my desk and practically dragged me from the bullpen into a small storage room that held evidence bags and cleaning supplies.

"Alex," he said before I could protest. "We have to talk." He had his hands on my shoulders and was bending down to get a good look at my face. His nearness, the warmth of his hands, the clean, musky scent of him, brought everything rushing back in vivid detail. I had to work to keep my expression stony and disinterested.

I stared up into his eyes, which were dark with worry, and shook my head. "Nothing to talk about."

"Like hell there's not," he exploded. His tone was low but so passionate his words had the intensity of a shout. "What happened last night—"

"*Nothing* happened last night," I cut him off. I tried to shake free of his hands but he tightened his hold on my shoulders, not letting me go.

"Bullshit," he said roughly. "Last night was one of the most important nights of my life and you're lying through your teeth if you say it didn't have some effect on you, too. Why is it that every time we start to get close you pull away? What the hell do you want from me, Alex?"

"I want you to take your hands off me, go back to your desk, and start researching new leads. In case you haven't noticed we're still in the middle of a homicide investigation." I deliberately kept my voice icy, fighting to ignore the effect the close proximity of his body to mine had on me.

"Fine." He dropped his hands, releasing me so suddenly I nearly lost my balance. "But you can't use that as an excuse forever. Sooner or later we're going to catch this guy and then..."

"Then we'll ask to be reassigned to different partners," I finished for him.

Cole's eyes narrowed. "What did you say?"

I shrugged, doing my best to be nonchalant. "You heard me. Look, Cole, we've blown it, and don't for a minute think that I'm blaming you. This is my fault as much as yours. More, probably. I never should have let you know...the things I let you know. I never should have encouraged you." I looked up at him, forcing myself to meet that intense gaze. "But the fact is that I can't work effectively like this. Not with all this..." I gestured vaguely. "...this tension between us. It's too much. We have to end it."

"Alex, no..." There was a look of almost pleading in his eyes now. "I know we probably shouldn't have done what we did last night but...but I can't lose you like this. I *can't*."

It took all my strength not to go to him then, everything I had in me not to put my arms around him and bury my face in his chest. I wanted him to hold me and tell me everything would be all right. I wanted him to love me, to comfort me, to need me the way I needed him. I wanted, in short, to let myself be weak. It was that thought more than anything else that made me straighten my spine and cross my arms over my chest.

Weakness and vulnerability—I'd enough of that to last me a lifetime in the past few days. What good would it do to let him gather me into his arms and tell me everything was going to be all right? Would it bring back his respect for me or my own self-respect? Would it rid me of my unwanted and unnatural desires? No and no and no.

"I'm sorry, Cole," I said as firmly as I could. "But I think we'd better get back to our desks before people get the wrong idea about us."

"What the hell," he said, his words tinged with bitterness. "Let them. It looks like I've had the wrong idea about us for years." He slammed out of the supply room angrily, leaving me to follow, trying to ignore the curious stares of co-workers as I made my way to my desk.

The rest of the day we spent chasing our tails, or that was what it felt like. We ran down every employee of the Liar's Club and most of the regulars too. None of them remembered any one man other than Cullen watching or interacting with all three of our victims. By eight o'clock that night we were still empty handed, every lead a dead end, a blank wall staring us in the face.

"There has to be something we're missing. Some key to this whole mess." Cole's voice was thick with frustration. He sat at his desk, running a hand over his jaw and looking as haggard as I felt. Despite the tension between us we'd worked as a team all day, putting our feelings aside for the good of the case, and the strain was showing on both of us.

"I don't know," I said. I felt nearly ready to drop with fatigue. I had been fighting with myself all day—fighting to keep from giving in to my weakness again. If only I could ask Cole for a neck massage—he always seemed to know exactly where I hurt and how to make it better. I caught myself missing his touch, remembering the way it had been between us the night before, and I had to push away my emotions again and again and remind myself that I was supposed to be stronger.

"What if we're wrong?" Cole looked up at me suddenly. "What if we're going at this from the wrong angle?"

"What do you mean?" I asked tiredly.

"I mean we've just been assuming that because all three vics had ties to the Liar's Club, that the perp picked them out there. But what if we're wrong? What if he's choosing them another way entirely?"

"How else is he choosing them if not through the club?" I protested. "The way he sets the scene, the way he stages them…it's classic BDSM."

"Your book theory—what you were saying about Sarah Michaels writing erotica and Lauren Schaefer researching for a book." Cole snapped his fingers excitedly. "What if Cynthia Harner was writing something, too? Didn't Love say she got interested doing some kind of research?"

I shrugged. "I think he said something like that, yeah. So?"

"So, don't we still have some of her personal effects? Harner said he couldn't stand to come get them, so they must still be in evidence."

"What do you think you're going to find?" I asked, feeling slightly ill. The "book theory" as Cole called it, had been a throwaway, just something to get his mind off what he'd seen on my computer the night before and back onto the case. I hadn't for a moment thought that the murder of these three women could have anything to do with what they were writing, and I still didn't. But if we started down that road, my dirty secret, the e-books I published, might be revealed, and I just didn't think I could take any more humiliation.

"It's got to be the club," I protested, but Cole was already on his way to the evidence room, looking more excited than I'd seen him all day.

"Look at this," he said triumphantly, pulling a new-looking Blackberry out of the white cardboard box. He turned it on and stared thoughtfully at the screen. "Give me a hand, here, Alex. You're better with these things than I am."

Feeling resigned, I took the Blackberry he was offering me and scrolled through the contents. I found what looked like an outline for a novel that Cynthia had apparently written herself called *Velvet Agony.* I recognized the title. It had been published online as an e-book, with a company called Candlelight Romance. A quick scan of one or two scenes made my cheeks flush—it looked like something I might have written myself. Was there more to my throwaway theory than I had imagined?

It made me wonder about Sarah Michaels—she had been writing the same kind of thing. At the time Matt had read part of her work aloud to us, I thought she was only writing for her own amusement. But had she, like Cynthia Harner, actually had her work published somehow—maybe somewhere online? And what about Lauren Schaefer?

"Well?" Cole looked at me eagerly.

"Give me a minute," I said. My lips felt numb. I scrolled to Microsoft Reader, which would hold the books Cynthia Harner had been reading. In my experience, if you write a certain genre, you read it as well. I wasn't surprised to find three books, obviously downloaded from the Internet not too long before her death. I even recognized the titles. *Sweet Submission, Painful Pleasures, Whispers in the Dark...* The last one gave me a nasty shock. I nearly dropped the small machine. Cynthia Harner had been reading one of *my* books!

"What is it?" Cole came closer, careful not to touch me, but looking very concerned. "What's wrong, Alex? You're pale all of a sudden."

"Just...just tired," I managed. I handed him back the Blackberry. "There's her reading list."

"Hey," He glanced at the small screen and then back to me. "*Whispers in the Dark*, by Victoria Tarlatan. Isn't this the same author whose book you were researching?"

"Um..." I was saved from having to say anything by the timely entrance of Captain Davis.

"Since it looks like we're not leaving, I'm ordering take-out. Who wants what?" She held up a menu from the Wok 'N Roll, a Chinese fast food place down the road.

"Wait a minute, Captain, I think I'm onto something." Cole was still holding the Blackberry like it was the Holy Grail, scrolling rapidly through the contents himself now.

"What is it?" She left me holding the brightly colored menu and went to look over my partner's shoulder.

Cole looked up, his eyes narrowed in concentration. "A lead—a strong one, I think. We've been working under the premise that the killer met all three of our vics at the Liar's Club because they all three had ties to the BDSM community and all three had been there. But what if that isn't the case at all? At least two of them were writing these..." He waved a hand excitedly. "These kinky sex books, and Cynthia Harner's was published online." He looked up at me, "What about Sarah Michaels? Was her stuff online, too?"

I shrugged uneasily. "Call Matt. I only got to see the print-out from her laptop."

Cole got on the phone immediately, taking my suggestion. When he hung up, his eyes were bright with the thrill of a breaking case.

"He's checking. Do you still have the number for Tate Zimmerman, Lauren Schaefer's writing buddy? Let's find out what she was writing and if it was published anywhere."

I closed my eyes, feeling sick. It didn't take long for Cole to get results—the book Sarah Michaels had on her laptop was *Sweet Submission*, published online by a company called Intimate Arousal, and Tate Zimmerman confirmed that Lauren Schaefer had been writing erotica as well. He couldn't remember the name but it had something to do with Pleasures. No doubt about it, the book was *Painful Pleasures*, and it had been published online by a company called Dark Fantasies.

When Cole got off the phone the second time, he was on fire. "This is it—this guy didn't have to know them at all. He read their stuff online and picked them out that way."

"Then that list of authors—" Captain Davis tapped the Blackberry's glowing screen. "—is also your list of victims. Cynthia Harner was Morganna Bloom, Sarah Michaels was Sylvestra Eden and Lauren Schaefer was..."

"Carolyn Sinders," Cole finished for her. "The question is, who is Victoria Tarlatan? Because she's next on the list. He could be outside her house right now! There has to be a way to find out who she is. We have to warn her—protect her." He clenched his fists and the muscles in his arms flexed, straining the long-sleeved dark blue shirt he wore. It was clear Cole wanted this guy badly, wanted to get to him before he got to the next victim. But he didn't know the next victim was supposed to be me.

I felt like I was going to be violently ill. But strangely, the thing that bothered me wasn't that I was apparently next in line on our killer's hit list, but that Cole and my Captain would find out my dirty secret. I could take care of myself—I knew I could. Being on his list didn't scare me; I'd blow the son-of-a-bitch away the minute he showed up at my front door. But if my partner and my superior officer learned about how I spent my free time...well, I'd be better off dead, I really would. Cole could keep it under his hat, although it would be horribly humiliating for me if he found out. But Captain Davis was an even bigger feminist than I was, and I was sure she wouldn't look kindly on my taste in literature.

There had to be some way to distract Cole from his theory. Some way to throw him off my track. I closed my eyes tightly, feeling like my brain was on fire. Suddenly, something occurred to me.

"I hate to poke holes in your theory, but you still haven't explained one thing." I was surprised at how cool my voice sounded.

Cole spun to face me, eyes narrowed. "What do you mean?"

"No forced entry. Three women alone at night—intelligent, savvy women, as I believe you yourself said, but no forced entry." I shook the menu at him. "How did he get inside to do what he did?"

Captain Davis frowned. "Maybe he was charming? Pretended he had a flat, needed to use the phone?"

I shook my head. "Captain, you live alone. Are you seriously telling me you'd let some strange man into your house after midnight to use the phone? In this city?"

"Reed's right." She looked at Cole. "He had to know them somehow."

"The club is still our best bet," I argued, halfway believing it myself. "The books are just a coincidence." I echoed the Captain's words. "He had to know them to get them to open the door."

"No. No he didn't." Cole shook his head, unwilling to abandon the new theory.

"Then why did he open the door?" Captain Davis arched a graying eyebrow skeptically.

"By presenting himself as someone they could trust, or at least someone they didn't have to be afraid of." Cole strode forward and snatched the Wok 'N Roll menu from my hand. "Remember, Lauren Schaefer ordered Thai food not more than an hour before she was killed."

"But the delivery boy turned out to be a girl," I protested.

"But it proves she was used to ordering out—too busy to cook. And do you remember that Sarah Michaels's roommate said she'd discovered the body when she went in to ask if Sarah wanted to order a pizza?"

"So two of your vics ordered out. So do most of the people in America." Captain Davis shrugged.

"No, Captain, *think* about it." Cole turned to face her. "You see somebody with a container of food and a hat or uniform on your doorstep—the automatic response is to open the door. Because he's not just some stranger—he has a function, a reason for being there."

"So our perp is some kind of a delivery man?" she asked.

"Yes, or playing one." Cole paced back and forth in the confined space of the mostly deserted bullpen. "And you know what we saw in the back of Jeremy Bruce's car? A Pizza Hut cap and one of those big red insulated bags. I asked him if he worked for them and he said it paid the rent."

"Wait a minute." The Captain frowned and crossed her arms over her narrow chest. "I thought Bruce had an airtight alibi."

"If you call sleeping with his favorite professor every night an alibi." Cole crumpled the menu in his large fist. "Dammit, I knew that was weak."

"Oh, my God." I put a hand to my mouth, unable to stop the words coming out.

"What?" Cole and the Captain both turned to face me at the same time. I sagged weakly back against the desk. "The last time we went to visit Harner, when I asked for a drink of water so you could snoop around his bedroom…"

"Yes?" Cole leaned over me eagerly, the awkwardness between us forgotten in the heat of excitement.

"He..." My throat felt dry. "There was a pile of pizza coupons on the table and Harner told me...he told me that a young man who had been a patient of Cynthia's had given them to him when he stopped by to offer his condolences after her death."

Captain Davis frowned and ran a hand through her curls. "*Was* Jeremy Bruce one of her patients?"

Cole snapped his fingers excitedly. "Remember that fresh scar on his face? I asked him if it was a defensive wound and he said—"

"He said he'd just had a mole removed," I finished for him, numbly. "Oh, my God, Cole. Just a regular mole, he could have had removed by a dermatologist, but it was on his face...he might have had it removed by a plastic surgeon—at Dr. Love's office."

Captain Davis's narrow face was lit by an inner fire. "You need to check that right now." Cole was already picking up the phone and speaking rapidly. She turned to me. "Can you tie him to the third victim too? Did he have anything to do with Lauren Schaefer?"

I shook my head. "I don't think so. The only think I can think of is that she was a PD so she might have defended him in court at some point. But he had no priors..."

"None that showed up with a routine check," she snapped, grabbing a phone herself. "But he's a kid—barely into his twenties. What if he did something while he was still a minor? If somebody with enough influence happened to be involved..."

She started dialing and then I heard her talking to someone in records, ordering an advanced search on Jeremy Bruce.

"Cynthia Harner removed a malignant melanoma from Jeremy Bruce's face a week before she died. Dr. Love's records confirm it, and he remembers the little shit. Says he seemed to have quite a thing for Cynthia—kept trying to flirt with her during the procedure. He was overseeing because she was still new." Cole slammed down the phone, a look of triumph on his face.

"Uh-huh, uh-huh, thank you." Captain Davis hung up her own phone and turned to face us. "Lauren Schaefer defended Bruce when he was seventeen on drug trafficking charges. She got him a suspended sentence with community service. And get this," She tapped the tabletop knowingly. "His dad's on the board at Busch Gardens—plenty of money to throw around. He went one better and got the record sealed—that's why it didn't show up on your routine background check."

"It all fits. I knew a guy who could afford the kind of car he was driving didn't need to deliver pizza to make the rent." Cole pounded on the desk for emphasis. "Goddammit—this has to be it, but we let that Professor Baird throw us off the trail."

"Okay—this is good." Captain Davis's eyes were shining with excitement and Cole was positively glowing but for once, I couldn't share in the electric charge of a breaking case. I still felt horribly nauseous.

We'd probably found our perp, true, but my secret was still going to come out sooner or later unless I was very lucky. I suddenly remembered the wizened little old black lady, Tante Jinnie, who we'd met while interviewing Sarah Michaels's neighbors at the Carlton Arms. She'd said that Sarah and I shared the same secret and that it might get me killed. At the time I had thought she was talking about our unnatural sexual desires, but maybe she was talking about the online books. Although, how could a woman who looked like she barely understood the use of a telephone know about the Internet? I supposed Sarah could have told her...

"...Reed."

I looked up, realizing Captain Davis was talking to me. I shook my head. "I'm sorry, what?"

"Are you all right? You look white as a sheet." She frowned at me.

"Fine, Captain, just thinking about the case." I straightened up and tried to smile.

She shook her head. "All right, if you say so." She sighed. "God knows this is wearing all of us down but for now, Reed, just try to keep up. Now, I was saying that we're going to split up. You two are going to get Bruce and his love professor, Baird, down here to the station and see if you can't poke some holes in those alibis. I'm going to get on the phone to the ADA and see if we can't come up with a warrant for his residence and car."

"It's going on ten o'clock," Cole objected. "You're going to be pissing off some judge somewhere to get a warrant this time of night."

Captain Davis looked grim. "I'm sure in light of what we just found out we can find a judge somewhere who's willing to sign it. The mayor will push it through if she has to. Remember, she and Lauren Schaefer were friends at law school. But let me worry about that—you two just go!"

"We're on it, Captain." Cole grabbed his jacket and I grabbed mine. "Special delivery coming up."

Chapter Thirty

Cole

"Stop protecting him, Professor, and just tell us the truth."

Professor Lisa Baird swept a stray lock of her luxurious sable-brown hair out of her eyes and gave me her blandest expression. "I told you, Detective Berkley, Jeremy was with me all three nights in question. And if you want my professional opinion, you're barking up the proverbial wrong tree. Jeremy isn't the type to do this sort of thing."

"This sort of thing is serial murder, Professor Baird, and I didn't ask for your professional opinion, just the truth." I sighed in frustration. The case against Jeremy Bruce would be so good if this damn woman wasn't stonewalling us. The thing was, I could tell she was lying. It was written all over her, in the nervous way she played with her hair and tugged at her skirt. She was struggling to control her voice but her eyes were wide and watchful. She knew something all right, and I was determined to get it out of her.

The worst thing was, we hadn't found Jeremy Bruce yet. According to the Pizza Hut (I'd been very surprised to learn that he actually worked there at all) he was out doing deliveries. So while Jeffries and Barkett chased him down, running his route, Alex and I were sweating Professor Baird. Or at least I was. Alex was sitting in a corner of the interrogation room, still looking pale and more and more ill by the minute. I was getting seriously concerned about her.

She'd been quiet all day, understandable considering the blow-out we'd had when she first walked in. At times I had gotten the almost insurmountable urge to touch her, to soothe her in some way, the way I used to before all this started. Only the knowledge that my touch was no longer wanted and would have anything but a soothing effect on my silent partner had made me keep my hands to myself.

The tension between us was high, and the case had been frustrating until it finally started to break. But Alex, who usually went into high gear when the pieces finally started to fit, had been getting quieter and paler as the night wore on. When we'd seen the list of names on Cynthia Harner's Blackberry and equated the authors with our victims, instead of getting excited, she'd looked genuinely ill. If we hadn't been in the middle of a breaking case, I would have insisted that she go home and get some rest.

I looked from my pale and silent partner back to Lisa Baird. The sooner we got what we needed out of her, the sooner we could wrap this mess up and go home. And after Alex had gotten a good night's sleep and wasn't looking so ragged, I fully intended to talk to her again. Never let it be said that Cole Berkley was willing to take no for an answer, especially when my gut told me the lady in question wanted to say yes. Case in point, Lisa Baird.

"C'mon, Professor." I took a seat opposite her, trying a different tack. "You can't expect us to believe that you really spend that much time with your students, even the ones you're sleeping with."

Her face colored and her voice shook slightly but she didn't waver. "I've already disclosed to your partner that I was—am, having a relationship with Jeremy that goes beyond the traditional teacher/student one. I have nothing to hide."

"Except that you're lying." I looked at her carefully, taking in the wide eyes and the hands fidgeting in her lap nervously. Something wasn't right. "Why are you covering for him? You're a good-looking woman, surely you can get someone besides a skinny kid with an Oedipus complex."

"Please don't presume to try and use your pop-culture psychology on me." Her eyes narrowed and flashed, and she lifted her chin defiantly. "I am a leader in the field, Detective, which is why I feel confident in saying that even if Jeremy hadn't been with me on the nights in question, he couldn't have committed these heinous crimes. The kind of sexual practices you've described to me disgust him—they're abhorrent to his very nature."

"A leader in the field, hmm?" I cocked an eyebrow at her and settled back in my chair. "Well then, Professor, I'm sure you publish a lot in the professional journals. Publish or perish—isn't that the credo of the academic world?"

"As a matter of fact I'm quite well published." She crossed her arms protectively over her breasts. "But I fail to see how my publishing record is relevant here."

I held up a hand. "Oh, I'm getting there, just bear with me." I stared at her intently until she squirmed in her seat. "So, if you're published in several of the professional psychiatric journals, it's safe to say that some of your writing ends up online. On the Internet?"

She shrugged. "I suppose some of it does, but why?"

"Ever try your hand at fiction—maybe a short story or a novel?"

"I...may have some time in the past, but I still don't see what that has to do—"

"And when you write fiction, do you use your real name or a pen name?" I interrupted her.

"Well, a pen name, actually."

"Have you ever used the name Victoria Tarlatan?" I looked at her intently but out of the corner of my eye, I saw Alex flinch. What was wrong with her? I became more determined than ever to send my partner home as soon as we had this case in hand.

"Well, no." Lisa Baird looked puzzled but I didn't get a sense that she was lying this time. Damn, I had been so sure that the professor was the next hit on our list. She certainly would have made the most sense if Jeremy was our perp, and I was sure that he had to be. I didn't let it rattle me, though.

"Well if you're not writing under the name of Victoria Tarlatan, some other woman is. And, Professor," I leaned forward, really getting in her face and forcing eye contact.

"Whoever that woman is, her life may be in danger right now. And *you* may have the power to save her, do you understand?"

"No, not at all, actually." Her voice was shaking more now, but she refused to drop her eyes. "Explain what you mean."

Briefly, I outlined the list of authors who also turned out to be victims and Jeremy Bruce's connection with each of them. As I spoke, I watched Lisa Baird's face getting paler and paler. Oh yeah, she would talk—I was sure I could get it out of her. "Now, you say that BDSM sex, like the kind that Sarah Michaels tried to get Jeremy Bruce to participate in, is abhorrent to him. Your words, not mine. Correct?"

Mutely, she nodded.

"Do you think those sexual practices are disgusting enough to him for him to want to punish someone who participates in them?" I asked quietly. "Or maybe that's not entirely it. Maybe this kind of thing both draws him and repels him. He feels compelled to try it and then feels disgusted with himself afterward. Has he ever talked about that in any of your little sessions?"

I could see by the look in her eyes that I was hitting very close to the mark. Her face was as pale as paper. "I...I..." she stuttered.

"Yes?" I leaned forward, eager to hear her spill it at last.

"I think I'd better have a lawyer," she said at last, dropping her eyes. "I don't want to talk anymore until I get one."

Bingo. It was frustrating, but at least I knew she was lawyering up because the alibis she'd been providing were false. But I had to try one more time.

"We can get you a lawyer," I told her. "No problem at all, but I want you to know that as things stand now, if we find out the alibis you've provided for Jeremy Bruce are false, we can get you as an accessory to every one of these murders. That carries some heavy jail time. Now, we may be able to work a deal but once the lawyer walks in the door, it's off the table."

"What?" she yelped, her eyes widening. "But I was never anywhere near—" She shut up abruptly, but it was too late.

"Listen, Professor," I said, getting down to her level, face to face again. "The life you save by telling the truth may be your own. Do you really think Jeremy is going to stop once he reaches the end of the list? He's got a real taste for it now—the killing. It excites him. Every crime scene we find is more elaborate and more lovingly detailed than the last. It's my experience that these people *do not stop* until we catch them. Are you really going to let him go free?"

"Well, I...I..." She looked up at me, biting her lip nervously.

"Look," I told her. "He's killing women he *knows*, and frankly, I'm surprised you weren't at the top of that list. But you can be damn sure you'll be somewhere near the bottom, and it won't take him long to get there at this rate." I got out of my chair and went around to kneel in front of her. I took her cold, clammy hands in mine and looked up at her. "If you don't do it for yourself, do it for Victoria Tarlatan, whoever she is. She's out there somewhere. Maybe she was his dentist, maybe another professor, hell, she could be his fifth-grade piano teacher for all we know. And she has no idea that she's on his list."

"All right...all right." The calm outer demeanor finally cracked and tears started pouring down her face, ruining a very careful make-up job. "We ate dinner the nights I told you, but after that we went our separate ways. He...we...we only made love once, but I was afraid someone would find out, that I could lose my tenure. And...and besides, I just didn't think that Jeremy would do that kind of thing. Oh, God—I still can't believe it." She pulled her hands out of mine and covered her face, sobbing. "I didn't want his life to be ruined but I didn't think..." She trailed off, obviously unable to continue.

"All right," I said softly, patting her shoulder. What I wanted to do was punch the wall. If this woman hadn't been so stubbornly assured of her own professional analysis of Jeremy Bruce, Lauren Schaefer might still be alive right now. But there was no bringing her back so instead I said, "Thank you, Lisa. For Victoria Tarlatan too, whoever she is."

There was a slight noise in the corner and when I looked over I felt my blood pressure skyrocket. Alex was slumped in her chair, her eyes rolled up until all I could see was the whites. She was in the process of sliding to the ground when I caught her.

"Alex," I said sharply. "Alex, can you hear me?"

She didn't respond to my voice but when I patted her cheek lightly, she moaned. Her pulse seemed steady but her breathing was light and rapid. I cradled her close to my chest and rushed her out of the room.

Chapter Thirty-One

Alex

"Alex...Alex?" Someone was calling my name and something cold and wet was on my forehead. Chilly, ticklish rivulets of water dripped down the sides of my face and neck. I opened my eyes to see both Cole and Captain Davis peering at me with worried expressions on their faces. I tried to sit up but two sets of hands pushed me back down immediately.

"Just hold still, Reed, the ambulance is coming." Captain Davis's eyes behind her glasses were large and worried.

"Ambulance? What are you talking about?" I struggled to sit up again and when Cole pushed me back down, I grabbed the dripping wet rag from my head and threw it at him. It bounced off his chest, leaving a big wet mark on his dark blue shirt and ended up on the floor. Looking around I saw that I was in the Captain's office, on the cot she keeps folded in the corner for the occasional all-nighter.

"You fainted." Cole looked terribly concerned, completely ignoring my petulant display with the washcloth. "I was sweating Baird and I looked over and you were about to hit the floor."

I vaguely remembered now, feeling worse and worse in the interrogation room, while he kept on talking about Victoria Tarlatan. As I sat and listened to him work on Professor Baird, it had hit me, in a much harder way than previously, that Victoria Tarlatan was *me*. That someone, apparently Jeremy Bruce, wanted me dead for some reason. I don't know why it suddenly bothered me, maybe it was the way Cole kept repeating the name. But the last thing I remembered was huge, slow-motion fireworks exploding before my eyes and then everything went black.

Of course, I couldn't tell them that I had fainted for an emotional reason because I would then have to explain what the reason was. It was embarrassing enough to faint at all without having to explain why. I had always prided myself on never fainting or puking at a crime scene, even the more gory ones, and now I had blacked out during a routine questioning. I would never live it down. Luckily, they didn't ask me to explain.

"I blame myself, I saw how white you looked earlier." Captain Davis frowned.

"It's my fault." Cole looked anguished, and I knew he meant my perceived illness was his fault in more than one way. He probably thought the mental and emotional stress we'd both been under was responsible for my collapse. He cupped my cheek gently, his eyes full of pain. For a moment, I let myself relax into his touch. It might be more weakness but it just felt so damn good, and I had been craving it all day.

"How is it your fault she fainted, Berkley? Did Reed tell you she felt sick?"

I looked up to see Captain Davis looking at Cole and myself with a sharp, suspicious look on her narrow face. Quickly, I pulled away from his touch before she drew the wrong conclusion. Or would that be the right conclusion? Cole and I were known to be touchy but he was taking it too far. Touching me like a lover and not just a partner. I turned away from the hurt look on his face.

"It's not Berkley's fault, Captain," I improvised rapidly. "He tried to make me eat but I just couldn't. This damn case has got my stomach in knots—guess my blood sugar got too low. But I feel fine now, see?" I sat up too rapidly and felt everything spinning again as the blood rushed to my head. I nearly slid off the cot but Cole caught me and seemed to have no intention of letting me go. I wanted to push him away, but I was too weak, both physically and emotionally. I gave in and let my head rest against his broad chest. Let Captain Davis think what she wanted.

"Yes, I can see you're in tip-top shape, Reed," she commented dryly. "Just peachy."

"I'll be fine as soon as I eat something, really," I protested as well as I was able from the confining shelter of Cole's arms. "Please, Captain, just give me a piece of fruit and let's get back to work. Cancel the ambulance, I'm fine, honestly."

She harrumphed, looking grouchy. "All right, I'll cancel it but you're not going anywhere but home to bed, Reed. And I expect—" The ringing of her phone cut her off and she talked rapidly for several minutes while we waited. I used the time to free myself from Cole's encompassing grip, trying to ignore the hurt look on his face as I did so. I needed to stand on my own two feet, both literally and figuratively. By the time Captain Davis was off the phone, I had managed it, feeling only slightly dizzy. Cole still stood protectively behind me, ready to catch me if I fell.

"That was Jeffries. They got Jeremy Bruce outside his last delivery stop. Guess which Pizza Hut he works for."

"The one closest to Bayshore," I volunteered.

Captain Davis nodded, "Got it in one. Now, the warrants for his car and residence should be in at any time. I'm going to have Jeffries and Barkett go over both with a fine tooth comb while Berkley sweats him."

"Sounds good." I straightened up, trying to make myself appear steadier than I felt. "Where do you want me?"

"Home in bed, Reed, just like I said." She looked at me sharply. "I don't want you driving, either. Berkley should have enough time to run you home and get back in the time it takes Jeffries and Barkett to get here from Bayshore."

"I'm fine," I protested, but I knew it was a losing argument. Captain Davis had that flinty look in her eye she gets when she's made a decision she isn't prepared to be flexible on.

"Just go. Get some sleep and something to eat, not necessarily in that order."

"I can't leave in the middle of an ongoing investigation," I protested. I swayed on my feet and Cole caught me from behind. I really did feel weak, and I began to wonder if maybe my blood sugar was too low. I struggled to stand on my own again but he wouldn't let me go.

"Reed, look at you." The Captain gestured at me. "You're weak as a kitten. We've got our perp, and you know it."

"We thought that before," I protested but she held up a hand to stop me.

"This time we're right. So go home and take the night off, what little there is left of it. Come back tomorrow when you're at a hundred percent. There's going to be plenty of paperwork for all of us by then."

"All right," I grumbled, admitting defeat, but not very gracefully. "But I can drive myself."

"Reed, enough bullshit already. I said Berkley's taking you home, and he is. Now get out of my hair, I've got to work on those warrants." She shooed us irritably out the door and I knew that was the end of it.

The ride home was mostly silent, but I had a feeling that Cole was keeping a lot he wanted to say bottled up inside. He had insisted on keeping a protective arm around my shoulders all the way out to the parking lot and then helping me up into the passenger side of his truck. I have to admit, I hadn't tried very hard to get away. I felt shaky both emotionally and physically, and I needed his touch more than I could admit to myself.

As we pulled into my driveway, I was swamped by a deep regret about the way things were between us. If only Cole and I weren't partners and were free to have a relationship. If only I hadn't allowed him to get inside my head and see my most secret and perverted desires. If only I didn't have those desires in the first place. If only, if only... Another one of my mom's sayings popped into my brain. If wishes were horses then beggars might ride. In other words, get over it because it isn't going to happen.

I became aware that the truck was no longer moving and that we'd been sitting silently in the driveway of my small house for some time. "Well, thanks for the ride." I said. I moved to open the door but Cole's hand on my arm stopped me.

"Alex." His voice was quiet and serious. I looked at him, not certain of what to say, so I kept my mouth shut. "After this is all over..." He cleared his throat and shook his head. "There's something I need to tell you. Something we need to talk about."

"Cole," I began but he shook his head and held up a hand.

"Not right now. There's no time. But soon." He reached out to cup my face again, as he had after I fainted, and for some reason I didn't shy away. His hand was large and warm and gentle, and he stroked my cheek as though I was made out of glass and might crack if he touched me wrong.

We sat that way for a moment, and I could feel him wanting to kiss me and I could feel myself wanting to kiss him back. But to do that would be to give in to weakness again, which would do neither of us any good.

"I'd better go," I said at last. With a brief sigh, Cole dropped his hand.

"All right, I need to get back and sweat this little bastard until he gives." He looked grim. "And he *will* give."

I gave a tired laugh that was more than half sigh. "Don't they always, Cole?"

He grinned at me. "Well, I can be pretty persuasive if I say so myself."

"You better get going," I told him. I opened the door and slid out, feeling for the ground with both feet. I didn't feel faint anymore, but I did feel terribly weak. Maybe I did need to eat something.

As though reading my mind, Cole rolled down his window and said, "Hey, get something to eat, will you? Order a pizza."

"Ha-ha," I said sourly. I knew it was a reference to our suspect being a deliveryman, but in this business if you don't have a sense of humor, even gallows humor, you won't get far before you crack. Cole was trying to cheer me up, and it almost worked.

"Seriously though, eat something," he said, and then, "Alex?"

I was halfway down the walk but the tone in his voice made me turn back. "Yeah?"

"Be careful." His face was troubled somehow, as though by the shadow of something he couldn't see but could only feel.

"I'll be fine," I said. I wrapped my jacket more firmly around me. "Look, it's freezing out here, I'm going in."

"Talk to you later," he said, and I knew he meant it in more than a casual way.

"All right," I said, resigned. It didn't matter how he put it, the facts of our lives were inescapable and undeniable. I loved him, and I wanted him more than I could say but we couldn't be together. But Cole, ever the optimist, didn't want to see it that way.

I felt his eyes on my back as I unlocked the front door and let myself in to the dark house. Only after I had flipped the switch and locked the door behind me did I hear the big engine under the hood of his truck roar to life and drive away.

I sighed and went into the bedroom, trying not to remember the events of the night before. Being handcuffed to the bed while Cole went down on me, the feel of his body thrusting into mine, the sound of his voice when he told me what a good girl I was for taking it all… I shivered, God—I had to stop thinking like this. Had to get a grip on myself.

I put the Browning in my nightstand drawer, its usual place when I'm at home, and went to take a long, hot shower. Afterwards I wrapped myself in my favorite fuzzy pink terrycloth robe and turned on the computer. I needed to relax and unwind, needed to forget the case and the stress of the day and most especially the problems I'd been having with Cole. I thought the best way might be to work on my book.

But when I brought up *Twisted Desire* that was exactly how I felt inside—twisted. I read the words I had written, but along with the flush of desire I felt, there was also a stabbing sense of shame. I had told myself when I started publishing the books online that it was only a hobby, just a game I was playing with myself for release. A form of mental masturbation. But look where this little game had gotten Cynthia Harner, Sarah Michaels, and Lauren Schaefer. All of them had the same sick fantasies I had myself, and all of them had dared to share their twisted longings with the world at large via the Internet. And Jeremy Bruce had killed them for it.

I remembered the look of disgust and revulsion in Jeremy's eyes when he spoke of how sick Sarah Michaels had been. He'd called her a freak, and I was sure he would see me the same way. My writing had certainly affected him that way—it was how I had ended up on his list in the first place. The worst thing was that I sort of agreed with him. Not to the extent that I deserved to be killed, but I was definitely not normal—not by any stretch of the imagination.

I flipped off the computer, not having written a word, and scrubbed a hand through my hair. There was no point in asking myself for the thousandth time why I was like this, but I felt my mind going there anyway, falling into the old familiar groove. If it was simply a matter of a few vague fantasies or half-formed desires, I could dismiss it easily enough. But it was a need, something rooted so deeply in my psyche there was no pulling it out, as much as I might want to. And, oh, God, I certainly wanted to.

I leaned back in my computer chair and thought of all the lovers I'd had since college. There weren't that many, considerably fewer than most women my age who'd never been married had had, I guessed. Dating a cop can be tough for any man. It seems like the minute they find out what you do for a living, they have to prove how macho they are. It was one reason my romantic relationships didn't last very long. The other reason was that vanilla sex didn't hold my attention or my affection. I needed something more to keep me in a relationship than a quick roll in the missionary-style hay.

But out of the men I had dated, I had only revealed my secret needs to one—to Jeff. And he distanced himself from me pretty quickly after I did. To tell the truth, I didn't blame him. Sometimes I thought *I* would get some distance from myself if only I could.

Only Cole, when faced with the reality of what I wanted, what I *needed*, in the bedroom, hadn't turned tail and run. He'd been upset at first and understandably confused by the strange dichotomy between my tough-cop image and my deeply submissive fantasies. But he had eventually come around—too far around, in my opinion. As my friend and partner he was the last person I should have acted out those fantasies with. I loved him with everything that was in me, but he needed more than that. He needed me to be strong for him, needed to know I would always be there to get his back. But now, how could he trust me when he'd seen me acting so...

"So weak," I whispered aloud. There it was, the root of my problem, the reason my needs and desires made me feel so dirty and wrong. It was the fact that what I wanted in the bedroom was the right to feel weak—to be vulnerable and lose control. But my whole life was about control and had been ever since I could remember. Being in control, being strong, being the best at what I was and never, ever letting anyone all the way in— that was my whole existence. Letting go of that, giving in, even for just a little while, was both seductive and terrifying. And utterly forbidden.

A part of me, a part I kept buried as well as I could, was still a little girl, starving for affection and attention I hadn't earned. I hadn't earned the right to let go, to give in and let someone else pleasure me the way Cole had the night before. I had no business allowing myself the luxury of weakness. No right to give in to my perverted fantasies and let my warped desires carry me away the way I had... Sick, weak, twisted...

My bitter musings were interrupted by the ringing of the doorbell. I frowned and glanced at the clock—it was going on midnight. Who could possibly be at my door at this time of night?

I got up, belting my robe more tightly around myself. I considered getting my Browning from the nightstand table but dismissed the thought as being stupidly paranoid. Jeremy Bruce was in custody at the downtown PD and I had nothing to worry about.

I went to the door, as I had the night before when Cole and I had acted out this scene. I stared through the peep hole and yelled, "Who is it?"

Chapter Thirty-Two

Cole

It was a long ride back down to the PD while I considered the words I hadn't said to Alex. I wanted to tell her that I wanted more from her than just her friendship, that I didn't want to lose her as a partner, and most of all, that I loved her. But the words had stuck in my throat and there was no time to get into what would probably turn into a huge argument once it got started. It was an argument I fully intended to win. That morning, Alex had tried to freeze me out. She said she wanted a new partner—that was equivalent to saying she wanted out of my life completely. But I wasn't about to let her go.

The caveman part of my brain was still insisting that she was *mine*, that I had claimed her the other night. Primitive and stupid, I know, but I couldn't help it. I'd always felt a certain amount of possessiveness toward my partner, and the mind-blowing sex we'd had the night before had deepened it considerably.

I promised myself I would tie her to the bed, if necessary. I would keep her in one place so she couldn't get away, so she would have to listen to my arguments until she came around. Because it was clear to me that she wanted to come around but was simply too scared and stubborn to admit it.

The way she'd leaned into my touch when I stroked her cheek and the way she'd responded to me last night proved there was something between us that even Alex couldn't deny. And whatever it was, all I wanted was a chance to let it grow. And if letting it grow meant going places sexually that I had never dreamed of before, so be it. I had decided I wouldn't reject anything she wanted to try in bed.

I've been a pretty vanilla guy most of my life, mostly because I was with Amanda, who, aside from her guilty passion for the cheesiest romance novels imaginable, was very straight-laced in bed. I had never felt like I was missing anything although our lovemaking could probably be termed prosaic at best, especially after Madison was born. And if anyone would have asked me a week ago if I thought I could get turned on by whipping Alex with a belt or handcuffing her to the bed while I had my way with her, my answer would have been an emphatic no. Of course, that was before I knew she *wanted* those things.

It felt funny to admit it, but I had actually *enjoyed* playing the dominant Master. And with a little practice, I thought I might get pretty good at it. Not so much that I could go out to bondage clubs and play the part every night—I was relieved that Alex didn't seem terribly interested in that. But in the bedroom, alone—that would be a whole different story.

I hadn't been sure, when I first learned of her desires, if I could stand to hurt her. But now, understanding the reaction erotic pain could generate in her, I thought I could easily spank her or whip her if she wanted me to. After all, anything that made her that wet and aroused could only be a good thing, as far as I was concerned. Yes, I was more than willing to try anything she could dream up, as long as we did it together.

My train of thought was interrupted when I pulled into the station parking lot. It was time to get my mind on the business of Jeremy Bruce. All I wanted to do at that point was get everything I could from the little bastard and get back to Alex as quickly as possible. I walked into the PD with that single thought on my mind, feeling focused and controlled.

What I wasn't prepared for was to see two suspects instead of one. Jeremy Bruce was sitting with his large knuckled hands folded quietly on the rough wooden table in interrogation room one. In interrogation room two was a kid roughly Jeremy's age but considerably taller and so thin if you turned him sideways he might disappear. A shock of rumpled reddish-orange hair stuck up in crazy corkscrews all over his head, not surprising since he was running both hands through it almost continuously. Watery blue eyes stared at me though the one-way glass almost as if he could see me, and I could see his lips moving in some kind of frantic, silent mantra.

"Hey, Berkley." I turned at the sound of my name and saw Brad Jeffries, one of the detectives Captain Davis had assigned to pick up Jeremy Bruce, coming toward me.

"Jeffries." I nodded, taking in his nicotine-stained fingers and rumpled suit. Jeffries always looks like he just climbed out from under the Salvation Army rummage pile, but he's a damn fine detective for all of that. Being a good detective doesn't mean he's not a pain in the ass, though.

"I heard about Reed—she okay?"

"Fine," I said, shortly. "Her blood sugar got low. She just needs to eat something."

He shook his head sympathetically. "It's a rough case, I guess it was too much for the little lady."

"Look, Jeffries," I said, getting in his face. "I'd rather have that 'little lady' watching my back than any four guys on this squad—she's as tough as they come. So if you're thinking of giving her shit for passing out, well, I wouldn't if I were you."

"Or what, you'll kick my ass?" Jeffries stood tall, but he still couldn't quite meet my eyes.

"No," I said, glaring at him. "I won't have to—Alex can kick your sorry ass herself when she gets back. Now, did you have something you wanted to tell me?"

Jeffries backed down and shook his head. "Bad news, my friend. Very, very bad news."

"We've got Jeremy Bruce right where we want him, how bad can it be?" I nodded at interrogation room one.

"What's so bad is that it looks like the little shit has an alibi for at least two of the three nights in question."

"How can you possibly know that?" I demanded, beginning to get angry. "Captain Davis gave orders for *me* to sweat him. I wanted to go at him fresh. Now I come back to find you and Barkett have already corrupted my suspect."

He held up his hands. "Hey, don't get pissed at me. Barkett's going over his car and apartment—the warrant came as soon as you walked out the door. And I didn't say jack to your suspect.

It's his little friend there who's been talking. In fact, he hasn't stopped talking from the minute we brought him in." He nodded at the tall skinny redhead in interrogation two.

"So what's he been saying?" I said, wondering how many people Jeremy Bruce would find to lie for him. I was as prepared to knock holes in this guy's story as I had been with Professor Baird's.

"Mostly that he doesn't want to go back to prison," Jeffries said dryly. "Name's Walter Torvald, and he spent about a year inside for drug trafficking already, which is exactly what we caught him and Bruce doing tonight. See, your suspect hasn't just been delivering pizzas to all those fancy mansions on Bayshore and apparently he isn't the only one. There's a whole damn ring of 'delivery' boys in the Bay area, catering to the upper crust."

"What does that have to do with Jeremy Bruce's alibi for the nights in question?" I demanded, watching the skinny kid pace and mutter to himself. His skin had the unhealthy pallor of a heroin addict and anybody knows you can't trust a junkie.

"What it has to do with it is that his buddy Walt, there, is being run by the narcs. Federal, no less. They've been keeping him and, incidentally, Jeremy Bruce, under observation for the past two months. The head guy is in Captain Davis's office right now screaming for blood, saying we're going to ruin their bust. They want Bruce and Torvald back on the streets pronto before the head delivery man can miss them."

"Like hell we're putting them back on the streets," I said, feeling rage build and tighten in my chest. "Jeremy Bruce looks fucking great for all three of these murders and if some federal narc thinks he can make me let him go so the little bastard can go do another one, he's out of his ever-fucking skull."

"Hey, you're a scary guy when you're angry." Jeffries backed away and nodded in the direction of the captain's office. "Go tell it to the man himself. I'm out of it."

I slammed into Captain Davis's office, ready to bring the fight home but what I saw on her desk stopped me dead in my tracks. Glossy colored surveillance photos, most of them showing Jeremy Bruce and Walter Torvald, littered its surface. In the right hand corner of each was a digital readout of the date and time they had been taken.

I looked at the top one. It showed our suspect handing a baggie in exchange for cash through an open door. The date on the bottom was November twenty-second at around midnight. It didn't take a mathematical genius to figure out that Jeremy Bruce couldn't have been raping and killing Cynthia Harner at the same time that he was selling heroin or speed balls or whatever the hell was in the baggie at the same time.

"Berkley." Captain Davis looked up, her narrow face lined and haggard. Beside her was a short, thick man in his forties with a luxurious mustache and a shiny bald head. "Meet Captain Martin from the Federal Drug Commission. They've been tracking the flow of heroin through Tampa International for the past several months."

"Is there a reason we weren't informed before now?" I asked tightly.

"The more people who know about an operation, the greater the chance it'll go down the crapper." Martin's voice had the harsh quality of a man with a four-pack-a-day habit.

"Which is where it's going right now if you don't release Bruce and Torvald right now."

Captain Davis spread her hands and shrugged regretfully. "I'm sorry, Berkley—they've got surveillance pictures of Bruce on every one of the nights in question. He's clear—at least with us."

"Well, why the hell couldn't they have told us earlier?" I demanded, turning on Martin. "We ran this same suspect in earlier this week, and nobody said anything. We've got a goddamn serial killer on our hands, and you people are sitting on vital information."

"Bruce isn't our snitch—Walters is," Martin said coolly. "It's not my fault if you people can't get it together enough to do your job and catch the right man."

I wanted to wring his neck, but there was no time to get into a pissing match. I turned to go.

"Berkley, wait," Captain Davis called.

I looked over my shoulder. "I don't have time. There's still a killer out there somewhere, and he's got another victim in his sights. We have to find out who Victoria Tarlatan is and get to her before he does."

Chapter Thirty-Three

Alex

Through the distorted, fish-bowl eye of my peephole, I could see that the man standing on my front doorstep was wearing a pizza delivery jacket and a ball cap with a long brim. He had his head tilted down so I couldn't see his face and one of those big red insulated bags that keeps the pizza warm until it reaches you. The night was chilly, so I didn't think anything of the black gloves that covered his hands.

"What do you want?" I said, still not opening the door.

"Delivery for Miss Reed." His voice was muffled by the jacket. A gust of wind blew across the porch and he shivered and tucked his head deeper.

"I didn't order a pizza," I said, exasperated. If this was a joke it was in very poor taste. Probably some of the guys back at the station had already learned about my little fainting episode and had sprung into action. They were always up for a practical joke.

Assholes. I should have thought up a better excuse for fainting than low blood sugar.

"Says here somebody sent it to you." He kept his head tilted down, his neck hunched into the jacket's collar, reading from the ticket in his hand. "A Mr. Cole Berkley. Paid for and everything."

Cole had sent me a pizza for real? I was torn between gratitude at his thoughtfulness and irritation at his choice of take-out. There *is* such a thing as taking gallows humor too far.

"So this is paid for?" I asked.

The man nodded. "Paid in full, lady. Even the tip."

I smiled to myself. It was like Cole to even think of paying the tip so I wouldn't have to open the door to a stranger when I was alone.

"Fine," I told the delivery guy. "Then just leave it on the front porch. I'll get it in a minute."

"You paranoid or something?" he asked.

"Maybe," I said. "Or maybe I'm just careful. After all, just because you're paranoid doesn't mean they're not out to get you, right?"

The delivery guy shrugged—obviously my humor was lost on him. "Whatever you say, lady." He slid a cardboard pizza box out of the insulated bag and set it on the porch. "You better get it quick. It's gonna be a frozen pizza if it stays out here too long."

"Thank you. I'm aware of how cold it is." I put a note of frost in my voice, letting the guy know I was waiting for him to leave. He shrugged again and turned, leaving my front porch, his head still tucked deep in his jacket.

"Nice night to you, too," I heard him say, and then the clunk of a car door opening as he went out of sight in my peephole.

I opened the door, shivering against the gust of cold wind, and reached for the pizza. "Let's see what you sent me, Cole," I muttered to myself. If my partner had remembered I liked veggie lover's with extra peppers, my gratitude would surely win out over my irritation. I felt my stomach rumble.

Before I could lift the box, the deliveryman was suddenly at my side, reaching into the big red bag he still held. "He said it was your favorite," he said, his voice low and menacing. He pulled something out of the bag and pointed it at me.

I stared in surprise at what he held in his hand. A gun.

Chapter Thirty-Four

Cole

"There has to be some way to find out who she is." I paced back and forth between my desk and Alex's, thinking out loud. I had tried to call her earlier, to tell her we were back to square one yet again, but she wasn't answering the phone. Probably either in the shower or the bath, was my guess. Alex loves long hot bubble baths, a fact her mother let slip when I was over at her house once. I had gotten my partner a deluxe basket full of Bath and Body Works products for her next birthday as a joke—a token offering to her softer, more feminine side, which she liked to deny existed. Alex had been pissed at me for a month afterward, but I knew she was using the products because I could smell them on her skin when we were together in the car.

"Uh, Detective B, you wanted me?" Matt appeared by my side, blinking his eyes groggily, his hair even wilder than usual.

He had on a too-tight, baby blue T-shirt that said, "I'm not your type—I'm not inflatable."

"Yeah, thanks for coming in this time of night, Matt. Or—" I glanced at my watch. "I guess now it's morning. Uh, nice shirt."

He looked down at himself and groaned. "Oh, man! This is Jennie's—my girlfriend's. It was dark when I got dressed. She's never gonna let me live this down."

"She won't have to find out if you can work fast." I told him about the necessity of finding out the identity of Victoria Tarlatan and contacting her immediately and the sleepy look left his eyes.

"She's next on the guy's list, huh? I'm on it." He sat down at the computer and started clattering away immediately. I watched for a minute and then tried to get Alex on my cell again. How long could she soak in the tub? I knew she would kill me if I let the re-activated case go down without her. She had only allowed herself to be persuaded to leave tonight because she thought we had the perp tied up in a neat little package. Well, it wasn't the first time we'd been wrong.

The phone rang and rang until eventually I got her prerecorded voice message. Listening to the message, which sounded flat and tinny over the phone, I felt distinctly uncomfortable. Why wasn't she picking up?

"Got it!" Matt's exclamation pulled me away from my uneasy thoughts, and I turned to see him pointing to the screen. "She's published two books with an online company called Loose Id. Strictly e-books." He moved the mouse, clicking on various links. "Most of these authors have their own web site but..." He frowned, disappointed. "Victoria Tarlatan doesn't.

Damn. Well, let's see if there's a bio…" More clicking produced no further information.

"Well?" I asked anxiously, leaning over his shoulder.

He shook his head. "Sorry, Detective B. Whoever this chick is, she's really careful not to let her real info onto the 'Net. Can't say that I blame her with the kind of stuff she's writing. Somebody might take it as an invitation and decide to pay her a visit."

"That's exactly what we're afraid of," I said grimly, staring at the covers of Victoria Tarlatan's e-books on the screen. Both involved women in positions of subservience, with arms bound behind their backs. Helpless, vulnerable—the sight sent a chill down my spine and an idea niggled at the corners of my brain.

"Keep looking, Matt. Whoever she is, she's bound to be local. See if you can't find some kind of connection that way," I told him. "I'm going to check something else."

I went to get Cynthia Harner's Blackberry and, with a little difficulty, found my way into the Microsoft Reader where her books were stored. A quick scan of her book, *Velvet Agony*, aroused my worst fears. There was a scene in the book where the heroine was bound to the bed and blindfolded while a man with black leather gloves has sex with her. I flipped to the next book by Sarah Michaels, *Sweet Submission*, and found a similar scene. Only in this book, the man whipped the bound and helpless woman's inner thighs before covering her in rose petals and making love to her. A quick click to Lauren Schaefer's book, *Painful Pleasure*, showed a scene of erotic torture involving hot wax.

Feeling my heart race, I clicked to the last book on the list, *Whispers in the Dark*, by Victoria Tarlatan. Sure enough, there was a scene with the heroine bound helpless to the bed. I scanned it quickly and then shut my eyes, unable to look at it any more.

My God, he was using their own books to choose the manner of their deaths. If we didn't find Victoria Tarlatan, and quickly, she was going to meet an agonizing end.

Chapter Thirty-Five

Alex

I've had a gun pointed at me before—being in my profession pretty much guarantees that. But I'd never had it happen in my own home before and never when I was unarmed and unprepared. My eyes widened as they flicked from the gun to the man holding it. "I don't understand," I said.

"You don't have to." He grinned at me, more of a snarl, and pressed closer.

I backed away and the gun followed me into the house, the muzzle looking as wide as a tunnel. It seemed to consume my whole field of vision. If I thought I could have gotten away with it, I would have slammed the door on his wrist, and caused him to drop it. But he was too quick for me, shoving the big black gun in my face, letting me know he could pull the trigger faster than I could make a move.

The minute we were inside, he snaked an arm around my neck and I could feel the cool press of steel as the cylinder nuzzled its way through my hair and kissed my temple. The oily metallic smell of it filled my sinuses like cold tears.

"You don't want to do this," I said, finding my voice again, as he kicked the front door shut with one booted foot.

"Oh, but I do. I want it more than you can imagine." His breath against the back of my neck was hot and smelled like rotten sushi—repugnant. I fought to keep from gagging.

"Let me go, and we'll talk about this." I put my hands up to his arm, which was in a chokehold around my neck, but his grip was like iron. I was reminded sickly of the way Cole and I had acted out this very scene the night before. Why had I opened the door? Why had I foolishly assumed I was safe? Just like all the other women, I was a victim of my own complacency—my own stupidity. Dimly, I could hear my cell phone ringing somewhere. Whoever it was would have to call back.

"I have a better idea—let's go into the bedroom." He guided me there as though he'd been there before. I felt a shiver run though me. How long had he been watching me, plotting his move?

"This isn't really you," I said, taking a chance, trying to keep my voice level. "You're a nice guy. Come on, let's talk about it."

"I think we've had enough talking." His voice was rougher and the arm around my neck tightened, choking off my air. I gasped and struggled until he loosened his hold. "All right?" he purred in my ear. Somehow, I managed to nod my head.

He guided me toward the bed, which was neatly made despite the turmoil my life was in. No matter how bad things get, it's always nice to come home to a neat house—another nugget of wisdom from my mom, the same woman who had taught me never to take candy from strangers. I wondered how she would feel when she learned that my killer had gotten into the house by offering me a pizza. No doubt she would be very disapproving.

You're not dead yet, I told myself sternly. *Although you're going to be if you don't do something soon. Once he ties you down...* Yes, once he had me helpless on the bed, then it would be game over. And a quick death would be preferable to what he no doubt had in mind. I didn't want to go down without a fight.

Taking a chance, I pulled back my arm and rammed it into his gut, twisting at the same time I drove my heel into his instep. If I had been wearing shoes and could've gotten better leverage, it would have been much more effective. As it was, I felt the stale gust of air rush past my face but his hold on me didn't loosen—it tightened. The muzzle of the gun pressed so hard against my temple I was afraid I'd have a permanent tattoo of it there.

"Try that again and you're dead. In fact, I think this would go much more smoothly without your participation." The arm around my neck tightened again, until my vision was shot though with veins of solid black. I scrabbled uselessly at his forearm but the jacket was too thick for me to use my nails.

I felt him lift me, one-armed, into the air, and I kicked back against his legs as hard as I could, which wasn't very hard with no oxygen in my lungs. I could hear him laughing at my feeble attempts as the view of my bedroom took on the same distorted fish-bowl look offered by my peephole. Useless, it was useless. He was going to kill me right now. Huge black flowers bloomed in front of my eyes for the second time that night. But this time Cole wouldn't be there to pick me up and put a damp cloth on my head. This time I was on my own.

"We'll have some fun when you wake up," I heard him say and then there was nothing. Nothing at all.

Chapter Thirty-Six

Cole

"I'm sorry, Detective B, still lookin'. Give me a minute more." Matt was typing furiously at the keyboard, the muted clatter filling the empty bullpen. I paced back and forth, thinking out loud.

"Local authors...romance authors...writers' groups... That's it! Matt, do a search for local writers' groups."

He was quiet for a moment, then he said, "Here we are, but I'm afraid there's a hell of a lot of them."

"Just look at the ones that focus on romance writing or, uh, erotica," I suggested.

The screen blurred and then Matt gave a short, sharp bark of a laugh. "Uh, Detective B, that's most of them."

"Damn!" I stared at the list he'd Googled for me, wondering which one to focus on. There was no way we had time to go through them all. "Start cross-referencing and see if her name pops up on any of those sites," I directed Matt. "Keep going, I have to make a call."

I turned away, trying Alex first, and getting her machine again. *Damn it, pick up!* I wasn't sure exactly what my partner was writing in her spare time (my guess was angsty poetry or maybe a book about being a woman cop), but I thought she might have some idea of the best place to start whittling down the massive list. I had a momentary spasm of worry for her but pushed it away. She was probably sound asleep already, and she could curse me out tomorrow for going on with the case without her.

The thought that she might be writing the same kind of books that all our victims had published had never entered my head. Alex was a very private person—I would have bet my salary for a month that she would never share her private fantasies with the world at large, even anonymously. Then again, a week ago, I would have bet the same amount that she wasn't into any kind of kinky sex. It was a bet I would have lost. I pushed the thought away—I had to concentrate on the case.

There was only one other person I could think of who might have an idea of what I needed to know, and I hated like hell to call her. But there was no other choice. Sighing, I cycled through my cell until I came to Amanda's new number. My ex-wife read romance books the way some people ate junk food— furtively and compulsively. I was hoping she would know something about the production of her favorite mental snack.

"H'lo?" She answered on the third ring, sounding groggy, and I had the momentary satisfaction of having been the one to wake her up instead of the other way around. "'Manda, who's it?" I heard a nasally voice in the background asking. Senior partner Bill.

"Amanda, it's me," I said without preamble, the same way she always did. "I need some information."

"Cole, it's past midnight, and I have to get up in four hours. What do you want?" There was a rustle of bed sheets, and her voice sharpened immediately.

"I need to know if you know anything about local writers' groups. Specifically romance writers' groups." I tapped against the desk with a pen impatiently.

"You called me at this time of night to ask me that? Forget it—I'm going back to bed."

"If you hang up without helping me, a woman is going to die." It sounded cheesy, but it was sufficiently dramatic to keep her on the line.

"All right, what do you want to know? I just read the stuff, I don't write it." Her voice was flat.

"I know that, but I was just hoping... If you did decide to write it, is there one local writers' group that would be the one to join? Any one organization that's at the top of the list?" Trust Amanda to know the highest echelon of any group or organization.

"Well, if you're talking about organized groups, that take dues and that kind of thing, I'd have to say the RWA." There was a muffled complaint in the background and she covered the phone and said, clearly enough for me to hear, "I know, Bill, but believe me, the easiest way to get rid of him is to just give him what he wants... No, I'll be off in a minute, I promise."

"The RWA, what does that stand for?" I was scribbling rapidly on my desk blotter.

"Romance Writers of America—that's the one I've heard about most often. Now look, Cole, I really have to go."

"Fine. Thanks."

"And we'll talk about Madison later," she added.

"What about Madison?" I asked sharply, momentarily distracted from the case.

She sighed loud enough that I pulled the phone away from my ear. "She's been begging me non-stop to come spend Christmas Eve with you, and I've decided to let her have her way just this once."

It was the first good news I'd had all day. "Thanks, Amanda," I said, really meaning it. "It means a lot to me."

She sighed again. "To her, too—she hasn't shut up about it since we saw you the other night. God knows what she sees in you, I certainly don't." Then she hung up without saying goodbye, the click loud in my ear.

I turned to Matt, who was still typing furiously. "Try the Romance Writers of America."

"Got it." There was another short, sporadic burst of keyboard clatter, and I watched the screen blink rapidly. "Okay, here we go—the local chapter's home page." Matt squinted at the screen. "We're in luck, there's a link to her books so this is probably it. But…still no dice on getting her real information."

"If it's a local chapter, somebody has to know. They must keep a list somewhere of their members. Is there a contact number for the person in charge?"

"Here's the chapter president, Rebecca Pollock. There's an e-mail addy but no phone number."

"Well, get me one," I snapped. I just hoped like hell the woman was home and not gone somewhere for the holidays.

Rebecca Pollock answered on the first ring, her voice surprisingly alert. I didn't tell her too much about the murders, just said it was an ongoing homicide investigation and that lives were at stake. "So I need to know which author uses the pen name, Victoria Tarlatan." I finished. "It's very important—urgent, in fact."

"I'm afraid it doesn't ring a bell, um, who did you say you were again?"

I repeated my credentials carefully. "If you don't know it, can you look it up? You must have a list of your members' personal information, don't you? Addresses, publishers, pen names..."

"Well, now, I just don't know. It's not a list we usually give out. Some of our authors prefer to remain anonymous. I'm sure you can understand." Her voice had a syrupy sweetness that denoted a lifetime of Southern living.

"Please, Ms. Pollock—this may literally be a matter of life and death. Now I can get a court order and compel you to release the list for me but by that time it might be too late."

"Oh, my." I could just picture her putting a hand to her bosom and shaking her head. "I want to help," she continued. "But how do I know you are who you say you are?"

I wanted to reach down the phone and strangle her but what I was telling her was the truth—if I had to go to the time and trouble of obtaining a warrant for her records, it might literally be too late. My gut told me that our killer wouldn't wait long to strike again. He might even be in action at that very moment, while I sat on the phone, helplessly chatting with Miss Manners.

"Take down this number," I directed and listened to her rustling around, getting a pen and paper. When she was ready, I recited the main switchboard number by heart. "When the operator answers, ask for Detective Cole Berkley," I told her. "All right?"

"I'll call you right back," she promised.

I waited impatiently until the phone on my desk rang, trying Alex on my cell twice more before it did. She still wasn't picking up. Where was she?

"Detective Berkley," I said, snatching up the receiver when the phone finally shrilled.

"This is Ms. Pollock," she said as primly as though we were being introduced over tea somewhere.

I bit back a sarcastic reply. "Yes, ma'am. Can you please fax me that list now?"

"I guess so," she said carefully. "I usually don't give it out except in extenuating circumstances."

"Oh? Has someone else asked for it recently?" I asked, feeling my heart rate suddenly pick up.

"Well, not very recently," she dithered. "But, one of our members was killed a little while back—Cynthia Harner, you know?"

"Yes, I know," I said, my fingers tightening on the phone until the plastic creaked. "Did you give the list out before that happened?"

"No, actually—it was after. To her husband, Mr. Harner." She made a tsking sound that hurt my ear. "Such a sweet man. He wanted to be able to invite Cynthia's fellow writers to her memorial service. Very moving."

My grip on the phone relaxed. James Harner had been in Denver during every one of the murders—I had seen the plane tickets myself. And besides, he had carpal tunnel syndrome. I doubted seriously he had enough strength in his hands to strangle anyone, even if he wanted to. Another dead end.

"Well, thank you very much, Ms. Pollock. This is my fax number." I recited it to her and added, "Please send it as soon as possible."

"As soon as I get off the phone," she promised.

We hung up and I fidgeted around the fax machine, waiting to see what it would spit out. While I was waiting the phone rang again. I picked it up, grinding my teeth. No doubt it was Ms. Pollock calling back to say she hadn't gotten the number quite right and could I please repeat it. But an entirely different tone answered when I picked up and identified myself.

"Oh, I'm sorry." The voice was high and younger than Ms. Pollock's syrupy drawl. "I was trying to reach Detective Reed. She said to call her anytime but she doesn't answer her cell number."

"This is Detective Berkley, her partner. You can talk to me," I assured her. "And you are…?"

"Theresa Peron. I'm just now returning a call that your partner made a couple of days ago. I'm, uh, afraid I kind of forgot until I saw him again tonight."

"What? I'm sorry, can you go back a little bit?" I kept an eye on the fax machine while I talked, ready to disconnect in a hurry if I had to.

"Sure. Um, a couple of days ago, Detective Reed called and asked me about a passenger of ours. I work at Tampa International—at the Delta boarding counter?"

"Go on," I said. Suddenly she had my complete attention. "Would this passenger happen to be James Harner?"

"Oh, yeah. Yeah, it is. That's who she asked me about. Anyway, I looked him up the computer for her and verified that he had bought tickets with us several times in the past couple of months. Only I didn't remember exactly who he was until I saw him again tonight. We see so many people, you know?" She sounded apologetic.

"That's all right," I said. "So you're calling to say he flew out to Denver again tonight?"

"No, that's just the thing. He was here and he bought the tickets but he didn't fly. Just like always."

"Excuse me?" I sat forward at my desk, the fax machine forgotten. "Could you repeat that?"

"I said, he buys the tickets, but he doesn't fly. It's happened like, four or five times now in the past couple months. He gets the tickets, even gets on board the plane, but then he can't go through with it, and they have to let him off."

My God. I gripped the phone harder and tried to keep my voice low and calm. "And you say he did it again tonight? At what time?"

"Um, around six, I guess. He was trying to take our six-thirty flight, but he just couldn't do it."

"Are you still at work now?" I asked.

"Yes, I just got off a long shift. That's why I didn't call sooner. Sorry."

"That's all right," I said numbly. "Can you look up the date of the first time Mr. Harner couldn't get on the plane?"

There was a distant clattering of a keyboard and then she said, "Looks like it was November twenty-second in the evening. He was scheduled to take the red eye to Denver but he backed out after he was already on the plane. I think I sort of remember that one, actually. He was on his phone and he wouldn't turn it off, you know the way the stews ask you to?"

I nodded and then, realizing she couldn't hear me, I croaked, "Yes? What happened then?"

She sighed. "Well, that time he claimed he had a family emergency and they had to let him get off the plane. The pilot was pissed—they had already shut the doors and everything. Now he claims it's a phobia he's trying to get over. Tonight he even told my friend, Paula, that his shrink told him he should keep trying. Like some kind of therapy, you know?"

"I know," I said numbly. "Listen, Theresa, you've been more help than you know. You say Harner was there around six this evening?"

"Uh-huh. Sorry I couldn't call sooner. I hope it helps."

I closed my eyes. Six. He'd gone to establish his alibi and then come back to grab another victim. It was long past midnight now. Whoever Victoria Tarlatan was, she might already be dead.

The humming of the fax machine behind me brought me out of my morbid thoughts.

"Theresa, I have to go but Detective Reed or I will definitely be in touch. All right?"

"Okay. Good-bye, then."

I hung up the phone without returning her words. As the first sheet of paper came out of the fax machine, I snatched it off the tray and studied it closely. The list was in alphabetical order and beside each name was a small space neatly labeled *nom de plume.* It was this second column that I scanned, looking for the last author on James Harner's list. I found what I was looking for about halfway down the page—Victoria Tarlatan.

I followed my finger across to find the identity of the last victim and felt my mouth go dry. Printed in the slot labeled *author* was the name Alexandra Reed.

Chapter Thirty-Seven

Alex

The shrill buzzing of my cell phone woke me up and I thought, *Gotta get that. It could be a break in the case.* But when I tried to roll over and grab it, I found I couldn't move my arms. Someone had tied me tightly to the headboard of my own bed. I became aware that my shoulders ached, probably because I had been slumped down, putting all my weight on them. My fingers felt numb and when I craned my neck to look at them, I could see that my wrists were encircled with black satin ties. Black satin ties...

Everything came rushing back to me, and I blinked my eyes. The groggy aftermath of unconsciousness dissipated when I realized the desperate situation I was in. I looked down at myself, fully alert now. I was naked and someone had covered me from head to toe in some kind of massage oil. The musky smell of patchouli invaded my sinuses, making me want to sneeze. My pale skin glistened in the dim lighting of my bedside lamp.

I rubbed my numb fingertips together and even they were oily—my toes, too. Someone had gone to a great deal of trouble to coat me thoroughly in the stuff—only my face was clear. Had he touched me while I was unconscious? While I was naked and vulnerable? The thought was unbearably disgusting. Horrible. But he hadn't only gotten oil on me—the bedclothes around me were soaked. Absurdly, the voice of my mother rose in my head, demanding to know how I was going to get the oily stain out of my nice down comforter. Then James Harner came into my line of vision.

"I see you're awake, Victoria." His smile, when he looked at me, wasn't the wide, leering grin of a lunatic. But the quiet, self satisfied smirk I saw on his narrow face was somehow worse. Here was a man who knew what he was doing and was enjoying every minute of it.

"My name is Detective Alex Reed, as you well know," I said, trying to sit up in the bed and sound confident. It's not easy to be confident when you're naked and tied up but I tried.

"Yes, but when you write that filth you peddle on the Internet, your name is Victoria Tarlatan. And *that* is the woman we are here to deal with tonight." His voice was gentle and reasonable and terribly frightening. I could see by the look in those pale, no-color eyes that he meant every word he said.

"Mr. Harner—James," I began, but he held up a hand to stop me.

"Victoria Tarlatan is the woman I have come here for, because she is the same woman who led my Cynthia into temptation and betrayal." He took a step forward, stabbing a gloved finger at me, the thin, pale face beginning to get some color. "*Your* books are what gave her the idea to start writing her own filth. *Your* books are what made her think she needed something else, something perverted and unnatural and wrong. Your books are what made her leave me." He was pacing back and forth beside my bed now, his face alight with the fire of rage. The black gloves he wore were shiny with oil. At least he hadn't touched me with his bare hands. The thought was a small comfort.

Harner stopped pacing and came closer to me, so close I could smell his rotting sushi breath. I flinched back but he leaned forward, pushing his hectic, flushed face into mine and continued his rant in a low, intense voice. "You woke the lusts of the flesh in her," he almost whispered. "You kindled her destruction with your disgusting ideas. If she hadn't read those horrible books of yours, she'd still be happy and safe at home with me, not cold and dead in the ground." His face twisted in sorrow for a moment, and two shining tears spilled over his red-rimmed lids. "*You* killed her, not me."

I wanted to draw farther away from him, from the stench of his breath and the crocodile tears standing in his watery eyes. But although I could pull my head back, there was only so far I could go, tied to the bed as I was.

"Mr. Harner, I had nothing to do with your wife's death," I said as calmly as I could. "From everything I've learned about Cynthia, she was a very ambitious person. She decided to go back to school. She decided to try her hand at writing. *She* decided she wanted more in the bedroom. My books are not to blame for those decisions."

"Shut up!" he said, fiercely. "I don't have to listen to your lies." He strode angrily to the other side of the room and ripped open the red insulated pizza bag he'd used to get me to open the door.

He saw me looking at the bag and smiled, a little of the tension leaving his lean frame. "I see you're admiring my props. Most useful, you know." He rummaged inside the bag, which seemed to have several things in it.

"The pizza coupons I saw on your table," I said dully. "You said they were from one of Cynthia's patients."

He nodded. "And so they were—it was what gave me the idea in the first place. Cynthia, of course, opened the door to me because she knew me. With the others, I had to find a way to convince them to open without making a fuss or a scene. I left one of the coupons on your door the other day, you know, just to let you know I was coming. Sort of my calling card, I guess you could say." He laughed, a high, nasal sound that send a chill down my spine. Maybe he *was* crazy after all.

He rummaged some more in the red insulated bag and then pulled out a roll of dull silver duct tape and a red satin mask edged in black lace.

I shook my head frantically. "No, please. I'm sorry."

"It's too late to be sorry. You killed my Cynthia, and now you must be punished." His voice had gone deep and sonorous now, like a prophet portending doom. He walked toward the bed, brandishing the tape in one hand and the mask in the other. "Don't fear, Miss Tarlatan," he said, smiling gently. "I have picked a scene from one of your own books to aid in your becoming. When I am done with you, you will be an entirely different creature—pure, complete…*dead.*"

"Mr. Harner, *please...* You don't want to do this. Let's talk about Cynthia. You must have loved her very much." I was desperate to keep him talking. Desperate to keep the tape off my mouth and the mask off my face. The minute I was completely helpless, unable to scream for him to stop or watch him do what he did, he would feel comfortable enough to start torturing me.

I flashed on the vicious whip marks on Sarah Michael's thighs and the hardened candle wax all over Lauren Schaefer's body. He had told me he had chosen a scene from one of my own books for my "becoming," whatever the hell that was. Was that the reason behind the elaborate crime scenes and his careful staging of the bodies? Had he been pulling scenes from his victims' books in order to punish them? To teach them a deadly lesson? I remembered the scene in my book, *Whispers in the Dark*, that involved body oil. It also involved a number of other components that I didn't care to think about.

"Please!" I said again when he didn't answer me. I yanked on the strips of black satin that held me to the headboard, feeling the greasy slide of patchouli oil along my arms and sides. The satin slid over my wrists, but the knots were tight—too tight. "Please, James, let's talk."

"Hush now," he said, coming toward me, fumbling slightly with the roll of tape. The black leather gloves were slippery and he couldn't pry up the end of the tape to tear off a strip. The mask was also stained and blotched with oil. He had taken off the jacket he was wearing when he first came to my door and rolled up his sleeves. His forearms were pale but wiry in the dim light.

"Your braces," I said, just to be saying something. Anything to forestall the tape and mask just a little longer. "You said you had carpal tunnel syndrome."

"I did, didn't I?" He nodded, pleased with himself. "They were easily obtained, you know and I wore them constantly after my Cynthia died. I thought it best not to shake hands with anyone, given my *modus operandi* of strangulation. I have quite a firm grip, you see." He put down the tape and mask for a moment, at the foot of the bed, and flexed his large hands in the black leather gloves until the knuckles popped. I shivered and pulled my legs up tight to my body.

"Do you like the gloves?" he asked, picking up the tape again and moving closer. "I wore them the first time for my Cynthia. I called her from the airport, that night. I wanted to talk to her once more before I got on the plane, and she said...she said she still wanted me." He grimaced. "She said if only I would *try* a few of the filthy new ideas she'd become so fixated on, maybe we could still make it work. So I got off the plane and rushed over, wanting to prove I could be the man she wanted me to be." He paused for a moment, yanking at the stubborn strip of tape, his tongue caught between his teeth in concentration.

"I put on the gloves, and I used the kit she bought," he continued, still struggling with the tape. "I tied her to the bed and did every sick, twisted thing she wanted. Do you know how hard that was for me, Miss Tarlatan?" He looked up at me, eyes wide, cheeks flushed. "It was wrong, but I did it anyway. I did it to prove to her that she didn't need it, not really. But... I got carried away." Suddenly the pale eyes were awash with tears again.

"It was a mistake," I said urgently. "Just an accident, James. You didn't mean to—I'll stand up in court and testify to that. I'll tell them—"

"No," he said gently, cutting me off. "You're never going to tell anyone anything again. Not with your mouth and not with your filthy, dirty books. It's time for your punishment. And after that, your becoming." He held up the strip of tape he'd finally managed to tear free and leaned toward me.

I shook my head wildly, feeling my hair stick to the skin of my shoulders, mired in the oil he had smeared all over me. "You don't have to do this," I told him urgently, trying to evade the tape.

"Oh, but I do." He threaded the fingers of one gloved hand through my hair and held me still by force although I was squirming all over the bed, as well as I could. I thought longingly of my Browning, nestled in the drawer of my nightstand, just a few feet from my head. If only I could get just one arm free... I felt the tight slide of the satin strips across my wrists but the knots were secure.

"I do this because I have been given a higher mission. Your punishment and the punishment of women like you. It is my duty—my calling. That way, you see, my Cynthia did not die in vain." Harner slapped the strip of tape over my lips, despite my efforts to evade it, effectively silencing me.

Panic welled up in me as my oxygen supply was cut in half. I felt my heart thundering against my ribs and my lungs screaming for more air than I could get through my nose alone. I yanked hard at the satin ties, feeling the slippery material slide over my skin. If only I could make just one hand small enough to pull through the noose that held it...

Harner leaned closer, this time with the mask in his hand and I went completely crazy, bucking and twisting, determined not to go without a fight. I couldn't let him cover my eyes—I just couldn't.

"Hold still, Miss Tarlatan, if you please." His voice was low and courteous, as though he were asking me for the time of day at a party instead of preparing to torture, rape, and strangle me. "After all—" He leaned closer and breathed in my ear. "—isn't this what you wanted? What all of you want?"

I shook my head wildly in negation. *No, never!* I wanted to shout. What I wanted, what I wrote, was all about a trusting, loving relationship. Not this hideous nightmare of pain and degradation. But I couldn't shut out the gibbering voice in the back of my skull that insisted that he was right—that this was somehow all my fault. My fault for daring to reach for what I needed, my fault for putting my desires in the hands of others instead of keeping them to myself. My weakness and my own twisted needs had put me in this position.

"It must be what you want—I read it in your book. I wouldn't be here, punishing you—helping you become what you most want to be—if you hadn't." It was as though he could read my mind, as though he could see my shame. Had all the women he killed felt this way?

I relaxed suddenly against the headboard, letting my body go limp. Tears leaked from my eyes. My fault. My fault for daring to dream. My fault for being weak.

"That's right, my dear. Just relax," Harner crooned. He had the elastic band stretched taut and was leaning over me when I suddenly brought my legs up again and kicked out with both feet. I caught him hard in the solar plexus and he lurched backward, an almost comical look of surprise on his face. The wind was knocked out of him in a ragged gust and he actually fell backward, his legs in the air. I heard a thump as his head connected with my carpeted bedroom floor and had a moment to wish that I had hardwood instead of Berber. Then he sat up, rubbing the back of his head with one gloved hand and scowling at me.

"That, my dear Miss Tarlatan, was a mistake."

I glared at him, wishing the tape off my mouth so I could give him a piece of my mind. I might have played a hand in my own destruction, but I was damned if I would go quietly. He shouldn't have mistaken my despair for submission. I would *never* willingly submit to a monster like him. *Never.* I pulled at the satin ties, feeling the maddening slide of satin that was just this side of too tight.

Harner stood, still rubbing his head, and retrieved the gun from its resting place by the red insulated bag. He was breathing hard. "Just for that I'm going to let you see what I have in mind for you." He nodded at me and reached into the bag with his free hand and pulled out something shiny and silver.

"Do you recognize these?" He walked slowly forward, the gun trained on me to keep me still. My eyes widened as he swung the object into my view. It was a set of nipple clamps attached at their ends by a chain. "From your book," Harner said, leering at me, as he swung the dangling clamps in front of me. "Just what you wanted."

I shook my head frantically—these were not the kind of clamps I had written about at all. The kind I had in mind were lined with soft rabbit fur. I had been anxious to experience erotic pain, but I have very sensitive nipples. The kind that

Harner was dangling in front of me looked like the alligator clips on the ends of jumper cables. Long silver snouts filled with bright jagged teeth glittered in the lamp light. I pulled hard on the satin, trying to make my hand long and thin, trying to slide out of the confining embrace.

"I'll just put these on you, shall I?" His face loomed in my vision like a diseased moon. I thought I felt a little give on the left side. I twisted my wrist desperately.

"Remember," he whispered, leaning even closer, the gun pointed straight at me, "no funny business this time. I won't shoot to kill, you know. I'll just incapacitate you—that way your punishment can continue without further interruption."

This more than anything else froze me in place. If he shot me in a leg or an arm, I would lose my last means of defense. I closed my eyes, not wanting to look as he pinched the end of the first clamp, opening it and exposing its needle sharp teeth.

"I had to search so long to find just the right kind," he crooned in my ear. "And I have a few more surprises in my bag for you—but I bet you can guess what they are."

Behind the tape I bit my lips hard as the wickedly sharp clamp enclosed my left nipple. The breath surged out of me in short pants as I fought to control my reactions and not panic. The pain was bad, but I could take it, I told myself. I concentrated on freeing my left wrist, exerting a slow, steady pull with my fingers bunched together and my thumb tucked in. If only I could get one hand free I could go for the Browning. Better to take a chance than be tortured to death.

The second clamp was tighter and it broke my concentration. I cried out—a muffled sound that didn't carry three feet, thanks to the tape, and felt tears come to my eyes.

"Now then, isn't that nice?" I opened my eyes to see Harner leaning over me, holding the chain that connected the clamps. The gun was still in my face. He gave a low chuckle and tugged the silver chain playfully. Sparks of red agony shot through me and I writhed helplessly, wanting to kick him again but not daring to.

"Now, I—" He stopped suddenly, his head cocked to one side, like a dog listening for its master's footsteps. Despite the rush of blood pounding through my skull, I heard it, too—a muffled footstep somewhere outside the door. My eyes widened in hope and disbelief—Cole!

Apparently Harner had drawn the same conclusion. Putting one black-gloved finger to his lips, as though I could speak, he withdrew to stand just to the side of the closed bedroom door, gun at the ready. My eyes widened further—he was going to shoot my partner! Cole was going to die because of me, because of my sick fantasies and twisted desires. He was going to pay for my weakness with his life.

There was another stealthy creak. Inwardly I cursed my old house, where every floorboard had a separate note. For a big guy, Cole was light on his feet but there was nothing he could do about the boards. I wanted to scream out a warning but the tape was firmly in place. The only thing I could do was pull at the satin band holding my left wrist and pray I could get free in time to go for my gun.

Once more I lengthened my fingers, tucking in my thumb and pulling with all my might. I felt the burn in my bicep and kept going, I was so *close*. The cloying patchouli oil helped and, little by little, I felt my hand begin to slip free. If I could just get the satin band to slide over the heel of my hand and the first joint of my thumb I knew I would be home free. I gave one last tug, feeling the give and then everything happened at once.

The bedroom door slapped open in one motion and Harner, who was waiting just behind it, caught it with his palm, aiming his gun with the other. I got one quick glimpse of Cole's face, dark as a thundercloud, and then I rolled to my side, my right wrist still tethered to the headboard. I fumbled open the nightstand drawer, clawing at the knob with numb, slippery fingers. I had just gotten the cool grip of the Browning settled in my palm when I heard the first shot go off.

I rolled back, nearly dropping the gun, and saw Harner and my partner facing off, both holding guns. They were both shouting but my ears were dazed by the loud noise in the confined space, and I couldn't make out anything that was being said. It didn't matter anyway. What caught and held my attention was a bright patch of scarlet spreading across the blue field of Cole's shirt. Bleeding—he was bleeding. Harner had shot him and if he died, I might as well have pulled the trigger myself.

I don't usually shoot left handed, but I raised the gun and took aim, feeling a blanket of ice drop over me as I leveled my sights. Harner must have seen me out of the corner of his eye because he swung toward me suddenly, his gun pointing at my heart. There was a crashing roar that I recognized as Cole's Glock and then I squeezed the trigger myself and heard the familiar hoarse cough of my Browning. Harner spun around like a toy tossed by a careless child, the no-color eyes going blank as a doll's. He collapsed bleeding on the floor with a muffled thump. The bright, bitter stench of cordite hung in the air like a choking cloud and coated my sinuses.

I screamed Cole's name, feeling like my throat would burst, but nothing came out because of the tape. The blood on his shirt seemed to be spreading. I yanked helplessly at my right arm, which was still tied tightly to the headboard, keeping me in place. He turned toward me. His mouth was moving but I couldn't hear anything coming out. The gun was still held tight in my fist. I had a thought that I should use it to shoot myself free of the damn satin band, but before I could, Cole was beside me, removing the tape and speaking softly in words I could barely make out past the roaring in my ears.

"It's all right, Alex. All right now."

He pried gently at my fingers, which seemed to be glued to the grip of my gun, until they suddenly relaxed and the Browning fell into his grip. Then he was gathering me close and holding me, careless of the oil that was getting all over his shirt. But the shirt was already ruined by the blotch of crimson, anyway.

I kept asking if he was all right but I couldn't seem to understand a word he said in reply. He reached over to untie the knot that still held me to the headboard and rubbed circulation back into my wrist. Then he looked down and noticed the cruel silver alligator clips, still clamped on my nipples.

"That son of a bitch!" he growled.

His face was dark and angry as he grasped the ends of the clamps and pinched them open, freeing me. I wasn't prepared for the sudden spike of pain that accompanied the action, as the blood rushed back into my starving tissues. I think I screamed and then the back of my head connected with the headboard of the bed with a dull crack as my back arched and I literally saw stars.

Cole reached for me, holding me close again and whispering into my ear. "It's all right, it's all going to be all right, Alex. All right, little girl…"

But I knew that nothing would ever be all right again.

Chapter Thirty-Eight

Cole

For a week afterward she wouldn't see me at all—wouldn't even speak to me when I called. I tried her mom's house daily but Mrs. Reed was playing the protective mother hen, a role heretofore unknown to her, and refused to bring her the phone. I thought about her constantly, thought of all the things I should have said before it was too late. I cursed myself for not staying with her that night, for not telling her how I felt, how much I loved her. I bought her a present, not knowing if I would ever be able to give it to her, and it sat under the tiny two-foot tree I had put up mostly for Madison's benefit, looking as lonely and bereft as I felt.

Finally on the twenty-third, I staked out the house. Alex and her mother have never been very comfortable around each other, and I knew with the two of them cooped up together, something would eventually have to give. My vigilance was rewarded around nine o'clock when I saw Mrs. Reed slam out the front door with a sour expression on her face. She slid behind the wheel of a Lincoln Town car and backed out quickly, driving away without looking over her shoulder. It was a good thing because I was only a few houses down on the right, and I really wasn't in the mood for a lecture.

It was getting chilly in the truck, and Christmas lights blinked softly all up and down the block. I drove a little closer, parked behind Alex's yellow Bug, and got out.

I thought of going and knocking on the door and then thought better of it. Instead, I walked to the front yard, stepping around the new landscaping, pulled out my cell phone, and called her. I let it ring probably twenty-five times before she finally picked up.

"Alex," I said before she could speak, "we need to talk."

There was a soft sigh on the other end of the phone and then a sound that might have been either a laugh or a sob—maybe a little bit of both. Then she said, "What did you do, stake out the house until Mom left?"

"I'm right outside," I told her. "It was the only way I could get through."

The curtains in the tall front windows twitched and I saw her face, pale and tired, staring out from inside. The big brown eyes were filled with sorrow I wanted to wipe away. I thought that if I could get my arms around her, if I could just get her to let me inside the barrier she kept so tightly around herself, I could make it all right for her.

"Hi," she said quietly, still looking at me out of the window.

"Hi," I said, standing in the front yard, staring at her.

"How's your arm?"

"Just fine." I flexed my bicep to show her I had full range of motion. "I told you the bullet only grazed me."

"I know, but there was so much blood. I thought…" She shook her head, obviously unwilling to continue.

"It's cold out here, can I come in?" I stamped my feet and blew on the hand that wasn't holding the cell phone to my ear.

She shook her head, her golden-brown hair brushing across the shoulders of the faded blue bathrobe she was wearing. "I don't think that's such a good idea. If my mom comes back and finds you here, she'll be pissed."

I laughed softly and shook my head. "You sound like a teenager, you know?" I walked closer, stepping between the bushes to get right up to the window. She stared down at me. Her eyes were solemn, but a small, sad smile quirked one corner of her mouth.

"When are you coming back to work?" I asked, looking up at her through the glass.

"I'm not," she said, and then added, "I can't."

"Because of what happened?" I felt the protective rage rise in me when I remembered the way I'd found her—tied to the bed with tape on her mouth and those damn torture devices clamped on her. "Goddammit, Alex, how could you go home alone knowing you were the next target. Why didn't you tell me?" I said.

"I didn't want you to know!" Her face, which looked thinner than the last time I had seen her, flushed red, then went pale again. "I didn't want anyone to know," she said, pressing the phone to her ear. She dropped her eyes. "And now everyone does."

I saw what she was talking about. "No," I shook my head. "The captain kept it quiet. The official story is that he was picking women at random and he fixated on you because we interviewed him after he did his wife. Nobody knows but you and me and Captain Davis."

She looked relieved for a moment, and then her face hardened. "That's still two too many people."

I wanted to shake her, I wanted to break the barriers that separated us and take her in my arms, but I forced myself to stay calm. I took a deep breath. "I didn't come here to fight with you. I came to invite you to Christmas Eve at my house. Or apartment, I guess. Will you come? Madison will be disappointed if you don't."

"Oh, Cole…" She shook her head. "I don't want to intrude on your time with your daughter."

"What are you talking about? Madison loves you." Madison got along a lot better with Alex than she ever had with Amanda, a fact that was a constant sore spot with my ex-wife.

"I don't know…"

I felt her wavering. "Please? No pressure, but we'd really like you to be there. And it's not like you'd be gone for Christmas, so your mom can't bitch *too* much."

She gave me a wan smile. "Now you're the one who sounds like a teenager."

I returned the smile with interest. "Yup. Guess I'm just young at heart." I reached up and put my hand on the chilly glass that separated us, wishing I could melt it with my warmth. "Please say you'll come," I said, softly.

Hesitantly, she raised her own hand and placed it over mine. I thought I could feel a small tingle of warmth through the pane. "All right," she said at last. "I'll think about it."

* * *

Christmas Eve was a success. Alex came around four, which was a damn good thing because, although I'm not completely domestically challenged, I did need help with the dinner. I had gotten one of those pre-packaged "homemade" dinners where supposedly, all you have to do is heat everything up, but it turned out to be a little more complicated than advertised. Alex jumped right in, showing the domestic side of herself that she usually keeps hidden, and got Madison involved, too. Before I knew it, Alex was sharing her mother's old Southern recipe for praline sweet-potato pie and both of them had melted marshmallow on their noses from licking the spoon.

It was good to see her loosening up and just having fun. I was afraid that the experience with Harner might have scarred her irrevocably, but that night she seemed like her old self again. I had managed to get out of her, before the paramedics took her away that night, that Harner hadn't gotten around to raping her yet, so that was one small bright spot. But you don't get over being tied to your bed and tortured overnight. I knew she had yet to go back to her house—at first because it was being treated as a crime scene and later because I guess she just couldn't stand to be there.

We finished dinner and opened presents—at least Madison did. Although she knew she didn't have to, Alex had risen to the occasion with a ridiculously elaborate Barbie dream house along with Barbie and some of her friends to occupy it.

"Thank you, Alex!" Madison crowed with delight when she ripped the wrapping paper off the huge cardboard box. We were sitting on the couch watching the fun. Despite the light-hearted mood, it was the closest I had been to her all night. I could smell her sweet, subtle scent and almost hear the soft brush of her hair over the back of her red sweater.

I nudged her with my elbow and murmured, "You're really going to be on Amanda's shit list now. She says Barbie objectifies women."

Alex grinned at me, but her smile looked more like a reflection of Madison's joy than genuine happiness of her own. "Yeah, I know Barbie's not politically correct, but I loved her when I was a little girl."

I groaned. "She'll have to keep it here to play with it and that house is going to be hell to put together." I looked at her hopefully. "Unless you bought District Attorney Barbie to live in it?"

"No, but I did get Policewoman Barbie and Doctor Barbie. They can live here with you, if you're not too intimidated by them." She patted my arm—the first move she'd made toward me all night. I felt like an electric current had passed briefly over my skin.

"Since when am I afraid of strong women?" I asked, giving her a sideways glance.

Alex dropped her eyes abruptly and shook her head. I realized that I had somehow said something wrong.

"What?" I asked softly. "Tell me."

She shook her head again and called to Madison, "Open the last one, honey, and show it to your dad."

Madison tore into the wrapping paper with unfettered delight and revealed that Alex hadn't just been pulling my leg. Policewoman Barbie had a blue and black uniform and stylish black boots to match.

"A policeman, just like you and Daddy." Madison took the doll out of its bright pink box and began playing with it.

"That's what you want to be when you grow up, huh?" I asked her.

Madison shook her shining river of blond hair. "Huh-uh."

"A lawyer like your mom?" Alex guessed.

Madison looked up. "I'm going to be a vet'rinarian so I can play with puppies all day long. Mommy won't let me have one at her house." She looked at me hopefully. "Can I have one at yours, Daddy?"

I had to grin at that—it was Amanda's bargaining gene coming out again. When Madison got a little bit older, my ex-wife wouldn't know what hit her. "Well, Sugar Bear, I live in an apartment right now, and there's no room. Puppies need a lot of space to run and play—they need a yard."

"Oh." Madison's face fell and she shrugged. "I guess you're right."

"Your dad can't have a dog, but I might be getting one." Alex's words surprised me into looking at her. I raised an eyebrow, and she nodded.

"Really? Are you really?" Madison jumped up and clapped her hands, Policewoman Barbie forgotten. "Are you going to get a sweet little pug dog? I love their smashed-in faces!"

"Well, I was actually thinking of something a little bigger," Alex said, and I knew she was looking to get a dog for protection. Maybe so she could stand to live in her own house again. The thought made me sad, especially since I knew how she felt about big dogs. But I guess she'd decided that getting over one fear might help her get over the other.

"Connolly over in narcotics has a Rott that just dropped a litter," I offered her. "That's a good, protective dog. A one person dog—very loyal."

"Daddy, what's a Rott?" Madison wanted to know.

I ruffled her hair. "It's a Rottweiler, Sugar Bear. A great big dog—bigger than you."

"Bigger than me?" She giggled at the thought. "Alex can ride him like a pony!"

"Maybe." A grin quirked Alex's full mouth. "Maybe I'll ride him over to your house and see you. How about that?"

Madison considered for a moment. "Only if I get to ride him, too."

"Of course." Alex nodded. "Wouldn't have it any other way. My pony-dog is your pony-dog."

"Pony-dog!" Madison chortled and broke up into a fit of giggles. I was glad to see Alex laughing along.

Just then there was a sharp, impatient rapping at the front door. I looked at my watch regretfully. Yes, past eight o'clock—it had to be Amanda. I never felt like I got enough time with my daughter, something I had promised myself to rectify in the coming New Year. Call it a resolution, but I intended to keep it.

"That's probably your mom, Sugar Bear. You better go let her in," I said. Madison jumped up to go to the door but Alex put a hand on her arm to stop her.

"No, wait." She looked at me and there was a fear in her eyes I had never seen before. "Cole, you go, okay?"

I tried to sound casual. "Sure, no problem." I got up and walked to the door when what I really wanted to do was gather Alex into my arms and erase that fear. But I knew only time could do that.

Amanda had her arms crossed and was already tapping her long French manicured fingernails impatiently when I opened the door. She swept across the threshold, but when she saw Alex she stopped short.

"Oh, hello, Alex," she said stiffly, arms still crossed.

Alex nodded and walked over to stand beside me. "Hello, Amanda. Merry Christmas."

"And to you." My ex-wife nodded back and then turned her attention to Madison. "You'd better start gathering up your toys, Madison. Mommy's in a hurry."

"Aww." Madison sighed, then brightened. "Can I take my Barbie Dream House, Mommy? It's a great big box. Will it fit in the car?"

I saw Amanda's lip curl, just a little, and she shook her head. "I'm afraid it most certainly will *not.* You can leave it here and play with it when you see your father."

"Aww..." Madison looked near tears until I told her that I would have the house all put together for her the next time she came to see me. Then she brightened. "Promise, Daddy?"

"Cross my heart, Sugar Bear. Get your other things together now, okay?"

"Okay." She started stacking boxes happily and I saw Amanda's lip twitch again. It had always been an irritant to her that Madison would do just about anything I asked while Amanda had to fight with her every step of the way.

"Did you and Bill have a good time at his parents' place?" I said, hoping to forestall an argument.

She nodded reluctantly. "They were disappointed not to see Madison, but I promised to bring her over sometime tomorrow." She turned abruptly to Alex. "I heard about what happened to you," she said without preamble.

I saw Alex's face pale and Amanda must have as well because she softened her tone and added, "No details—only that you had a rough time. I'm... I'm very sorry."

"I survived." Alex lifted her chin, her brown eyes locking with Amanda's sharp blue ones. It was my ex-wife that dropped her gaze first.

"I see," she said. She turned to Madison again. "Hurry up, Madison."

"Coming, Mommy. Almost done," my daughter chirped. She ran up with an armload of packages, and Alex and I both hugged her and wished her Merry Christmas.

Amanda ushered her out the apartment door and then looked back at us. "I hope... I hope you'll be happy together," she said at last, as though the words were a bone stuck in her throat.

Alex's eyes widened and she shook her head. "I think you have the wrong idea, Amanda."

"Oh?" My ex-wife's eyes sharpened as she took in the two of us standing side-by-side. "I don't think so," she said. Then she turned and swept down the walk, urging Madison to hurry.

"Bye, Daddy! Bye, Alex!" Madison called over her shoulder.

"Bye, baby," I called.

And Alex said, "Next time I see you, I'll have that pony-dog."

Madison's high, warbling laughter filled the night like silver bells until she and Amanda got into my ex-wife's Lexus and drove away. We went back into the apartment.

"Well," Alex looked around my place, apparently uneasy now that Madison was gone. "I guess I should get going," she said. She wrapped her arms around herself, as though trying to ward off something she couldn't see.

I took her hand, deliberately invading her space. "Stay a while," I said, softly. "I can't offer you a romantic evening by the fire since I don't have one, but I thought we could make some hot chocolate."

She looked up at me, and I could feel her hand, which had been very cold, beginning to warm in mine. She sighed. "Well, for a little while, maybe."

"Great, come help me make the cocoa." I led her into the kitchen, not letting go of her hand. It wasn't that I really need help with the hot chocolate, which was a mix, but that I was afraid if I let her out of my sight, she'd slip away.

"Hand me the milk," she said, taking charge at once when we entered the kitchen.

Instead, I pulled her close. "I love you," I said. It wasn't how I had meant for it to come out. I had been meaning to lead up to it, but somehow the minute we were alone it just slipped out. I guess I couldn't hold it in anymore.

Her face got pale, but she didn't struggle to get away. She didn't say anything, either.

"Look me in the eyes and tell me you don't have some feeling for me," I said—demanded, rather. "You tell me that, and I'll drop it and leave you alone forever." I knew I was taking a chance, but I also knew Alex was too honest to lie about something so important to me or to herself. I looked at her intently.

She dropped her eyes. "It doesn't matter how I feel, Cole. We're partners—at least for now. Partners don't make good lovers, and lovers don't make good partners. You know that."

I shook my head. "I thought we did okay together the week before last. We would've done better if we had been honest with each other, though."

She shook her head. "No, we would've done better if we had never started this at all."

"But it's too late now," I said softly. "You can't run away from this, Alex. Getting another partner and transferring to another department won't help."

"I just... I just can't." She shook her head again, and she was doing that thing with her mouth she does when she's trying hard not to cry. I decided not to press it.

"Forget the hot chocolate and come back in the living room," I said gently. "I almost forgot—I have a present for you."

"What? Cole, that's not fair. I didn't get anything for you," she protested. "We *never* exchange gifts." It was true, we never gave each other presents on our birthdays or holidays because it's not something you do with your buddies at work—not at my work, anyway. But I saw Alex as more than that now; she was no longer just one of the guys, and she never would be again.

I thought about trying to tell her that, but it seemed complicated. Instead, I shrugged. "Well, never is a long time. C'mon."

We went back to the wrapping-paper-strewn living room and sat on the couch. Through it all, I never relinquished Alex's hand. I wasn't letting go of her if I could possibly help it.

I reached under the two-foot Christmas tree, which was set up on a card table, and felt around under the red skirt that covered its green plastic base. I had hidden Alex's package under there because I didn't want Madison to unwrap it by accident. That would have been cause for a lot of explaining, and Amanda would have been considerably more pissed off than she was about the Barbie house.

I handed it to her a little awkwardly. "It's two things, actually, I just wrapped them together."

"Cole, you shouldn't have." She took the rectangular package wrapped in reindeer paper and opened it slowly. "*The Story of O*," she said in a low voice, looking at the top book.

"I know you've probably read it," I said quickly. "I mean, they said at the store that it was a classic. But this one is a special edition—leather binding, illustrated..." I trailed off, watching her face and hoping I hadn't made a huge mistake.

"Cole," she said quietly, after a long moment. "I don't know what to say."

"I don't either," I said. "It's, uh, it's why I bought the book. I mean, I don't even know if you're into that anymore after…after what happened."

She looked down at her hands. "I don't know what I'm into right now but I know…" She looked up at me. "I know that I still have dreams about that night. That I wake up sweating and shaking…"

"Nightmares," I said sympathetically. "About Harner. But he's dead, Alex. He'll never be able to hurt you again, you know that."

She shook her head. "I'm not talking about that night, Cole," she said in a low voice. "I have dreams about that, too, but I'm talking about…about the night before it."

I looked at her in surprise. "Oh, the night you and I…"

She nodded. "Yeah." She rubbed her thumb thoughtfully over the rich leather binding of the book in her lap. "So, yes, as sick as it sounds, I guess I'm still into 'that' as you put it."

"Alex," I said softly. "I never thought you were sick, and I still don't. By giving you this book—these books, I hoped I could make you understand that. Go on, look at the other one."

She lifted *The Story of O* and looked underneath. "*When Someone You Love is Kinky.*" She looked up at me, a small, sad smile playing around the corners of her mouth.

"I know, I know, it's a cheesy title. But it's actually a pretty good book." I shrugged. "I've, uh, been doing a little homework."

"So I see," she said.

"Alex," I said. "What you do—what you need, it doesn't bother me. How many ways can I say it?"

She looked away. "Well, maybe it bothers me."

"Why?" I asked. "Because you think it's perverted or sick or wrong? Hell, I'm the one who was raised Catholic, not you."

She shook her head. "It's more than that now. What I wanted—what I wrote—it nearly got both of us killed."

"That wasn't your fault." I took one of her hands in mine. "Harner was a sick bastard who killed his wife and wanted to justify himself. If it hadn't been your book on Cynthia Harner's laptop and PDA, it would've been somebody else's. If she hadn't been reading and writing erotica, he would've found someone or something else to blame. Anything as long as it shifted the guilt to somebody else's shoulders." Alex had told me briefly what Harner had said to her so I knew I had to be hitting a nerve here. "It's not your fault," I said again.

"But…but why am I like this? I *shouldn't* be," she burst out, pulling her hand out of mine and running it though her hair.

"Like what?" I said quietly, wanting to hear her say it—knowing she needed to.

"So twisted, so needy…so *weak*." Her eyes were suspiciously bright, but she still held back the tears. The same old Alex, hating to cry or show emotion.

"Is it weak to want to be loved the way you want to—the way you *need* to?" I asked her softly. "You know what Mistress Samantha told me? She said some people have to be tied down to feel free." I took her chin in my hand and tilted her face up to mine. "Alex, from the minute I met you, you've always been the toughest and the bravest and the smartest. You don't take shit off anybody, and you're the best cop I know."

She dropped her eyes. "How can you say that? Now that you know what I need? What I *am?*"

"Because it's still true," I said softly. "You're still that person, and there's nobody else in the world I want getting my back but you. You're the best partner a guy could ask for. But recently—" I ducked my head to get a look in her deep brown eyes. "Recently, I've seen a whole other side of you. Softer, vulnerable, feminine and so damn desirable it makes me ache." I stroked her cheek lightly and she shivered, a slow blush spreading over her cheeks. "That's the Alex I want to get to know better," I told her. "But knowing that part of you exists doesn't make you any less in my eyes."

She looked up at me, eyes wide and soft, and I felt my heart clench for a minute. "What if it makes me less in my own eyes?"

"Why should it?" I pulled her closer and leaned down to brush her lips with my own. "Let me love you, Alex, the way you need to be loved. It won't make you weak," I whispered. "And if it does, strictly in the bedroom, of course, is that really such a bad thing?"

She pulled back. "It's always been the worst thing there is, in my book."

"Well maybe it's time for a rewrite." I picked up *The Story of O.* "Something along these lines. If you want to?" The look in her eyes answered my question clearly.

She sighed. "I still say it's not wise to get involved with your partner."

I shrugged. "I'd say it's too late for that particular worry. Besides, I'm not asking you to run away to Vegas. I'm saying let's take it one day at a time. Let's try it out." I didn't tell her that I never intended to let her go, that I wanted that one day to turn into a lifetime. I didn't want to scare her by saying it out loud, but I think she understood anyway.

"All right," she said softly, a genuine smile lighting her face for the first time that night. "We can try it…" She looked at me, an expression of fear and longing taking the place of her smile. "Master," she whispered.

Epilogue

Alex

It took me a while to get over what had happened that night with James Harner. I still woke up with chills in the middle of the night, feeling my wrists for satin bands and my mouth for tape. But when I did, Cole was right there beside me. He would pull me into his arms and hold me close, rubbing my back in long, soothing strokes until my shivering stopped and I was able to go back to sleep.

At first I resisted him, not wanting to let myself get too weak or emotionally dependent. But Cole simply wouldn't take no for an answer. He'd hold me close until I stopped struggling and let the tears come. I always felt better afterward.

In time I learned to trust what he said. At work, he treated me no differently, going out of his way to be sure our professional relationship remained completely intact. It was only when we walked in the door of my house or his apartment that his buddy-partner attitude changed to one of dominance and possession. Outside the bedroom he never treated me as anything less than an equal. It was that, more than anything else, which finally allowed me to accept my desires and needs and move more deeply into the lifestyle.

I could never stand to be tied up again, although handcuffs didn't bother me. Cole and I actually did go back to Mistress Samantha for some lessons. He learned how to discipline me just the way I needed it and even took a few of her classes, including Erotic Biting and the Sensuous Art of Caning. In a few months, he had become a very accomplished Dom, and I was a more-than-willing sub.

By mutual consent, we didn't go out into the scene. But in time, our bedroom activities grew to include most of our off-hours together. Calling him "Master" still made me wet, and the feel of his hands on me, gentle and forceful at the same time, was an erotic thrill no e-book could ever duplicate.

Of course, we curtailed our activities on the weekends we had Madison. Cole actually went to court and compelled Amanda to give him more time with his daughter. He spent every morning with her and took her to breakfast before dropping her off at school. Also, Amanda wasn't allowed to rearrange the weekend schedule to suit her own whims. I thought she might never forgive him for that—talk about a woman with control issues. I thought of suggesting to Cole that we buy her a free session with Mistress Samantha, but somehow I didn't think she'd appreciate it.

It was a little more than nine months after I promised to try taking it "one day at a time" with him, that I came home to find him waiting for me with a blindfold in one hand and the demi-cup leather bustier he'd bought me as a birthday gift in the other.

"Put these on and don't ask questions," he commanded in his Master tone. I had been late at the station finishing paperwork, and I hadn't expected anything like this, but I was more than willing to obey him.

"Yes, Master," I whispered, feeling a small chill of anticipation crawl down my spine.

I started to go into the bedroom to change, but Cole stopped me.

"No. Change here. I want to see your naked body, Alex. I want to kiss you before you get dressed."

The shiver of anticipation had turned into a river of need, flowing through me. I did as he asked, taking off everything down to the black lacy Victoria's Secret panties I happened to be wearing before Cole stopped me.

"That's good, sweetheart," he said softly, using the endearment he knew I loved. He brought me close to his broad chest and held me. I pressed my face against his crisp, white shirt and breathed in his spicy, masculine scent. My nipples were stiff from the cool air circulating through the house, and I gave a little moan of pleasure when Cole pinched them lightly.

"What are you going to do to me, Master?" I asked, as he ran one large, warm hand over my cool skin, caressing from the nape of my neck to the small of my back.

"I have something a little different planned for tonight," Cole told me. He pulled away from me and started to help me into the bustier. It laced up the back, and he pulled the laces expertly to just the right degree of tightness so that I felt confined but in a loving way. My breasts rested on the demi-cups like ripe fruit on a platter, and my nipples were already hard with anticipation.

Cole stood back for a moment to admire me. "I'm glad you're wearing those sexy black lace panties," he said. "Your breasts are the only thing I want on display right now."

"Why?" I dared to ask, but he only shook his head.

"Time for the blindfold," he said. I went to him submissively and let him wrap it around my eyes.

"Now, Alex," he whispered in my ear, when he was certain I couldn't see anything through the thick black velvet. "I want you to know that what I have planned for tonight will hurt a little bit, but not more than you can stand. I'm going to be with you the whole time, touching you and making sure you're okay. And afterward, it's going to be more than worth it, I promise you."

My breath began to come faster, and I bit my lip and nodded that I understood. Cole hadn't asked me if his hurting me in the course of our pleasure was all right with me, and I didn't want him to. I loved the way he took charge of my body, took responsibility for both my pleasure and my pain.

"Good." Cole led me to the couch and seated me on it, positioning me the way he wanted me with my legs pressed together and my arms at my sides. "I want you to stay that way," he told me. "Don't move no matter what you hear or feel." Then he moved away from me, and silence fell in my living room.

I bit my lip and wanted desperately to fidget, but I knew that Cole was probably still somewhere nearby, watching me. Sometimes we played games where I disobeyed him on purpose, so he could have a reason to punish me. But I sensed that this wasn't one of those times. So I resisted the urge to move and sat still as a statue, my back straight and my breasts thrust out, the nipples stiff with anticipation.

After a few minutes I heard a knock on the door and Cole opened it. There was a low murmur of male voices and then someone new was in the living room. I stiffened, torn between wanting to hide myself and obeying Cole's orders. Why would he bring a strange man into my house to see me half-naked like this? I was fairly sure he wouldn't initiate a ménage à trois—he had told me many times that he didn't want to share me with anyone else. So I couldn't imagine what he had planned or how the strange man figured into it.

It is a measure of how much I trusted him that I managed to hold still and keep my arms at my sides, even when the stranger's footsteps stopped right in front of me. Then Cole settled on the couch beside me and put an arm around my bare shoulders.

"Alex," he said, speaking in a low voice directly into my ear. "This is Javier. He comes highly recommended by Mistress Samantha."

I relaxed a little when I heard that. Mistress Samantha wouldn't recommend anyone who wasn't a true professional—someone who was both skilled and completely confidential. Now I knew why Cole felt comfortable enough to invite a strange man into the house. But I still didn't know why he was here. Anticipating my question, Cole went on.

"Javier is a piercing artist, Alex," he told me. His breath was warm on the side of my face as he spoke. "He's going to pierce your nipples." He flicked my hard nipples, and I gasped in surprise at the unexpected sensation. I opened my mouth to object, but Cole anticipated me again. "I've picked out some very small gold rings that won't set off any metal detectors," he continued, a slight hint of humor in his voice. "This is going to be our little secret."

I nodded my head mutely, unable to speak. My breasts felt terribly exposed and extremely sensitive. I fisted my hands at my sides, waiting for what I knew was coming.

Soon enough I felt a latex clad hand swabbing alcohol over my right nipple, which tightened even more in protest as the cold liquid dried on my skin. "You're going to feel a small pinch," Javier explained in a soft, soothing voice. "There will be hardly any bleeding but you're going to be tender for a while. All right?"

I nodded again and then something sharp and cold and pointed bit into my right nipple, making me gasp. The pain was a bright white sensation behind my eyelids, like a shooting star that was there and gone so fast I could scarcely believe it had happened at all. It left behind a warm throbbing, and I realized I could feel a new, slight weight dangling from my newly pierced nipple.

The entire time, Cole's large warm hands were caressing my shoulders and back, and he was whispering endearments and encouragement in a low voice, meant for my ears alone.

The left nipple was harder. When I felt the stinging cold of the alcohol swab touching my flesh, I started to draw away instinctively. But Cole held me still and whispered in my ear.

"It's all right, Alex. It's okay. I know it hurts, but I need you to do it anyway—need you to relax and let it happen."

I felt myself getting wet at the low, commanding tone of his voice, and I knew I could stand anything for him—any amount of pain or pleasure he wanted to give me—because he was my Master, and I trusted him completely.

I sat forward on the couch, thrusting out my breasts again, waiting for the second piercing. Beside me, Cole murmured his approval.

It was over and done almost before I could take a deep breath, and then Cole left the couch. I heard him thanking the technician before shutting the door firmly behind him. When he came back he took my hands and pulled me up, leading me still blindfolded through the house.

"Now," he said, after he had me in place. He was standing behind me, and I could feel his larger body, warm and protective at my back. He took the thick black blindfold carefully off my eyes, and I blinked in the sudden light. When my eyes adjusted, I saw that I was standing in front of the bedroom mirror.

"Look at yourself," Cole commanded me, his breath warm on the back of my neck. I looked and saw a woman I still scarcely knew, although I was getting to know her bit by bit. The Alex in the mirror wasn't the tough police detective, and she wasn't the furtive writer, so ashamed of her secret desires that she had to hide them in the pages of a book.

The woman in the mirror looked softer, and her face was more open, more accepting. It was the face of a woman who had gotten wet from having her nipples pierced, not necessarily because of the pain but because her Master had commanded it, and she had obeyed him. And she—no, *I* wasn't ashamed of that fact. The thin gold crescents of the rings Cole had picked out glimmered as they rested on the curves of my areolas, mellow gold against the dark pink of my flesh. They were beautiful. *I was beautiful.*

"Beautiful," Cole echoed my thoughts out loud. He reached in front of me and cupped my breasts, being careful not to touch the tender new piercings. "When they heal, I'm going to buy you a chain to wear between them," he murmured in a low voice. "I want to tether you to the bed by your breasts, want to see you on your hands and knees, helpless to move while I fuck your sweet pussy, Alex. Would you like that?"

"Yes," I whispered, shivering at his hot words. I understood now why he had wanted the piercings. I still liked to have my nipples played with and teased, but I was shy of nipple clamps now, and Cole wanted to be able to do other things with his hands while keeping me stimulated above the waist.

I let myself lean back against him, feeling supported and protected by his large body. Very gently, Cole caressed my nipples with his warm, blunt fingertips. The mingled pain and pleasure that shot through me drew a moan from my lips.

"Please," I whispered, barely able to speak as he stroked me. "Please, Master..."

"What is it you need, Alex?" he asked softly. "Don't be afraid to tell me anything you want or need."

"Need you inside me," I told him, meeting his piercing blue eyes in the mirror. "Need...need you to fuck me. Please, Master." Even a few months before I would have been unable to voice such a request, but Cole had taught me that no need, no wish was too much to ask of him. If I needed him to kiss me, he would do it. If I needed him to spank or cane me, he could do that, as well.

He growled low in my ear, a sound of possession and lust. "That's exactly what I'm going to do with you, little girl," he promised me. "I'm going to fuck your sweet little pussy." He slid one large hand down my body, over the curve of my hip to the damp black lace panties I wore. I moaned again as he cupped my mound in his palm, and bit my lips as he started the rub the silky material.

"You're wet, aren't you?" he whispered in my ear. "Wet for me, ready to take me. Ready to come all over my cock when I fuck that sweet pussy."

"Yes, Master," I whispered as he rubbed his fingers against me. Instead of moving my panties aside, he pressed the silky material of their crotch into me, parting my pussy lips with his fingers and circling over and over the swollen bump of my clit.

"So soft," he murmured. "So hot and wet. I can't wait to put my cock inside you and fuck your sweet cunt."

I blushed at the dirty, forbidden word, but I felt a fresh surge of wetness between my thighs. Cole seemed to know that his blunt language turned me on, and his bedroom conversation was often peppered with words that he would never use at work.

He kissed the side of my neck possessively, nipping just hard enough to make me moan again but not hard enough to leave a mark. I liked him to mark me, and he often did—but on my inner thighs or other places where his marks of possession wouldn't be visible at work.

"Come on," he said, leading me to the bed. "Take off your panties. I want you now—on your hands and knees, Alex."

I obeyed him without question, slipping off my panties and crawling onto the large bed, feeling it give slightly under my weight. I loved when Cole took me this way—it felt so primal, so animalistic—and it reminded me of the first time we had nearly made love. I felt his heat against my back as he climbed onto the bed behind me.

"Spread your legs. Wider." His voice was a low growl, and I shivered and did as he said, spreading my legs wide for him. My wet sex opened with the movement, and I moaned when I felt the broad head of his cock brush against my slippery folds.

"You like that?" He repeated the action, sliding the length of his shaft against the tender bump of my clit until I cried out. "Or this?" He pulled back, and I felt the head of his cock enter me—but just the head—no more.

"Please," I gasped again, needing him so badly I could barely breathe. "Please, Master."

"What do you need, Alex?" he asked, pulling out a little, then pressing forward so another inch of his cock entered me. "Tell me, and maybe I'll give it to you."

"Please, Master, I need you to fuck me," I gasped. "I need your cock inside me—all the way inside me."

"Good girl," Cole murmured, and I felt his thickness sliding home inside me, filling me completely until the broad head of his cock bottomed out at the end of my channel. "You're such a good girl, Alex."

His words of praise almost as much as his cock inside me made me gasp and push back against him, wanting more. I felt his warm hands on my hips, holding me in place, and he growled warningly in my ear. I knew that he wanted me to stay still, to submit to his fucking. I let my head hang down, my hair getting in my face and my breath coming in pants and moans.

Cole drew out and rammed into me again, spreading me wide to accommodate his thickness. His large hands bracketed my pelvis, his fingers digging into my hips in a way that was painful and pleasurable at the same time. I knew he was marking me, that I would see the bruises on my pale skin the next day and remember this experience, and I loved it.

"Who do you belong to?" Cole drew out again and thrust into me again, being deliberately rough, just the way I needed him to be. "Who, Alex?" He drove into me again, setting a slow, deliberate pace that seemed designed to drive me wild. At the same time, one large hand found the place where we were joined, and I felt his blunt fingertips rubbing gently against the sensitive bundle of nerves at my center.

I opened my mouth to speak, to tell him that I belonged to him and only him but the pleasure that Cole was building inside me with his rough, luscious fucking was almost too much. For a moment my vocal chords locked up, and I couldn't say or do anything—could only hang my head and try to endure what he was doing to me, the way he was taking me, owning me.

"Who?" Cole demanded again. "Who do you belong to, Alex?"

At last I felt the orgasm he had been pushing me to taking me over, rolling over my body in a huge, warm wave of sensation and light. And at the same time, I found my voice.

"You, Master. You, Cole. Only and always to you." I gasped, feeling my body tighten around his as the waves of pleasure pulsed through me. "Oh, God, I'm yours. I belong to *you.*"

"Alex!" Cole groaned my name, and I knew my admission of his ownership of me was making him come as much as our lovemaking. "God, love you so much," he gasped as he thrust into me as deeply as he could. I felt his shaft inside me, pulsing into me as he came in my unprotected sex, giving me every bit of himself as I had given him every bit of myself. It was a completion I had never known was possible, a connection I had never felt with anyone else. To my surprise, I actually felt tears in my eyes at the thought.

"Alex?" Cole pulled me down so that we were both lying on our sides. I must have been crying harder than I thought because he sounded concerned. He rolled me over to face him and stroked my cheek tenderly. "You okay?" he asked. "Did I hurt you too much?"

"No." I wiped my eyes with the heel of my hand and gave him a watery smile. "No, it was just…intense. I guess I just love you so much. And I love that you're willing to do this for me—to give me what I need."

"What do you mean 'willing' to do this?" he growled. "Don't you know I like it, too? I love doing this with you. Love being the one who owns you. Love being the one who makes you come."

"Cole," I whispered, snuggling against him. "I meant what I said a minute ago—I'm yours. For always."

"And I'm yours, sweetheart." He kissed me on the neck. "I love you, Alex. This—what we have together, what we do together—is what I want. What I've always wanted, I guess. I just never knew I wanted it until you showed me."

He wrapped his arms around me and held me close, and I let my eyes drift closed, feeling safe and secure in a way I never had before.

Some people have to be tied down to feel free. I have finally found my freedom.

Evangeline Anderson

Evangeline Anderson is a registered MRI tech who would rather be writing. She is thirty-something and lives in Florida with a husband, three cats and a college-age sister but no kids because enough is enough already. She had been writing dirty stories for her own gratification for a number of years before it occurred to her to try and get paid for it. To her delight, she found it was actually possible to get money for having a dirty mind and she has been writing steadily ever since.

You can find Evangeline Anderson on the Web at www.evangelineanderson.com, or feel free to send her an email at vangiekitty@aol.com.

Printed in the United States
96892LV00002B/277/A